QUEEN'S GAMBIT

KAREN CHANCE

CHAPTER ONE

Dory, Cairo

The one-hundred-eighty-degree sweep of floor to ceiling windows normally would have been a little odd for a ball room, but when you have an uninterrupted view of the pyramids, you make sure that everyone knows it. And I had to admit, it was pretty spectacular. The sun was setting, giving the golden hued monuments a salmon, tangerine and navy backdrop, with the latter including a few faint stars overhead. It looked like a postcard, although it was hard to concentrate on it when there was something even more dazzling standing in front of it.

"Some view, huh?" Raymond Lu, my self-described go-to guy, had sidled up with a couple of champagne flutes.

"You mean the pyramids or the man?" I asked.

Raymond frowned. Maybe because he was uncomfortable. His shock of black hair was slicked down and behaving, but he was tugging on the collar of his perfectly tailored tux and shifting from one foot to the other, like his shiny dress shoes hurt his feet. His usual idea of dressing up was a multicolored snakeskin jacket that had fallen off the back of a truck, paired with a black silk shirt and a lot of gold chains.

Ray was out of his element.

Of course, so was I. My work uniform was jeans and a T-shirt, with maybe a black leather jacket thrown over it when the weather warranted. I liked boots with a heavy sole and a steel tip in case I needed to kick down a door, and a duffle bag full of illegal weaponry in case the boots didn't work.

But no such luck tonight.

Tonight, I was in a slinky black silk number, cut down to here and up to there, and a pair of shiny black stilettos. The get up went well with my short dark hair, giving off vaguely nineteen twenties vibes, although it would have probably gotten me arrested in the twenties. But it made me have to watch every movement so that I didn't flash somebody. Plus, the thong it pretty much required had migrated inward.

Again.

I resisted an urge to dig it out and drank champagne.

Raymond scowled. "He needs a scar."

I assumed he was talking about my new husband, Louis-Cesare, who was standing on a dais at the front of the room, surrounded by beautiful people who looked completely at ease in their clothes. And jewels. And elaborately made-up faces that were laughing at something my lover had just said. I saw several women shoot me envious glances and raised my glass to them.

"Die mad about it," I murmured, despite being pretty sure that they could hear me. We were across a crowded ballroom from each other, but vampire hearing has exceptional range. And they were all vamps, members or high-ranking flunkies of the North African Vampire Senate.

It was a subsidiary of the huge African and Middle Eastern Senate, which had so much land to cover that they'd had to split it into more manageable chunks. But it was all under the control of its iron fisted consul, Hassani. He was here, too, his handsome, bearded face—a glamourie but a good one—shown to effect in a turban and a blindingly white burnoose. He and Louis-Cesare were soon to make pretty speeches about the current war and the great victory that our united front had won us.

Then would come the presentation of gifts, including

4

spoils taken from the plundered capitol of an alien world. They were already on display, in warded cases scattered around the large room. I was supposed to be over there, smiling and schmoozing and explaining the exotic booty to all and sundry, in order to help shore up the tentative alliance between the world's six vampire senates.

It had been forged after some home-grown enemies joined up with the fey king Aeslinn to wreak havoc, and the only way to get them to stop had been to invade Faerie and kick some ass. Only nobody knew how to fight a war on another world. So, we'd united our forces, for the first time ever, with old enemies forged into reluctant allies by a serious threat.

But that threat was over, wasn't it?

So, what happened to the alliance now?

It was a problem, since the threat wasn't really over. We'd won a battle—a major one—but a battle wasn't a war. Yet people who hated each other's guts tended to forget that, especially when they were also worried that the consul of the North American Senate, who headed up the shaky coalition, might decide to make her rule over vampire kind permanent.

After all, it was what they'd do.

Enter Louis-Cesare and me, on a good will tour to hand out largesse and compliments in equal measure, and try to keep the allies allied.

So far, it wasn't going great.

I didn't know whose brilliant idea it had been to send a dhampir, the traditional enemy of vampire kind, on a diplomatic mission, but it wasn't working. I made the locals nervous simply by being in the same room, which was fair. You spend five hundred years bringing back their heads in a bag and it tends to cut into the general sense of goodwill.

I'd noticed that whatever display case I was standing by suddenly got very lonesome, and when I walked through a room, people tended to step over each other to get out of the way. I'd smiled at one woman, whom I'd mistaken for a human servant, and she'd passed the hell out. I'd retreated to my corner after that, allowing my famous, gorgeous spouse to take over the schmoozing, which seemed to be working better.

Maybe a little too much better, I thought, eyeing the admiring throng.

And then eyeing him, mostly because I enjoyed it.

His fashionably pale skin—or fashionable for vamps, anyway—was as flawless as the mane of burnished auburn hair that fell half way down the muscular back and was currently being limned with fire by the setting sun. It had been leashed tonight, as much as possible, by a tortoise shell clip at the base of his neck. It was a popular compromise by the men in the family, who understood that styles had changed but were damned if they were going to wear the short hair of a peasant. In Louis-Cesare's case, the sleek style only served to highlight a profile that would have made an ancient Greek sculptor weep, and was accompanied by the rest of the Greek god package: broad shoulders, long legs, and the best butt in memory. And I had a long memory.

Damn, I hated being the ugly one.

I glanced at Ray, who was scowling even more furiously. "A scar?"

"You know." He drank champagne. "Something to give his face some character."

"It has plenty of character."

"Yeah, if male model is considered character."

"You're just jealous."

"Damned right, I'm jealous. I'm five foot seven; he's six four. I look like a penguin in this get up; he's Mr. Universe. Plus, I got hair on my ass, and I bet his is silky smooth—"

"Don't start about your ass."

"I was just making the point—"

"Well don't."

"—that I gotta shave to get my trousers to lay right, while he—"

"I'm not listening." I walked out onto a terrace.

Unlike most vampire courts, which tended to be underground, cramped and inward looking, this one was wide open, with the sand-colored terrace outside almost as expansive as the ballroom within. I took my champagne over to some stone benches that looked like they'd been looted from an ancient temple, and prepared to try to enjoy myself. Of course, Raymond followed.

"Why aren't you in there, anyway?" he demanded.

"Needed some air."

"No, I mean *in there*. At the front of the room, smiling with the bigwigs."

"When I smile at people, they tense up."

"That's 'cause you don't really smile. You grimace, and half the time, you show fang."

"You show fang."

"Yeah, but I'm not a diplomat."

"Neither am I."

"Ah." Ray settled down on the organically curved piece of granite, which was high enough to leave his legs dangling. "Then you know."

"Know what?"

"That Louis-Cesare married one woman, but he wants another."

I felt my hand move instinctively to the stake I'd shoved into the top of my thigh high. "Oh," I said nonchalantly. "Which one?"

Ray rolled his eyes. "That's not what I meant. If there was a rival here, do you think I'd tell you? What, am I crazy?"

"Then what did you mean?"

"Look," Ray said, and his face in the odd, pinkish light was earnest. Which meant that either I was about to get played, or he was actually serious. "I don't want to tell you your business—"

"Since when?"

"—but you're a *killer*, and we're at *war*. What the hell are you doing here?"

"Getting more well-rounded?"

"I'm serious."

"So am I. At least, that's what I was told." I drank champagne.

"And you *believed* it?"

"I believed I was going to get divorced if I ran off on another errand for the senate. Remember what happened last time?"

"That was not our fault." Ray looked indignant. "And we saved a city!"

"It's never our fault, and we almost got killed. Louis-Cesare thought I was safe at home, only to discover on waking that I was halfway around the world battling an ancient demon. He . . . didn't take it well."

Of course, that might have had something to do with the fact that we had just, and I mean *just*, finished fighting a queen of the light fey, during which time his body had been taken over by an outside force and used as a weapon to try to kill me.

He had very nearly succeeded.

He had also been seriously traumatized by the whole affair, more than I'd realized, frankly. And then my unexpected side trip took place and . . . well. After I recovered, I'd been forcefully reminded of the fact that my husband had red in his hair. He'd presented me with an ultimatum and I chose him.

Ray was eyeing me. "If this is some kind of extended honeymoon, then why did you call me?"

"Call it an itch."

I got up and walked to the railing. Damn, it was beautiful here, and romantic—or it would have been, had Louis-Cesare and I gotten half a second alone. Instead, we'd been wined and dined and escorted to that famous site and this ancient statue, as the local senate pulled out all the stops for their illustrious guests.

Well, guest, anyway.

"What kind of itch?" Ray asked, joining me, although his eyes were darting worriedly around the terrace. There was nobody else out here, with the main event about to start inside, but I didn't blame him. We'd been through a lot lately. "You mean, like intuition?"

"No, I mean like being on unfamiliar ground with a famous senator during a war. The consul's control over the alliance is tenuous and everybody knows it. If Louis-Cesare was to get assassinated, it might tip the political balance. He wants me on this damned tour because he thinks it's safer. *I* think—"

"That he's a target."

I nodded.

"You're a senator now, too," Ray pointed out. "Why aren't *you* a target?"

"I'm not a dueling champion. If anyone wants to be considered a legit successor to the consul, they have to duel her, and she's named Louis-Cesare as her champion before—"

"Dory—"

"—so why not again? Nobody wants to fight him, and a war is the perfect time to take him out before a challenge is even issued and blame it on somebody else—"

"You've thought about this."

"Of course, I have. Two birds, one stone. Weaken her politically and make the challenge easier at the same time. It's how they think; you know it is—"

"Dory!" Ray put a hand over the one I had clenched on the railing. "He's a dueling champion surrounded by vamp bodyguards. I think he's fine."

I eyed the four huge vamps inside, who were dimly visible through the striations of setting sun on the glass. They were trying their best not to look like gorillas in their tuxes, which was a complete waste of time standing near my elegant husband. They were big, they were badass—or so they thought—and they were all but useless against the kind

9

of things we had been fighting. And I didn't mean just our enemies.

I narrowed my eyes at Hassani, who had started life as an expert assassin and, as far as I knew, had never gone out of practice. I hadn't had to ask if he wanted to head up the new Vampire World Senate. He was a master vamp; he wanted it. And Louis-Cesare could be his ticket to ride.

Especially when the so-called bodyguards were busy scanning the crowd, while completely ignoring the much more dangerous man standing right beside them!

Not that I really thought that Hassani—or anyone else —would try something so openly, but vampires were tricky, especially the old ones. You never knew how their minds worked. And, yeah, I was paranoid, but I had reason to be, and my nerves—

Were a little on edge, I thought, realizing half a second after it happened that I had whirled, my body splayed out in a lunge, to hold a terrified waiter at knife point.

He didn't move and he didn't scream, although the front of his nice dark trousers got a little darker as we stood there in our little tableau, staring at each other.

"What?" I asked, realizing that Ray had said something.

"I was gonna ask why you don't rate any guards," he said dryly.

"Two of them are mine. I put them on Louis-Cesare," I said, and pulled the knife back.

It was at the other end of the stake for convenience, and thin enough not to bulge my dress. I'd been flashing it all night anyway, whenever I moved just right, like a gunslinger in the Old West with a .45 under his arm. But I was past caring.

Screw diplomacy; my party was going home with all their limbs attached, and if Hassani or anybody else had something to say about it, they could—

The waiter dropped his tray of drinks and screamed as the delayed reaction hit, then fled. Several people glanced outside, with the bored disinterest of beings who had seen everything and didn't think much of it. There wasn't even a break in the subtle ebb and flow of conversation.

"Sorry," I told Ray, taking the handkerchief he proffered to wipe the spilled champagne off my hand. "I've just been a little on edge late—"

"Shit!" he yelled, and tackled me.

I heard it a split second after he did: a high-pitched whistle, unmistakable to anyone who'd ever been at war. A missile, incoming. And then here, a split second after Ray threw us behind one of the massive old benches, which I guess were as sturdy as they looked. Because the explosion tore around and over us, but not through us.

Not through *us*.

I was on my feet and tussling with Ray, who despite appearances was a vampire and a master at that, while debris was still in the air, while heat was still radiating outward in waves, and while the wind of the explosion was still blowing my hair around. I didn't care. I threw him off and ran, into a once nice ballroom that was currently falling to pieces.

Damn it, I knew it!

"Louis-Cesare!"

I didn't see him. I did see a jagged-edged hole in the sky outside the windows, or more accurately, in what I guessed was a shield surrounding the ballroom and terrace. The pretty view was still being projected onto the inside of what was left of it, while everywhere else . . .

Was destruction. A heavy ceiling tile crashed to the floor at my feet, sending sharp edged shards to pepper my legs and the arm I threw over my eyes. Blackened furniture, much of it still on fire, lay scattered around; destroyed columns were in chunks on the floor, one of them crushing a servant; smoke filled the air, chokingly thick; and the charred bodies of vamps and glassware crunched underfoot.

But there were signs of survival, too.

There was movement amongst the fire, with the power

levels of those in attendance on clear display. The weakest were burnt corpses, mere shells of gray ash that puffed away into nothingness as I passed. Those with more years and more power under their belts were stirring, some weakly calling out for help in a dozen languages, the stronger struggling to get up or staggering back to their feet. But the masters . . .

Were *furious.*

A woman jumped up beside me with a snarl, her finery burnt away except for a few scraps clinging to her blackened, naked body. Much of her henna dyed updo was also missing, and the rest was down around her shoulders, one of which was smoldering like an ember. She clawed it out, grabbing a chunk of her own damaged flesh and tearing it off before it took the rest of her along with it, then ran to the other side of the room. Others were congregating there as well; rallying around Hassani, who was suddenly surrounded by an army of his creatures, blackened and bloody, but still deadly.

And they needed to be. Because the missile had only been the first volley. It had somehow broken through the shield surrounding the court, like a medieval trebuchet making a breech in a wall, and now the army was pouring in.

Only an army of what, I wasn't sure.

They were human in shape but swathed in black, including their heads, so I couldn't tell much about them. Most were on the short side and thin but fast, even by vampire standards, being mere blurs across my vision unless they paused for half a second. And they were strong—insanely so.

One lunged for me and I ducked, came back up and got my knife in his neck. But that gave another a chance to grab me from behind, and for a second, I couldn't break his hold. Because I'd been treating him like a human, which judging by the rapid heartbeat against my back, he was. But that wasn't human strength. So, I switched tactics, shucked my shoes, ran up a cracked support column and flipped over his head.

And slit his throat.

I looked up, panting, but while there were plenty of black clad forms running around, no more were targeting me. Maybe because Hassani had just given a shouted order and his vampires had rushed the invaders, making me think for a second that it was all over. But the army in black pushed *back* against what should have been an overwhelming show of force, half of them somehow stopping the charge while the rest . . .

Went for the warded cases of artifacts.

And I finally got a clue. This wasn't an attempted assassination; this was a *heist.* Somebody wanted the fey artifacts badly enough to risk attacking Hassani's court for them—and they were getting away with it.

An explosive charge was slapped onto the blue column of a shield to my right, and I heard it go off as I ran. Another just ahead wreathed a shield in black smoke, and a second later it cracked and then shattered like glass. Artifacts disappeared into black plastic garbage bags, which would have usually gotten a reaction from me, since they were our responsibility. But right then, I couldn't have cared less.

"Louis-Cesare!"

I finally saw him, over near the shattered main shield, looking down over the city. He turned his head to stare at me for a second, before yelling something that I couldn't hear over the fires and cries and roar of a furious Hassani. Who leapt over the fleshly breakwater of clashing forces with a scimitar in one hand and a long knife in the other, and began demonstrating, that, yes, his assassination skills were as sharp as ever.

The enemy army broke and stumbled back into me, and the vampires yelled and charged. And by the time I fought my way through all of that and ran over to the opening, Louis-Cesare was gone. Or almost.

I spotted him in the distance, running hard into the night, chasing . . . someone. It was almost dark and I couldn't make out who it was. But I could see the shadows that peeled off the walls all around and followed.

Goddamnit!

"No," Ray said, running up beside me as I tore the trailing hem off the damned evening dress. "No, you are not going to —"

And then I threw myself onto the roof below, and took off.

CHAPTER TWO

Dory, Cairo

Open space is at a premium in Cairo, so many people live partly on the rooftops. And even those not made up like an outdoor living room are full of stuff: laundry flapping in the breeze, satellite dishes—so many damned satellite dishes—old tires, abandoned refrigerators, piles of rubble and broken furniture that someone intends to do something with at some point, *inshallah*. But not today, which left it in my way.

It didn't help that Louis-Cesare had had a head start, and was faster than me, although usually by only a fraction of a second. But tonight—tonight he was *flying*. I'd never seen him move like that; hell, I'd never seen anybody move like that.

Except for the creatures pursuing him.

There were dozens of them, leaping across the rooftops of Cairo like mad things. And they didn't look like the shorter types doing the heist; they were at least as tall if not taller than he was. At least as far as I could tell, based on the brief glimpses I got around old stone walls, flapping sheets, and five thousand damned satellite dishes!

I jumped onto a terraced rooftop, grabbed a ladder to vault up to the taller story, and paused. Adrenaline was telling me to *hurry, hurry, hurry*, but older instincts, the kind that live in the lizard brain, were telling me something else. And I learned a long time ago to listen to the lizard brain.

I glanced around, while palming my knife.

The whole area was dark, with the last rays of the setting sun having just disappeared over the horizon. The only light came from the stars overhead and a few dim windows of illumination, darkened by curtains, in the surrounding buildings. Nothing moved; nothing stirred. My straining ears could hear only distant traffic, faint Arabic from a T.V., and the cooking sounds of somebody fixing dinner in a nearby apartment.

And the tell-tale slice of a blade through the air.

I lunged to the side, a split second before a knife appeared, vibrating in the wood of the ladder. I grabbed it and threw it back—in the same direction that it had come from, because you learn a thing or two in five hundred years. And finished my turn to see it sticking out—

Of the chest of Anubis, the jackal headed god of death.

All right, I thought.

I had not seen that one coming.

The maybe nine-foot-tall creature stepped forward, seeming to coalesce out of the shadows. Starlight limned the muscles on the broad, human-like chest, on thick arms banded by gold, and on strong, athlete's legs. The latter emerged from under a white linen, pleated skirt, the ancient Egyptian version of a kilt, with a golden jackal's head in place of the sporran. But they ended with huge, very non-human clawed feet, which along with the elongated snout on the head and the slitted, golden eyes, were enough to give me the creeps even before a spear the size of a small tree was shoved at me.

I caught it in a rung of the ladder and sent it spinning off into the night. Only to have the creature materialize another out of thin air. And then three more jackal headed bastards leapt into the fray from the terrace above.

Okay, then.

Done here.

The creatures came along as I jumped for a nearby roof,

slashing and hacking at me while we were still mid-air. I received an impromptu haircut from a razor-sharp sword, watched the inch-long fringe arc against the starlight, and got my own knife in my attacker as I hit down, rolling. And saw the creature pull eight inches of steel out of its side and throw it away as if it had been a splinter.

All right, then.

A little-known fact about dhampirs is that we are *fast*. Not Louis-Cesare fast, but compared to almost anybody else . . . yeah, I could move. Which I proved by taking off like a bat out of hell.

And had one of them pass me in a classic flanking maneuver, without so much as breaking a sweat.

Son of a bitch, I thought, ripping up one of the ubiquitous satellite dishes and flinging it at the nearest snout. Only to have it be caught midair and snapped back, so fast that I ended up bending over backwards to miss it and fell off the building. I grabbed a laundry line on the way down, which would have been more of a comfort if one of my attackers hadn't immediately started reeling me in.

I began overhanding it for the other side—fast—only to find that there was a jackal on that end, too.

Why they didn't just skewer me on one of those huge spears I didn't know, but it wouldn't matter in a minute.

Dorina, I thought, *some help here!*

And I wasn't talking to myself.

Well, okay, I sort of was, but . . . it's complicated.

My name is Dory Basarab, daughter of the famous vampire senator and general Mircea Basarab, and recently a member in my own right of the North American Vampire Senate. I'd been promoted for two reasons: it was assumed that I'd vote the way that daddy wanted, thus giving his faction on the senate additional power. And because of Dorina—my "twin" as she called herself—which I guess was a reference to Siamese twins.

Only instead of being joined at the hip, we were joined

everywhere.

We'd been born one person with a dual nature—half human, half vamp—but a single consciousness. Until, that is, our father Mircea—a master mentalist—had decided to put a barrier between our two halves when I was just a girl. The idea had been to give the human side of me a chance to grow up separately from my vampire nature, which had already been stronger than I could handle.

That was why so few dhampirs lived for very long: their two sides ended up at war with each other, and ripped their minds apart. Mircea had helped Dorina and I to avoid that, but at the cost of remaining separate people for something like five centuries. And a division like that . . . tends to be permanent.

I hadn't even known she existed until recently, when Mircea's barrier finally failed, since we had never been awake at the same time. I'd just thought I had fits of dhampir-induced madness when I blacked out and killed everything in the room. It had kept me apart from society for most of my life, under the assumption that I was a dangerous monster.

It didn't help that I was sort of right.

Not that Dorina was a homicidal maniac, but she had all the ruthless practicality of a vampire, blended with centuries of being a virtual prisoner in my mind. Mircea had left human-me in charge of our union, which allowed her limited freedom, mainly when I was asleep or freaked out and my control lessened. She was therefore both very old and yet also strangely naïve in how she thought about things, with much less real-world experience than I had.

And, like a child, anything that startled her was likely to get beaten up.

But damn, if I couldn't use some of that ferocity right now.

However, Dorina had the ability to leave our body behind for mental jaunts on her own, and this looked like one of those times. Meanwhile, I was getting my ass handed to me—possibly literally in a minute—by creatures faster and stronger and more numerous than I was. And my damned purse, which had some items that might have evened the odds, was back on the terrace, assuming there was a terrace anymore.

I was starting to find Egypt less romantic.

And then somebody grabbed me—from behind, just as I was being hauled over the edge of the roof.

"If you stake me, I swear to God!" Ray shrieked, before I could retaliate. Or figure out what was happening. Because we were going up, I realized, as one of the jackal-headed bastards jumped for me—

And missed.

I saw the creature flail in the air, its fingertips just missing the fringe of what appeared to be a rug from somebody's living room, which I'd been slung across. It was an ugly rug, and its fringe was an unraveled mess. Even stranger, it appeared to be the only thing underneath us at the moment.

"Hold on!" Ray yelled. "I don't know what the hell I'm doing!"

That's reassuring, I thought, as we took off, soaring over the rooftops of Cairo on what appeared to be a flying carpet. At least as far as I could tell with the wind throwing what remained of my hair in my eyes and my fisted hands clutching the hard-to-grasp surface for all I was worth. I almost fell off three times anyway, felt my stomach lurch alarmingly when we jackknifed around a building, and then we stopped—abruptly enough that I did hit the ground.

Or another dusty rooftop, at least, with my head spinning and the stone underneath my hands feeling like it was undulating while I stared up at Ray. "What the—"

He was off the rug with a hand over my mouth before I could blink. "Shhhh! I don't know what kinda hearing those things have, all right?"

"Whhmpphwhhmmmmhhh?"

"What?"

I removed his hand. "Then why did we stop?"

"Why did we—" he looked at me incredulously. "I don't know how to drive that thing!"

He gestured back at the rug, which was levitating a couple feet above the roof and looking pathetic. Like, really pathetic. For one thing, it wasn't even close to being a rectangle, which was one reason I'd had so much trouble holding on. For another, it had a "pattern" that would have embarrassed a cross eyed two-year-old, with nothing repeating or making sense. It looked like somebody had scribbled a picture . . . in a hurry . . . in the dark . . .

I glared at Ray. "Son of a bitch!"

"Shh! Shhhhhh!"

"Where is it?"

The blue eyes shifted. "Where is what?"

"You know damned well!"

"All right, all right! Keep your voice down—"

I didn't wait for him to finish pulling an object out of an inside pocket of his tux, and instead jerked it out myself. And then shook it under his nose. "You said it wasn't finished yet! You said—"

"I say a lotta things," Ray hissed. "Cause I got a master with a death wish! I wanted to test it out first—"

"Well, it obviously works!"

"Yeah." He glanced back at the lopsided rug. "You know. Kinda."

"Close enough."

I stood up and looked around, but as I'd feared, there was no Louis-Cesare. There were no jackal-headed thugs, either, including the ones that had been after me. And there'd been at least a dozen, as more had zeroed in on my location from surrounding buildings.

What the hell was going on?

"How does this thing work?" I asked Ray, returning to the business at hand.

He shrugged. "Same as the other, more or less."

I examined it. It resembled a child's toy pistol, but with an extra-large barrel. But what it shot out wasn't water.

Ray and I had gotten the idea for a new weapon from a recent adventure in supernatural Hong Kong. A hidden city that existed out of phase with the normal world, it didn't have to hide its weirder elements like most enclaves did. That had allowed some . . . peculiarities . . . to become every day sights, including magical ads that could jump off their billboards and follow you down the street.

They were "drawn" onto the side of a building by a gun-like object that contained a reservoir of magic and a spell to animate it. You sketched whatever you wanted on a little screen, pointed the gun, and presto! An instantly mobile, and occasionally vocal, advertisement.

Thanks to a buttload of magic supplied by a crazy war mage we'd met, Ray and I had managed to use the gun to animate ourselves a little help. Giant ads had become warriors in a very strange battle, and while their fighting ability had been debatable, they'd served admirably as a distraction for our attackers. But a distraction wasn't what I needed right now.

I drew a figure, aimed the gun at a wall, and pulled the trigger.

A second later, what had been bare bricks had a glowing, golden stick figure on them, the size of a six-year-old child. I waited, biting my lip and hoping this would work. Ray and I had taken the idea of the makeshift weapon we'd put together on the fly in Hong Kong to a master wardsmith—the father of a friend—who liked to tinker with crazy magic. He'd refined it, upgraded it, and added some special features.

Including that one, I thought, as the "child" started spilling off the wall like an accordion, not one figure anymore but dozens.

"Thought you were an artist," Ray said, checking out the toons' oversized, lopsided heads and mismatched eyes.

I ignored that. The dial control on the device was as hard to use as an Etch-a-Sketch, which probably explained the rug. I pawed through my oversized purse, which Ray had slung over his back, pulled a picture of Louis-Cesare out of my wallet and held it up in front of the nearest little glowing stick figure. It had been toddling around aimlessly along with the rest, having received no instructions yet.

So, I gave it some.

"Find him—fast—and signal me when you do."

The lopsided head got a little more so, tilting in an almost human-like way as it regarded the picture with its big, mismatched eyes. I hadn't bothered to fill it in much, so it was mostly just a collection of glowing lines, showing the darkened city scape beyond. But there was obviously something at work inside that empty head. Because a moment later the stick guys were gone, just golden blurs against the night, shooting off in all directions.

"Get on!" I told Ray, while clambering back onto the rug.

"Yeah." He eyed it. "Only I was thinking maybe you could make another one. I was kinda in a hurry and—"

"It'll do. Come on!"

"—it ended up too small. And lopsided. And—"

"Ray! The magic cartridges are $10,000 a pop—"

"I know that—"

"—so I'm not making another one. And, anyway, we don't have time. Get on!"

Ray was not getting on. Instead, he was backing up, his eyes on the tiny sort-of rug that I was straddling like a motorcycle. He did not appear to want another go.

"Did I ever mention I get airsick?"

And then a couple of jackals jumped onto the roof, and Ray screamed and threw himself at me. "Go! Go! Go!" he yelled, which I guess was all the command the little rug needed.

It took off like it had been shot out of a cannon, with Ray's last word being exaggerated into a single long line that I thought might actually *be* his last word, as we dodged spears and flipped over and somersaulted in mid-air, which had me wanting to scream, too, only I was the master.

It wouldn't have been dignified.

We finally stabilized high over the city, with Ray in front and me holding on behind. Old Town was spread out in a warren of broad avenues and narrow alleyways below, through which my tiny golden men were flickering. Not running down the streets as humans would, but appearing briefly on walls, on parked vehicles, and on the shuttered side of shops, the corrugated metal making their distorted shapes even more so. But they were flickering fast.

"Come on," I breathed, watching them. "Come *on*."

And then I saw it: a little man who was no longer golden. He was red—blood red. And no sooner had the color washed over him than it spilled outward to his closest brothers, who turned unerringly on his location. And then more did and more, until I had a bright red arrow spread out below me, fritzing like a neon sign in the darkness—

And pointing straight at where my lover was likely fighting for his life.

"There!" I yelled, gesturing—and forgetting how the carpet worked. The syllable had barely left my lips when it leapt ahead, causing Ray to yelp and me to clutch his waist as we took off at what could only be described as an extremely unwise pace.

I didn't care. "Faster," I breathed, and swore that I felt us speed up even more.

"Shiiiiiiiiiiiiiiit!" Ray screamed, because there were no safety protocols on this thing, which had just fallen like a stone. But it had fallen in a slanting, forward motion-y kind of way, which literally seconds later had us hitting the Khan-el-Khalili, the huge bazaar in the center of the city.

I'd heard of this place, of course; everyone had. It was almost as famous as the pyramids, with its narrow, cobblestone streets, soaring arches, and limestone walls practically unchanged for seven hundred years. I'd heard tales of towering mosaics, of intricately carved wooden doors, of sagging wooden balconies hanging over shops filled with everything from cheap tourist crap to genuine finds. I'd been planning to visit before we left and maybe pick up some souvenirs for the folks back home.

But not like this.

Because our turbo charged ride did not seem to understand the difference between flying unimpeded through the air and flying through a still-crowded marketplace, where colored glass lanterns cast rainbows over what had to be hundreds of people—touts, tourists, locals, guides, and shop owners with their merchandise.

Especially their merchandise.

"Ow!" Ray yelled, batting at a hanging garden of copper pots, pitchers and platters that batted us back. And then at some blue beaded chandelier things outside the entrance of another shop, the strands of which hit us in the face like hail. And then through a lamp seller's inventory, which—gah!

"Down!" Ray gasped, as glass shattered and sprayed everywhere. "Take us down!"

We went down, plowing through a shoe vendor's rack, sending multiple pairs of leather slippers flying like a flock of startled birds. And then through another rack of brightly colored outfits, shimmering with beads and sequins, half of which clung to us. And then behind a local man on a motorcycle, who was staring over his shoulder with the panicked, disbelieving eyes of a guy being chased by a couple of djinn on a flying carpet.

Which only got worse when an Anubis jumped off a building on top of him.

The man and his ride went skidding into a café, sending the patrons screaming as we tore past. And then was thrown off altogether when he hit a wall. The crash didn't seem to faze the ancient god, however, who swiftly righted the bike and used it to come after us.

"Give me the gun!" I yelled at Ray, who had shoved it in his pocket.

"What?"

"The gun!"

He gave me the gun.

I sketched something appropriate and pointed it at a wall. But we were going so fast that the pic got a little overstretched. Which resulted in a twelve-foot-long scorpion that . . . yeah. Worked really well, I thought, as I gestured at the god of death coming up fast behind us.

"Kill it!"

The scorpion seemed enthusiastic about this idea, leaping off the wall and tackling the motorcycle riding asshole. At least, I assumed so, judging from all the yelling going on behind us. I would have turned around to see, but another huge assailant had just jumped down and caught hold of the back of our ride.

And Ray—God bless him—made sure that he regretted it.

Ray had the front of the rug in a death grip, and was using it to steer by tugging this way or that—and he'd gotten pretty good at it. Because we slung around corners, sped down avenues, and zipped across cross-streets. And in the process smashed our would-be assailant into beautiful old geometric wood paneling, into plastic mannequins wearing belly dancing costumes, into glassware, copperware, and shelves of obsidian statues—some, ironically, of Anubis himself. We plowed him through displays of carved wooden boxes and dishes with shimmering mother-of-pearl inlay, and a huge brass hookah taller than he was. We slung him into a couple of massive alabaster vases outside an antique shop and then through a spice seller's baskets of cinnamon, peppercorns, and cardamom.

If there was a shop we missed, I'd be surprised. And when we weren't crashing into something, we were dragging him over rough-edged cobblestones, scattered café chairs, and a fountain of very hard ceramic tiles. Which I guessed wasn't fun judging by the sounds he was making.

And all the blood he was shedding.

Strange that Anubis bled like a human I thought, and reached around to grab hold of the elongated snout, which had yet to move despite all the noise.

And pulled.

"Oh, fuck!" Ray said, staring over his shoulder at the long spill of silver hair that flowed out of what was now quite obviously a mask. "Is that what I think it is?"

"Fey," I agreed, and put a knife in its eye.

But these weren't ordinary fey, if there was such a thing. I'd met the silver haired bastards before, and while they were taller, stronger and faster than a normal human by an order of magnitude, they weren't this strong. Or this fast. Or this numerous, because the marketplace was suddenly crawling.

And they didn't like that I'd just killed their friend.

"Go up, go up!" Ray screamed, as half a dozen fake gods leapt for us.

The rug went up. Unfortunately, our enemies were up there, too. Running across rooftops, jumping from balconies, throwing huge spears like freaking rain and causing our little conveyance to have to dodge here, there, and everywhere along the narrow alley, goddamnit!

"Need some help?"

I felt a familiar, cool presence slip inside my skin, or our skin technically, since my alter ego was back. And just in time. "Is that supposed to be funny?" I yelled, as five jackal-headed thugs dove at us like they were trying to set an Olympic record.

And fell in pieces on the ground a second later, because—

"Where did you get that?" I demanded, looking at the bloody scimitar in my hand.

Dorina gestured vaguely behind us, to where I guessed she'd ripped off a vendor as we flew past, or mugged a fey, before I'd even realized she was back. Which she definitely was. Because instead of gripping the little rug with both knees and at least one hand, I was now standing up on the tiny surface like a surfer on a board, and slashing at jumping fey with a bloody sword.

"Dorina?" Ray guessed, staring up at me.

"What do you think?" I yelled, trying to focus past the panic and find—

Him, I thought, half in joy, half in shock, as we slung around a minaret, above a cobblestone courtyard where I finally spotted Louis-Cesare, fighting alone, and surrounded by what had to be three dozen massive, jackal headed assailants.

My heart seized as Ray circled 'round again, as half a dozen spears flew up at us, and as I scribbled as fast as I could one handed—

"Got it!" I yelled.

"Got what?" Ray demanded, looking at me over his shoulder. "What is that thing?"

"Horus."

"What?"

"The king of the gods!" I yelled, as a huge falcon tore off the side of the minaret, its wingspan big enough to threaten to block out the sky. I don't know how large it actually was; I was kind of distracted. But I'd poured the rest of our magic into it, and I guess that reservoir had been worth the money. Because in that place and at that moment, it looked like a jumbo jet.

It soared into the air, then matched speed with us, the mighty wings knocking over a shop stall or two in the process.

"What the hell?" Ray demanded, staring at it.

"We just pulled rank!" I pointed at Louis-Cesare, and saw the bird's great head turn with my movement. *"Save him!"*

And Horus did.

Ray and I landed in a nearby alley to watch the show, because our ride was running out of juice. Sort of like the fey, I thought, watching the giant beak savage the no-longer-huge-looking creatures. It was a bloody slaughter, and I had no idea how we were going to explain this to Hassani, assuming he hadn't engineered the whole thing, not to mention cover it up. But when I saw Louis-Cesare running toward me across the square, slicing and dicing fey as he went, it suddenly didn't matter anymore.

Love . . . is a strange emotion, Dorina commented.

Couldn't argue with that.

"You owe me an Omega for this," Ray piped up, from behind me.

"What?"

"You know, the watch? The kind James Bond wears."

I glanced back at him. "What about it?"

"I been thinking, and that's what I want as a master's gift."

"Come again?"

"Masters always give their Seconds a gift, something to show off, only you haven't ponied up yet."

"I'm not much of a master," I pointed out, watching Louis-Cesare decapitate two fey at one time without breaking stride.

"But I'm a *great* second."

Yeah, I thought. He kind of was.

"What kind of Omega?" I asked, glancing back again—

In time to see him torn limb from limb by four fey.

"Ray!" I screamed, while someone else shouted: "Now!"

The alley lit up with a strange purple light, and something hit me like every freight train on Earth, all at once. I didn't scream, but only because I couldn't. I couldn't do anything, including fall, despite the fact that I'd been caught halfway through a leap. Except watch as what looked like a stone hockey puck—one of the captured fey artifacts—sent purple lightning scrawling up the alley walls.

I could feel Dorina struggling as hard as I was, but we remained suspended in mid-air while the lightning built and built above us, raising the hair on our head and arms and sending painful chills cascading up and down our body. And then it came crashing down, all at once, a searing torrent that felt like it should have incinerated us on the spot, or cooked our bones inside our skin. But it didn't kill us. I didn't know what it did, other than make me feel like I was coming apart at the seams.

And maybe I was.

A portal opened up in the opposite wall, and from the strength of it, it was headed a long way away. I barely noticed. A horrible ripping, tearing, sundering feeling had hit me, and suddenly, there she was, standing in the alley bedside me: Dorina, but not in the ghostly way she sometimes appeared when we had a chat. But solid. Real.

She touched my hand, looking as shocked as I was. For a second, we just stared at each other. And then a group of fey tackled her like linebackers, and all of them disappeared through the portal.

It immediately closed up behind them and I fell to the ground, the strange light dying at the same moment. Louis-Cesare grabbed me a second later, right before I passed out, yelling things that I couldn't hear over the pounding of my heart. Because I'd just realized something.

He hadn't been the target, after all.

Dorina had.

And now she was gone.

CHAPTER THREE

Dory, Cairo

I awoke in the dimness of an unfamiliar room. It was lit only by a few low burning oil lamps and the starlight drifting in through some large, floor to ceiling windows. My sleep-muddled brain finally recognized it as the suite that Louis-Cesare and I had been assigned at Hassani's court, all golden stone, cream draperies, and medieval architecture that, in the low light, could have been mistaken for a pharaoh's palace.

That was especially true in the lamplight, with the tiny wicks dancing in the soft breeze blowing through the windows, and throwing veil like shadows on the walls. This place had electricity, as well as all the other modern conveniences, or it had for the past week. The fact that it didn't now informed me that the main wards were online, the big boys that didn't play well with electrical systems, even before I felt the frisson of their power brush across my skin.

Hassani wasn't taking any chances, I thought, and felt a bolt of pure rage shoot through me. No, he wasn't taking chances now. Now when Dorina was gone and Louis-Cesare had almost died and Ray—

Ray was in pieces.

I sat bolt upright in bed, a scream building in my throat as I remembered that scene in the alley. Ray's face, looking startled and then horrified when he realized what was happening, his eyes going to me for help I couldn't provide. And the blood, so much of it, like a mist coating everything. I could still taste it on my tongue, smell it in my nose, feel it gunking up my eyelashes. Ray . . .

I felt Louis-Cesare move behind me. He was naked, with the lamplight sheening all that creamy skin, turning it to gold. He had been draped over me like a weighted blanket, only even more comforting. Now I felt his arms go around me, and his body sit up behind mine, preserving the closeness.

It didn't help.

A strange, hollow feeling lay under my breastbone, like a gaping wound. It was so real that I slid a clumsy hand down there, to see if I had been put to bed half gutted. My hand met only smooth, sleep warm skin, without a cut or flaw. Yet I could still feel it: a deep, echoing nothingness, like my soul had been carved out of my body.

Or half of it, I thought sickly.

Dorina . . .

I could see her in that alley, too, as naked as the day we were born, because whatever had happened to us had not transferred over any clothes. She had looked newborn in other ways, too. Her face had been as soft and vulnerable as a child's, her eyes huge and dark and startled, her body hunched and small, silhouetted for an instant before the manic green fury of the portal.

And then she was gone.

I had lost both of them in one night.

"Shhh," Louis-Cesare murmured against my hair, his arms tightening around me. "You're safe. You're safe and it's all right now."

I wanted to scream at him that it wasn't all right, that it would never be all right again. But I couldn't. If I did, that horrible mewling cry I was barely keeping behind my teeth might escape and I couldn't risk that. Couldn't let him know how weak I felt, how vulnerable without my other half.

Sister, I thought, and felt my face crumple.

A strong hand cradled my head, and pulled me against a chest that was warm, hard and comforting. I'd always felt safe in Louis-Cesare's arms, peaceful and calm, like nothing else mattered. But not tonight.

Tonight, I was about to crawl out of my skin.

I knew he could feel it, could detect the minute tremble I couldn't control. Could hear the rapid beat of my pulse, the fight or flight response kicking in with a vengeance. Could smell my emotions on the air: sweat, adrenaline, and all the unnamed chemicals that passed humans by without notice, but to a vamp . . .

Said more than I wanted them to.

But he didn't try to pressure me to talk. Instead, a rhythmic massage of my scalp began, by fingers strong enough to punch through a wall. But with me they were gentle, so gentle, with just enough pressure to ground me and keep me from falling over the edge. I'd always been the excitable one, the fly-off-the-handle one, the impulsive, crazy one.

Or so everyone had said. Tonight, for the first time, I agreed with them. Tonight, I wanted to scream, to cry, to savage those who had destroyed my family.

Dorina, my sister, and lately, my friend. Louis-Cesare, my lover, and brand-new husband. And Ray . . .

Ray hurt worst of all, maybe because he was my direct responsibility. Or because I had seen what happened to him. Dragged through the portal, not by the fey, who had thrown him aside like so much garbage, but by the power of the vortex itself.

My stalwart defender, he'd had no reason to trust a dhampir of all things, had no reason to trust anyone after the life he'd lived, but he'd pledged himself to me nonetheless. Even without the usual blood bond, which I could not do, he'd been loyal, more loyal than anyone, and I'd lost him. I'd lost both of them. And now I was doing it, I was crying and screaming and clinging to Louis-Cesare, who I vaguely realized was rubbing my back in long strokes up and down the spine that did no more good than anything else. The pain was too great. I couldn't think past it, I couldn't breathe, I *couldn't—*

I couldn't bear it.

He held onto me when I tried to get up. I didn't know where I was going, but the crushing guilt and anger and horror all set in at once, making me need to move. And when I couldn't, to fight the very man who was trying to help me.

"Let me go. Let me *go!*"

Louis-Cesare did not let me go.

"I understand," he said instead, his grip gentle but implacable. "It is the worst feeling in the world, when a master loses a Child. I have seen some go mad with grief, have felt the red claws of it shred my own soul. I have lost servants, too."

"Ray wasn't a servant," I said harshly. "He was my *friend.* And he died because those bastards ... those *bastards* ... and I didn't ... I couldn't—"

"You did everything you could have done." He pulled back far enough to look at me, and his face tightened at whatever he saw. "This was not your fault, Dory. It was mine."

"Yours?" I stared up at him, his image blurry through my furious tears. "How the hell was it yours?"

"You would not have been out there except for me. The fey dangled the bait in front of my nose, and I fell for it, utterly and completely—"

I stared up at him. He wasn't making sense, or else I couldn't think straight. Either could have been true right then.

"What bait? What are you talking about?"

"You didn't hear me?" he frowned. "I called back to you, but then, the ballroom was deafening. I should have thought ..."

I vaguely remembered seeing Louis-Cesare shout

something, just before leaping through Hassani's shield. I hadn't been able to hear what it was, but it wouldn't have mattered. There was nothing he could have said that would have kept me from following him.

"But I wasn't thinking," he continued, his voice ragged. "I was reacting, and stupidly so. I lost your sister, I lost Raymond, and I almost lost you." His arms tightened, bruisingly hard.

I pushed at him until he let me go. "What are you *talking about*?"

"Jonathan," he said, uttering the most hated name I knew, and one of the few that could focus even my currently jumbled thoughts.

"What? That's impossible."

Louis-Cesare shook his head, his jaw tight. "He was there, outside the ballroom, smirking at me. I went for him without hesitation. And in doing so, I endangered all of us."

I stared at him, my head spinning. I was still half asleep, and what few faculties I had were stuck on horror—and that name didn't help. It was even worse than the damned Svarestri, the silver haired bastards in jackal's clothing that we'd fought tonight.

Jonathan was a nine-hundred-year-old necromancer who had been using stolen magic to unnaturally prolong his life. But taking other people's magic into your system was like taking a drug. Yes, it could give you a high, as well as extra stamina for spell casting, but it also built up a dependency. One that required more and more over time to achieve the same result.

And that went double for anybody taking enough to elongate their life more than four times the average for magical humans. Jonathan wasn't just addicted to magic anymore, he required it to live, and had become very creative at coming up with new ways to get it. Including trapping and draining a master vampire to the brink of death day after day after day.

Louis-Cesare had eventually escaped his imprisonment, but the experience had left him deeply scarred. I wouldn't have blamed him for taking off after Jonathan tonight. Except for one thing.

"He's dead," I said harshly. "We saw the body—"

"And I *know* him! Do you understand?" The gentle expression of a moment ago was gone, and the blue eyes blazed. "All those days at his mercy, all those nights—" he cut off abruptly, his jaw clenched.

"A glamourie, then. A good one—"

"Do you know what Hassani's master power is?" Louis-Cesare demanded. He was speaking about the unusual abilities that some of the very oldest vamps acquired. I'd assumed that Hassani had one or more; anyone able to hold a consul's position practically required it. But I'd never heard what it was.

"No."

"He sees through glamouries, including fey ones. They say there is nothing his eyes do not perceive truly, and many of his Children have this same gift. The fey did not want us to know that they had kidnapped Dorina. You have enemies; as does your father. If we did not see them, it would widen the field of our search considerably."

"And slow us down."

He nodded. "The fey could therefore not have used glamouries at this court and have expected them to work. *And neither could Jonathan.*"

I frowned, trying to think past the pain, and finding it hard going. "But it couldn't have been him. *We saw the body.*"

"Yes, we did." Louis-Cesare's voice was grim. "But the Circle refused to release it."

He was talking about the Silver Circle, the world's leading magical authority and a frequent pain in my ass. They'd had Jonathan in one of the cells at their main headquarters in Stratford, until he had a little 'accident.' They'd made us travel all the way to England to see what was left.

"That's my point," I said now. "You thought it was him, said you were sure of it—"

"As sure as I could be. But the stench . . ."

My nose wrinkled in memory. The Circle's HQ was underground, almost like an ancient vampire lair, with a maze of twists and turns and a thousand dark doorways. I'd stopped trying to memorize our path after I saw one suddenly fill in and another casually move itself further down a hallway. But instead of the fine furnishings and unctuous servants of a vampire abode, there had been the reek of potions, so thick that it had permeated the very walls, and cold-eyed war mages fingering their weapons as we slowly walked by.

The cell we'd been escorted to had been even worse than the rest of the place, being small and cold and vaguely damp, a miserable spot to spend any time at all. But Jonathan hadn't been there long. Because the best security in the world won't help you if you manage to seriously piss off a demi-goddess.

I didn't know the whole story there, what exactly he'd done to deserve having his heart aged to powder even while it was still beating. Yes, he was a leading figure among our enemies, coming up with new ways to use old magic and giving us a series of migraines in the process. But you don't risk alienating your allies in the middle of a war just to execute a guy who was already on everybody's shit list.

No, it had been personal, whatever he'd done to her, just as it was for me. And despite everything, I hadn't been able to suppress a vicious smile at the expression on the body draped over the thin cot. He'd been on his back, his arms flung out, his face caught halfway between surprised and apoplectic.

Even in death, he'd looked furious that anyone would dare to cross him.

Only now I had to wonder: had she?

"I couldn't get a good scent read," Louis-Cesare was saying. "The mages say we live like snakes in holes in the ground, but at least we clean ours. They had decayed protection wards like spider's webs in every corner, with new ones merely layered over the top. There was potions' residue, some of it going back centuries, like pepper in my nose. There were spells, crawling all over each other, and snapping and snarling everywhere I turned, or whenever a war mage passed too close to another . . ."

I nodded. The mage who had been chosen for our escort had been civil, at least, and had managed to keep a sneer off his face most of the time. But his damned coat had shocked me every time I got near it, which was difficult to avoid in some of those narrow tunnels. Not that I could have anyway. I'd initially thought that I was just being clumsy, having been thrown off my usual game by the level of creepy, but no.

I'd looked down after the fifth or sixth shock to see the damned coat *reaching out for me* with its hem. Like leather fingers ready to pinch. As a result, by the time we'd reached the cells, the only thing I'd been able to smell was my own searing flesh.

Damned mages.

"I couldn't scent Jonathan through all that," Louis-Cesare added. "But tonight was different. The taste of his blood on the air, the stench of corrupt magic—it was exactly as I remembered. I've never smelled it as strongly on anyone else, or in precisely the same combination. It may as well have been his signature cologne."

I sat there, and despite the complete sincerity in my lover's voice, I was having a hard time with this. "But I talked to her. She assured me—"

"You mean the Pythia," he said, referring to the chief seer of the mages, who pretended to preside over the whole supernatural community.

I nodded. Despite her court's claims, and my father's best efforts to seduce her to our side, she mostly worked with the Circle. Of course, she'd lie if they asked her to. Rumor was she was even dating a war mage these days.

But I'd been in a business where judging people accurately was important for a very long time, and I remembered the intensity in those strange, too-pale eyes, when she'd told me what had happened. She'd shifted into my room at the consul's court without warning—a demigoddess's privilege, I supposed—and practically scared me to death. One second, there'd been nothing but air behind me, and the next—

A skinny blonde chick with weird eyes and weirder clay earrings had been standing there. She'd seen me notice the latter and said that some of the young initiates at her court had made them for her. They were supposed to be chocolate kisses, her favorite candies.

They'd looked more like poop emojis to me, but I hadn't been dumb enough to say so.

She'd stood there awkwardly for a moment before blurting out that Jonathan was dead and she was sorry she couldn't have saved him for me. And I'd promptly forgotten about terrible earrings and good manners and the fact that people who ruled whole countries were on a waiting list to see this woman. And just turned around and ran. News travels fast and I'd wanted to get to Louis-Cesare before he heard it from someone else.

I'd made it, if only just. And then we'd gone to see for ourselves, because neither of us could believe it, otherwise. And damn it, maybe I should have stayed and questioned her some more, but I still didn't think she'd lied!

Yet it seemed equally unlikely that she could have been fooled. She was the damned Pythia. I just didn't know anymore.

"You're saying that the mages deceived us somehow," I said.

Louis-Cesare shook his head. "I'm saying that it was Jonathan. How he came to be there I do not know."

I frowned. My head hurt; my *heart* hurt. I wasn't up for this.

And Louis-Cesare didn't look any happier. "If I'd stopped, even for a moment," he said, his eyes distant. "But there he was, leering at me from underneath one of those black masks, having evaded death yet again. He took off and I went after him—immediately, not pausing to think that of course it was a trap. But not for me."

"Or for me." I put my head on his chest. "They wanted Dorina. They left me lying in the street, while eight or ten of them shoved her through that portal."

"I know. I saw. I tried to reach her, but I wasn't fast enough."

Neither was I, I thought, and shivered. His arms tightened. "I'm sorry," he said roughly. "We shouldn't be talking about this now."

"Except that I want to talk about this now. I need—"

I stopped because I wasn't sure what I needed. I hadn't felt like this since I lost my mother, all those centuries ago. I'd found the village where she'd lived blackened and corpse-like, under a blanket of new fallen snow. Plague, they'd said. It had had to be burned.

They'd lied.

She'd been murdered, and I hadn't been there to save her. She'd been lost to me, because I was too slow in tracking her down. I'd been nine at the time, a skinny, pale, dark eyed waif, but a dhampir nonetheless. The Roma, who had taken me in as a baby after she was forced to give me up, had known what I'd become: a predator, one who could fight off their enemies.

But I hadn't been able to save them in the end, any more than I had her. I didn't seem to be able to save anyone. And, suddenly, the torrent of emotions I'd felt then burned through my veins again: fear, anger, hatred, loss. I suddenly knew what I wanted, as I had all those years ago, and it wasn't sitting here grieving uselessly.

I wanted a *target*.

And now I had one.

CHAPTER FOUR

Dory, Cairo

"**N**o," Louis-Cesare said, his voice hard as I struggled against his hold. "No!" he said, as I fought to get out of bed, to find the bastard who had done this to my family. "*No!*" he said, as I swore to make Jonathan bleed.

"Why are you doing this?" I yelled in my lover's face, because try as I might, I couldn't break that iron grip.

"I failed you!" he said, his color high. "I failed you tonight, and as a direct result, you lost two whom you love. You lost a part of yourself. I won't fail you again!"

"Then get off me!"

"Dory." I found my face captured between two huge hands. Sometimes I forgot just how big Louis-Cesare was. Before I met him, I'd usually gone for shorter men. At five foot two, nearly everyone was tall to me, and it made the height difference less ridiculous. Yet who had I married?

A six-foot-four-inch giant with matching hands and body, the latter of which was pressing me down into the mattress, forcing me to listen. I didn't want to listen. And while I'm not as strong, I'm wily.

A second later, Louis-Cesare was sprawled on the bed, face up because I'd just flipped us. "I'm going after him!" I snarled.

I found myself flipped back again, and this time, he had a foot hooked under the bed, giving him leverage. Damned long legs! "I understand," he said tightly, "You're angry, and rightfully so. But you're not thinking—"

"I don't want to think! I want to *kill something*!"

"I know. I've been there. And I've seen others who experienced the loss of a Child. But I've also seen more than one master dead because they didn't stop to heal—"

"I'm not a master," I said, fighting him. "I'm not even a vampire. Without Dorina, I'm *nothing*—"

"That's not true—"

"It's completely true and you know it! Nobody gave a damn about me until they found out about her, so what difference does it make—"

I stopped, but not because he had said anything. But because he hadn't. Not a word, yet the expression on his face was eloquent.

I had rarely seen Louis-Cesare angry. When you're as powerful as he is, that sort of thing is dangerous. He usually kept himself on a tight leash.

But I was seeing it now.

The aristocratic face had gone deathly white, except for two little spots of color high on his cheekbones. His hair was everywhere, a tousled auburn mess, and the sapphire blue eyes were as bright as I'd ever seen them. He wasn't angry, I realized. He was *furious*.

I stopped struggling.

"*I* give a damn," he finally said, his voice harsh. "I didn't fall in love with Dorina. I still barely know Dorina. I fell in love with *you*."

He got up suddenly and walked away, not bothering with the opulent robe that somebody had draped over the end of the bed. I didn't go after him. I was angry, too, more so than I'd been for a long time. He had no right to keep me here!

But he had positioned himself, whether intentionally or not, directly in front of both possible ways out. He was standing between me and the door, and looking out of the sweep of windows that were currently showing a fake, or at least very enhanced, view of the desert. We weren't anywhere near the desert, being in the middle of Old Cairo, but the wards here were determined to present a pretty picture.

It was pretty, although not because of the sweep of stars or the moon silvering the sand dunes or the wind whipping a few palm trees around. I barely noticed them with my husband standing there. That word—husband—still felt strange, while lover rolled easily off the tongue. Maybe because I'd had lovers before, while the other . . .

I was still getting used to.

Lovers didn't tell me what to do; lovers didn't care. At least not the lovers I'd ever had. Some of them had been okay people; some had been outright bastards. But none had ever cared enough about me to get wounded by anything I said.

And yet choose to stick around anyway.

I hugged my knees and wondered what I was supposed to do now. I didn't talk out problems; I hit things. But I didn't want to hit Louis-Cesare. So, I sat there and stared at him instead, trying to come up with an argument that might get me out that door. It didn't work, but the view was nice. The view was incredible.

He was powerfully but elegantly made, with long, graceful lines that flowed smoothly from the muscles of his shoulders and back to the smoothness of his buttocks and thighs. The lamplight loved him, glinting off the hints of red in that glorious mane, gilding the smattering of freckles on his shoulders, and turning the blue eyes to tawny gold.

But while anyone else who looked like that would have been trying to distract me, using his body to get me into another frame of mind, Louis-Cesare wasn't like that. He wasn't like anyone I'd ever known. It was probably why we kept bumping heads.

Even now, even after marrying the guy, I didn't really understand him. I knew things *about* him: he was every inch the aristocrat from another age, with crazy ideas like *noblesse oblige*, the concept that rulers had a responsibility to the ruled, and that power came mixed with duty. That idea was woefully out of fashion among humans, and it had never been in style with vamps in the first place.

I knew that he had serious trust issues caused by a series of important figures in his life walking out on him —something we had in common. In fact, we had a lot in common, including a lifetime of being lied to, left behind, betrayed, and discarded. It had resulted in both of us having issues opening up and being fully honest, even with a partner, something we were still working on.

I knew that he was a mass of contradictions, with nature and nurture in his case having come into serious conflict. He was generous to a fault with money, but often stingy with his thoughts. He was kind and patient with subordinates, but could be harsh and irritated with those on his level who were behaving badly. He was willing to roll up his sleeves and do menial work when required, but he was proud, even haughty, with his fellow vamps, holding them to a code of ethics that they'd never subscribed to.

He was stubborn, my God was he stubborn! But he could be strangely open minded, too, accompanying me to shows for artists he'd never heard of, or listening—with the strangest look on his face—to some of the garage and neo-punk bands I liked, trying to see the allure. I don't think that had worked, but we had discovered a mutual appreciation for trashy novels and spicy Sichuan cooking, so I supposed that was something.

But, no, I didn't pretend to understand him. I'd partly agreed to this trip hoping to get away from the war and spend some quiet time together. And we *had* had a single, wonderful day. Hassani had been held up from playing chaperone by some court issue a couple of days ago, so we'd been given a local guide and a trip to the temple of Abu Simbel, the famous memorial to Ramses II and Queen Nefertari.

Fortunately, we never made it there. I was already tired of aging stone monuments, desert sand, and heat. Instead, when our airplane stopped at Aswan, the nearest airport, we discovered a Nubian market and fell in love. Or, at least, I did, and Louis-Cesare hadn't seemed to mind the idea of spending the day among a gorgeous collection of blue, yellow and green buildings, with colorful murals and quirky inhabitants, instead of a long, dusty trip into the desert.

So, we'd overruled our guide and gone shopping.

We'd started with a visit to a local family, who gave us bright red hibiscus tea while we tossed treats to their pet crocodiles. Crocs were everywhere in the village: alive, and waiting for their next snack; dead and carefully mummified; tiny and perched on a local man's shoulder; or huge and skinned and splayed out above doorways. The usually vicious creatures had been tamed by being hand reared, along with being fed a hefty diet of chicken and fish, to the point that several of them were positively potbellied.

The left-over dinosaurs were well taken care of, being an important money maker for the locals. It was much needed after the famous Aswan Dam took their land away, which they were still waiting to be compensated for. The crocs were also a nod to the crocodile-headed, ancient Egyptian god Sobek, who ironically, like the dam, was supposed to control the flooding of the Nile.

Afterwards, we'd eaten an early lunch of *hawawshi* bought from a street vendor, which turned out to be a crispy pita bread stuffed with beef, onions, peppers and chilies—basically an Egyptian taco and every bit as good as it sounds. Then we wandered the streets, marveling at the artwork on the houses, which was huge, in your face, and exuberant. There was everything from abstract designs to full on murals, including a beautiful one of feluccas sailing on the Nile; from dusky Nubian beauties in traditional attire, to gorgeous Arabic calligraphy flowing along the sides of buildings like water; and, in a memorable instance, of a bunch of pert camels, one with his tongue sticking out.

Speaking of camels, the real things had been everywhere, with happy-looking pom poms dancing on their bridles in every color of the rainbow, to lure in tourists whose feet were starting to hurt. I had eyed them speculatively, but we'd chosen to walk to the market instead, where the hunt was soon on for the tackiest souvenir possible for my uncle Radu. He managed to combine deep pockets with Liberace taste, so it had been a struggle to find something suitable.

We'd finally settled on a *galabeya*, one of the full-length robes worn by men and women all over Egypt, in eye searing purple, with a shimmering phoenix on the back in gold paillettes and sequins. I was pretty sure it was supposed to be for a woman, but Louis-Cesare knew his Sire. He'd immediately declared the search over, and that Radu would love it.

He was very likely right.

The day had ended with savory-sweet chicken tagines with preserved lemon at a colorful restaurant overlooking the Nile. We'd completed the meal with spicy Nubian ginger-coffee made on charcoal and hot sand, while a glorious orange sunset splashed our faces. It was one of those perfect days, a picture postcard glimpse of a life that could be, and one that had given me unrealistic expectations for the rest of the trip.

Because that had been our only night off. I hugged my knees and jealously recalled the dreams I'd had for our honeymoon. Of lazy days sailing down the Nile, of a selfie on top of the tallest pyramid, of an evening making love in a tent in the desert with nobody but our camel around to hear . . .

Okay, maybe not that last one, since November could be chilly at night. Like this room. Like the knot in my gut, because I'd alienated the only person I had left and I wasn't even sure why.

I bit my lip, my own anger having drained away as fast as it had come, which was normal for me. My husband tended to take a little longer. I found myself wanting to go to Louis-Cesare, but not sure that it wouldn't make things worse.

Dhampirs didn't do relationships. Dhampirs were lonely by nature. We had to be, as most of us weren't much saner than the things we hunted. I'd always been more stable than the norm, but grouping with other people had been a rarity and usually short lived. There'd been hunting parties to take down bigger prey, even a few that lasted a week or two. And desperate groping sessions in the dark sometimes, with other hunters as lonely as me.

But nothing like this.

Nothing close to this.

Louis-Cesare was the longest I'd ever been with anyone, and I was pretty sure I was screwing this up. Make that definitely sure. I was also freezing without his warmth, in more than one way.

But Hassani's people had thought of everything, and along with the luxurious sheets and warm blankets on the bed, there was a barbaric looking fur heavy enough to have been a rug, just in case the little half human got cold.

I sat up and pulled it close about me. And then decided what the hell, and dragged it off the bed to join my lover at the window. It felt barbaric against my naked skin, and looked it, too, with the dark brown color sheened by golden lamplight, the same that played over Louis-Cesare's body. The wards around this place assured that we weren't flashing the locals—probably—not that I cared much at the moment.

I didn't say anything, not sure what would help, and for a long moment, we just stood there. Me wrapped in my fur, him wrapped in lamplight, neither speaking. I wasn't even sure that he would.

But after a moment, he broke the silence.

"I almost lost you tonight," Louis-Cesare said roughly. "I know you're hurting, but did you stop to think how I would have felt if my stupidity had cost . . . even more than it did? You say you're not important, that you can go running after your revenge and it won't matter what happens to you. How can you not see—"

He broke off. He was still staring out the window, never having turned around, so his expression was hidden from me. I didn't need it. There was pain in every line of his body, although not the physical kind. His healing abilities had already erased the signs of battle as if they'd never been. But there were other ways to hurt, and the stiffness of his stance and the almost painful rigidity of his spine spoke of deeper wounds.

The kind that even a vampire couldn't always heal.

I put a hand on his back, and it felt like velvet stretched over steel. I smoothed it around his side, until I felt the warm, inward dip of his stomach, the ladder of his ribs, and the springy hair and soft indentations around a nipple. There was nothing to say, so I didn't say it. But my touch seemed to be doing something.

Slowly, I felt a little of that awful tension start to ease.

I lay my cheek against his back and continued to say nothing. I didn't pretend to understand everything that was going on with him, but I got part of it. I got enough.

Louis-Cesare and I weren't the greatest with communication, but we were learning. It was like two skittish horses getting to know each other; there had been a lot of rearing and even some biting, but also some snuffling and staring and deliberate prancing, just to see if the other noticed. And, lately, some genuine intimacy, although with serious side eye, both wondering if the other was about to bolt.

But we were talking—about some things. About us. But there was one conversation we continued not to have. One topic that was still off limits.

Jonathan.

Not that I hadn't tried. But nothing made Louis-Cesare close down faster, or clam up more completely. Maybe because he was the only creature in living memory that had made my husband feel weak. Powerless. Afraid.

A first-level master rarely experienced those emotions. He'd not only left behind human weakness, but had also forgotten what it was like to be a lower-level vampire, ordered about by the god-like beings on top of the heap. And that was truer for Louis-Cesare than for most, as even among first-level vamps, he was unusually strong.

He had been a dueling champion for the European consul, Anthony, for centuries, helping to support that crumbling wreck of a court. Because as lax as Anthony was, he was far better of a ruler than some who might have replaced him. And at the same time that Louis-Cesare was almost singlehandedly propping up a failing consul, he was also keeping another first-level master in thrall.

That was right: Louis-Cesare had kept one of the most powerful vampires on the planet under his control, bending him to his will in order to save the life of a woman he despised. But he had felt responsible for her, and he was honorable to a fault. So, he had expended a huge amount of power to make sure that she was safe.

Yet Jonathan had found a way to bring that same man to his knees, over and over and over again. Draining him of power and thereby of life, and in doing so, forcing Louis-Cesare's family to have to scramble to find enough energy to support their master, feeding him everything they had through the blood bond to sustain him. Only to have most of it go to his tormentor.

Jonathan hadn't merely victimized Louis-Cesare; he'd held the whole damned clan for ransom. It was a master vampire's worst nightmare, that he would not be able to protect his family. So, yes, he did know what I was feeling.

The tension had slowly leaked out of him while we stood there, until he was leaning back against me. I put my arms around him from behind, dragging the fur along with them so that it covered us both. With his regal bearing, long, loose hair and fur draped form, he could have been a king from another time, or a Viking warrior lost on a raid and washed up on Egyptian shores.

But I'd seen plenty of beautiful bodies through the years; I'd seen far fewer beautiful souls.

"I'm sorry," I said.

One of those large, yet elegant hands covered mine. "You mean everything to me," he said hoarsely. *Everything. Promise me—*"

"I promise," I murmured, my cheek flat against the warmth of his back. "I won't do anything tonight."

I felt a little more tension melt out of his spine. "I swear to you, if they live, I will find those who hurt you. And wreak a bloody vengeance on our enemies."

Our enemies, I thought, a little startled. But, from a vampire perspective, they were, weren't they? Louis-Cesare and I were married, meaning that my rag tag crew also belonged to him now. And anyone who hurt one of his . . .

I smiled against his back. "I know."

He turned and swept me up in a kiss, so sudden that it took my breath away, although it probably would have done that anyway. Louis-Cesare knew how to kiss, but tonight . . . tonight there was something fierce in the way he gripped me, his fingers digging into the skin of my back and upper thigh. Something possessive in the way he picked me up and carried me back to the bed. Something savage in the way his lips plundered mine, and yet also shook slightly against my skin.

I was part of his family, and he'd almost lost me, I realized. He was trying to comfort me, while feeling the same way that I did. He wanted to go after them, too, the ones who had hurt me, wanted it desperately. But he would put that need on hold to make sure that I was all right.

Tears wet my cheeks, and I couldn't tell if they were his or mine. If anyone ever asks why I married him, I thought. This, this is what I'll tell them.

CHAPTER FIVE

Dory, Cairo

Louis-Cesare was usually a tender lover, but not tonight. That was all right; I didn't want tender. It would have ripped me apart, sent me screaming into the void. I wanted a partner who could meet my frustrated fury with his own, and turn the terrible need to hurt into something else, something glorious.

The light from the nearest lamp threw our shadows on the wall and I laughed, because together, we made a monster. A hunched backed, multi-limbed thing that would have sent anybody else scrambling for the hills. That was good; that was perfect. I'd been called a monster all my life, and for once, I was fine with it. Let the fey find out exactly what they had awakened.

Louis-Cesare seemed to understand what I wanted without my having to tell him. Although perhaps my body was already doing that. I scratched my nails down his back, hard enough to leave bleeding lines in their wake, and he healed them before I finished the movement. But his eyes caught fire, turning blood red in the lamplight, and I laughed again, baring my throat.

He already wore my mark, the one I'd given him on the night we chose each other, the one that made him mine. But he'd never reciprocated, I didn't know why. But this seemed like the perfect time.

"Take it," I urged. I wanted to feel his fangs in me, wanted the distraction of the pain, but also the sense of belonging that such a bite gives, a closeness beyond anything else I'd ever experienced.

But he shook his head. "No." It was raw.

"Why not? I'm giving it to you—"

"I don't want a gift!" The strange eyes blazed. And no, that wasn't lamplight. "I want to earn it. I want to deserve you—"

"And you think you don't?"

"After tonight?" It was his turn to laugh, and it was bitter. "No, I think I don't."

He tried to get up, but I wrapped my legs around his waist and hung on. I could feel him next to me, hard and thick and long and perfect, but it wasn't his body I craved. All right, it wasn't *only* his body. I wanted to wipe that expression off his face, the one that said that all the titles and money and success in the world didn't matter. That to him, he was still that little boy inside, the one whose family had abandoned him, had locked him away, had left him to rot.

Louis-Cesare had never felt like he belonged anywhere, deserved anything, although I'd thought that had changed after we found each other. And maybe it had, to a degree. I'd never seen him happier than after I claimed him—me, a lowly dhampir, who had dared to mark that aristocratic neck. Any other vamp would have been outraged, appalled and possibly homicidal.

He had been incandescent.

But he'd never done it back.

I turned his face to me and kissed him, gently, sucking on the full lower lip for a moment before nipping it hard enough to draw blood. I smeared it with another kiss, white hot and burning, and then pulled back to watch his body absorb it. That never got old.

"We're really screwed up, you know that?" I whispered, and felt rather than heard him laugh.

"So I've been told."

"Some say it's a danger fetish, having a dhampir

51

girlfriend."

"A dhampir *wife*," he said, and the bite in the tone told me that he'd heard them, too: the nasty little comments, the furtive looks, the smiles quickly hidden by a fan or a hand. 'She's pretty enough, but so is a viper. And you wouldn't see me letting one of those near my—'

Louis-Cesare slid against me, making my breath catch in my throat, as if he could hear my thoughts. But he couldn't. Not anymore. Dorina had facilitated that on the few occasions when it had happened, or I had by borrowing her gifts. And now she was—

"Don't," he said, watching my face.

He kissed me between my breasts, which was nice but not what I'd asked for. He kissed my stomach, my thighs, the knee I'd unconsciously pulled up beside his ear, opening myself, offering. He kissed me there, too, longer, slower, sweeter, but it still wasn't enough, wasn't what I—

He bit me, finally, and despite it not being on the neck, not being a claiming bite, it was still perfect. I arched up with a cry, the pain and pleasure of a vampire bite being heightened in that particular area to something approaching ecstasy. Make that all the way there, I thought, half delirious in seconds, especially when his tongue joined the action, to kiss and suck and lick the tiny wounds better. Oh, God, so much better!

If they could put this in pill form, they'd addict the world.

As it was, the monster on the wall was bucking and flailing and yelling 'now, damn you' within seconds, but to no avail. The long, slow warm, wet torture continued, because he wanted me to lose my mind, I thought, panting. If I lost my mind, I couldn't think . . . about anything . . . oh, *God!*

When I could breathe, I pushed him back, caught him behind the neck and sat up, taking him fully inside me as I did so. And groaning as I sat down, straddling his lap as he shivered against me, inside me. He was big, and I wasn't quite ready, but the stretch and burn were exactly, *exactly* what I wanted tonight.

When I finally had him all, I stopped, panting, and stared into his eyes as his forehead came to rest against mine. "You don't have to prove anything," I said. "Not to me."

"I know," he said, and then gasped, because I'd just pulled up again, sliding along the full length of him, giving him no rest.

"Do you really know?"

"Dory—"

"Do you really, *really* know?"

His face flushed, possibly because I was working him harder now. Or possibly because I had leaned back, supporting myself with one arm on the bed and one on his forearm, giving him a view all the way up my body. Everything from where we were joined to my sweat-slick abs, tightening under the workout they were getting, to his favorite parts of all, which had started bouncing in time to the rhythm I was setting, which meant that they were bouncing hard.

I had never thought of myself as beautiful before I met him. My looks were something I played up when it would help me bring in a bad guy with a decent bounty on his head, but somehow, they were almost something outside of me. Another tool to be used, not something that mattered.

Because, when people find out that you're dhampir, not much else does.

But with him . . . I saw myself through different eyes. His eyes. And in those eyes, I was beautiful.

Even better, the next moment, his head was thrown back, his own eyes closed, and his face, while still flushed, was somehow calmer. Fiercely determined but also at peace. It was a strange combination.

But it was better than the anguish I'd seen there before, the struggle of a man who insisted on taking the weight of the world on his shoulders, even when he didn't have to. I loved him, but he drove me crazy sometimes, as crazy as I was determined to drive him. Which wasn't all that difficult, frankly.

I clamped down, hard, and he growled and rolled us off the bed. We hit the floor, taking one of the lamps with us, which sloshed out enough oil to set the rug on fire. "Leave it," Louis-Cesare said, and I arched an eyebrow.

Vampires went up like kerosene-soaked tissue paper when exposed to flame, but I guess tonight was about conquering fears. Or something. I was having a hard time concentrating, since I had ended up on the bottom, with the powerful vampire on top seemingly determined to pound me through the floor.

Or maybe that was the door, I thought, unsure of where the hammering was coming from. Or my heart, I thought, getting sloppily romantic, because the orgasm of the gods was about to hit and hit hard. "Louis-Cesare!" I screamed, and I guessed it had been the door, after all. Because it practically blew off the hinges and there they were, half a dozen of Hassani's servants staring at us.

They had buckets of water in their hands, I didn't know why. The sprinkler system seemed to be working fine, I thought, as it proceeded to douse us along with the flames. "Get out," Louis-Cesare suggested, pulling the crimson and gold robe down from the bed to cover me.

The servants just stood there, looking appalled, because I guess Hassani didn't run a den of iniquity sort of court.

"Get out!" Louis-Cesare ordered, and put some power behind it.

They got out, which I appreciated considering that he had never stopped his current occupation, or indeed so much as broken rhythm.

"They're definitely going to gossip about us now," I told him, giggling.

"They would have been disappointed otherwise," was the blithe response.

"And we wouldn't . . . want to do . . . that," I agreed, as

his pace picked up, and my head encountered the bedpost a few too many times, and my butt threatened to freeze to the chilly stones on Hassani's now waterlogged floor.

I decided I'd live.

And then, just in case the bastards were listening outside, I gave a few screams of appreciation. And then a few more. And then I was basically screaming all the time and I am not a screamer, particularly in bed. But that . . .

Damned well deserved it.

I stared upwards afterwards, panting and lightheaded, my body tingling and throbbing in places I had not known that it could tingle and throb. And watched a diligent little sprinkler overhead shower me with ice cold water. Too late, I told it, grinning sloppily.

Much too late.

* * *

Round two was in a new room down the hall, which we'd found open and empty after a foray wrapped in a half-drenched fur. The servants had fled, so we weren't caught *in flagrante delicto* with our bear skin, instead of on it. And the bed in our new digs was just as big as the old one and, soon, just as well used.

Louis-Cesare sprawled on his stomach afterwards, boneless and effortlessly graceful. We hadn't thought to bring a lamp, so he was lit only by moonlight. It was a good look on him.

Silver limned his face, turning it dark blue in the hollows and bleaching the lashes almost white. It did the same with the tiny, soft hairs along his spine, running down to the sweet rise of his buttocks and thighs, before deepened into the nest of curls that showed briefly between his spread legs. I let my eyes wander down the smooth line of muscle running from hip to knee, and then again from knee to long, elegant foot. The bottoms of his feet were as smooth and uncalloused as a newborn's, thanks to vampire healing abilities.

He cracked an eye, feeling the weight of my gaze. "You wish to go again?"

"Just looking."

He appeared vaguely relieved. I grinned. So much for vampire stamina.

In reality, I wasn't perving . . . much. I just couldn't believe that this was real. Any of it: my marriage, my new status, the fact that I was an honored guest *at a vampire court*. But especially that I had someone to come home to. Someone to grieve with. Someone . . .

Who gave a damn.

That wasn't supposed to happen and it kept freaking me out.

A strong, long-fingered hand lay limply on the mattress. I picked it up and a faint roughness met my touch along the pads of the fingers and ball of the hand. It shouldn't have been there. Fighting with a rapier doesn't usually leave callouses, and his body should have erased any damage before it could build up anyway.

But it existed, nonetheless.

Relics of early sword practice, I thought, my fingers tracing the lines. I closed my eyes and could almost see him, from all those years ago. An earnest faced little boy, probably still redheaded at that point, holding a wooden practice sword. Running around a courtyard with his fencing masters and studying everything about them, from their stance to their finger positions to the direction their eyes darted before they struck, giving away the direction of their lunge.

I bet he'd been a quick study, that he'd surprised them.

He constantly surprised me.

Like tonight. I'd been furious when I thought he was trying to keep me from pursuing my enemies, from avenging two of the only people who'd ever fought for me. But in fact, he just didn't want me running off exhausted and vulnerable and alone. He wanted me to understand that this wasn't my hunt; it was ours. That this wasn't my family anymore; it was ours.

And that I never had to hunt alone again.

"Something pleases you?" Louis-Cesare asked. I opened my eyes to find that he'd turned on his side, watching me as I explored him.

"You please me," I said roughly, not knowing how to process this much emotion, all at once.

I smoothed a hand up his arm, wanting to touch, wanting something to ground me. But it was caught before it got very far. Clasped and held and then examined, as I had been doing to him.

I didn't like that. My nails were short and utilitarian, and my skin bruised from some part of tonight's adventures. There was nothing to admire there.

But Louis-Cesare didn't seem to agree.

A kiss to the back of the hand, another to the wrist. Blue eyes looking at me with his lips still pressed against my flesh. "You please me, too."

My breath started coming faster in my chest.

I reached out with my other hand, desperate to feel all those little details: the chest, hard and lean and beautifully defined; the Adam's apple that moved so temptingly under my fingers; the shoulder blades with their dusting of freckles that matched the ones on his back—another relic of a former life. The skin was different there, light golden brown instead of the cream of areas further down, speaking of long days spent shirtless under the French sun.

I wondered if it would have a different texture under my tongue. If I could close my eyes and map his body as easily by taste and touch as by sight. I bet I could—

But he wouldn't let me.

I'd closed my eyes again in preparation, but a second sense had me opening them again. And discovering that my lover had moved, in that so quiet way that vamps have, to the point that I hadn't even noticed it. Of course, I'd been distracted, I told myself, staring directly up into blue, blue eyes.

"What?" I asked, a little breathlessly.

A faint tilt to the edge of the lip, and a glance that seemed to rake my body with an actual, physical touch, did not help my breathing.

"What?" I said again, as he slowly gathered my hands, holding them together in one lazy, iron-fisted grip, above my head.

"*What?*" I demanded, as he went back to that disturbing exploration.

He kissed my forehead. "My turn," he whispered, and my whole body shuddered.

He took his time, examining every inch of me, refusing to stop when I squirmed. I supposed it was fair, but I couldn't imagine what I looked like: beaten and bruised, bangs half gone, sweaty from previous sessions . . . not too tempting. But he didn't seem to see it that way.

A big, elegant hand dragged those callouses from breast to thigh and back again. He seemed fascinated by the color difference between his hand, probably the darkest shade of gold on his body, and the milkiness of my skin. I'd seen the sun plenty in my lifetime, but dhampirs don't tan. The same healing abilities that prevented me from wearing earrings or bleeding out after a battle also erased a sunburn in a day, often less.

It was annoying, as dead white skin was a fashion no-no these days, but Louis-Cesare didn't seem to mind. Or maybe it was the textural difference that intrigued him. The rough spots on his skin found no purchase on mine, sliding easily back and forth, back and forth, back and—

"Stop it," I growled. "I don't like—"

"To be admired? Why? You are exquisite."

I stared at him. "Yeah, that's why most people run at the sight of me."

"They're intimidated." He kissed my stomach. "Do you know how many people I saw watching you tonight?"

"Afraid I'd steal the silver. Or possibly stab them with it."

He looked up, and the dark eyes were serious. "They were admiring glances. Do you have any idea what you looked like then? What you look like now?"

I started to make a joke, but the look in his eyes stopped me. "No."

"Then perhaps I should show you."

I'd thought he meant in a mirror, but apparently not, because a warm, wicked mouth captured a nipple. The talented tongue played with it for a moment, swirling around my softness, then playfully biting the little nub he'd teased up until I was aching with it. Before abruptly starting to suck.

And, okay, I thought, that's—that's not fair.

Louis-Cesare did not appear to care. In fact, he compounded the issue by slipping that talented hand between my thighs, where he found another little nub. And, for the record, callouses on certain things are . . . nice. Very nice. *Exquisitely* fucking nice and suddenly I was squirming constantly.

I may have also started to vocalize, just slightly. I wasn't screaming—I was not a screamer—but I might have been panting a little. Which was completely understandable considering the twin provocations. And then maybe a moan or two slipped out, and some Romanian curse words that I thought I'd forgotten but apparently not, and then a few things that might qualify as shrieks, only they were way softer than that and they should probably come up with another word but I couldn't think of one right then, maybe because I was having problems remembering my damned name.

And then the shrieks became louder, but I didn't care, because you try to stop it when he's—and then he—and oh, yeah, oh yeah, right there, *right there*.

"No, go back! Go back!" I shrieked, when he deliberately strayed off target. And it *was* deliberate. The wicked little glint in his eye gave it away, as well as the fact that he went back to the exact spot as soon as I said something, finding it with no problem whatsoever, the *bastard*.

And, all right, there might have been a little screaming going on at the end, but I can't be sure because I think I blacked out for a second. When I came around, he had a self-satisfied look on his face and my body was quivering and shaking and moaning in a way that would have been embarrassing, but I was past that. Way past.

"In case you were wondering," he breathed in my ear. "Darkly dangerous, seductive red lips, sleek dark hair, black stilettos and a thin, barely-there dress that flashed open now and then to reveal a *stake*. At a vampire ball."

I cleared my throat and tried to remember how to talk. "Well, I wasn't going to go in unarmed—"

He laughed suddenly, full throated and genuine, and his cheek came to rest on my stomach. His eyes met mine. "I do love you."

I'd been about to point out that he hadn't been unarmed, either, but at that, I stopped. I found that I couldn't speak, suddenly. My fingers found his hair, and I let them comb through it until his eyes closed and his breathing evened out, and the powerful limbs went slack. And then I kept on doing it anyway, just because I could.

"I love you, too," I whispered, and finally went to sleep.

CHAPTER SIX

Dorina, Faerie

"Augggghhhhh!"

Somebody was screaming.

I did not think that it was me. It was hard to tell over the sound of the portal roaring like a hurricane in my ears, and the violent green of all that swirling power searing my vision. I had many ways to see, but the raging energy of the line negated most of them.

That was all right.

I did not need to see my attackers to kill them.

Their scent was strange in my nose, and their bodies showed up as cool spaces in my mind's eye against all that pulsing power. They did not seem to have the same ease at detecting me, however. Several were turned in completely the wrong direction, while others were moving around with their arms out, trying to locate me after I tore away from them in the initial confusion.

I helped them out with that, slitting the first creature's throat before he knew I was there and then had two more jump me, zeroing in on his aborted cry. I whirled, dancing away from one and slashing another with my blade, where it stuck in the bone of his arm. I tried to cut through and then I tried to pull out, either of which would have worked easily with a human. But he wasn't one, and my blade stayed trapped.

We circled each other, him trying to get a knife in me

while I tried to free myself. I finally cracked through the bone with sheer brute force. But instead of falling away into the electric tunnel we were traveling through, the severed arm began orbiting us, like a piece of clothing thumping about the laundry machine back home.

There were other body parts tumbling around, too, one of which was still screaming. It was part of the small vampire that Dory liked. He must have been close enough when the portal opened to have been swept inside along with us.

My eyes were adjusting now, to the point that I could see the fey as dark shadows silhouetted against all that leaping color. I still couldn't make out any details, but the vampire . . . yes, I could see him. Because he is family, I thought, and smiled.

I cut off a fey's head and offered the vampire the bleeding stump, but he only stared at me. Another fey jumped onto my back while a second grabbed my wrist—the one with the scimitar in it. I dropped the body of their compatriot and snatched a tumbling arm as it fell past.

"Is this yours?" I asked the vampire.

"What?" He stared at me some more.

"Does this belong to you?"

"No?"

"Good." I used the jagged femur to stab the fey on my back through the eye. And when he let go, I slashed it across the other's neck.

I picked up the decapitated body and offered the vampire the stump again.

He did not seem to understand.

"Feed," I urged him.

"What? I *can't*!"

Of course, I thought. He has no arms. I dragged the body up to his mouth, to the point that the fey's blood smeared his lips.

"Gah! Gah! Gah!"

I pulled it back. "Is there a problem?"

"Is there a problem? *Is there a problem*?" Blue eyes blazed at me. "I get my limbs torn off, get kidnapped, and now you're trying to *poison* me—"

"It is not poison."

"—and you ask if there's a *problem*?"

I decided that he might be in shock. Just as well. There were four fey still on their feet, including the one with the missing arm, and they were coming.

I broke off half of the scimitar's blade in the first one's neck and kicked a second far enough away that I should have had time to deal with the remaining two. But he only stumbled back a short distance before hitting and then splaying against something that I couldn't see at all. Something that appeared to be rotating and was taking him along with it.

Dodging a blow, I watched him circle against the primordial fury of the line. Ley lines were fascinating: huge rivers of magical power that flowed around the Earth and then beyond. It was said that their energy could dissolve a human in seconds, and a vampire even faster. No one traveled through them without a shield of some kind.

Like the one gleaming all around us, I realized, as two of the remaining fey jumped me.

I slammed their heads together, somersaulted over top of them, and then did it again from behind. They had thick skulls; they did not go down, and one even spun and swung at me. But I twisted away and pulled back out of reach, taking a second to think.

Why did we need a shield inside a portal, which was already a shielded pathway through a line? That was the reason people made such things: to provide safe passage from one point to another. Why bother with a second layer of protection?

Unless they were more interested in keeping something in than keeping something out, I realized.

This wasn't an assassination; it was a kidnapping.

Fear and panic swept through me at the idea of being caged, so much so that I lost myself for a moment. I lashed out, beating my fists and feet against the sides of my prison, and then against the jailors who had stupidly locked themselves in here with me. The shield, which had already been spinning wildly from the tumult inside began rocking alarmingly, sliding and sloshing us around.

The rocking motion became so violent that it brought me out of my fit. It was just in time to see us burst through, not the gate on the other end of the portal, but the side of the portal itself. And go spinning off into the fury of the ley line.

Suddenly, everything changed. It was like the difference between riding down some white-water rapids and surfing the crashing ferocity of an ocean in a major gale. We plummeted down what felt like a fifty-foot wave, then rode another back up, only to be spit out the top and do it all again. And again.

I was overwhelmed for a moment, and I suppose the fey felt the same, because the attacks had stopped. Or perhaps there was another reason for that. A vortex of orbiting body parts beat on me as we spun about, as their owners could no longer do. But some bruises were less of a problem than the reason for the fleshly storm: we were tumbling out of control, and I did not know enough about shields to stop us.

But someone else did.

"Goddamnit!" The vampire yelled, his body, or what was left of it, thumping about the shielded circle. "Hold me up. Let me see!"

"Let you see what?"

"That!" He nodded vigorously at something. "The control!"

"This?" I touched something about the size of a crystal ball. It was on a stick, protruding waist high from what was probably supposed to be the stationary middle of the shield, but which was now slinging all over the place.

"Yes, hold me up, damn you!"

I held him up.

"Fuck," was his verdict.

"Is that bad?"

"No. It's peachy fucking keen, what the hell do you think?"

He gave me a rapid-fire stream of directions that involved turning the ball this way and that, which did not appear to have any effect on the spinning. But the wild, leaping color around us slowly became softer and hazier, like veils across the horizon. Until we burst out of the line, into bright blue skies filled with puffy white clouds and startled birds.

Who were less startled than us when we abruptly plummeted through the air.

"Auggggggghhhhhhhh!" the vampire screamed. "Augggggghhhhhhhh!"

The shield remained in place as we fell, which surprised me. I was under the impression that they did not work outside of the lines. But then, this was a fey shield. Perhaps they were different.

"Augggggghhhhhhhh!" the vampire screamed some more. "Augggggghhhhhhhh!"

We hit the ground and bounced, what must have been fifty feet into the air. And then did it again and again, while also rolling down a steep incline. It was covered in flowers, predominately purple with a few yellow and white ones mixed in.

Beautiful.

"Augggggghhhhhhhh!" the vampire yelled. "Augg—*bump* —auggggh—*bump*—aughhhhhhh!"

We finally rolled to a stop.

I found myself slightly dizzy, but mostly unharmed.

The same could not be said for the vampire, who continued to scream, albeit weakly. I shook my head to clear it, which did not work as well as I would have liked. I still felt as if I was surfing the biggest storm in history, with my stomach doing flips inside my body. It was not a wholly unpleasant sensation, but it did make it hard to move about.

I did so anyway, crawling across the gory floor to gather up the body parts that belonged to my companion. It was easy to tell them apart, as his were smaller than those of the fey. I finished and looked up.

And saw him lying on the bottom of the shield, near the control mechanism, panting and shrieking softly whenever he found enough air. He was covered in blood, his eyes were wild, and he was trembling. I needed to get him somewhere safe, as I did not know if the fey could track their device.

But first, I had to deal with more pressing concerns.

"Hold still," I said, tugging on what remained of his tuxedo.

"Ahhh!"

"I know it hurts. I am sorry."

He stared up at me in apparent shock. His eyes searched my face, as if looking for something. Probably signs of the woman he knew, which he did not find. Dory was not here; I could feel her absence like a missing lung, leaving me breathless. We had never been apart, not even when I took an occasional mental flight away from our body. There had always been a tether there, a strong, unbreakable connection to my other half.

But not now.

It made me feel dizzier than the ride, and more than slightly horrified. I did not know what had been done to us, but this was not the time to think about it. This was the time to survive; thinking would come later.

The vampire seemed to feel the same. He tensed as if bracing himself. And then he nodded.

I held up one of his severed arms and looked at it. It had lost the sleeve, but the arm itself was more or less all right, except for the raw, red meat and shattered bone at the end. The fey hadn't cared how much damage they did, merely wanting to put him out of commission. I felt anger well up in me, red hot and burning, but tamped it down.

Later.

We would have our revenge on whoever had ordered this, but for now, I needed to heal the vampire.

"Ray," I said, suddenly remembering. "Your name is Ray."

"Raymond Lu," he said, his lips white. "I'd shake your hand, but . . ."

"You will in a moment." I regarded the arm again.

It was weakly moving, but not in any purposeful way. A master should be able to control his body parts, even when they were not attached, but Raymond had lost too much blood. He was almost exsanguinated, and that . . .

Would be very bad.

We had avoided exiting through the other end of the portal, and had thereby missed the reception that undoubtedly awaited us. But we weren't scot free. I paused, looking about.

We'd come to rest on the side of a hill, where a goat trail from below divided and created a small plateau. To our right and below was a verdant valley with a large river running through it, and bright green fields with grasses so long and thick that they moved like water under the breeze. To our left was a dense old forest, with tree trunks as big as houses and a canopy so solid that I did not know how any rain penetrated.

It was beautiful, but it was foreign. I could not name a single type of tree, a single bird, or even the variety of grass, which had odd, purple tips. My tongue flickered out, tasting the air. Cool and faintly scented, but also strange. Alien.

Faerie.

It had to be.

We must have traveled too far to reappear on Earth when we exited the ley line, falling instead into the land of the fey, just not where they had intended. I felt a shiver go through me, but it wasn't one of fear. It was excitement, curiosity, the thrill of the new. I was on an alien world that I knew nothing about—

So why did something smell like home?

"Wait," I told Ray, who nodded weakly.

I searched around the gory bodies on the floor, and discovered that they were a bit gorier than I'd expected. Eight times more. There had been eight fey warriors in all, and each of them had on his person a small bag.

A bag of blood.

One of them had ruptured during the fight, but the others were intact, inside of clear packets that looked like plastic but felt like paper. It was very odd. I had no idea what they were doing there.

But they were a lifesaver, possibly literally.

Ray did not seem to want the fey blood; perhaps it was too strange to nourish him? But he had to have something. I tore the corner off of one of the packets, to make sure that my nose wasn't deceiving me, and he made a soft sound. Yes, it was human. I stared at it some more. It appeared to be fresh.

I glanced back at Ray.

Normally, I would never have thought to give a possibly adulterated substance to an already weakened ally, but I did not think that this was poisoned. I could detect no corruption, and in any case, what choice was there? Even were there humans to be found in this place, I did not know how to find them.

And Ray did not have much time.

Exsanguinated vampires could be brought back, but if his limbs were not reattached before he bled out, they could shrivel and die. Leaving him as a stump of a creature for the rest of whatever life remained to him. And while I could spare enough blood to sustain him, at least for a while, I could not give him enough to heal.

We had to risk it.

I held the bag up to his slack mouth, and dribbled a little inside. There was no reaction. He was fading quickly, and would soon go catatonic.

"Ray." The blue eyes opened, but did not focus. They were not fixed, not yet, but it wouldn't be long.

"Ray!" I gripped his chin, and saw him frown. But he didn't curse at me, which I had learned from Dory was not a good sign.

I forced more of the blood down his throat, massaging it to make him swallow. It did not make any difference that I could detect, other than for a faint tinge of color in what had been the dead white mask of his face. So, I gave him some more, emptying the bag and starting on another, and kept going until he had drained that one as well.

But still, he just lay there.

I knew that he'd absorbed it; otherwise, it would have been trickling out of his wounds. But it did not appear to be enough. I fed him a third bag, and when he still gave no sign of returning to life, I began to panic.

"Ray!" I slapped him across the face, not knowing what else to do.

"What?"

I blinked. It had been faint and crabby, but nonetheless discernable. "Are you alright?"

"Do I fucking look alright?"

I sat back on my heels, a smile stretching the skin of my face. "You are not dead."

"Not for lack of trying. The goddamned fey." His eyes finally managed to focus on something—his arm beside me. "You don't have that on yet? What the heck have you been doing?"

"I am remiss in my duties," I said, and saw him narrow his eyes.

"Was that sarcasm? Cause in case you didn't notice, I'm in pieces here! Can I get some help, preferably before the fey find us and finish the job?"

"Yes," I said, biting my lip. "I will help."

"Damned right." He lay there grumpily while I worked to reattach the arm.

It was easier than I expected. Vampire bodies are largely self-healing, if there is enough blood to use as fuel. Ray had just ingested at least three pints, which was a full meal for his kind, and his body wanted to use it. I had barely put the limb in place when the bones were reknitting, when jagged flesh was flowing back together and smoothing out, when veins were squirming out of the wound like little worms, reaching for—

"Hey! Do you mind?"

I looked up. "What?"

"I could do without the commentary, okay? Little worms . . ." he shuddered.

I sat back on my heels in surprise. "You could hear my thoughts?"

"Why so shocked? You're my master, right? And where's my other arm?"

I regarded him for a moment, and then fetched the other arm.

"Great. It's got nasty fey blood on it." He scowled.

"Technically," I reminded him, as I worked to get the second arm back in its proper place, "Dory is your master. You pledged yourself to her."

"Yeah, only you *are* her, right? I mean, kind of the hardcore version, but . . ."

I shook my head. "We are different people."

"Uh huh. Who happened to start off as one person and share the exact same DNA."

"Twins start off as one person. And they share DNA."

"But they aren't born as one and live that way for eleven or twelve years like you guys did!"

"They also don't live more than five centuries." The bone was knitting wrong. I adjusted it. "The percentage of our lifetimes that we lived as one is becoming an insignificant figure."

"Yeah, but like . . ." He scowled. "Trust me to get into a deep philosophical discussion when my head's pounding and my eyes are crossing and I still don't got legs yet."

"Your arms are healing. Trying to do too much at one

time—"

"Yeah, yeah. You're the expert." He closed his eyes.

I was not, in fact, having spent far more time killing vampires than healing them, but thought that this might not be the best moment to point that out.

We sat there quietly for a while. He looked so thin and pale, like a teenager, with his hair falling over his clammy forehead and his face speckled with fey blood. It had dried brown and looked almost like freckles.

And even when healed, he would not be a large man, or a particularly strong vampire. He was a master, but he would never reach the upper rings of power. I had seen enough to know.

Yet, he had been brave today, and honorable, and loyal. I had known far stronger men who would have fled at one look at what we faced. But he had stayed, and he had helped.

I did not think I would have made it out of the ley line without him.

"I would also be your master, Raymond Lu," I finally said. "If you wish it."

The eyes opened, and as always, it was a surprise to see that they were blue. He was half-Dutch and half Indonesian, I remembered Dory saying. A bastard child never wanted by either parent, on his own in a hostile world far sooner than he should have been. And then a vampire with a master who, while not abusive by their standards, had not valued him. He had been given as a mocking sort of gift to Dory, discarded after centuries of service, like a dirty handkerchief.

But she had recognized his worth, as did I.

"You would?" he asked, sounding confused.

"It would be an honor."

Ray stared at me. He seemed to do that a lot. "Well." He cleared his throat. "Well, all right, then."

"I am happy to have you with me on this journey, Raymond Lu." I looked around at the still intact shield. "Do you happen to know how we get out of here?"

CHAPTER SEVEN

Dorina, Faerie

Ray was cursing again, probably out of frustration. I was feeling rather like that myself. I could see the world spread out so invitingly all around us, could watch a couple of bright yellow birds chase each other across the sky, could feel the wind that rustled through the treetops, even smell the flowers. But I couldn't touch any of it.

We could not get *out*.

"They're gonna find us," Ray said, pacing back and forth across the bodies. His legs had been reattached, but they were not functioning very well yet, or perhaps he was tripping on the corpses. "They're gonna find us in the middle of a pile of their people who we obviously killed—"

"Perhaps they died in the crash?" I offered.

"And we didn't?" He whirled on me. "Plus, you cut that guy's arm off! You think they're not gonna notice that?"

I regarded the fey in question. Ray had a point. He was looking a little worse for the wear, with a missing arm, a proud, blood splattered face, and long, red-stained, silver blond hair. They were so beautiful, these creatures, like their world. I felt a certain . . . not regret, but melancholy, that they'd had to die.

And then I remembered them ripping Ray apart so callously, and I wanted to kill them all over again, but they were already dead.

Although at least this one was still clothed, unlike several others.

I had stripped them to provide Ray and I with something to wear. Whatever had happened in that alley had given me my own body, but it had not transferred over any clothes. That did not bother me, but it might be a problem if we met anyone, as I did not know the customs here.

Unfortunately, the fey leggings had been far too long for either of us, as well as too large. But the tunics had proven easier to work with. I had hacked off part of the sleeves so that they did not cover our hands, but otherwise hadn't needed to do anything. The one I was wearing was knee length on me, while Ray's was a little below mid-thigh.

They were also very fine. Ray's was brown, although that word didn't do it justice. It had a luxurious, velvety nap, which turned a beautiful russet shade if smoothed one way, and a light sable when pushed the other. I had settled on calling it brown, but it was more like the hue of the forest floor: different every time you looked at it from another angle.

My tunic was simpler: a pale gray that did not change color. It was technically quite plain, with neither embellishment nor embroidery, but it was not peasant garb. It had a silver sheen to it when the sun hit it, and while it was a thick, heavy weave that was as warm as wool, it felt as light as silk. It looked like what it was: the clothing of an aristocrat.

It appeared that the fey had sent elite soldiers after me, ones willing to die to complete their mission, and yet they had equipped themselves so poorly. There wasn't a sword in the group, and only a single knife, and it was quite small. I had found a leather belt with a scabbard attached, into which I'd already placed the knife for ease of transport, although it didn't fit. It was more like the kind you would normally slip down a boot, in order to hide it.

But why would the fey have to hide their weapons? And why did they have so few of them? It looked as if the larger knife had been left behind, and just the empty scabbard taken into battle.

Even if they had planned merely to push me into the trap they'd laid, and had not thought to get caught inside with me, surely it would have been better to be cautious? Going practically unarmed into battle against a largely unknown enemy, and one with backup nearby, with almost no weapons? It did not make sense.

Like carrying pints of human blood.

I could only think of one reason the fey would have blood. They must have thought that dhampirs were like vampires, and that I would need it to heal should I be wounded in the fight. They clearly wanted me alive, for what purpose I did not know, but they wanted it badly.

Enough to strip their soldiers before battle?

All except the one with the knife hidden in his boot.

"Dorina?"

Ray snapped his fingers in front of my face, as if he had been attempting to get my attention for a while. Or, to be more accurate, he tried to snap them. It would probably be several days before his coordination fully returned, after his nerve endings healed. That put us at a disadvantage in a fight, and I was little better.

I had tried to manifest my spirit form a few minutes ago to scout out the area and see if I could spot any silver-haired fey. Or determine if there was a village nearby where I could nudge help our way. But it had not worked. I did not know whether that was because Faerie had different magic from Earth, or whether I was merely too tired. The two fights had taken a great deal out of me, and my spirit form took considerable energy.

But it was not encouraging.

And no weapons to speak of was even less so.

"Damn it, are you listening to me?" Ray snapped.

His temper seemed a little worse for the wear, too.

"Of course, Ray." I looked down at the dead fey again.

"Perhaps if I mushed him some more?"

"Mushed him? Did you just say *mushed him*?"

"Or I could set him on fire." I wondered if any of the fey had been carrying a flint? I started to check, when Ray grabbed my arm.

I looked up into angry blue eyes and flushed cheeks, I supposed because he had some blood to work with now. "Yeah. That's just great. You need to *breathe*, okay? Die of smoke inhalation and you leave me all alone in Faerie and that's not happening, all right?"

"I would never—"

"Which means you don't die, I don't die, nobody freaking dies! We got that? *Are we clear on that point?*"

I did not think it was particularly up to us, but doubted that this was the time to mention that, either. "Yes."

"Good." Ray went back to thumping the crystal ball some more.

It did not seem to help.

"I think that it is broken," I said.

"I know it's broken!" He tried to push some hair back from his forehead, but only succeeded in poking himself in the eye. "Damn it!" He glared at me through the limp black strands. "The problem is that the shield is *not* broken, and the fey are *coming*, and we gotta get out of—what are you doing?"

"The fey warriors were not well equipped," I said, tugging on a bloody corpse. "None of them had a sword and mine broke during the fight. They do not appear to make the souvenir versions combat ready."

"So?"

"So, all we have is a broken sword and a knife. I thought that I would make us some more."

"Some more what?"

"Weapons. We don't know what we might be facing, and Faerie is said to be treacherous."

"But how are you planning to—" He stopped abruptly, his eyes going from me to the fey, whose leg I was currently working on, and back again. "You thought you would make us weapons . . . out of their *bones*?"

I knew that look. It was the one Dory sometimes gave me, when I had accidentally done something unacceptable. I put the tibia back.

"No?"

"My God," Ray said, staring at me. "I don't believe my life. I just don't, you know?"

I didn't say anything. After a moment, he went back to trying to break the small control sphere, in the hopes, I supposed, that it would also destroy the shield. But even vampire strength did not seem to be up to the task.

I watched him while checking out the fey's body through my peripheral vision. Their bones were nice and thick and very hard. They should take an edge well, instead of shattering as human bones were wont to do. I just needed to gather up a few more, lower leg bones usually worked the best, and—

Ray started shrieking.

"I'm sorry," I said, dropping the bone again.

The shrieking did not stop.

"Ray, I was only trying to—"

I stopped talking when I noticed that he wasn't looking at me; he was looking at something behind me. I turned and saw nothing for a moment, merely the dark green forest, with its old, old trees in the background, their twisted trunks a stark contrast to those of the saplings nearer the road. Some of the latter of which were rustling.

And then a very small creature came waddling out of the tree line.

I was immediately enchanted.

It was so *tiny*. It looked like Dory's roommate, but it had miniscule wings and big, jewel-like eyes and a little baby snout, and was so pudgy that its scale-covered legs had fat rolls. They had *rolls*.

Its coloring was various shades of gray, with almost

white scales on the fat little belly. But there was enough pink on its back and, especially, down the spine, to hint that perhaps it would be more colorful when grown up. But now it was just a tiny, roly-poly creature with bright, curious, sapphire eyes.

It was adorable.

And then I noticed that one of the trees was moving strangely behind it. Only no, that wasn't a tree, was it? Trees didn't have scales. That was a—

"Dragon!" Ray shrieked, right before I realized that the tree was something's leg.

Something huge.

"Oh," I said, and quickly got up to join him in pushing against the shield.

I thought that he had the right idea: roll us a little farther away, and make it clear that we were no threat to the child. But the shield was surprisingly heavy, or perhaps that was all of the bodies, and it had landed in a slight depression. It did not want to move.

Even worse, the tiny creature had the curiosity common to all young things, and was coming closer, probably wondering what this strange device was. The mother let out a bellow of warning that . . . was quite something. It was so loud that it was almost literally stunning, to the point that it upset my balance and had me stumbling about instead of Ray.

But the child paid no mind.

"Freaking brat!" Ray said, looking wildly over his shoulder. "Go away!"

It did not go away. In fact, our now somewhat desperate rocking was merely making it more curious. Another, even louder bellow broke the silence, which, if there was any fairness in life, would have also broken the shield, shattering it like glass in the presence of an opera star.

It did not shatter, but a moment later we were on our way, nonetheless. Not because of our combined effort, but because of the footsteps of the giant creature, which were thudding this way. They began moving the ground so much that we started moving, too.

One of the footsteps jumped us out of the depression and back onto the road, wobbling about like a giant ball. The baby laughed delightedly, and crashed into us, its little paws scrabbling at the shield's surface, its bright eyes peering inside curiously. That didn't add much in the way of momentum, as it couldn't have weighed more than a few hundred pounds.

It did, however, terrify Ray.

"Get away! Get away!" he screeched, while apparently trying to take his own advice. He ran straight into the shield and then kept going, even when it began to revolve. He reminded me of a hamster on a wheel, if the hamster was a traumatized master vampire with superhuman strength and considerable motivation.

We started to roll, something made easier by the flat, trampled dirt of the road, which appeared to be well used. That would have been a considerable improvement, except that the plateau wasn't as flat as I'd thought. It looked to be so, but was in fact slanted.

Which was why we had started rolling back toward the larger dragon.

Ray screeched again and threw himself sideways, and we left the dirt road for the verge, which was grassy and strewn with wildflowers and rocks. The latter made us judder every time we hit one of the latter, and then bounce, which made it difficult to steer. Not that that mattered after a moment.

Not when we dropped off the plateau entirely and headed toward the valley below, all while being chased by the small dragon and what I assumed was its mother.

"I think it believes we're a toy!" I yelled, as the baby rolled past us, all scrunched up in a little ball and giggling. It seemed to find this whole thing amusing. Raymond did not.

At least, I didn't think so. He was no longer pushing

as there was no need, as we were speeding down the steep mountainside. Instead, he had braced himself against the shield bubble, his newly reattached limbs splayed out, to try to keep from thumping about as the fey were doing, I supposed. But his face was almost blank.

It looked as if he might be having trouble processing his emotions right now.

I smiled at him encouragingly as I ran to stay upright, which did not appear to help. I could sympathize. I frequently felt the same, and without Dory, who I looked to for clues on how to behave, I was at a loss.

Particularly when I discovered that there was something that could crack a fey shield, after all.

The paw that came crashing down on us from above was longer and heavier than a car, and with far more force behind it. Fortunately, the shield was as slick as glass. It slammed into the dirt, but then shot out from underneath the huge foot before the web of cracks above our heads became a full-on structural failure.

"See," I told Ray, who was staring at me with huge, blank eyes. "That was lucky, wasn't it?"

And then the massive tail hit us.

We shot off the side of the mountain as if we had just come into contact with the biggest baseball bat in the world. I had my first look at the full-sized dragon as we tore through the air, and she was magnificent. At least the size of a five-story building, she made Dory's friend look petite. I hadn't realized it when we met, but Claire—the half dragon's human name—might still be an adolescent, the equivalent of a teenager in their world.

I did not think that this one was.

She ran after us—moving gracefully in spite of her size —and then flew, taking off from the steep mountainside as easily as a human would step off a stair.

I watched in awe as she launched herself into the air, leaving an avalanche of dirt behind her. Unlike her baby, she was all shades of blue, from the acre of pale, silver-blue scales on her belly, to aquamarine on her sides, to sapphire on her back and, finally, to midnight along the heavily ridged spine. The darkest hues blended beautifully with the iridescent color of her wings, which was variously black, navy and silver when the sun hit them just right.

No, not the sun, I thought.

An alien star . . .

I felt dizzy again, and only came back to myself when someone began tugging on my clothes. I looked up and realized that Ray had found an emotion at last. Unfortunately, it appeared to be terror, because he was screaming again. And pointing ahead to where something else was hurtling at us through the sky.

Or perhaps we were hurtling toward it, I thought, or we were both rushing at the other, which might explain the speed at which—

"We're gonna crash!" Raymond shrieked, as whatever was in front of us tried desperately to turn.

It succeeded, although not in getting away. We hit it broadside, and at such a rate that all I saw was a massive explosion of shattering wood. I hadn't had a clear view of the craft or whatever it was, but it must have been big judging by all the fey suddenly falling everywhere. And getting plucked out of the air by the mother dragon, who seemed to have forgotten us in the face of an easy meal.

For our part, we continued racing ahead, and then falling so quickly that we splashed down in water what felt like only seconds later. I was still looking behind us, at a wooden platform that was all that remained of whatever we'd hit. It was listing around the skies, half a dozen fey holding onto the edges and another few trying to haul them back up, while a dragon picked them off like appetizers from a canapé tray.

I've been here for an hour, I thought, blankly.

I've been here for an hour, and look what I've seen.

What will I see next?

"Don't turn around," Ray said conversationally, sitting beside me.

He no longer appeared terrified, and in fact, seemed unusually calm.

"Why?"

"We landed in a river and we're about to fall over a great bloody waterfall."

I looked over my shoulder. He was right. "Faerie is . . . unpredictable," I commented, not sure what to say under the circumstances.

"That's one word for it," he agreed, as the current took us.

This time, I was the one who screamed.

CHAPTER EIGHT

Dory, Cairo

I woke up—again—in a strange bed—again—although the sheets smelled of butterscotch, so I wasn't too worried. I'd never told my lover that he reminded me of my favorite candy and couldn't now because he was gone. Maybe off explaining to Hassani why we'd switched rooms.

And torched his rug.

And scandalized his servants.

Or, knowing Louis-Cesare, who had the aristocrat's disdain for explaining anything, he hadn't so much as mentioned it.

Yeah, that was absolutely what he'd do, I thought, grinning slightly and getting out of bed. I padded over to the bathroom, which was huge and luxurious. Because Hassani might have the reputation of a scholarly monk, but he didn't live like it.

I eyed the stone pool—that was the only word for it—that took pride of place in the center of the room and easily fit two. It would probably fit ten, but we hadn't had ten this past week, when we'd thoroughly enjoyed the one in our old suite. I thought that was just as well. Ten Louis-Cesares would probably kill me.

I opted for a shower this morning because it was quicker, then got out, dried off, and ran a comb through my hair. The Svarestri had almost scalped me on the left side of my bangs, so I parted the hair on the right to hide it, and decided it would do. This whole goodwill tour had required me to seriously up my game, not just wardrobe-wise but makeup-and-hair-wise as well. But today I was working, and I intended to look like it.

Fortunately, my luggage had been transferred over and placed just inside the foyer of the suite, and I'd remembered to pack some normal looking clothes. Black jeans, a matching t-shirt, and a pair of scuffed boots and I was feeling much better. Throw a leather jacket over this lot, and I might look like myself for the first time in weeks.

I smirked at a pair of four-inch pumps, and dropped the lid on them with finality.

Not today, assholes.

Not today.

I was zipping up the bag when I noticed that, while my luggage had been brought over, Louis-Cesare's hadn't. The set of soft brown calfskin was nowhere to be seen, not even the matching alligator toiletry bag I'd bought him for his birthday, because he used more shit on his hair than I did. I wondered if Hassani was trying to separate us after our wild night, before we corrupted the Children.

Good luck with that, I thought, and flung open the door.

And met the man himself on my way out of the suite.

He was dressed more like an Arab sheik today than an Egyptian, in snowy white robes and a black and white keffiyeh tied into a turban. In fact, he was neither nationality, being Persian by birth, although he'd studied in Egypt as a young man. But I guessed that, these days, he needed to appeal to a larger audience and had expanded the wardrobe.

He bowed as elegantly as if he'd expected to be almost run over, and maybe he had. With vamp hearing, not much surprises them. Although my outfit seemed to, maybe because it wasn't some sort of fetish wear.

I'd never trust my uncle Radu to pick out my wardrobe again.

However, it probably wouldn't have mattered what I

wore. I'd gotten the impression that Hassani viewed me less as a person and more as a kink of Louis-Cesare's. And, from his perspective, the evidence was on his side.

Christine, my husband's first long-term girlfriend, had been a centuries old revenant—one of the mad vampires who results when a Change doesn't take properly. They're considered extremely dangerous because they attack with no provocation or concern for their own well-being, like rabid dogs. They can do a boatload of damage even to older vamps as a result.

There's a whole story there about the fact that Christine wasn't really Louis-Cesare's choice, that he was guilted into a relationship he didn't want, and which had ended up saddling him with Tomas, as well. He was the first-level master that Louis-Cesare had kept in thrall for so long. Another consul—Alejandro of the Latin American Senate—had gotten control of Christine, and used her to blackmail Louis-Cesare into fighting a duel against Tomas for him.

Louis-Cesare had won—to no one's surprise—but he'd felt sorry for Tomas, who hadn't challenged for wealth or power, but out of a justified, seething hatred of Alejandro. The consul was a piece of work and Tomas wanted him dead, and was willing to risk his life to achieve it. Louis-Cesare had therefore refused to kill Tomas at the end of the duel, probably sympathizing with his point of view. And in retaliation, Alejandro had refused to release Christine.

That was a problem since revenants were to be killed on sight by senate law. But Louis-Cesare had been the one to Change Christine—another long story—and felt responsible for her affliction. He was afraid that, if he didn't get her back, eventually someone would realize what she was and destroy her, but he also couldn't kill the innocent Tomas. He had chosen, therefore, to keep Tomas in thrall so that he couldn't hurt Alejandro, although it drained his power and weighed heavily on his conscience. In return, Alejandro was supposed to guard Christine.

Of course, he'd ended up letting her escape instead, and the whole, massive cluster fuck had only ended with Christine's long overdue death at my hand. It had been in defense of others—the bitch really was dangerous as hell—but it hadn't been in time to keep what she was a secret. Louis-Cesare had lost his senate seat as a result, which he'd only gotten back due to the war, but he'd also acquired a reputation.

I mean, I knew how it looked: one girlfriend a deadly, centuries old revenant, the next a five-hundred-year-old dhampir . . . people were bound to make the connection. Both were the kind of things that gave good little vampires nightmares, both were legal to kill on sight, and both were deadly. Add that to keeping a first-level master vamp as essentially a house pet, and Louis-Cesare started to look like he really did have a danger fetish.

It was bullshit, but things kept conspiring to add to it, because people like a salacious story. Like the vamps last night had probably reported that Louis-Cesare and his dhampir were getting busy amidst the flames of hell, or some such. When in reality, the fire had been well away from us, and was being handled by the room's sprinkler system. We just hadn't wanted to pause what we were doing to clean up right then.

But to people who didn't know the truth, it probably sounded pretty convincing. And judging by the looks Hassani had been giving Louis-Cesare all week, he hadn't appreciated him bringing his latest freak to court, even if she had been named a senator due to her father's influence. I'd never met a vamp prude before, but I kind of thought I was looking at one now, and he clearly didn't think much of me, either.

Just as well I was leaving, then.

"White would be a better choice," he said, after a brief pause. "It reflects the sun and will keep you cooler."

"Keep me cooler where?"

"Djeser-Djeseru, the mortuary temple of Pharaoh Hatshepsut." I stared at him blankly. The tiniest of frowns creased the sun bronzed skin of his forehead, which even death hadn't managed to fade. "It is on the day's schedule?"

I finally caught a clue, although I found it hard to believe. "You're going ahead with that?"

"Of course. Why would we not?"

"You were *attacked*?"

"An unfortunate interruption." Hassani brushed it away. "My apologies for any inconvenience you were caused."

"Inconvenience?"

"And my condolences on the loss of your . . . assistant . . . Raymond, I believe his name was?"

"Raymond was—is—my Second," I said sharply, wondering why he hadn't mentioned Dorina. "And we don't know what happened to him. That's one of the things I need to find out."

Hassani shook his head sadly. "One no more powerful than he, and with such wounds . . . he is likely lost to us, as were many of my own people. But they will be avenged, I assure you. In the meantime, if you would care for breakfast before we leave?"

"I'm not hungry. What I want is—"

"It is a long way, even by air," Hassani protested. "A good breakfast is essential—"

"Consul—"

"Teacher, please. I prefer it as a title."

"As you like. But I don't need breakfast because I'm not going anywhere. At least not into the desert."

"You are mourning for your assistant," he said. "It is understandable, but in these difficult times, the best we can do for those who look to us for leadership is to show them that nothing has changed. That we are proceeding as normal."

"But things are not normal," I said, struggling to hold onto my temper. "And Ray wasn't my assistant, he was—is—

my Second! Now, I will need some information, everything you have on what happened last night—"

"But that is not technically true, is it?" Hassani broke in, scratching his beard.

I stopped mid-sentence. "What isn't?"

"A dhampir, if you will forgive me, has no Second. And Senator Dorina was captured, as I understand?"

I stared at him, a strange feeling starting in my belly. "What's your point?"

"That you are welcome here at court despite your . . . disability . . . due to your father's position. And your own as envoy from the North American Vampire Senate. But as for the rest . . ."

"What about the rest?"

"Well, if you will forgive me, the details of last night's events are senatorial business. I cannot release that information to one of your status."

I felt my blood pressure rise, to the point that Hassani could probably hear it pounding against my veins. But although he had a curved dagger at his waistband—a beautiful thing in carved steel, the only ornamentation he wore—he didn't twitch so much as a finger toward it. Of course, he didn't.

Dhampirs were a problem for lesser vampires, and the revenants that used to provide most of my income. But for someone like him? We were gutter scum. I was probably expected to be grateful that he wasn't chucking me into a ditch.

But then, he couldn't, could he? Because I might not be a senator anymore, by his reckoning, but I was still married to one. And Louis-Cesare could get all the information he wanted.

"Then tell Louis-Cesare," I said tightly. "The point is—"

"But I am afraid I cannot do that, either," Hassani said, looking remorseful.

"Cannot do what?"

"Give any assistance to your lover—"

"My husband! And why the hell not?"

A sly smile, the first real emotion I'd seen from him, flickered across his face for a second, before being replaced with more faux concern. "My apologies. I thought you knew."

"Knew what, damn it!"

"Why, that he left this morning."

I stared at him for a moment, then tore across the corridor and down to our old suite of rooms, where I found the door open and half a dozen servants cleaning up and repairing the damage. But no Louis-Cesare. And no luggage.

I stood there for a moment, vibrating.

Louis-Cesare had deserted me once, to run after Christine, despite the fact that she was a complete psycho. He'd received word that she had escaped from Alejandro, so he hadn't really had a choice, but the fact that he'd gone without so much as a word had almost ended us before we began. The one, absolute, unbreakable rule of our relationship was that we communicated. If one or the other had to leave unexpectedly, fine, but at the very least we left a note.

I did not see a note.

I did not see anything, except for people mopping up what could be water from last night. Or what could be signs of another fight, one that I'd slept through. And that meant—

Fear clutched at my heart, sharp and dizzying, and a cold hand stopped my breathing. I whirled on Hassani as he followed me inside, as unhurried as if we were having a stroll through a garden. He didn't so much as blink when I snatched his own knife and held it to his throat.

He did look faintly surprised, however.

"If you've killed him—" I growled.

"Killed him?" he blinked at me.

"Louis-Cesare! If he's dead—"

"Oh, I sincerely hope not." A finger pushed the knife away. "That would be . . . difficult to explain."

I saw red. And this time, it wasn't from Dorina, who wasn't here to help me. But then, she hadn't been for most of the last five hundred years. She'd intervened on some occasions, when she happened to be in residence and judged me to be out of my depth. But the rest of the time I'd been on my own, and fighting creatures far more powerful than me.

And I didn't fight fair.

I grabbed a small tab from my jacket, slapped it to the front of his clothes, and sprang away. I didn't want to be caught in an inverse shield, one that contracted upon contact, trapping the subject. Usually trapping the subject, I revised, as Hassani broke out of it pretty much immediately.

Okay, upgrade, I decided, and threw a golden spider instead.

My arsenal used to be limited to what I could beg, borrow or steal, unless I'd actually lucked out and gotten paid. And even then, magical weapons—particularly the unlicensed, not exactly legal variety—are expensive. I'd had to be judicious about what I used.

But while senators don't get a salary, I'd discovered that they do get one very big perk of the job: access to the senate's extensive arsenal. Which was not only well equipped, but also contained all the fun little toys they'd confiscated from the bad guys. And the bad guys knew how to party.

Which was why the tiny spider had babies immediately upon contact, who went scurrying all over those snowy white robes. Hassani watched them with distaste. "It doesn't matter what you throw at me, dhampir. It isn't going to—"

He stopped talking abruptly, probably because the big spider had just webbed up his mouth. The babies quickly did the same to his body, wrapping him in layers of fine, white silk, like the mummy he wasn't. And then contracting the web, causing him to topple over onto his back.

He hit the floor with a thud, one of the servants screamed, and another jumped for me—and got slapped with one of my little tabs for his trouble. He didn't seem to find it as easy to break out of as his master, who was thrashing about on the floor, having managed to halfway free himself already. But that was the beauty of Spider's Bite, as the golden spell was called: the more you fought, the stronger it got, pulling power from its victim.

And Hassani had it to burn.

In another moment, he actually did look like a mummy. The thick, white strands, maybe a foot deep at this point, had covered his eyes and muffled the rich tones of his voice. And then cut them off altogether.

That appeared to be the last straw for the servants.

They ran, stampeding over themselves to get out of the door, except for the one now frozen in what looked like plastic wrap. He stared out at me, perfectly fine since vamps don't need to breathe, like a vintage Ken doll still inside his box. But he wouldn't stay that way for long.

Others were coming.

I closed and locked the door, which activated the ramped-up shields. But that wouldn't stop Hassani's children, who would rip it apart with their bare hands if necessary, to reach their master. Teacher, I corrected myself, pulling a knife and cutting away the webbing from over his face.

Pretentious twat.

But the pretentious twat wasn't stupid, and had finally stopped struggling.

I didn't have much time, and he knew it. He also knew something else. "You won't kill a consul," he told me, the rich voice untroubled. "It would destroy the alliance."

"But you would kill a senator?"

Hassani looked aggrieved. "Right sleeve."

"What?"

"Check my right sleeve, you annoying woman!"

I checked his right sleeve. That required cutting away more of the webbing, which I doubted my tiny allies had the strength to replace. Not that it mattered; the door to the suite was already starting to shake.

I pulled out a folded letter, and knew immediately who it was from. My name was on the front, and that perfect, copperplate handwriting belonged to only one person. I unfolded it and—

Don't kill Hassani.

Motherfucker.

"You could have just given this to me," I pointed out, to the smarmy bastard on the floor.

"I always heard dhampirs were mad," he countered, staring prayerfully at the ceiling. "I did not think it actually true."

I ignored that and went back to reading.

Dearest, I expect that this will not please you. What would not please me is your death. We do not know the effect that halving a soul might have, but it would be inadvisable for you to enter combat at the moment.

"Ironic," Hassani offered, because he was reading over my shoulder.

I jerked the letter away.

Please do me the honor of fulfilling our mission in Egypt. In return, I will fulfill the vow I made to you last night. Those who have hurt you will pay; I promise you that. And if possible, I will also retrieve those we have lost. I will be in touch.

Louis-Cesare

I just knelt there for a moment, rereading the letter. Then I read it a third time, before it really sank in. And I felt my face burn.

I guessed I knew what that look of peace had been about last night, huh? He'd suddenly been calm, but not because he was with me. Not because we'd comforted each other, and were about to chase down our enemies together. But because he'd decided what he was going to do. Which involved leaving the little woman behind while he ran after Jonathan.

Alone.

He was chasing the one man who'd ever beaten him, but he didn't want backup? Bet if Dorina was still here he'd have wanted some goddamned backup. But plain old Dory? Nah. What the hell could I do for him?

I heard the letter crumple in my fist.

Hassani sat up, having freed himself as far as the waist. "You see," he said, watching me. "You could go to the queen's mausoleum, after all."

I shot him a look of pure fury. "Is that what you'd do?"

"No. But I am not a dhampir."

The look didn't change.

The door burst open, and at least a dozen master vampires tore into the room, blades out and faces set on hate. Hassani held up a hand and they stopped, so suddenly that some of them ran into each other. One toppled Ken, who fell onto his face, still unmoving.

Hassani regarded them calmly. "Children, a teachable moment. As it is written, 'Repel evil with what is better; then you will see that one who was once your enemy has become your dearest friend.'"

One of the vampire's hissed, and another bared fangs.

"So, I'm evil?" I demanded.

Hassani brushed it aside. "Exaggerated for effect."

"Do they know that?"

He freed himself the rest of the way and took his time standing up and shaking out his perfect clothes. A number of tiny golden bugs fell out and rattled against the floor. He sighed.

Then he looked at me, and the dark eyes were somehow different than before. "Come. There is something I want to show you."

CHAPTER NINE

Dory, Cairo

We headed to a part of the complex I hadn't seen before, with sets of rock cut stairs going down into limestone caverns well below city level. Going down also meant going back in time, apparently, as layers of the current city peeled back like an onion to show earlier habitations. And then to reveal another city altogether, as we came to several stories of medieval brickwork.

It featured the curved archways and pierced stone of Fustat, the original city built here by the first Arab conquerors, which predated Cairo by centuries. I remembered one of our guides telling me that Old Town overlapped its borders somewhat, or what was left of it. But we didn't stop there.

Maybe seven levels down we branched off the main stairs and cut through some rock hewn, sepia-colored rooms. They had traces of age-old pigments on the walls, and cartouches containing hieroglyphs I couldn't read. Hassani paused like a good host whose guest has seen something that interested her, and the lantern boy he'd brought along stopped, too.

The kid was a vamp but just barely, with big dark eyes and a nervous disposition. He had on a simple djellaba—the local robe that reminded me of a long nightshirt—with pale blue and white stripes. With the simple leather sandals he wore, and the old-fashioned lantern he carried, he looked like he'd stepped out of another time.

As did everything else. The abrupt halt set the light swaying and the carvings flickering like an old news reel. I expected to see Howard Carter show up, any time now.

"Heliopolis," Hassani said, looking approving of my interest. "You are standing in the remains of the first city ever built on this spot. The City of the Sun, as the ancient Greeks called it."

"I thought Fustat was the first on this site."

"Oh, no. In fact, the temples and other buildings of Heliopolis were scavenged for materials to build Fustat and then medieval Cairo, just as the pyramids were."

"The pyramids?"

Hassani nodded. "The monuments used to be faced with pure white limestone in ancient times, so highly polished that it was said to be blinding under the sun. But taking their facing stones was easier than quarrying new material, so." He shrugged. "You can see the stones of temples like this one in the walls around Old Cairo."

"This was a temple?" I glanced around. I supposed I should have figured that out. The paintings were faded almost to indecipherability, but there were a lot of them, covering even the ceiling, which was so high that the light barely touched it. And while the stone pillars guarding the doorways were bare of pigment, their surfaces were beautifully carved, with the tops looking like lotus flowers opening under the sun.

That sort of thing was expensive in the ancient world, where everything was done by hand. Palaces and temples were virtually the only spots that received such treatment. Well, and tombs.

For some reason, I felt a shiver go across my skin.

Hassani did not appear to notice, maybe because he was busy tracing another carving on the wall. "Oh, yes. Heliopolis was full of temples, to the point that the Greeks named it after the god they associated with the deity worshipped here.

In ancient Egypt it was known as the House of Ra. You see? This is his cartouche."

"Ra? He was the sun god, wasn't he?"

Hassani wasn't called Teacher for nothing. I'd thought it was more of a religious title, but he seemed genuinely pleased that his strange visitor knew something, at least. I was grateful for the guide to Aswan, who had basically never shut up. "Yes, indeed. Heliopolis was the center of his cult, going back as far as history does. It predated the dynastic period, you see."

"Dynastic?"

"The era of the pharaohs."

"And what was before that?"

He shot me a look. "Why, the time of the gods, of course."

We went on.

There were more stairs, and more descent into darkness. The underground temple was vast enough for me to wonder why a good chunk of Old Cairo hadn't collapsed into a massive sinkhole. I assumed that something had been done, magical or otherwise, to shore it up, although there were no signs of anything. No magic glistened anywhere, and the only scent I could detect was dust.

Well, and an odd, skin ruffling odor that tickled my nose occasionally, from different directions, as if born on a breeze that didn't exist down here. It was acid-sharp and bitter, and disturbing because it was impossible to identify. It didn't help that the rooms we'd transitioned into were smaller and interconnected, and as dark as pitch before our completely inadequate light source lit them up. I was starting to wonder what had possessed me to accompany Hassani down here in the first place.

He had promised to take me to the morgue where they were keeping the attackers' corpses from last night. Louis-Cesare had already seen them, and probably gotten a clue as to where to start his search. It was something he hadn't bothered to share with me, forcing me to retrace his steps in the hope that I'd notice whatever he had—which had sounded like a perfectly reasonable plan upstairs.

Here . . . was a different story.

This place was seriously creeping me out, and my overly suspicious brain was taking full advantage. It was busy pointing out that this was a damned long trip to the morgue, wasn't it? One with no witnesses to anything that might happen along the way except for Lantern Boy, who was Hassani's creature. The consul hadn't hurt Louis-Cesare because that would have been tantamount to declaring war on our senate, but a filthy dhampir who had just attacked him? And who he probably blamed for the assault last night?

Shit.

My mood wasn't improved when we entered yet another area of the temple. I still couldn't see squat—even less than before, in fact, since the lamplight was no longer able to reach the ceiling. But whatever we were walking through suddenly felt bigger and airier, with our footsteps echoing loudly in absolute silence.

Well, almost absolute. The vamps weren't bothering to breathe since they didn't need it, but my own breaths sounded loud and ragged in my ears. Calm the hell down! I told myself sternly.

My adrenal glands told me to get fucked and pumped out some more energy I didn't need and couldn't use right now. It buzzed around in my veins, threatening to make me clumsy, although the crappy lighting and uneven floor were already doing that. The tiny puddle of lantern light seemed vanishingly small, leaving me feeling like I was walking through a big, black, echoing void, with the only thing keeping me from falling on my face the small area of rough-cut stone that I could see directly in front of me.

And, eventually, that wasn't enough.

I tripped on the crack between two huge stones and went down to one knee, and then almost jumped out of my skin when a hand cupped my elbow.

"My apologies," Hassani said, his voice repeating eerily from all directions. The handsome, bearded face bent down into the puddle of light. "Our people see so well in the dark that I sometimes forget that others do not. But you should experience this."

"Experience what?" I asked hoarsely, and heard my own voice echo.

I was pretty sure that I didn't want to experience shit down here.

But it wasn't up to me. Suddenly, a series of light flashes all but blinded me, to the point that I threw an arm over my eyes. And when I lowered it, blinking in a dazzling flood of illumination, I saw . . . something incredible.

I had wondered why Hassani's court was smack in the middle of Old Cairo. Vampire enclaves tended to hug the outskirts of cities or be off in the hinterland somewhere. Wards were good, and the ones upstairs were next level. But they couldn't hide everything as last night had proven. It was easier to make sure that any oddities were well beyond the range of prying eyes.

But now I understood.

Holy shit.

"The ancient Egyptians knew how to build," Hassani said, appearing pleased by my reaction as he helped me back to my feet. And kept a hand on my arm to steady me, which I actually appreciated since I probably would have fallen again otherwise. I still might, I thought dizzily, staring up and then around a long, octagonal chamber that could have fit three or four football fields. And their stands. And parts of their parking lots.

The damned thing was *immense*.

The ceiling soared out of sight, claimed by darkness despite the fact that each of the dozens of huge stone pillars supporting it had lights branching off of them. The massive torches were at least ten feet tall, but they looked tiny in comparison to everything else, and were woefully inadequate. And, damn it, I wanted to *see* this.

I fumbled in my jacket and came up with a small, golden bird that looked a lot like the spider I'd thrown at Hassani, which was probably why he eyed it apprehensively.

But this one was for me.

I tapped it against my temple, and the magical tat dissolved into my skin, leaving not so much as a raised outline under my fingertips. Had I had a mirror, I would have seen a faint blue outline of a hawk next to my right eye. And I would have seen every tiny feather of it, because my vision had just gone high-def.

But the help came at a price, namely a hit to my reputation. Vampires didn't need magical tats, which were mostly designed to improve areas they already had covered: sharper senses, greater speed and boosted strength. As a result, they tended to be viewed, at least by mainstream vamp society, as another example of human inferiority—needing magic just to compete with a bargain basement vamp.

I expected, at the very least, to get a sneer or two.

But I was surprised.

"Ah." Hassani nodded gravely. "It is good that you know of such things."

"What?" I touched the bird self-consciously. "Why?"

"I will explain later. But for now," he stepped forward and threw out his arms in a gesture that would have been overly dramatic anywhere else, but here just seemed to fit. "Welcome to the House of Ra-Horakhty, the greatest temple in a city of temples, and the only one to survive intact from ancient times!"

The words echoed impressively around the huge hall, then slowly faded into silence. Hassani waited another moment, then looked back at me expectantly. This was one of those times that I could have really used Louis-Cesare, who always seemed to have some flowery French compliment to fit the occasion.

I, on the other hand, was speechless. It was like something out of an Indiana Jones movie, only with a better budget. *Way* better.

I just stood there, staring around like an idiot. Unlike Lantern Boy, who put down his burden and began furiously to clap. Hassani shot him a dark look and he stopped.

We eventually moved forward, the consul apparently realizing that I needed some time to take all this in.

He was right.

The sheer size of the place was breathtaking, but what it contained was even more so. There must have been a charm active in here, after all, or else an army of painters had been doing touch ups, because the faint images on the antechamber walls were nowhere to be found. Instead, dazzling murals many stories high blazed with color and hints of gold on both sides of the elongated body of the great room, showing a panoply of ancient Egyptian gods.

Closest was Taweret, the somewhat comical looking hippo-croc goddess, with her strange head and very pregnant belly, who protected women in childbirth. The murals were done in bas-relief, with the paintings protruding from the background slightly, and embossed with different types of semiprecious stones. In Taweret's case, her crocodile-like snout gleamed with what appeared to be malachite, the dark veins in the rock convincingly replicating scales.

Next in line was ibis-headed Thoth, the scribe of the gods, with a scroll clutched tightly in one jeweled hand. More jewels gleamed from his golden armbands and from the matching belt he wore, and glittered on the collar of the small baboon perched on his shoulder. The hair of his companion was made out of what appeared to be thousands of long, thin flakes of carnelian.

Anubis was next, looking frighteningly like the creatures we'd fought last night, with the sleek black head gleaming in the firelight. The eyes looked like two huge yellow diamonds, although I assumed that they were actually some sort of quartz as each was as big as my head. They reflected the flames of the torches, giving them an ominous, life-like quality.

Of course, that was true of all the gods, a seemingly endless procession on either side of the room, leading up to a long set of rock cut stairs at the far end. A throne sat at the top, with its gilt wood looking as fresh as if it had just been completed. And although it was empty, behind it was the biggest mural of them all, towering what had to be six stories high.

"Ra-Horakhty," I guessed, as we started the long approach.

"Indeed." Hassani's voice was quiet now, as mine had been. It was that sort of place. I could easily imagine it awing the hell out of some ancient worshippers.

It was doing a pretty good job on me.

"Ra was the original sun god," Hassani explained, "usually identified as the noon day sun, when it is at its most powerful. He is often depicted, as he is here, with a falcon's head. Horus was another popular sky god, and the two became associated with each other over time. Thus Ra-Horakhty, 'Ra who is Horus of the Two Horizons.'"

I nodded, looking up at the figure of a young man's sun bronzed, muscular body, with gold glinting at the neck and wrists and sandal clad feet, as well as on the elaborate, jeweled overskirt he wore. I didn't know how some ancient sculptor had managed to make the skin look smooth and touchable, and the rock cut underskirt appear as filmy and diaphanous as fine silk, but he had. Ra was the very image of an ancient king, even with the huge falcon's head growing out of his shoulders.

Or maybe because of it.

In most of the portrayals I'd seen, the combo had looked like a guy wearing a bad Halloween mask. But not here. The artist had carefully shown the transition from skin to feathers, with the color starting well down his chest and shading darker as it flowed up the fine muscles of his torso, to the huge pectoral he wore.

The broad piece of gold was studded with what looked like genuine lapis, turquoise and red carnelian. Likewise, the plumage that started around the edges of the necklace and continued onto the head was carved from some kind of blue stone—agate perhaps? Whatever it was, the fine striations perfectly mimicked the look of feathers.

The head itself was a masterpiece, fierce and intelligent in its expression, with a vicious looking beak and gleaming dark eyes. And even more than the rest of the murals, this one was done in deep bas-relief. To the point that it looked as if Ra was stepping out of the wall, about to descend on us puny visitors.

I belatedly noticed that we had been included on the murals, too, or people like us. Small brown humans, hunched over in deep obeisance, littered the area around the gods' feet, not even coming up to their knees. No jewels had been wasted on them, nor any differentiation in the features. They could have been clones of one another, with the only variance being dresses for the women instead of the loin cloths the men wore.

Way to let us know our place, I thought. Although, in comparison to Ra, the gods weren't in much better shape. Not only were they smaller than the big, main mural, they were also bearing gifts, their hands clasped around boxes and baskets overflowing with grain, incense, gold or jewels, which they were about to present to their lord and master. Those near the front of the line were already beginning their obeisance, sinking to one knee with their offerings raised high above their heads.

The message was clear: gods they might be, but one was far above the rest, as much so as they were above the pathetic humans.

"There, you see?" Hassani said, pointing, and jolting me out of the almost reverie I'd fallen into. "There is the sun disk, above Ra's head. It was the symbol of godhood to the ancients, and became the royal emblem of pharaonic Egypt as well. The cobra that surrounds the disk was even added to the royal crown."

I nodded, but I was finding it hard to focus on where he was pointing, because the disk in question was blinding. Instead of the usual, plain, orange-red sphere that decorated tourist statues and tomb walls alike, this was a huge, polished bronze mirror, which reflected the firelight like the sun's rays, spearing them out to all points of the hall. It was dazzling.

But after a moment and some squinting, I finally located a black cobra wrapped around and then protruding outward from the sun. It looked like its scales might be obsidian, but I couldn't look at it long enough to tell. It was also probably as big as me, but from this angle, it looked tiny.

"Is there a story behind it?" I asked, because I assumed so.

Hassani chuckled. "There are always stories in Egypt, and many for the Uraeus. I have my own theory as to its origins, but many believe it to be the symbol of Wadjet, a flame breathing snake god who destroyed Ra's enemies."

I blinked. "That's . . . pretty hardcore."

"Indeed. What I find most interesting, however, is that the pairing is similar across so many cultures."

"The pairing?"

"Sun gods and serpents. Take the Aztec snake god, Quetzalcoatl, for instance. He vanquished an early sun god, Tezcatlipoca, and took his place during the second age of mankind—"

"The what?"

Hassani flipped a hand. "Part of the Aztec creation myth. Likewise, the sun god of the current age, Huitzilopochtli, was conceived on Mount Coatepec, 'Serpent Hill', and held a scepter in the form of a snake. And in Toltec mythology, the sky is symbolized by the sun god looking out of the jaws of a snake."

"That's . . . very interesting," I lied. I wanted to run across the hall, to examine a voluptuous version of the cat goddess Bastet, who was wearing a net-like dress that concealed basically nothing, but appeared to be woven out of genuine diamonds. They weren't faceted like modern stones, but they caught the light in unmistakable ways, casting dancing prisms all around her, which I thought low-key hilarious.

It could have been a coincidence, but I liked to think that some ancient sculptor had enjoyed the idea of her chasing the lights cast by her own dress.

"It is, isn't it?" Hassani smiled at me. "For their part, the Maya worshipped Kukulkan, a divine snake that served as a messenger between the king and the gods. He is still remembered among the modern Maya as a pet of the sun god."

"Fascinating."

"And we find the same sort of thing in other mythological traditions. The Babylonian god Marduk, a child of their sun deity, vanquished the great snake Tiamat and used her flesh to make the world. He also had as a companion and protector a "furious serpent" known as Mushussu. Indra, the sun god of the Hindu pantheon, likewise fought and defeated the great serpent Ahi."

"You don't say," I said, wondering how I ended up in this conversation, and how I was supposed to get out. There was so much to see, but Hassani was fixated on snakes for some reason.

"Then there was Apollo—god of the sun to the ancient Greeks—who defeated the Python at Delphi, which afterward became one of his symbols. That is why the staff of Asclepius, his son, has a snake entwined around it. Likewise, Helios, the god whom the Greeks identified with the sun disk itself, had a chariot pulled by serpents instead of horses. And Sulis-Minerva, the syncretism of a Celtic sun goddess and the Roman goddess of wisdom, had a snake for an emblem."

I decided that it was just possible that Hassani's devious

plan was to bore me to death.

"But it was here where the most references are to be found," he continued obliviously. "There were many snake gods in Egypt, either helping or opposing Ra. However, you see a difference over the dynasties. In the earliest records, snake gods are almost always seen as helpful to Ra, and many are depicted wearing his solar disk above their heads, linking them to him and his children."

"His children?" I asked, desperate to change the subject.

Hassani didn't look at me that time, but something changed in the air. As if the rest of this had been a prelude, and we were finally getting down to business. Whatever the hell his business was.

"Do you know how the pharaohs justified their rule?" he asked, his voice deliberately light.

"Through armies, like everybody else?"

His lips quirked. "That, too. But it helped to have some other basis as well, or else the next person with an army could come in and have just as much legitimacy as you. In Europe, that basis was normally a particular bloodline: the British royal house still claims the throne by right of descent from William the Conqueror, for instance. In China, it was the Mandate of Heaven, the idea that the ruler was divinely appointed and, as long as he ruled well, the people were required to obey. Whereas in Egypt . . ."

Hassani, usually so loquacious, suddenly trailed off.

"In Egypt?" I prompted.

He had been staring up at the huge statue of Ra, which did tend to draw the eye. But now he shook himself slightly, and glanced at me. And his gaze was strange, almost . . . searching.

"They combined the two ideas," he said, after a moment. "In pharaonic Egypt, it was said that the queen was visited by the god Ra, who impersonated her husband. And that her child was therefore a demigod, divinely appointed to rule over the population."

"Divine right of kings taken to the next level," I said dryly. "Not just appointed by a god, but sired by one."

"Exactly so. Although in Egypt's case, it wasn't mere propaganda. The creature who ruled these lands before me was such a man."

I blinked a little at that, wondering if I was being had. But it had been said so matter-of-factly that I doubted it. "You mean, a demigod?"

"You sound skeptical."

"A little." I knew a supposed demigod—although I had my misgivings. Poo emoji earrings did not inspire a lot of confidence. But even assuming that she was the real deal, the bastard kids of ancient gods were not exactly thick on the ground these days.

But Hassani was nodding. "Understandable, but true, I assure you. An Egyptian of the lower classes, he was cast out of his family and would almost certainly have died had he not been taken by the god Ra to be experimented upon. He was infused with some godly DNA in a process that he once described to me as a rebirth, and in a way, he was right."

"In what way?"

"Why, the same way that our Children are reborn, after the Change. He became the world's first vampire."

I went another yard before what he'd said sunk in. I turned around to see Hassani standing there, in the middle of the puddle of lantern light, waiting for me to catch up. He was gonna need to wait a little longer.

"I—what?"

He smiled at me, and this time, there was a glint in those too-innocent eyes. "Oh. Would you like to see him?"

CHAPTER TEN

Dory, Cairo

The entrance to the tomb was on the dais, through a small door situated directly behind the throne. The reception chamber was even more impressive from this angle, with the procession of glittering gods flickering in the firelight, giving them the illusion of movement. All those jeweled eyes gleamed knowingly at me, as if to say: "We were here before you, and we will be here when you are dust."

Yeah, but I can leave, I thought back, and damned if that didn't sound like a good idea right about now.

And, for a moment, I thought we'd have to. Despite vampire strength, it took Hassani putting a shoulder to the wooden door to move it, which was painted to blend in with the stone and seemed almost as heavy. And when it did finally burst inward, it let out a breath of stale air like, well, like a tomb.

After a brief hesitation caused by what was left of my good sense, I followed the consul inside. And immediately regretted it. I stopped abruptly, staring around at a cave full of bodies, all of which seemed to be staring back.

Okay . . . not expecting that.

There were dozens of them, maybe more because I couldn't see well in here. The torchlight from outside was little more than a thin veneer on the darkness, and Lantern Boy wasn't helping. I glanced over my shoulder and saw him hanging back, just outside the door, and looking unhappy.

Vamps used glamouries so much that I'd almost stopped paying attention to their appearance whenever I met a new one. It was easier—and safer—to go by feel: how much power were they putting out? How much of an atmospheric disturbance did they cause? If it felt like a gravity well had opened up beneath my feet when I approached them, or like a couple extra atmospheres had suddenly descended onto my shoulders, then yeah. They were old.

But this kid didn't have a presence at all. He wouldn't even have registered as a vamp except for the fangs he kept forgetting to hide. And, yes, there were vamps so good at concealing their power signature that they could fool anyone, including me. But I didn't think he was one of them.

He kept cutting his own lip on the aforementioned fangs, which were growing because he was nervous and sensed danger, and then being retracted because he was with his master and was supposed to show some decorum. Out in; out in. The result was a polka dotted lip that didn't scream "ancient vamp" to me.

Hassani shot him a longsuffering glance, but didn't comment. Except to me. "Prisoners," he said, before I could ask.

"Prisoners?" I glanced at the bodies again. I thought that was a strange word to use for dead men.

"At one time. In our court, as in most, serious offenders are left out for the sun or staked, at the consul's pleasure. But my predecessor . . . preferred a different solution."

"Your predecessor? You mean—"

He nodded. "He wanted anyone who moved against him to know what they risked. That there would be no swift end for them, no easy death. Indeed, no death at all."

"No death? Then what . . ."

I trailed off, taking a closer look at the nearest "prisoner."

He was just inside the rock cut door, propped against the wall, but not in the way that a human would stand. He was as rigid as a block of wood and pretty much the same color. Old, leather like skin had desiccated and the flesh underneath withered to the point that it looked like a thick coating on a bunch of old bones. As if a skeleton had been dipped into a vat of brownish-yellow lacquer that had adhered to the frame, covering but not hiding it.

I could see every rib, every bone. Even the skull, with a few, dusty strands of hair still clinging to the surface, looked more like a leather mask. Only the dim, flickering lamplight gave the body any semblance of life at all.

And yet, there was something there. I couldn't put my finger on it, and it was certainly nothing like the flood of power coming off of the consul. It wasn't something I would normally have noticed at all, like the faint, background hum of a lightbulb, which in a crowded room can be almost inaudible. But on a basement staircase at night, with your heart thrumming in your ears because *something is down there*—

It's as loud as a dropped cymbal.

And I was suddenly hearing crashes everywhere.

Eyelashes still visible on a corpse in a corner quivered slightly, although there was no breeze to move them; a few tiny scratches on another's thigh, from long, overgrown nails, looked fresh; the tell-tale throb of a vein in a third's temple was almost invisible, but still moving something along . . .

"Vampires do not die of starvation, you see?" Hassani told me quietly, his hand catching my arm again, before I even realized that I'd stepped back. "They go mad, if deprivation continues long enough, then wither as these have done. After a very long time, they become inert, incapable of movement, of feeding themselves—of anything."

"How," I felt my tongue flicker out to wet my lips. "How long?"

"Over seven hundred years, in this case. They tried a rebellion. It did not succeed."

No shit. And then what he'd said registered. "Seven *hundred*?"

I gazed at the closest prisoner again. There were eyes in those deeply pitted sockets, small, pebble-like and dark, like two of the dried figs they sold in the marketplace. There was no sheen to them after so long, and no movement. I couldn't tell if he could see me.

God, I hoped not. I hoped that he, whoever he'd been, was in a deep, restful sleep. Not staring at the backside of a door for centuries. Just the thought . . .

I dug my nails into my palm to stop a full body shudder.

"We believe that that may have been where the mummy's curse foolishness began," Hassani said. "Some humans stumbled across a desiccated vampire who had a little mobility left. And who then pursued them, driven mad by hunger, but failed to catch them due to the rigidity of the muscles."

"And they mistook him for a mummy due to—" I waved a hand at the withered forms.

"Just so. It is one reason we left these down here, to avoid any . . . unfortunate encounters."

I stared at the face of the still living creature. I couldn't seem to look away, although my lips felt numb. I'd seen plenty of bodies in my time, but this . . .

"Why keep them at all?" I asked roughly. "Is it just to torture them?"

Hassani looked surprised at the question. "Torture them? No. They are quite mad, and know nothing of what is happening to them. Indeed, they are not even conscious unless fed."

Uh huh, I thought, staring at that vein again. That's what people used to think about coma patients, too. Turned out, plenty of them heard every word.

"Then why not just end this?" I asked harshly.

His eyes became distant. "They were warriors once. Good men; brave men. Some were my friends. What was done to them was shameful, but giving them a coward's death, the same one reserved for lawbreakers and evildoers . . ." he shook his head. "I could never countenance it. I keep them here as I found them, for they are beyond pain at this point, hoping that Allah will someday show me a way to end their days with dignity. Although that day has yet to come."

I had a sudden, vivid recall of the first time I'd seen Hassani, at a party given by the North American consul. She'd had anti-glamourie charms layered all over her court, in case any fey tried to gate crash, I supposed. Therefore, my first look at him had been more than a little disturbing.

I'd had no idea what was wrong with him at the time. But based on what I'd just been told, I assumed that he and his elder Children had been given the prisoner treatment at some point. Maybe by his predecessor, after a failed coup? Not that they had looked this bad. But they had been gaunt and haggard, with sunken, leathery cheeks and hollow eyes. It was bad enough for me to guess that they'd been well on their way to starvation when they . . . fought their way out? Were released after having learned their lesson? Were rescued?

I didn't know, and it seemed impossible to ask. But it gave me a new respect for the African consul, which was only heightened after we passed through another room that must have once held the prisoners, or ones like them. There were deep scratches on the walls, ceiling, and floor, thousands of them. As if, in their madness, they had tried to claw their way through solid rock.

Even more disturbing was the fact that they hadn't managed it.

Limestone was fairly soft as rocks went, and the prisoners were vamps. The only scenario I could come up with for why they hadn't been able to literally move a mountain was that they had already largely atrophied by the time they were entombed here, and were so weak that their best efforts only made scratches. To be so desperate, and yet be unable to get out, knowing the fate that awaited them . . .

I did shudder then.

Ray, I thought suddenly, Ray would have been cussing up a storm right about now and dragging me out of here. Ray was a smart man. I guessed I was less so, because after a brief pause, I followed Hassani into the burial chamber.

It turned out to be a huge room with a gorgeous sarcophagus carved out of the same yellow limestone as everything else, but long as a yacht and taller than my head. It would have fit a giant—or the actual statue of Ra outside, had they folded it up a little. But I didn't think that was what was in there.

No, I didn't think that at all.

I guessed Lantern Boy didn't, either, because he was shaking enough that golden light shimmered around the room like water. It splashed the walls and made the hideous thing festooned above the sarcophagus and draped around the room also seem to move—and thus making him shake even more. It got bad enough that Hassani took the lantern away and held it up himself, which . . . yeah.

Could have done without that.

"He ruled over the vampires of this land for time out of mind," Hassani said, his voice hushed. "Before the pyramids were built, he ruled. Before there was an Egypt, he ruled. Before civilization itself, he was here, and he ruled."

I didn't say anything. Diplomacy required an answer, but fuck diplomacy. I stared upward and hoped like hell that the cracked and dusty thing up there didn't fall on me. Or I was gonna do a Ray, I swore to God.

Hassani glanced at me, and a small smile flirted with his lips. "It is a bit much, all at once."

Yeah, but at least I finally knew what that smell was. It permeated the air, thick and old and musty and horrible. I'd been in some bad places, and smelled some pretty terrible things. But nothing that stuck in my throat, feeling like it was clogging and burning it at the same time, quite like that.

I really envied the vamps their ability to just not breathe.

But worse than the smell was what it was coming from. Papery thin pieces of scale-covered skin draped the room like evil bunting. In some cases, there was coil after coil of it, what looked like a hundred layers all rolled up together. In others, those layers had burst apart, like the most God-awful Christmas cracker ever, leaving fluttery ends waving about in the air in abstract shapes yards long, and a foot-deep confetti of smaller pieces on the floor that crunched and crackled horribly underfoot.

I shuddered again visibly, and didn't give a shit.

"After his death, he was brought here, to the seat of his power, to possibly regenerate," Hassani said. "He had been able to do it before, and his supporters thought that, despite the damage, their god might yet return. But not this time."

There was a certain vicious satisfaction in the consul's voice that I didn't understand, and he didn't give me a chance to ask.

"The bones put out flesh and skin, more than once," he continued. "But the final push back to health, to life, eluded him. In the end, even his most fervent supporters had to admit that he was gone."

"He was a *snake*?" I croaked, finally managing to get my head around the image of a shed snakeskin at least twenty times bigger than I was.

"It was his master power, the ability to transform," Hassani said. "Or one of them, I should say, as he had several. As Apollo's son, he grew more powerful in the sun, for instance, instead of being consumed by it—"

"What? Wait."

Hassani did smile then. "I know how it sounds. But he was the first of us, the very first vampire ever made, and thus a . . . prototype, if you will. He was enormously strong, able to redirect the sun's rays to consume his enemies, among other things. It was the reason we entombed him down here. To deny him his greatest weapon, should he ever return."

I wasn't listening. I'd made the mistake of looking closer, and—shit. It wasn't just a snakeskin. Cracks in the shed epidermis showed that there were *bones* in there, including a spine as long as a train and three-foot fangs. I wondered what the hell they'd buried, and then remembered what Hassani had said: this thing regenerated. I stepped back, really glad not to have met this bastard in person.

Really, really glad.

"The ancient Greeks named this city Heliopolis, after Helios, their original sun god," Hassani continued. "But they were wrong to do so. They saw the suns portrayed everywhere, and naturally thought of Helios, who was the personification of the sun disk itself. But Apollo was the god who used the sun's power, and thus aligned more accurately with Ra, while our friend here—"

"Was the cobra," I whispered, remembering the tiny snake on the statue outside.

"Exactly so. The statue shows the god, the source of his power, and his defender. The ancients understood, even if modern man has forgotten."

"What happened to him?" I asked, after a pause, because clearly something had.

Hassani glanced at me. "Your father never told you the tale?"

"My father?" I frowned. "What would he know about this? Didn't that thing die . . . well, a long damned time ago?" This whole place reeked of age and dusty centuries forgotten by time. The man—the vampire—must have died thousands of years ago.

But Hassani was shaking his head. "He lived until the year 853 in our calendar, which would be . . . 1449 in yours. And even then, it was not so simple. After his bones were brought back here—"

"Wait. *Wait.*" Hassani obligingly waited. "You're telling me that that . . . thing . . . died less than *six hundred years ago*?"

"Yes." Hassani regarded me mildly. "In Venice."

"In Venice. He died in Venice in 1449." I did some mental math, and didn't like what it was telling me. I scowled. "*What* didn't Mircea tell me?"

"Anything, apparently. My apologies; I assumed you knew."

"Knew what?"

"That it took three of them to take him down. Your consul, the European consul Antony, and your father."

"My father . . . killed *that*?"

"Helped to kill that. You see, your consul and Antony were Changed by . . . well, we called him Pa-neck, meaning the serpent, although not to his face."

"Yeah." I stared up at the huge, fanged skin above me.

"His parents named him Sokkwi, 'Little Fool', but he took the reign title of Setep-en-Ra, 'Chosen by Ra.' He was quite capable, by all accounts, when young, and a fierce defender of his adoptive father's interests. Some have even surmised that the serpent above Ra in the early portraits wasn't Wadjet at all, but Ra's chosen defender, emblematic of the army he was building for himself."

"The army."

This was starting to sound eerily familiar.

"Yes, the gods were constantly at each other's throats in those days, some five thousand years ago—"

"This thing is—was—*five thousand years old*?"

Hassani blinked. "Well, I did say he was the first of us."

I shut up.

"In any case," he continued. "The old gods were a quarrelsome lot, and a selfish one, with each wanting to rule over all. But they were too well matched to be able to win a decisive victory. They therefore decided to change humans, or whatever creatures came to hand, improving them and forging them—"

"Into armies to fight their wars for them."

The dark eyes narrowed. "This is not the first time you have heard this."

"No." I thought back to a strange creature I had met several times recently, the last in Hong Kong during the desperate fight for the city. He had died there, but not before telling me a story that didn't seem all that relevant at the time. But then, his kind were basically the secret service of hell: fallen angels with a network specializing in information who frequently seemed to know more than they should about what was coming.

I stared up at what remained of an ancient demigod, and wondered what he'd known about this.

"An Irin told me," I said.

"Ah. Fascinating creatures."

That was one way of putting it.

"Well, the Irin was absolutely right," Hassani said. "The gods made themselves armies, but they did it so well that they began to worry. The creatures were made to battle other gods, after all. What if they decided to turn on their makers? That is why later generations had limitations added deliberately—vulnerability to sunlight, weak points at the heart and neck, helpless early years—"

"I wouldn't say helpless," I muttered.

"—but Setep-en-Ra had none of these. He was virtually indestructible physically."

"And mentally?"

Hassani shook his head. "He grew progressively more paranoid and detached from a world he no longer recognized. After the gods were banished, he began to think of himself as a god himself, and his delusions grew. As his strongest Children, your consul and Antony plotted to take him down, although in the end, they were not enough. Your father had to assist—"

"At *two years old*?" Because that was what father had been, at least in vampire terms, in 1449. He should have had trouble defending himself, much less . . .

I looked up again, and shivered.

Hassani smiled. "He was always very clever, your father,

and sometimes, that is more useful than power."

I crossed my arms. "Is there a reason you're telling me all this?"

"Yes, in fact. I—"

Hassani stopped suddenly, and cocked his head, as if listening to someone. Which he probably was. Vamps' ability to communicate mentally with members of their family, or in the case of someone as powerful as Hassani, with virtually any vampire in the area, was one thing that made them so deadly.

I waited it out, my arms wrapped around myself and that horrible, decaying stench in my nose. I didn't understand why we couldn't have had this conversation upstairs. I didn't understand why we had to have it at all. Old vamps liked to be mysterious, and centuries of having people kowtow to them hadn't helped encourage them to get to the damned point already. But I really wished he'd hurry up.

I'd been in some creepy ass places before, but this one was really starting to get to me. And I wasn't alone. I glanced back at Lantern Boy to find him looking miserable, his mouth turned down and his eyes darting here and there, as if anticipating an attack.

And then widening in apparent horror, as if witnessing one.

I looked quickly back at Hassani, expecting I don't know what.

But there was nothing happening. The consul still looked a little zoned out, but perfectly fine. Until he suddenly reached out and *touched the shed skin.*

Lantern Boy made a sound and I sucked in a breath, even though it didn't make sense. Whatever this thing had been, it was long dead now. But I still didn't like him touching it.

Hassani, however, seemed to like it fine. He rubbed a bit of the brittle skin between his fingers for a moment, then crushed it in his fist. Lantern Boy gave a bleat of terror and fled, while I just stood there, frozen in place. But Hassani wasn't done. He suddenly jerked at it, not a piece but the whole thing, and he put a master's strength behind it. He pulled not once or twice, but over and over and over, until the entire, carefully displayed snakeskin was on the floor and broken into pieces.

I joined Lantern Boy in the creepy, scratched up antechamber, mainly because I couldn't breathe in the burial chamber anymore. Pieces of ancient god fluttered through the air and dusted my lungs, even out here. While inside . . .

I didn't know what the hell was going on inside.

There was a noise, which I thought was a cough. But it kept going and going, and gaining in strength until it echoed loudly around the chamber. And even then, it took me a moment to identify it, because it was so strange under the circumstances.

But yes, I realized.

Hassani was *laughing*.

"I was so afraid of you!" he yelled. "So afraid! And look at you now! Dead and dusted and *gone*, like all the gods' children, while ours—*ours are still here*. Who inherits the Earth now, you bastard? Who rules *now*?"

There was no answer, unless you counted Hassani's own devilish cackling. The kid and I looked at each other, and then back at the boss, who had found a piece of snake skin he liked and was holding it to the lantern flame. And *shit*!

The dry old stuff went up like a torch, but Hassani didn't drop it. He wrapped the end in a piece of his robe and shook the heavily burning taper around the room, giggling like a madman as he did so. Soon, the whole place was burning.

Flames ran up the walls, finding pieces of shed skin that I hadn't even noticed, and forming garlands of fire. It ate across the huge skin on the floor, making it twist and writhe as it was consumed, as if, in its last moments, it lived once more. The fire consumed the main part of the skin, then swept the ground, setting all the smaller pieces aflame, too.

And threatening Hassani himself.

I turned to Lantern Boy, because it was definitely save-the-boss time, but he had clearly had enough. He must have understood some English, or perhaps he'd just decided that the consul had gone crazy, and the better part of valor was called for. He ran.

I, unfortunately, did not have that option. I was a shitty ambassador, but allowing a consul and ally to die on my watch was a bit much. Not to mention that I had no idea how to get out of here alone. This place was huge; I could end up wandering for days.

So, I womaned the hell up, threw an arm over my face and went to rescue a possibly crazy and certainly disturbed master vamp.

Which is when things got weird.

CHAPTER ELEVEN

Dory, Cairo

Hassani was just standing there, surrounded by flames, I had no idea why. And then I realized why. The snakeskin was burning up, but as it did so, it was throwing out more than just sparks.

Two chariots raced, neck and neck, the black flanks of their horses gleaming, the sun on the golden armbands of the drivers blinding, the sand spraying from under the wheels like waves in the air. A crowd roared as one chariot pulled ahead, crossing a line in the sand a split second before the other. But the winner did not look pleased.

Instead, he jumped off his vehicle before the horses had even stopped, hit the ground and rolled, but not to his feet. He knelt, despite the fact that the burning sand must have been all but cooking his flesh. "Please," he begged.

It was not enough. The whole point of these games was to remind the people who ruled—and why. Seeing a human best a god at anything might lead to the idea that the gods could be bested at other things, could even be driven out.

No, not close to enough.

The god glanced up at the sun, his father's symbol, boiling hot and brilliant overhead. And then just as hot down here, as a column of blinding white light surged earthward. The charioteer's screams echoed around the racetrack, turning to shrieks and then to gurgles as his skin sloughed off, as the meat cooked on his bones, as he fell over, toppling to the ground as his pharaoh lifted a hand.

And the handlers released the lord's favorite dogs, free now to enjoy their freshly cooked meal.

The vision shattered and I stared around blindly for a moment, before realizing that my left sleeve was on fire. I shook it out and grabbed Hassani. "Come on! Come on, we've got to *go!*"

But we weren't fast enough.

The pool sparkled dimly in the lantern light, throwing golden ripples on the dark water. Inside, a dozen hand selected girls bathed under the watchful eyes of the harem eunuchs. The women came from all over Egypt and beyond: nubile temptresses from Ta-Seti and Punt, their skin as dark as midnight and lustrous with lotions and perfumes; golden skinned beauties from Canaan and Lebanon, with rippling tresses that almost reached to their feet; and rare, moon-skinned lovelies from further afield, acquired through trade with slavers from faraway lands.

The girls had noticed his entrance, flanked by sumptuously dressed servants, and felt the weight of his gaze. Some slid farther down in the water, their hands moving to conceal their bodies. Others did the opposite, putting their charms on display, hoping to be the lord's next wife.

But it was one of the former that caught his eye. "That one."

The royal scepter singled out a girl with hair like flame and skin like milk, little more than a child with her breasts just beginning to form. Two eunuchs pulled her from the pool and brought her, dripping and naked and trembling, before the god. She knelt and one of them lifted her chin to show him her face; she was breathing hard, her skin flushed, and her eyes—

"Closer."

She was pulled to her feet and brought forward, and yes, he had thought so. Her eyes were as unusual as her other coloring, like the water in the shallower reaches of the Nile. Beautiful—

and rare.

He smiled in approval. After a nudge from her handlers, the girl smiled hesitantly back. Until she saw the fangs.

She screamed, a small, brief cry that was quickly silenced, for the god could drain a vessel in seconds. She sagged in the hands of her holder, withered and lifeless, and hidden from the others' eyes by the eunuch's bulk. She was carried away, and the son of Ra surveyed the pool again.

"That one."

The vision shattered—just in time. I ducked, and dragged Hassani down with me. A piece of the burning tail slung by overhead, shedding an arc of sparks in its wake. They rained down on me harmlessly, but Hassani was not so fortunate.

"Fuck!" I yelled, as the consul went up like a roman candle.

I always carried temporary shields in my arsenal, but I hadn't activated them. I'd thought that this would be a quick in and out; my mistake, and possibly Hassani's death if I didn't do something. And a shield wouldn't help here.

There was no time for finesse. A grab in a pocket, a tear of his clothes, a slap to his chest, and a small golden charm sank into his skin. I just hoped it wasn't already too late.

With the typical vampire flammability, Hassani already had orange-red wounds opening up all over his body, with the skin blackening and tearing and splitting around them. He had seconds at best. But that was before the charm started spitting out little tattooed rain clouds that shot in all directions.

They were supposed to be used for camouflage: to raise a rainstorm to disguise the sounds of a getaway, or to wash away evidence, or to persuade nosy humans to run inside. They were meant to be deposited on the side of a building or shot straight into the air. They were not intended for use on a body.

But necessity is the mother of stupidity, and sometimes,

stupidity works.

Well, sort of.

The room should have been awash in water, with a literal rainstorm blowing up inside the walls. But charms like this had to draw their resources from the natural world. They didn't contain water; they just pulled whatever was available in the vicinity together. And there wasn't much in the bone-dry temple to work with.

But they were finding something. Because, every time a spark on Hassani's skin turned into a conflagration, they were there, enthusiastically showering the hell out of it. We didn't get a rainstorm, but we got enough to keep him from dusting away to nothing, although it came at a price. We were both drenched in seconds from the enthusiastic sprays, and when I finally did activate the shield, the small bubble it projected around us quickly started to fill with water.

I sloshed for the door, while images from the beast's life hammered at my cranium, trying to force their way inside. I managed to hold them off, grateful for once that Dorina wasn't here, because the mental gifts were on her side of the brain. I was all but mind blind without her, dull as a block of wood, which was usually a problem living and working with people who could talk as easily mentally as physically.

But not today.

Today, it was a gift, and one the consul did not have. Hassani was catatonic, caught in whatever vision had contorted his face and widened his eyes as I dragged us toward the door. I'd been pulling on his clothes, but the robes were weakened by fire, and the piece I was holding split in my hands. And, as soon as I touched his skin, a sneaky little vision caught me, leaping from him to me like lightning and throwing us both to the ground.

"Nothing to say?"

The speaker was a small man, thin, brown and bald, someone you might have passed in the street and never looked at twice—except for the haughtiness of his face. That much arrogance was reserved for kings and gods, the latter of which he absolutely believed himself to be. The son of Ra . . .

I felt my lips, bone dry as they were, crack into a smile.

"To who?" My voice, usually one of my best qualities, was little more than a dry rasp in my throat. I persisted anyway. "To the child unwanted even by his own parents? What was it they called you? Sokkwi? They knew what they'd birthed, and nothing ever done to you afterward has changed that. Little Fool you were; Little Fool you remain."

"You see this, captain?" The fool—and the monster—glanced behind him. "I share secrets with him, and he uses them against me. Trying, in a clumsy fashion, to persuade me to anger, hoping I'll kill him, no doubt."

"Yes, Lord."

The monster smiled gently at me. "It will not be that easy. Not for you. I wondered when those others rebelled, who was behind it. Wondered which of them was smart enough to plot so cunningly and so well. They never told me, did you know? They're here still, downstairs, dried up like old firewood. Perhaps that is what I'll use them for, someday."

He laughed, and the captain of his guard, a huge man with a scarred face, laughed with him.

"Perhaps, one day, I shall afford you the same privilege," the fool said. "But not yet. And not soon." He glanced about the room, to where my friends and supporters were chained, suffering as I was. Then he leaned in. "Do they hate you yet? Before I'm done with you, they will."

He left, but the captain stayed behind. And in a moment, I felt it—the coolness of metal in my palm. I looked down to see a key glimmering there. I looked up—

And found him gone.

Of course; he couldn't risk so much as a word. Neither could I. But words were not what was needed here.

I started working on the lock to the magical cuffs that held me; not that they needed magic. Not anymore. I had no idea how

I would get through the door in my current state, or past the soldiers who would doubtless be guarding it.

But when it came to it, the door was open, and the soldiers gone.

My people looked at me, clear eyed and stalwart, despite all that they had endured. They did not ask any questions. Even in my head their voices were silent, too exhausted to manage a simple connection. But I knew what they wanted to know.

"Someday," I croaked. "Someday, we will light the biggest bonfire in the world over his corpse. But not today. Today, we live."

I slammed back into myself with the words still echoing in my brain. Today, we live. Today, we live. Today, we *live*.

I knew the door to salvation was just ahead, even if I couldn't see it. Grayish white smoke billowed around the outside of the bubble, blocking my view and threatening to choke me, even through the protection the shield offered. Worse, that protection had become our trap, filling up like a water balloon while I was out, leaving Hassani floating and me rolling uselessly around the floor.

So, I dropped it, heard the water hiss away into steam, felt the heat slam into me like a hundred ovens opened at the same time. The air was hot enough to sear my skin, even without the fire touching me. It didn't matter.

"Today, we live," I rasped at Hassani, and crawled toward safety, dragging him behind me. "Today, we live."

It wasn't easy going. Mind blind I might be, but the visions coming off the dead god were getting wilder and more numerous. I'd felt them batter me as soon as the shield dropped, in a hurricane of little bits and pieces, like the patches of shed skin burning up in the air all around us. And each of them seemed to have a story to tell, an attempt to drag me back inside a memory and leave me helpless.

One of them succeeded.

A huge palace, surrounded by date palms and sycamore figs, a man-made oasis where none had existed before. Stars overhead, brightening the otherwise solid black of the skies. The dark of the moon: beautiful, but deadly.

With no light, they would never make it out of here.

"I will burn, and light the way."

It was Zakarriyyah who spoke, he whose master power was to resist flame. I could not see his eyes, but I knew they were burning, too, with the resolve he'd always shown. He had the stoutest heart of all my people; he would gladly die to save us.

And slowly burn to death, over the long journey across the sands.

But I could not let him. "My Child—"

A hand covered mine. It was rough and dry, more like clasping wood than flesh. We were all so weak, so close to turning into living statues. That is what the fool would have us be, to decorate his palaces, something to be used to cow any who would challenge him.

"We cannot be that," I said roughly, as a tremor went through my Children, some pieces of my thoughts bleeding over. "We were not the first, and will not be the last to oppose him. Those who come after us must believe that they have a chance."

"Teacher—" Zakarriyyah pleaded.

"And they will. We will. And you will be among us when we do."

"Not if we do not escape tonight!" The hand grasping mine trembled, but there was resolve in his voice. "Let me do this. Let me help—"

"Have you fools never heard of lanterns?"

The hissed words came out of the darkness, almost in my ear. I turned, human slow, to see the slim figure of the monster's chief Child standing there, a lantern in each hand. I did not have time to greet her, or to attack. I could not think clearly enough in my current state even to determine which would be best.

And she did not give me the chance. The dark-haired beauty sat down the lights we so desperately needed, and a moment later, a pack hit me in the face. It was clothing by the feel, which we also needed, as our tattered rags would give us away wherever we went.

"One to each," she said, her voice low, and two maidservants hurried to obey.

I watched, uncomprehendingly, as packs were distributed to each of my people. Until a rough hand jerked me around. "Feed."

I stared at her. She was offering her own arm. It made no sense.

"He will kill you for this," I rasped.

"If you keep standing there, looking at me, very likely!"

I looked at her arm instead, gleaming golden bright in the lantern light. "I cannot partake when my people starve."

She said something shockingly rude in Greek. And then I found myself grabbed by my rags, and dragged down to her face. Her fangs were out; a breach of etiquette at court. She did not look as if she cared.

"Listen to me, old mummy," she hissed, "and listen well. If you want to live, you will do exactly as I say. Feed, enough that your eyes aren't crossing and you can think to lead your people. Ride for Fustat—it's due east. Get there before sunrise, or you will surely die. Even your masters have no strength left. Go to this address," she pushed a piece of parchment into my hand. "The man there knows me; he will hide you, find blood pigs for you. Drink; recover. Then get as far away from these shores as you can."

She did not wait for me to reply. She slit her own flesh with a dagger like fingernail, and shoved her arm into my face. And the smell of it—

Ah, it would take a better man than I to resist!

I drank, so briefly, and she turned to go.

"Wait." I called her back.

She spun. "I must leave! I have been here too long already."

"First, tell me why you help us. You owe us nothing—"

"This isn't for you," she spat. And then her eyes went to the *palace, and the expression in them . . . even in darkness, it was palpable.*

The enemy of my enemy, I thought, and understood.

"One day," she told me, and then she was gone.

Rain hit me in the face, bringing me back, and I looked up to see a tiny cloud on Hassani's shoulder, busily putting out an ember and squirting me in the face in the process. I opened my mouth, caught a few drops on my tongue. Thought I'd found paradise—

Only to feel the excruciating pain of the other place, as the vision fully released me.

I screamed, my hands and arms and back burning, while what was left of my leather jacket melted to my flesh. This wasn't a normal fire; this wasn't a normal anything. And then I coughed, retching and hacking, dizzy from the lack of air. Hassani said and did nothing, still lost in his dreams—

And, suddenly, I understood. They *were* his dreams. The fluttering bits of memory or whatever they were coming off the dead demigod weren't the problem. The first two, yes, but these last—they had both been through Hassani's eyes. I couldn't shake them off because I was touching him, but I couldn't get us out unless I did!

But my jeans were full of black edged holes, with burnt red flesh peeking through. And I had nothing else to use, unless I stripped my flesh off with my jacket! Hassani was no better, in tattered rags half burnt away, and weakened to the point that they ripped as soon as I touched them. There was nothing—

Well, almost nothing.

I grabbed a piece of the dead demigod, no longer caring when it crinkled under my hands, and used it like an oven mitt to keep from touching the consul. I still saw images: the mad dash through the desert, the furtive days of hiding that followed, the creak of a ship sailing God knew where. But they were distant, transparent, a glaze on the burning, smoke filled hell we were crawling through, nothing more.

And we started to make headway.

I doubted we'd have made it if not for the little rain clouds. They kept dashing us with water every few seconds, less than before, as whatever resources they had found dried up. But enough to keep going.

Only where I was going, I wasn't sure.

I couldn't see anything anymore. Smoke billowed everywhere, coating my throat, stopping my nose, obscuring my vision. The world had been reduced to heat and ash and the sharp reek of the fiend behind us, who was trying to kill us even in death.

But, once again, he failed.

A sliver of cool air from outside reached out like the hand of an angel, guiding me forward. I followed it until warm stones replaced the burning ones under my body, the first indication I'd had that we'd found the elusive doorway.

I would have laughed if I'd had enough breath, or cried if I could have spared the moisture. As it was, I just increased my speed, dragging the consul because he was too tall for me to easily carry. And that was assuming I could have managed it with so little air in my lungs.

Make that none at all, I thought, as my airway closed up completely. I'd been coughing and hacking, feeling like I was going to bring up my lungs with every breath, but this was worse. This was endgame.

The lack of oxygen made me weak, and made the simple matter of traversing a few, smallish rooms feel like a marathon. But the temperature continued to drop, becoming cooler and cooler as we moved ahead, giving me hope. Until my torn and burnt hands were freezing, the coldness of the outer rooms coming as a blessed relief.

We reached the prisoners again before I could see anything, their bodies appearing out of the smoke, still stacked like wood against the cold stone walls—and probably flammable as hell. But I couldn't help them. I could barely help myself.

My strength was almost gone, and without Dorina, I had no reserves to draw on. But I could see the damned throne room now, glimmering ahead like a mirage. Could feel the cold air on my face. Could hear the echoes of running feet and shouted voices—was it another vision?

I couldn't tell; didn't know. I didn't even remember what I was doing anymore. The burning in my lungs eclipsed my world, and nothing else mattered, nothing else was real.

"Dory!"

I thought I heard Louis-Cesare calling my name, but it couldn't be him. He wasn't here. He'd left me and he wasn't here.

And then neither was I, as darkness finally overwhelmed me.

CHAPTER TWELVE

Dory, Cairo

Yells, screams and curses hit my ears, quickly followed by the clash of blade on blade. But fast, inhumanly so, as if someone was playing the castanets. With a rapier . . .

The thought jerked me awake, and it was no gentle return to consciousness. Alarm bells were going off all over my body. My lungs were struggling to drag in enough oxygen while also hacking up vile black phlegm; my skin was screaming in pain, and feeling like only half of it was still adhered to my body; and my stomach was warning of an eruption.

Oh no, you don't, you bastard, I thought. You didn't have breakfast or dinner, either. So, don't threaten me!

I rolled over and tried to get to my hands and knees, but my hands were screaming, too. Everything was screaming. My body felt like it was still on fire, and I could smell my burnt hair. But I was up. I was swaying on my feet and the room was spinning, but I was up.

Where was he?

I was at the top of the stairs with an expansive view, but my eyes kept trying to cross. That wasn't helped by the rapid-fire sound of metal on metal that echoed around the room, confusing my sense of direction. And my sense of balance, apparently, because I promptly tripped over something.

Hassani, I realized. And looking better than I'd expected. I watched a nasty burn on his face slowly close up, while being lovingly watered by a tiny, cheerful cloud.

My life was . . . odd.

Lantern Boy was there, too, kneeling by the boss's side. I guessed he'd come back while I was out. Maybe he'd felt bad about abandoning his consul.

Which he damned well should, I thought evilly. Vampire strength could have gotten Hassani out of there a lot faster than I'd been able to—assuming that the kid hadn't burnt up right along with him. Which come to think of it . . .

I decided that maybe it was better that I hadn't had two fiery vamps to deal with, and patted his shoulder.

He started sobbing then, while his hands continued what they'd been doing, which was to uselessly stroke the boss's arm. I guessed it made him feel better. I staggered off down the stairs.

A vampire lunged for me and I threw something at him. Wasn't sure what, 'cause my head felt weird and everything was swimmy, to the point that I was faintly surprised to have found a weapon in my hand. But that'd do it, I thought, as a tiny golden tiger went glimmering along its arc, vivid against the gloom. And turned into an eight-hundred-pound fluffball with fangs and claws before it hit down.

It jumped one of Hassani's masters, making the man's eyes go big.

"Did the same thing to me, when I first met him," I slurred, as the two rolled back down the stairs in a ball of orange fury. "He grows on you."

The vamp didn't answer, unless you counted screaming.

So, what was I—oh yeah. Louis-Cesare. I had this weird idea that he was here, although I didn't see—

And then I did. Leaping out from behind one of the huge pillars, a rapier in one hand and a flaming torch in another: my hubby. My old man. My ball and chain.

I stopped two thirds of the way down the stairs to leer at him affectionately. He didn't notice, maybe because he was facing off with what had to be twenty guys. Or maybe ten; my eyes kept trying to cross. A lot of guys.

Make that a lot of masters, I thought, as four or five rushed him, all at once.

Not fair, I thought, and threw some more stuff.

There was a glittering rain of gold, and then there was a variety of things that should not have been sitting in an ancient throne room. Some of it, I admit, was not technically relevant. Like the easy chair and dorm style fridge—so nice for stake outs—that popped into being in the middle of the air and fell onto a vamp's head. Or the case of disguises, which deposited a blonde wig on another vamp, and a fake beard and glasses on a third. Or the bright red motorcycle that suddenly appeared and skidded into a pillar.

An inflatable life raft, on the other hand, which hit the floor as a tiny charm and bounced a couple of times, sprawled out full sized in the midst of a vampire charge.

It didn't do much damage; it was a raft. But the fact that it was there at all seemed to confuse them and several tripped and fell. It did not confuse Louis-Cesare, who stared around wildly until he saw me. And, for some reason, looked stunned, appalled, and furious by turns.

Hope the latter wasn't directed at me, I thought, and waved.

"Hey!" I yelled.

"Dory! Go back where you were!"

"No. You're in trouble. M'gonna help you." I smiled at him sloppily.

Then I remembered that I was mad at him about . . . something. I pushed it away. Kill vamps now, figure out why I was mad later.

Having formed a plan, I weaved my way forward.

Louis-Cesare tried getting in between me and a group of vamps that had just peeled off of the main bunch and headed my way, but they were sneaky. They jumped onto the pillars, high above his head, clinging to the surface by the tiny ridges left by the carvings. That was impressive enough, but then they started leaping on all fours from column to column, as easily as I'd walk down a street. They looked like . . . like . . . like those climbing things, I thought, my brain not cooperating.

Little brown fuzzy creatures with long tails. An 'M' word. Moose? Mice? Manatees?

No, that wasn't right.

"Motherfucking lemurs!" I yelled triumphantly, causing some of the vamps to stop and stare.

But others kept coming, and they didn't look happy. Of course, they looked a lot less so a moment later, when they were tackled by the remaining elements of my arsenal. And these *were* relevant.

A pair of flying bolos wrapped around a couple of vamps' necks, dragging them off of the columns and into the air, feet kicking and eyes bulging. Three razor-edged disks knocked down half a dozen more and chased them across the room, slinging about like deadly Frisbees whenever they tried to double back. Meanwhile, Kitty—aka the tiger, aka the charm I'd borrowed from a friendly triad and failed to return—was going ham on the rest.

Well, most of the rest.

There was a pile of bodies on the floor a little way from Louis-Cesare that didn't look dead. They were still moving, writhing and groaning and being dragged off by other vamps who were making a hash of it, because they were trying to keep on eye on him at the same time. I didn't know why; he seemed pretty busy. He'd put his back to a pillar, had a vamp under one arm and his rapier in the other, which he was holding steady on a second vamp on the floor. A semi-circle of snarling masters surrounded them, but at a distance, as if they were afraid for the life of their friend if they came too close.

Which didn't make sense. Judging by the furious, peppery smell coming off of floor vamp, he was a high-ranking master. One of those could heal a blow from a metal weapon in seconds, even to the heart.

Or maybe not, I thought, noticing something weird about the rapier.

"What's that?" I asked, wandering over after Kitty ate a hole in the semicircle.

"Dory." Louis-Cesare looked conflicted. Like he wanted to grab and hug me, but that would have required letting go of one of his captives.

I squatted down, and then almost fell on my ass.

I'd had better days.

But this was new. It was a highly polished wooden tip that had been affixed to the end of Louis-Cesare's rapier. Turning it, effectively, into a stake without interfering too much with the functionality of the blade. Huh.

"Where did you find that?" I asked, looking up.

"I didn't. I had it made—"

I grinned at floor vamp. "My hubby, the inventor."

He just stared at me.

I thought he looked familiar, but couldn't place him. Tall and lanky, with a hooked nose and dark brown skin. Bald. Maybe I'd seen him at the party?

Seemed plausible.

"Dory, perhaps you should sit down," Louis-Cesare said, sounding a little strangled.

"No, no, I'm fine," I assured him, just before my butt hit the floor. Guess my body had other ideas. "Where'd you come up with it?"

"Come up with what?"

"The wooden thing." I pointed, more or less. "What's it called?"

"A *col de mort*, and I didn't—"

"A . . . death collar?" I translated. It was harder than it should have been.

"Yes, but I didn't—"

"Didn't what?"

"Didn't come up with it!" Louis-Cesare was looking exasperated. "We need to get you to a healer!"

I looked around. The circle had closed back up, and the people didn't look friendly. "Well, that's gonna be kind of hard."

"You're never getting out of here," floor vamp said. "Kill me if you will, but there are hundreds between you and the exits, each willing to die—"

"For what?" I asked curiously.

"—to see that neither of you escape alive!"

"Well, technically one of us is already dead," I pointed out, lying down.

Oh, yeah.

That was better.

"Dory!" Louis-Cesare's voice snapped. "Do not go to sleep!"

"Okay." I yawned, and listened to Kitty savaging something in the distance. "I'm just gonna close my eyes—"

"I read about it in a book!" he said, sounding desperate.

I opened an eye. "Read about what?"

"The *col de mort*."

"You didn't invent it?" I frowned.

"No. No, it was in a detective novel, a metal tip used to make a training sword deadly. But I thought—"

"That wood would work the same way on vamps." I sat up. "You *did* invent it!"

And then I felt dizzy.

"Dory!"

"M'kay." I caught myself with one hand. It hurt. I picked it up and looked at it, and all the skin was burned off the palm.

How'd that happen?

"She isn't." Floor vamp laughed. "You're both going to die."

"Why?" Louis-Cesare demanded furiously. "We came in peace to your court—"

"Does this look like peace?" the vamp snarled, and started

up, until the *col de mort* bit into his chest. He froze.

"This is of your doing," Louis-Cesare said. "I came back for my wife. All I want is to take her and go—"

The vamp snorted. "I'm sure you do!"

"Zakarriyyah," I said, finally placing him. I tried to snap my fingers, but that doesn't work with no skin.

Startled, dark brown eyes met mine. "How did you know my name?"

"You were at the palace, in the desert. You were going to set yourself on fire to allow the others to escape." I looked at him soberly. "That was very brave."

Louis-Cesare and the vamp were both staring at me now.

"How did you know about that?" the vamp whispered.

"Saw it. Hassani showed me."

"Before or after you tried to kill him?" Another vamp snarled. He was the opposite of the skinny, bald guy on the floor, having a full head of hair, more muscle than he needed, and a beard that looked like it was trying to eat his face.

Oh, that would be one of mine.

I grinned at the piece from my disguise bag that had gripped him and wasn't letting go.

And then I remembered what he'd said.

"Kill him? I saved him." At least, I was pretty sure.

My head hurt.

"She has bleeding on the brain," the vamp woman under Louis-Cesare's arm said, speaking for the first time. "I'm a healer. I can help—"

"No!" That was the big bearded vamp. He looked at Zakarriyyah. "You saw what they did upstairs, the monsters they unleashed on us!"

"What monsters?" I asked.

"Do you mean the fey?" Louis-Cesare demanded. "We fought them; we didn't send them!"

"And that was last night," I told Zakarriyyah. Talk about holding a grudge.

"If you don't let me—" the woman began.

"Do it," Zakarriyyah ordered, but of course, that required somebody's else's approval, too, didn't it?

"She will soon have irreversible brain damage," the woman said, speaking slowly and distinctly to Louis-Cesare. "It is a common side effect of smoke inhalation."

Louis-Cesare didn't move.

"Your toys will not last much longer," the woman said. "And then it will be out of your hands. But it may also be too late."

"It's okay, you can trust Zakarriyyah," I said. "He's a good sort."

The vamp in question stared at me some more.

"And if you choose to kill her instead?" Louis-Cesare said viciously.

"I don't have to kill her!" The woman struggled uselessly against his mental grip. "She'll die without treatment!"

"You have me captive as well," Zakarriyyah said slowly, still looking at me. "If your woman dies, my life is forfeit."

That was apparently acceptable, because Louis-Cesare let the healer go. And, immediately, she was by my side. I didn't even see her move.

Of course, there might have been a reason for that. It felt like my brain had started skipping, like a video with bad editing. Suddenly, I was on my back again on the cold stone floor, staring up at the pretty vampire's face. She looked Egyptian, but not like modern Egyptians, who have a good deal of Arab blood from the invasion in the Middle Ages. But like a frieze off a tomb wall.

"You should be wearing pleated linen and gold in your hair," I told her seriously.

"I will consider it," she said, and put a hand on my forehead.

My brain skipped again, and I guess Louis-Cesare and Zakarriyyah had made up. The latter was no longer on the floor, and they were talking in hushed voices along with several other vamps. That included the big guy and another who could have been his twin except that he was bald and had a chest so hairy that it looked like a fur carpet had been stuffed inside of his shirt. I could see it through the rents in his clothes that matched Kitty's claws, but he must be pretty high ranking, as he'd already healed the body underneath.

There was no problem hearing them, despite the low tones. The acoustics in here were really something. But I didn't understand what they were saying.

"—impossible! Do I look like a necromancer to you?" That was Louis-Cesare, sounding furious.

"And we are to believe that you don't have one on staff?" That was the big guy with hair. He had managed to lose the fake beard, only to reveal that he had a real one underneath.

"I don't, as it happens! And if I did, I wouldn't be using him to attack you!"

"And why should we believe you? Why should we believe anything you—"

Zakarriyyah lifted a hand. He looked at Louis-Cesare narrowly. "You say you know nothing about this?"

"Nothing. I left this morning thinking that my wife would continue the diplomatic visit here, while I traced our attackers—"

"But you came back!" The big, bald vamp looked like he thought that proved something.

"Yes, I came back." Louis-Cesare was holding onto his temper, but you could hear it in his voice. At least, I could. And from the way the surrounding vamps, who hedged the smaller group at a safe distance, were fingering their weapons, it looked like they could, too.

We were the diplomatic dream team, I thought, and laughed.

"Try to stay still," the healer said, her hand cool on my brow.

I tried.

"And we're not to assume that you left to call your creature and coordinate *this*?" the big, bearded vamp demanded.

"I left for the reason I said," Louis-Cesare snapped. "I returned for the reason I said! That is all you need to know."

And there it was, why my hubby had no more business on this mission than I did. 'King to peasant,' I'd heard my father say, when describing Louis-Cesare's more aggrieved tones, and it had not been approving. Mircea had been a king once, too, or something very close to it, but he had learned how not to sound like it.

Louis-Cesare had not, and the vamps clearly thought so, too.

"Ah, *malik*, do forgive your humble servant," the big, bald vamp said, giving the most sarcastic salaam I'd ever seen. The '*malik*' was sarcasm, too; it meant 'lord' or 'king', and from what I understood, was once a common designation across the Middle East. But this group didn't strike me as people who liked kings.

The female version was '*malikah*', meaning queen, which I'd been called frequently since I got here.

It hadn't been meant kindly, either.

"You're forgiven," Louis-Cesare said coldly.

I rolled my eyes.

"Perhaps we should ask your woman," the big, bald vamp said, glancing at me.

"My *wife*," Louis-Cesare snapped, and okay, things were heating up.

"Can I move yet?" I asked the healer.

"No."

I sighed.

"Don't ask me what's going on," I said, staring at the ceiling. "He ran off, leaving me at a court where I'd just been attacked, to chase an old enemy who may or may not be dead —"

"I had every reason to assume that you would be safe here!" Louis-Cesare said.

"Yeah, feeling real safe right now."

"They were supposed to be our hosts!"

"And you were supposed to be guests! Not assassins!" the big, bald vamp said angrily.

I laughed.

"You think this is funny?" he demanded, and started towards me, only to find Louis-Cesare in the way.

"Not really."

"You laughed!"

"At the irony. You're a cult of assassins, or you started out that way, but now you accuse us—"

"With reason!"

"Rashid," Zakarriyyah said, cutting off big, bald and hairy, who stayed almost nose to nose with Louis-Cesare, but didn't try for me again. "You were saying?" Zakarriyyah asked me politely.

"I was saying . . ." I didn't actually remember what I was saying. Oh, yeah. "He abandoned me," I said, flapping a hand at Louis-Cesare.

Who frowned. "I would never abandon you—"

"You left me to run after Christine."

"Who is Christine?" the healer asked.

"His old girlfriend."

And now we were both looking at him accusingly.

"It . . . wasn't like that," Louis-Cesare said.

"And then when you stole Ray's head—"

"He stole a head?" the healer looked appalled.

"It was my head," I clarified. "I mean, I'd chopped it off—"

"You cannot take another's trophy," the big, bearded vamp said reprovingly. "Even a filthy dhampir's."

"Call her that again—" Louis-Cesare threatened.

"Why do you care? You abandon her and steal from her."

"Mostly abandon," I agreed, looking at my old man. "Like when you ran off with that fey queen—"

"I was possessed!"

"Still. It's a pattern." I didn't know what the healer was doing, but it had wrapped me in a warm, fuzzy blanket of a feeling, which was not enough to mask a stab of pain. I suddenly remembered why I was mad at him. "My sister was taken, leaving me alone for the first time in my life, and what do I find when I wake up? You're gone, too!"

"I was trying to protect you!"

"I didn't need protecting. I needed *you.*"

The healer put a soft hand on my shoulder.

Louis-Cesare looked conflicted. He clearly didn't want to talk about this now, which was too bad, because I did. "What is it?" I demanded. "You think that, with Dorina gone, I can't handle myself? You leave the little dhampir to drink tea and look at pyramids because she'll be a drag on you?"

"That's not—"

"Then what was it? I mean, you didn't even talk to me—"

"He didn't talk to you?" the healer repeated, sounding appalled.

"Stay out of this!" Louis-Cesare snapped.

"No," I said. "No note, no anything—"

"I gave Hassani a note," Louis-Cesare said defensively.

"Yes. Hassani. Not me."

"I wanted to make sure that it reached you—"

Okay, now I was pissed off, because that was a lie. "You wanted to make sure you didn't have to face me. You left Hassani to do your dirty work and ran off—"

"I did not run! I was following a lead—"

"Yes, without me! And without telling me what it was so I couldn't follow you." I sat up and, this time, the room stayed mostly steady. "Do you know what I was doing down here in the first place? Hassani was taking me to the morgue so I could try to figure out—"

"Dory—"

"—what you'd seen and where you'd gone. Because somebody hadn't bothered to tell me anything in that damned note that wasn't left with me in the first place. Despite the fact that this is about *my sister*!"

"Okay, this is getting good," the big, bearded vamp said.

"Bahram," Zakarriyyah reproached.

Louis-Cesare ignored them. "You're being unfair," he told me.

"Unfair?" I stared at him. "What about that was unfair?"

"All of it!"

"Then give me a reason—a better reason—"

"I don't have to give you a reason!"

The healer gasped.

"Oh, son," Bahram said, wincing and shaking his head. "How long have you been married?"

"At least not here," Louis-Cesare amended.

I narrowed my eyes at him, and got unsteadily to my feet. "Here."

"Dory—"

"Now."

"You can't ask me—"

"I damned well can."

"You shouldn't need to!" The blue eyes, pained a moment ago, suddenly blazed. "Look at you." He grasped my shoulder, the one that still had clothes covering it, but carefully, as if he was afraid that I might break. "Look at you! *Mon Dieu*, have you seen yourself?"

"No, and that's not the point—"

"It is exactly the point!" I found myself crushed to a chest that was breathing hard, despite the fact that he didn't have to. His hand started to cradle my head, and then jerked away. "Your hair," he whispered. "Half of your hair is gone."

Was it? Shit. "It'll grow back—"

He did not seem to find that very reassuring. "I could have lost you."

"Then I was right. You think I'm not strong enough—"

"No—"

"That I can't do my job without her—"

"You're taking this the wrong way—"

"How else am I supposed to take it? You think I'm weak!"

"This isn't . . . that's not—"

"Then what is it? You said—"

"I know what I said!"

"And what else could you have meant?"

"That *I'm* weak!" He pulled away suddenly and turned his back on me. "I'm the weak one! Is that what you want to hear?"

I stood there, feeling seriously unwell but also nonplussed. "What?" I finally said.

There was silence for a moment, and when his voice finally came, it was rough. "When I was with Jonathan, I thought that he had done his worst, that there was nothing else he could take from me. I was sure of it—and I was right. Until I met you." He turned around, and one look at his face and I understood why he hadn't wanted to talk about this here. "Now, I am afraid all the time, and it is affecting my judgment. I left, thinking I was protecting you, and then I realized: what if he came *back*?"

And, finally, I got it. Louis-Cesare hadn't told me everything that had happened with Jonathan, but I'd gotten the gist. But despite that, his worst nightmare wasn't falling back into that monster's hands. It was having me do so, and him be unable to stop it.

"He isn't coming back," I said softly, walking over. "He has what he wants. He left me lying in the street—"

"*He* didn't. The *fey* did. Their interest may be in Dorina, for whatever reason, but his—"

"You think he might try to get at you through me?"

"I don't know. I don't know what he might do. I just—" he looked at me, and there was no deception on his face this time. None at all. If I'd wanted honesty, I was getting it. "I only know that I left for the right reasons, and that I returned for the wrong ones. Because I was afraid, and I am weak."

"Oh, yeah, you're weak, all right," Rashid said sarcastically.

The healer smacked him.

"No," I said, putting my arms around Louis-Cesare's neck

and pulling him down to me. "You didn't come back for that."

"Then why did I come back?" The blue eyes were haunted.

"For the same reason you left. For love."

And then, right there, in front of them all, I kissed him.

CHAPTER THIRTEEN

Dory, Cairo

"This is all very touching," Zakarriyyah said dryly. "But can we please get back to the point?"

"Which was?" I asked, still hanging onto my lover.

"To discover who sent our attackers. If it wasn't the two of you—"

"What attackers?"

He looked irritated, probably because he'd already explained this to Louis-Cesare while I was out. But I hadn't heard it. And I still didn't.

Because someone cursed and someone screamed, and every vamp in the semi-circle surrounding us suddenly looked like they'd seen a ghost. Several fell to their knees and several more fled, dropping their weapons and running for the exit. And the rest were staring in what looked like horror at something behind me.

I turned, but all I saw was an elongated shadow flickering in the firelight and rippling down the stairs. It didn't look like a man; it didn't look like anything, at least not from this angle. And before I could look up and see what had cast it, the healer's pretty face was in my way.

"Do it," Louis-Cesare said roughly. "Now!"

"What?" I asked, turning back toward him.

And never completed the motion. A soft, cool hand slid onto my shoulder, and I realized what was going on—half a second too late. "Don't you da—" I began.

Then I was out.

I woke up furious—and disoriented, because I was staring up at a huge dwarf. He had to be three stories tall and was carrying a basket filled with giant emeralds. He looked like he'd tripped, and some of the stones were tumbling out and cascading to earth like the world's costliest waterfall. I was lying right underneath, and the view up the glimmering cascade was seriously trippy with only half of my brain working.

Bes, the demon fighter, I thought vaguely. God of war and parties, which didn't seem to go together to me, but the ancient Egyptians had liked him. One of our guides had said that dancing girls often had a tattoo of him on their upper thigh . . .

Then the rest of my brain came online, and I abruptly sat up.

Son of a bitch!

The world went violently swimmy as soon as I moved, as if I was in a boat on the high seas. I clutched the cold stone underneath me and stared around, waiting for my eyes to adjust and my stomach to settle down. I didn't get any help with that, because the healer—damn her—was missing, although that might have been her screaming somewhere in the distance. I couldn't tell. It was a woman, but there were men's shouts, too, and bangs and crashes and—

I grabbed my head, feeling cold hair on one side and bumpy, burnt flesh on the other. It was concerning, but less so than the pain. What had that bitch done to me?

I didn't know, but I slowly realized that I'd been moved into the shadow of the great stairs, as had Hassani. He was lying nearby, with the remains of his smoke blackened robes still white enough in places to show up in the gloom. He was out cold, but since he hadn't dusted away, I assumed he was in a healing trance.

Lantern Boy was there, too, standing a little way off and

bisected by a jagged backdrop of half-light, half-dark from the slant of the staircase. It lit up his own white and blue robe and the hand he was using to clutch the stone. I couldn't see his face, but his body language read "freaked out" loud and clear.

Makes two of us, I thought, and rolled to my knees. This did not improve the massive migraine that the vamp hereafter to be known as That Bitch had given me. But I somehow managed to drag myself back to my feet.

The fury helped. It helped a lot. I'd been left with a half dead consul and a kid who couldn't be more than a couple years into his vampy life.

"*I'm* the weak one," I heard Louis-Cesare say again.

Sure, asshole.

Which is why you stuck me at the kiddie table.

We were going to have words about that, oh, yes, we were, but first I needed to find out what the hell was going on. And there was only one person to ask. I tried a few steps, managed not to fall on my face, and limped over to junior. Only I guessed he hadn't noticed.

"Hey," I croaked, and had to jump back to avoid his swinging fist.

He recognized me after a second and stumbled back against the stairs, a hand clutching the fabric over his no longer beating heart. Vamps are hard to sneak up on, but this was one was clearly not doing well. The huge, liquid dark eyes were wide and panicked, and the already mangled lip had been bitten all the way through a couple of times. He had one fang up and one down, and was looking frankly deranged.

I frowned at him. "What's wrong with you?"

This was not the right question. The result was some more bruises courtesy of a pair of slender hands that forgot to be gentle when they grabbed my upper arms, and a panicked torrent of part English, part Arabic, and part something I couldn't identify with my head swimming and people screaming and what sounded like a full-on battle happening on the other side of the stairs. But my lack of comprehension seemed to disturb him even more, because after a moment, he shook me.

"Do you understand?"

"No."

And then something flew by overhead, big as a small airplane, and briefly blocked out what little light there was. Lantern Boy ducked with a shriek, his hands over his head, and something hit the far wall of the chamber like a bomb. It rocked the room, sending shrapnel flying everywhere, and dust billowing like a desert storm had blown up inside.

"The *hell*?" I coughed, and hugged the side of the stairs myself.

I didn't get an answer. Not that I really needed one. A piece of stone the size of a VW Beetle had hit the wall beside the dwarf and spun to a stop, showing a curved shape with familiar carving on it.

I stared at it, slowly coming to terms with the fact that one of the massive columns that supported the roof had just been launched across the room. I had no idea how, and wasn't likely to get one with my only informant huddled and incoherent. I decided to see for myself.

There was a lot of dust floating around beyond the stairs, and some large piles of rubble that had probably been pillars a little while ago. A torch still burned over the closest heap, on the side of a still intact column that the rubble had washed up against. It was sending flickering shadows to lick the floor, although they didn't help much since the torch was guttering, and the debris blocked much of my view.

I glanced around, but didn't see anybody brandishing weapons, or anybody at all. This area seemed completely deserted. I took a chance and ran, reaching the bottom of the rubble pile safely, and intending to climb up for a better vantage point.

That turned out to be harder than I'd thought. My hands

were fumbling and clumsy, and my feet were no better, acting as if the rubble was on some kind of conveyor belt. Which wasn't far from the truth, as it was loose and moved every time I did. Damn it, how could this simple thing be such a royal pain in the—

There!

I felt an inordinate sense of accomplishment after finally surmounting a hill that had started to feel more like Everest. The damned torch was right overhead, searing my eyes and making it impossible to see anything. But I instinctively hugged the rocks, anyway, staying low, staying out of sight.

Battlefields were no place to poke your head up.

Not that I could hear much fighting anymore, come to think of it. Or any, really. Things were suddenly very quiet.

I shifted position, putting myself in the flickering shadows along one side of the heap, next to the still intact column. The dimness helped my vision, but not my mood. Because the huge room was littered with corpses.

And some of them were still stumbling around.

There was a burned and blackened . . . thing . . . nearby that I only identified as a man by the overall shape. The skin was flaked up, like black, crispy shingles, the left arm was mostly gone and the head was on fire. It looked like a human torch, burning brightly enough to actually light up some of the surrounding rubble. One of the cheeks flared as I watched, and I actually gasped, a lifetime of shit still apparently not enough preparation.

It was a small sound, but the thing's head immediately turned my way.

It didn't have eyes, it didn't have ears, it didn't have most of a head, but it was coming. And it was coming fast. Fortunately, it seemed to have as much of a problem with the rubble mountain as I had. Unfortunately, its struggle had attracted the interest of a couple buddies, who headed over to help.

And I finally caught a clue.

The human torch was tall, maybe six feet or more despite missing most of a head. But the backup guys were shorter, were wearing identical black outfits, and did not look like they'd been hanging out in a bonfire. They were very clearly dead, with slack features and obvious wounds, with one still having a knife sticking out of his eye. They were also familiar.

I realized that I was looking at two of the small, ninja type guys who had attacked Hassani's place last night, in order to steal the artifacts. Two who hadn't made it back out, by the look of things. So, what were they doing hanging out down here?

"Somebody make the bodies from last night go," a low voice said from behind me.

I turned my head to see Lantern Boy clinging to some rubble, and eyeing the sparks flying out of the guttering torch warily. He still looked freaked out, but there was also a stubborn tilt to his jaw. As if seeing a beat-up woman head out when he wouldn't had wounded some male pride.

"They carry them to morgue for study," he continued. "But then—" He suddenly splayed his fingers, like fireworks going off. Or, I guessed, like zombies sitting up. Because that was absolutely what those things were.

Looked like Louis-Cesare had been right, after all.

"They attack our people," Lantern Boy added. "That why master set fire to monster."

I nodded. A necromancer, especially one as powerful as Jonathan, could probably animate any corpse in the area. Hassani's people must have mentally communicated with him about what was happening at the morgue, so he'd decided to make sure that the big boy didn't get in on the act.

Which, points for proactivity, but he could have said something!

Of course, that didn't explain why he'd wanted to show me the creepy thing in the first place, but that could wait.

"Only it not work."

I'd started digging in my jacket, to see if I had anything that might help with the current problem, so it took a second for what Lantern Boy had said to register. I stopped and looked back at him. "What?"

He nodded solemnly. "He return. He always return."

I knew—I *knew*—I was going to regret asking this. "*Who* returns?"

The boy's eyes flickered ominously, or maybe that was just the light. Most of the fuel had been knocked out of our torch during the impact with the other column, leaving it with only a few knotted reeds and some small sticks in the metal holder, most of which had been consumed. But dark red embers still glowed at the base, and deep in his eyes.

"Gods not like us," he told me. "They not die, you see? They . . ." he stopped, as if searching for the right word. Which I guessed he didn't find, because he looked frustrated. "Like torch, about to go out."

He waved a hand at the fading item over our heads.

"They burn lower?"

He nodded. "Yes, they go low. But not out. They just need —"

"Someone to add more fuel," I said numbly, wondering why what remained of my skin suddenly felt like it was about to detach and crawl off.

A massive crash shook the rubble underneath me, and another pillar disintegrated into pieces. It was on the far side of the room, in an area of mostly shadow, but that didn't matter. From this vantage point, I could see perfectly well. And what I could see . . .

"He glow bright now," Lantern Boy whispered.

Yeah, I thought, staring at the creature emerging from the curling clouds of dust.

Yeah.

It was a snake, if snakes were as big as buildings. A cobra by the look of it, with the typical wide spread hood and flickering tongue, and black as sin. But not like the zombie, which had been darkened by fire. This thing looked fresh out of the box new, without a mark on it. The black was a shiny, lustrous gleam of a color, like the paint on a luxury car, or the patina of black pearls. It was broken up into a thousand small scales—if the size of a medieval shield is considered small—that shaded to gray and then to white on its belly, getting smaller and tighter as they went, down to maybe the size of my fist.

I shouldn't have been able to see it so well from this distance, but I guess my hawk charm was still functional. Because I was getting a perfect view of round, wicked black eyes reflecting the lamplight like golden suns. And of fangs longer than my body. And of a tongue flicking out in between them, as if testing the air, looking for . . .

Something.

My stomach gave a lurch, but I didn't have time to decode the message it was sending before the burning zombie lunged. How it had hoisted itself up Mount Rubble I didn't know, and didn't care. I put two bullets in what was left of its brain and kicked it back into the other two, who were also clumsily headed up. More of the creatures turned their heads my way, as if on a string, drawn to the echoing sound of the bullets.

But not the main event. It just stayed where it was, swaying back and forth and occasionally striking down at . . . nothing, as far as I could tell. But it wasn't nothing.

Please God, I thought fervently. Please, just one time. Just this one, fucking time, don't let it be—

Goddamnit!

The creature turned suddenly and I spotted Louis-Cesare, clinging to the side of its neck, just under the great hood, with a sword in his hand. He clearly intended to use it to chop off the head. Which would have been fine, which would have been great, except that that wasn't going to work, and where the *hell* had I put—

"Where he come from?" Lantern Boy shrieked, spotting

him, too, and then clapped a hand over his mouth, not that it mattered at this point.

"He does that," I muttered, searching frantically through my jacket.

"Does what?"

"It's called the Veil. He goes . . . dim," I explained—badly, but who had time for—

A muffled scream from Lantern Boy had me looking up, just in time to see my lover hit the far wall of the great chamber, hard enough to leave a Louis-Cesare-shaped divot in a cavorting goddess. I didn't know who she was, but she had a tambourine in her hand and was wearing a ton of golden spangles, each of which appeared to be made out of actual gold and was as long as a spear. Which became a problem when Louis-Cesare fell to the ground and they stabbed down on top of him.

He was a master; they wouldn't kill him. But they could pin him for a second, and a second was all that thing needed. And if there was anyone else still able to help, I didn't see them.

In a split second, I spotted hairy chested Rashid, his bald head gleaming in the torchlight, his body writhing on a spear half buried in solid rock. Nearby was bearded Bahram, on his feet but wrestling with half a dozen energetic looking zombies. Zakarriyyah was also still standing, in front of a pile of the wounded, defending them alone with a single sabre. Even That Bitch had gotten in on the act, with twin daggers in her hands and a snarl on her pretty face, as she stared down two partially burnt corpses.

But no one else had been crazy enough to take on the main event, no one but my husband. Who was about to pay for it. The huge, hooded head reared back, the fangs descended, the body lunged—

And was hit by a double barrage of bullets as I sped across the floor, a bright red crotch rocket between my thighs, a defiant scream on my lips, and two .44 Magnums in my hands.

The bullets didn't hurt it; I hadn't expected them to hurt it. The damned thing had survived a funeral pyre and come out shiny and spit polished. But they got its attention.

Oh, boy, did they get its attention.

And goddamn, the creature was fast. It didn't so much stop its lunge as change direction, almost quicker than my eyes could track. One second it was spearing down at Louis-Cesare, and the next—

It was right in my face.

CHAPTER FOURTEEN

Dory, Cairo

It was impossible, just impossible. And this was coming from someone who had once stared down a fully grown dragon. I'd thought that was intense, but after this, I was going to have to revise my personal scale.

Holy shit just got a brand-new definition.

Of course, that depended on me surviving this at all, which . . . yeah.

Fortunately, the senate didn't buy cheap shit, and while I wasn't the best on a bike of anybody I'd ever seen, I was motivated. I threw a couple of magical smoke bombs, skidded around in the resulting confusion, saw that giant head strike down all of an inch away from my right leg. And knifed the bastard in the eye.

It reared back, an unholy ululation of surprise and pain coming out of its mouth, so human-sounding that it had every hair that was left on my body saluting the insanity. And then it was coming for me as I rocketed ahead, with a sound like all the sandpaper in the world being scraped across all of the stone. The dragging shhhhSSSSHHHSSSHHHHHSSSSSHHHHHH noise made my ears want to join my skin wherever it had fucked off to.

And damn it, I tried. I was *flying*, straight back the way I'd come because that was the only exit I knew, and I was getting the fuck out of here! And so was someone else.

A second earlier, Lantern Boy had been on top of the rubble heap, hiding like he maybe had some sense. Now he was sitting behind me, holding onto my waist, and screaming in my ear. *"Take a left!"*

"What?"

"After you leave the chamber, go left!"

I went left.

"What are you doing?" I yelled, staring at him over my shoulder as we plunged into darkness, and thus getting a perfect view of the wall behind us blowing out.

"Helping you!"

We started down a long set of narrow stairs with almost no light at all, which wasn't the best place for a conversation. "W-w-w-w-w-why?"

"I fail you. I fail *him*. I not fail again!"

Well, that's optimistic, I thought, as the stairs disintegrated beneath us. That probably had something to do with the fact that an ancient demigod was smashing through them like they were tissue paper instead of solid stone. Or maybe it was just trying to fit its bulk down a passage completely unsuited for it.

Either way, it wasn't fun.

That wasn't the worse part, though.

A foul, lung shriveling stench flooded the air as my tires struggled to find purchase on the disintegrating floor, while chunks of stone tumbled down the stairs from behind me. It was so bad that I almost couldn't breathe again, not because there wasn't air, but because my body didn't want it. I had to force myself to take in any oxygen at all, which was probably just as well.

Imminent asphyxiation gave me something else to concentrate on other than imminent death.

But that wasn't the worst part, either.

"Left!" Lantern Boy screamed, and I hung a left, despite not being able to see a damned thing. But I could feel, and there was suddenly solid stone under my wheels again. I tore ahead, straight into a group of—

What was this shit?

I still couldn't see too well, although the dead blackness of a moment ago was gone, but not for any good reason. We'd just plunged into the middle of what appeared to be a glowing crowd of mummies. They weren't glowing much, but down here, any illumination seemed bright. And they *were* mummies, as in the ancient Egyptian, covered in bandages, barely shuffling along variety.

They weren't attacking us, unless you counted getting in the way, so I guessed they weren't part of Jonathan's forces. It looked like whatever spell he was using to animate the dead had some spillover, and whoever had been buried in the temple's crypts had gotten caught in it. As to why the hell they were glowing a faint greenish white, I had no idea.

But it was pretty damned startling, and the ancient demigod apparently thought so, too. Or maybe he just got confused. Whatever the reason, one of the creatures was snatched up from beside us, and—

"Fuck!"

"The god, he has poison," Lantern Boy informed me.

No shit. The mummy was no sooner pierced by those fangs than it began writhing and flailing, almost like it was alive and in pain again. Only no, I realized staring over my shoulder. The reason was the same one that caused a piece of paper caught in a fire to dance for a second, before curling up and dusting away.

Or in this case, to fall to pieces and then into nothing within seconds, like it had been hit with the world's fastest acting acid.

Okay, I decided sickly.

That was the worst thing.

And then I floored it.

"Left! Left!" Lantern Boy yelled, as we skidded through another doorway, but there was no left anymore. The giant snake head had just taken it out, along with everything on that side. We slid through the collapsing door, scraping sparks off of the floor, then straightened up and went barreling ahead—

And found out where all the mummies had come from.

For the record, riding through a long, dark tunnel of a room, with a bunch of sarcophagi on either side, the lids of which are either off or rattling, is a fairly pants wetting experience. Especially when paired with mummies disintegrating left and right as spirts of acid hit them. And a goddamned Lantern Boy yelling "LEFT!" loud enough to rupture an eardrum.

I veered left, which was heart attack inducing itself as I couldn't see squat, and we were going about sixty miles an hour, and there was no actual corridor there. Or a room or even another crypt. Any of which would have been preferable to—

"Stairs!" And worse, they were going up.

We crashed into them, almost flipped, and did stand on end for a second before I could sort us out. Mummy light is not good light, but by this time, I was mostly going on feel anyway. That and sheer terror.

"Sorry!" Lantern Boy yelled from behind me as we started up.

He didn't sound sorry. He sounded hyper, as if whatever passed for an adrenaline system in vamps had hit overload, enough to short out his good sense, fully extend his fangs, and probably tent the front of his robes if I could see them, which thankfully I could not. But it was indisputable that I had a hopped-up teenager determined to prove himself to his possibly dead boss, and for some reason, I was taking orders from him.

I wasn't sure which of us was crazier.

But I didn't know the layout down here, so I just kept going. When a spurt of pure acid hit the wall beside me, melting ancient stones into goo, I kept going. When the ceiling started to collapse, sending huge rocks tumbling down at us, some bigger than we were, I swerved and kept going. When Lantern Boy shoved a hand in my jacket, and sent every charm I had left tumbling down what remained of the stairs, including one that transformed into a cute little Citroën that I'd never even had a chance to drive, I Kept. Fucking. Going.

I heard the car crumple between the too-narrow walls behind us when it expanded to its full size, and wedged itself there like a barricade. One that lasted about a second when hit by twenty tons of godly fury. I heard the brain altering sound of an entire car getting crushed like a soda can as we burst out into a suspiciously well-lit tunnel. And then—

"Left!"

"You asshole!" I yelled, because sure enough, the damned kid had brought us right back where we'd started.

Well, almost. We were on the other side of the great hall now, where a Louis-Cesare-shaped hole was to be seen on our right, in the midst of a field of golden spikes. There were crumbled pillars and piles of rock everywhere, shambling zombies in the shadows, and vampires, beaten and bloody, but back on their feet, why I didn't know.

And then I did, along with why Lantern Boy had suddenly gotten so perky.

The boss was back.

When I'd first seen Hassani at our consul's court, I'd thought him fairly menacing, and not just because of his looks. He'd had an air about him, not of danger exactly, but of something. He had been completely believable as a thousand-year-old assassin and the head of a group of equally badass characters.

Which was why I'd been surprised when Louis-Cesare and I arrived in Egypt and met a mostly gracious, scholarly type with ink-stained fingers and rosy cheeks above his carefully tended beard. He'd reminded me of a cross between a younger version of Santa Claus and a medieval monk. It had been . . . disappointing.

I wasn't disappointed now.

Now he looked more like Gandalf, only not the kindly, firework-wielding version. But Gandalf the White, come back from the brink of death to kick butt and take names, and he was all done taking names. But not of thundering one from the top of the stairs, his arms raised like Moses, if Moses had wielded a sword in either hand.

"Sokkwi you were, and Sokkwi you are, and ever shall be, no matter how many times you return. But you will not return again, Little Fool. Today will see your end."

He didn't even raise his voice, not that he needed to with those acoustics. And yet I was shivering. And skidding around, throwing an absolute wave of sparks into the air from a fender sliding across rock, which the tide of vamps rushing at me didn't even flinch away from.

I guess fear was relative, and nothing looked intimidating next to what was chasing me.

So, I didn't understand why, instead of running to back up the boss, they grabbed me and started dragging me back. "That thing will kill him," I said, fighting. "Don't you get it? *It will kill him!*"

"No, it won't," Louis-Cesare said, pulling me back, pulling me away. Leaving the tiny looking man in the burnt and filthy robes, standing all alone at the top of the massive staircase.

But not for long.

The wall I'd just driven through exploded, sending huge stones tumbling over the floor, each as big as a small house. Fortunately, we'd retreated out of the way, into the shadow of a lion headed goddess whose name I couldn't remember. Right now, I could barely remember my own.

Because the giant shadow of the great beast had just fallen over the stairs, blocking out the light, leaving Hassani all alone in the darkness.

"We have to help him," I whispered.

But Zakarriyyah was shaking his head. "He has all the

help he needs," he said softly.

I had no idea what he meant. There was nobody else here. And, worse, the trip through the crypts hadn't put a mark on the creature. That armor-like hide was a little dustier, but if it had picked up so much as a scratch, I didn't see it.

How did you fight something like that? How did you even start? If massive boulders hadn't hurt it, I doubted any weapon we had was going to do any better. Not that I had any left in the first place—

And then the snake *started talking*, and I forgot to care. I forgot everything except the words echoing and echoing— inside my mind.

It was like a thousand voices speaking at once, each in a different language. But the English words were louder, or maybe they were just louder to me. So loud they hurt, like nails scraping the inside of my brain.

Until Louis-Cesare's arms tightened, and the screaming became softer. More like a shout in the ear instead of a megaphone. Not pleasant, but bearable.

"I won't have to come again, young one. This time, I am not leaving. This time I will carve a bloody path of vengeance through those who have wronged me. Their corpses shall litter the Earth, as will those of any who—ah!"

The voice broke off abruptly, I wasn't sure why. And then I heard it, another voice behind the first, too quiet to make out. But whispering, whispering.

"Save your breath, mage!" the monster hissed. "You do not control me. Did you think you could use a god as your puppet?"

Jonathan, Louis-Cesare mouthed.

"I will take your power," the thing that had been Sokkwi said, "and once I am back in the sun, I will add to it such a mighty sum that all the Earth shall tremble!" The huge head was suddenly back in Hassani's face. "But you first."

I started fighting again, knowing what was coming even if the others didn't. I'd just seen it, and it had been memorable. And, sure enough, the burst of caustic venom hit Hassani dead center barely a second later . . .

And kept on going.

"What the—" I stared. I'd seen that shit dissolve solid rock! How was he just standing there?

"One of the Teacher's master powers," Zakarriyyah murmured. "To project an image somewhere he is not."

"So, where is he?" I asked, because I only saw one of him, standing calmly in the middle of a torrent of poison that couldn't hurt him, because he wasn't really there. But he was somewhere, and I didn't think playing hide and seek with a demigod was going to work for long.

And neither did the demigod.

"I don't have to look for you," the voice in my head echoed again. "You will come to me. The only question is, how many of your people do I have to kill first?"

"Scatter," Zakarriyyah said—unnecessarily. We were already doing it, with me and Louis-Cesare heading for my bike until it was crushed under the massive body slithering this way. It loomed up in my vision, a solid wall of gleaming scales, blackness smothering the light and swallowing the earth—

And swallowing us, or flat out running us over, crushing our bones into powder. Except that I'd been wrong earlier. Louis-Cesare hadn't used the Veil, his own personal master power, after all. It took a huge amount of energy and couldn't be deployed again for hours.

So, if he had, I wouldn't be looking at the world through a haze of white, like a London fog had just rolled in.

Or staring in disbelief as a river of scales slammed into me, yet didn't hurt.

The creature passed right on through us and out the other side, leaving me staring around wildly, confused, disoriented, and seriously skeeved out.

"All right?" Louis-Cesare asked.

I nodded breathlessly. That was a lie, but the truth

wouldn't help us right now. Not when I could still see the massive creature stopped in the middle of the room, not ten yards away.

But it couldn't see me.

Like Hassani, I simply wasn't there anymore.

Louis-Cesare was able to slip out of phase with the world for a short time, transitioning into some kind of non-space I didn't fully understand. I doubted he did, either, since he couldn't stay there for long. A minute, maybe two—probably the former since he'd dragged me along with him—and that was it.

We didn't have much time.

"Come on!" I said, pulling on him, but he wasn't budging. Unless you counted going the other way—*toward* the snake. "What are you *doing?*"

"You bought us time; we used it," he told me. "But we have to finish this—"

"How?" I demanded, holding onto him.

"—and the chance will pass by if you don't trust me."

"Like you trusted me?"

He at least had the grace to blush. "Dory—"

"Later," I said, and released him. He nodded, although he did not appear to be looking forward to later. Personally, I'd just be grateful if we had one.

Especially when he started *climbing the goddamned snake.*

I married a crazy man, I thought, hugging myself to keep from going up there after him. Louis-Cesare could survive being flung against a stone wall. I doubted that I could, especially now.

But damn it, climb *faster.*

The great beast wasn't making it easy. The skin was slick, and the creature wasn't staying put to hunt for us, because we weren't the target. Hassani was. And to flush him out, any of his people would do.

The huge body suddenly moved like quicksilver, spotting some of the fleeing vamps and crossing the room after them in seconds. But they weren't staying still, either, and had jury rigged a few surprises in the short time they'd had. Including working together to topple one of the already cracked pillars, sending it crashing down onto the beast and causing huge, broken pieces to scatter everywhere.

One passed through me as I ran after them, but didn't kill me because of the Veil. But we had seconds left there at best, and Louis-Cesare wasn't even half way up the great body. I could see him through the dust and debris, looking impossibly small next to those acres of scales.

Hurry up, I thought savagely. Whatever you're going to do, do it now! Before we're both—

Back.

A flying bit of rock cut a line across my cheek, a burning warning as I stumbled back into real space. I looked up, and sure enough, Louis-Cesare was visible, too, clinging to the great hide as the creature lunged after the fleeing vamps. Who were suddenly fleeing the other way.

I stared in disbelief at those crazy bastards, who swarmed the huge body, not one or two of them, but all of them, all at once. It was futile, like a bunch of ants charging a bull elephant. But for a brief moment, it worked, causing Sokkwi to pause in confusion.

And a moment was enough.

A blade flashed, high on the scaly hide; the great head reared back as if in pain, and a stream of poison spewed wildly everywhere. Several of Hassani's people cried out and then were silenced, their bodies dusting away to ashes when the droplets touched them. And something that looked a lot like a long, jagged fang arced through the air—

And was caught, but not by me.

Not by Hassani, either, although he was there, in the shadows of the great stairs as another army joined the fray. One composed of emaciated brown bodies that reflected the torchlight like lacquer as they surged down the steps, including the one in front, whose shriveled, date-like eyes I'd seen staring at a door for centuries, waiting—

For this.

Louis-Cesare jumped free, unable to use the weapon he'd provided them without dusting to powder. But the poison didn't seem to have the same effect on the prisoners. Their skin burned with it, but they didn't disintegrate, I didn't know why.

"They're his Children," Zakarriyyah said, coming up beside me. "It gives them limited immunity."

Limited being the word, I thought, watching great wounds open up in that strange skin, but the prisoners didn't seem to care. They waded into the fray, the fang held aloft in the leader's hand, who used it like a dagger to do what steel never could, and tear open the belly of the beast. The prisoners immediately swarmed into the flood of viscera, tearing, clawing, biting.

And laughing.

Terrible, yet joyous laughter rang around the room and echoed off the stones, sending hard chills climbing up and down my body, while the monster writhed and twisted, trying to throw off his tormentors. Only they weren't there anymore. They were *inside*, ripping their former master apart from within, eating him alive even as they were themselves consumed.

Hassani staggered over, pale as a ghost, which he nearly was. The rich blood of a consul had gone to feed the prisoners for this, their final battle. But it seemed almost futile, with what we knew.

"He'll just come back," I said hoarsely.

"Let us test that theory." Hassani looked at Louis-Cesare, who had come up on Zakarriyyah's other side. "If you would be so kind?"

Louis-Cesare handed over his rapier, with the *col de mort* attached, which Hassani threw to the leader of the prisoners. He'd been waiting alongside the great wound he had made, waiting while his skin burned and his people died, waiting, for what I didn't know. Until one of them brought it forth: a huge, still beating heart.

"Your consul didn't understand the need, when she fought him," Hassani said, his usually rich voice a soft rasp. "He was but a pile of bones. What could bones do?"

A lot, I thought dizzily, if they happened to belong to a demigod.

"My friend, the honor is yours," Hassani said to the leader.

I didn't know if it would be enough; Hassani had said that Sokkwi did not have the same weaknesses as other vamps. But the next moment, the air was suffused with ashes, a huge swirling storm of them, coating our eyes, our ears, our tongues, everything. And when we finally emerged from the choking cloud, we stared around in wonder.

The great body had disappeared.

The gods, it seemed, weren't so immortal, after all.

CHAPTER FIFTEEN

Dory, Cairo

Vampire monks, or so I'd been told, knew how to party, but I wasn't sure if I was going to this one. I'd had all day to rest, while being attended by an absolute throng of servants, to the point that I'd finally had to lock the door to keep them out of the room so I could nap. It was night again now, and I was feeling surprisingly well, all things considered; that wasn't the problem.

That was the problem, I thought, staring into the mirror.

"You look lovely," the woman behind me said.

It was That Bitch, whose real name was Maha. I'd been told that it meant "Beautiful Cow" which . . . okay. Different strokes. She and I had made up, and as a peace offering, she was in my bathroom, attempting to get me ready for the party to end all parties, celebrating the death of the bastard downstairs.

There was just one problem.

"I don't think it fits," I said, tugging on the latest fake hairdo.

She had come up with a selection of wigs to cover my no longer burnt, but terribly bald head. There was everything from short and blonde to vibrant red and flowy, along with a brunette that almost matched my real hair in cut and style. Because it turned out that, while vamp healers could repair a damaged brain and heal baldly burned flesh, they could not regrow hair.

Not that I was totally bald. It was more like a third of my hair that was missing in action, all along the left side of my head, from above the ear to the nape. But it was not festive.

"You just have to get used to it," she told me, with her own long, lustrous, beautiful hair rippling down to her butt. She'd had it up before, in a no-nonsense bun, but tonight it was down and it was glorious.

I sighed.

"Can I see the brunette one again?"

She obliged and I tugged it on, but the same problem persisted. It's hard to fit a wig, any wig, when your own hair is so lopsided. After a few frustrating moments, I pulled the dark, shiny mass off again and stared at my terrible reflection.

Maybe I'd just get room service.

"There is another option," Maha said, holding out her hand. On the palm was a familiar sight, although not a familiar shape. I picked up the little golden item she was offering and frowned at it. It was beautiful, like a delicate brooch made in the form of a spray of flowers, with the gold work so fine that the tiny stems quivered whenever it moved.

But it wasn't a brooch. The tell-tale thrum of a magical tat vibrated against my palm, although softer than I was used to. Not weaker but . . . different. There was magic here, but not a kind I knew.

"It's a weapon?" I asked, looking up at her.

Maha laughed. And then the laughter faded, and her face became somber. "What kind of life have you lived?" she asked softly. "That that is the only magic you know?"

"It isn't the only kind," I said, feeling defensive. An emotion that melted away into wonder when she turned me around to face the mirror again, and placed the tiny object— not in my hair, as I'd expected, since I didn't see what else she could do with it. But on my bald skin.

No, make that *in* my skin, I realized, as it melted into the surface the same way that my little bird had done. But while the birdie had had an immediate effect on my senses, this charm didn't seem to make any difference at all. And then the most amazing thing happened.

"Do you like it?" Maha asked, watching my face.

Well, obviously, I didn't say, but not because I was practicing my diplomacy. But because I was honestly speechless for a moment. The delicate spray of stems, flowers and leaves had expanded, twining along my bare patch of scalp until they covered it in an exuberance of beauty. And unlike most tats, even magical ones, this wasn't a mere blue outline. This looked like the tattoo had been made with liquid gold.

It glimmered against my skin and set off my dark hair like a diadem. I laughed in wonder, and felt it gingerly when it finally stopped. It was solid and cool under my fingertips. It was amazing.

"I look like that chick from *Hunger Games*," I said. "You know, the one with the camera crew?"

"You look beautiful," Maha said, and it sounded genuine.

I met her eyes in the mirror. "Thank you."

She ducked her head. "There is a command for when you wish to remove it. I will write it down for you."

"I'll return it in good condition," I promised.

She looked startled. "But it is a gift."

"A gift?" I put a hand back to the delicate tracery, feeling it slide solidly under my touch. "But . . . I couldn't. It's too much —"

"Too much?" Those beautiful eyes flashed.

"Uh, I just meant—"

"I know what you meant." It was grim. "I have seen how you have been treated since you arrived. I did not add to it, but I did not object, either, to my shame. The men's crude comments; the women's jealousy; virtually everyone declining to so much as touch your hand, thinking you tainted. And for what? An accident of birth you could not control, and which gave you the abilities to save us all?"

I blinked at her. "I . . . didn't exactly—"

She didn't want to hear it. "You saved our *consul*. Our leader for time out of mind, and my Sire. I will not forget that. I do not speak for the others, but as for me, you have made a friend this day, Dorina Basarab."

"Dory," I said, and tried to ignore the pang that the other name caused. It was hard considering that, while I may have helped to solve a problem for Hassani, I hadn't done a damned thing about finding my sister. She'd been gone for almost a day, and I knew little more than I had when she was taken.

I needed to change that.

"Thank you," I said to Maha. "I don't have a lot of friends. I'll be grateful to count you as one."

She smiled, and then impulsively hugged me. "I will leave you to change."

"Is Hassani going to be at the party?" I asked, because I had a few questions for the wily old consul.

"Yes, he says he is feeling up to it." She looked fondly exasperated. "And none of us would gainsay him."

She left and I turned to the next challenge: what to wear.

Twenty minutes later, I was still working on it, thanks to dear uncle Radu.

I hadn't had a lot of time to prep for this mission, and my wardrobe was seriously deficient for a high-level diplomatic trip. I'd made the mistake of calling on Radu for help, as he had the time and was interested in fashion. And, yeah, I don't know what I'd been thinking, either.

Laid out on the bed and hung around the room were a couple dozen evening outfits. All of them were beautiful, all of them were expensive, and all of them would have looked perfectly appropriate on a high-priced hooker. Radu's idea of diplomacy apparently involved vamping the hell out of whoever I met by showing as much skin as possible.

In fairness to him, the sexy all-black, all-silver, or all blood red color scheme, and the sleek, sultry lines worked great at our home court, where they complimented my father's minimalist Armani wardrobe and heightened the already strong family resemblance. Clothes were weapons there, designed to remind people of your age or power or family affiliation. And the Basarab faction was looking strong these days.

But it couldn't have been more out of place here.

Maha had had on a white and gold caftan like garment with long, fitted sleeves and delicate gold embroidery over the shoulders and down the front. It had covered her from neck to toes, yet hadn't looked restrictive, moving gracefully when she walked and highlighting her dark beauty. I needed something comparable, something elegant but classy, something . . .

Completely unlike any of these.

I sighed, biting my lip. I had never cared much about clothes, but these people . . . they were trying, suddenly. I'd been mobbed all afternoon by shamefaced men bearing flowers and embarrassed looking women inquiring after my health and plying me with food I didn't want, because whatever sedative Maha had given me had shut down my system. We'd all misunderstood each other, but now . . . well, I wanted to show that I was trying, too, by respecting their customs. But the only caftan-y thing I owned was—

Well, there was a thought.

I walked over to my luggage and pulled out the package from Aswan. It was wrapped in simple brown paper, which seemed completely inadequate for the spill of royal purple that fell into my hands, shimmering softly. The color had been in-your-face glaring in the simple market stall, but now it looked deeper, richer, and far more luxurious. I hesitated for a moment, then shucked my bathrobe and pulled the swath of silk over my head. I was careful not to catch it on my new floral accessory, but needn't have worried. The smooth, golden lines stayed flat against my skin, and the garment itself was surprisingly light.

Despite the embroidery, it felt soft and filmy, almost like I wasn't wearing anything. But it fully covered me from neck to feet. And the fact that there were only a couple of short slits at the sides that didn't even make it to my knees, the modest vee of the neckline, and the full length, loose sleeves meant that, for once, I didn't have to worry about flashing anyone. I might even be able to wear normal panties!

I found myself getting ridiculously excited by the idea, before calming back down.

I hadn't seen what it looked like yet.

There was a full-length mirror in the bathroom, but I didn't need it. The one over the dresser was big and showed something like two-thirds of my body from this far back. I kept my eyes closed, bracing myself, and uttering a little prayer that this would work, because I didn't know what I was supposed to do otherwise.

It's gonna be bad, I told myself. Just accept it. The question was, is it better than the others?

I opened my eyes.

Royal purple wasn't something I normally wore. For years I'd dressed for the job, and that meant midnight blue, which is actually harder to see at night than black, or black, or—if I was trying to seduce a target long enough to get him away from his goons—bright red. But maybe I ought to rethink that.

Because purple . . . looked pretty good.

Make that very good, I thought, surprised. It was kind to my complexion and brought out heretofore unnoticed depths in my hair and eyes. The gold spangles, which had looked so gaudy amid sweaty tourists and a profusion of other colors and fabrics, looked strangely fitting here. The embroidery work was really very fine, and even the huge phoenix on the back didn't take away from the whole. In fact, it added a merry, what the hell quality to it.

This was a happy, party sort of robe, swishy and fun.

And I was pretty sure that I even had the right shoes to go

with it.

I got so involved in finding the goddess sandals, with flat soles and gold leather, that Radu had insisted on packing, and then doing my eye makeup—because when else were Cleopatra eyes gonna be suitable—that I failed to notice I had an observer.

Some sixth sense had me looking up, to find Louis-Cesare leaning against the door, holding a huge bouquet and smiling slightly as he watched me. I checked out the flowers in the mirror, which were beautiful but unnecessary, especially since it looked like he'd bought out the shop. I finished the eye I was working on, completing my over-the-top look, and turned around to lean against the dresser.

"That's not gonna help you."

He produced a ridiculously huge box of chocolates from behind his back.

"And neither is that."

Then he brought out the big guns, and proffered a bottle, which initially confused me, because where did he get three hands? But it turned out that the flowers were actually in the crook of his arm, so that was all right. I walked over and regarded the bottle, which was a distinctive shape.

"You're really sorry, huh?" I asked, taking the fat little jug of Louis-XIII, better known as the cognac of the gods.

And then he ruined it.

"I am sorry you were upset," he informed me.

I looked up in surprise. "Oh. So, we're gonna fight?" I waggled the bottle at him. "Then why bring out the good stuff?"

He frowned. "I have no desire to fight. But I cannot apologize when I did nothing wrong."

I bent over and carefully placed the bottle onto the bedside table, because there was no reason to risk good cognac. Then I stood up and smiled. Louis-Cesare started to look worried.

"Nothing wrong?" I asked. "You're seriously leading with

that?"

His back straightened.

Yeah, we were gonna fight.

"Are you seriously telling me that you didn't see that . . . thing . . . target you?" he demanded. "It chased you halfway around the temple!"

"Because I was shooting at it—"

"Or because Jonathan told it to!"

I scowled. "You heard what it said; it didn't take orders. And anyway, Jonathan doesn't care about me. Jonathan probably doesn't even remember me—"

"He remembers you." It was grim.

"Isn't it more likely that he was here for you? He's obsessed with you—"

Louis-Cesare brushed it away. "It amounts to the same thing. If he caught you, he knows I'd do anything, give him anything, even betray the family to keep you safe."

I'd been about to say something else, but I stopped, wondering how I was supposed to reply to that. It was often a problem with us; Louis-Cesare could be incredibly tight lipped when he wanted to be, but when he did talk, he just laid it all out there. He somehow managed to be infuriatingly stiff necked and completely vulnerable at the same time, and it never ceased to throw me.

For once, I decided to reply in kind.

"And if he caught you, do you really think I wouldn't come after you? That I'd just sit around and let him do whatever he wanted? *That I wouldn't gut him for touching you?*"

Louis-Cesare blinked, and I wondered just who the hell he'd thought he married. Did he think Dorina was the only savage part of me? Did he not realize that, on most of my hunts, she hadn't even been awake?

And there'd been plenty of carnage, all the same.

"I'm a hunter," I reminded him. "It's what I've done most of my life. I'm good at it."

"I know."

"Then let's hunt him together." I put a hand on his arm. It was tense, but it had already been that way before I touched him, and he didn't pull away. I tightened my grip. "I can track him. I can track anyone. Together, we can—"

"No."

It was flat—and exasperating. And if I'd thought it was coming from a place of 'me man, you woman, you do as I say,' we'd have had a problem. And in fairness, I didn't know that that wasn't what this was.

But it didn't look like it. His jaw was hard and set, but his eyes were haunted. Something about the expression made me want to protect him, which was absurd. Louis-Cesare didn't need anyone's protection. But it didn't feel that way right now, and emotion softened my tone.

"We complement each other," I said. "You can do things I simply can't, especially now. I can do things you won't, or wouldn't think of. And Dorina is my sister. He knows where she is. We find him, we find her, or at least where to look for her—"

"I said no!" The blue eyes, so vulnerable a moment ago, blazed. And he did pull back then, an angry, abrupt gesture.

I let him go. "And you think that ends it?" I demanded. "That you forbid it and that's it?"

"I think I know Jonathan a little better than you do! If you would listen—"

"I can't listen when you're not talking to me."

"I've told you all I can—"

"You've told me nothing—"

"Damn it, Dory! Let it go!" He threw out an arm, which happened to be the one cradling the flowers. They went tumbling to the floor and, apparently, the silken ribbon keeping them all together hadn't been tied properly, because they scattered everywhere. I got down on my hands and knees to gather them back together, and after a moment, Louis-Cesare joined me.

For a moment, we just picked up flowers.

"It isn't enough," I finally said.

He didn't reply.

"Why is this so hard?" I asked. "I thought we were a team —"

"We are a team."

"But not on this. I want to understand. Explain it to me."

More nothing. It was starting to piss me off. I felt for whatever he was going through, I really did, but I was going through something here, too.

"Okay, then I'll explain it to you," I said, sitting back on my heels. "Dorina is my responsibility. Ray is my responsibility. I don't know what happened to either of them, but I'm going to find out, and Jonathan is the key."

"The fey—"

"I don't know the fey. I can't track the fey. I can track him." I met his eyes. "And I will—with or without you."

I had expected anger, possibly even an explosion considering how things had been going. I didn't get it. Instead, Louis-Cesare looked . . . bewildered, as if he'd never before been confronted by someone he couldn't simply order around. You, sit there. You, come with me. You, hang out and do your nails until I return.

Assuming I ever do.

"Boy, did you marry the wrong woman," I told him frankly.

"I didn't." It was rough. "I love your spirit, your independence—"

"Except right now."

He paused, but he was fundamentally an honest person and always had been. "Except right now," he agreed.

He sat down among the profusion of flowers, some of which were clinging to his trousers. I picked off a rose that had gripped him by its thorns so that it wouldn't stain. It was blood red and velvety soft—the petals, anyway. It reminded me of the ones he'd scattered on our bed on our original honeymoon, which had been in the room I was renting from a friend, because things had been too crazy to allow us to get away right then.

They had stained, too, crushed and ground into the sheets by morning to the point that I'd had to throw that bedding away.

I grinned.

Worth it.

"Why are you smiling?" Louis-Cesare asked, watching me.

I twirled the rose around in my fingers. "I was thinking about Radu," I lied, because I wasn't ready to make up yet. "He'd love it here. He'd be in full-on Napoleon-during-his-Egyptian-campaign mode: flowing burnoose, silk cummerbund, turned up shoes—"

Louis-Cesare's lip twitched.

"—maybe he could even talk some sense into you."

The smile faded. "I'm not the one who needs to see sense. I want you protected!"

"And I want to find my sister—"

"I will find your sister. I promised—"

"To never treat me like an inferior again." I looked at him. "Or did that only apply to Dorina?"

I was referring to another, similar incident, when Louis-Cesare had taken it on himself to try to fight one of my battles for me. That had not ended well, with Dorina coming very close to attacking him for the implication that she couldn't handle herself. That sort of thing was not only incredibly rude in vamp circles, it was dangerous.

In a society where people were constantly jockeying for position, appearing weak was an open invitation.

Louis-Cesare didn't answer. But, this time, there was a pregnancy in the silence that hadn't been there before. He was finally listening, and he was thinking. I just wished he'd do it out loud, so I could figure out how his mind worked.

But my hubby was not a talker.

"If we do this," he finally said. "If we hunt him together . . ."

"Yes?"

"I take him down. When I tell you to back off, you back off, no questions asked. You do not engage him yourself—"

"Is this about his magic? Because I know about magic—"

I suddenly found my wrist clutched in a grip of steel. "This is about you doing as I ask! Promise me!"

There was something in his face that stopped the response that trembled on my lips, something that kept me from pulling back and telling him off. It wasn't anger, or even the wounded pride of a master not used to being challenged. It was worse.

It was fear.

I searched those blue eyes, but couldn't tell if it was fear *of* Jonathan or *for* me, or a combination of the two. I only knew that this issue frightened my husband when nothing else did, so it frightened me as well. Which only made me more determined that, whatever had put that look in his eyes, he would not face it alone.

"Of course. He's your kill."

"I mean it, Dory. I know how you are—tenacious, brave, stubborn. But no arguments. Not on this. When I say you leave, you leave. Immediately."

I sat there for a moment, wanting to ask what the hell Jonathan had done to him, what there was that I didn't already know. But I bit my tongue. He would tell me when he was ready, or he wouldn't. He'd already made a big concession tonight, one that he obviously did not want to make.

It was enough.

"I promise," I said.

CHAPTER SIXTEEN

Dory, Cairo

F inding Hassani, I realized, might be harder than I'd thought. The party that we joined after a quick trip upstairs had spilled out onto multiple rooftops, with vamps casually jumping from one to the other on a whim. That wasn't such a big deal in some cases, where the buildings were basically sitting cheek by jowl, but with others there was a significant gap. Giving me the visual of men in tuxes and women in sparkly, high fashion gowns leaping through the air like gazelles.

Not that everybody was all dressed up. I'd worried about my outfit being too touristy or too spangly or too something, but it would have been hard to pick something that wouldn't have fit in here somewhere. Because each rooftop seemed to be doing its own thing.

One had sleekly dressed people in mostly Western clothing holding champagne flutes, although they were probably filled with the same nasty, non-alcoholic stuff we'd been served since we got here. Hassani did not approve of the devil's brew, despite the fact that vamps can't get drunk, at least not off of Earth hooch. But the partiers made it look good, quietly talking or slow dancing together as if they were at a high-end supper club or a refined house party.

Another gathering, right next door, had the vibe of a bunch of old friends, casually attired and sitting on plastic chairs, playing cards, smoking hookahs, and relaxing. Well, except for the three guys in the back. They were trying to hide the keg they'd smuggled in by nonchalantly throwing a tablecloth over it and planting a candlestick in the middle.

Damn, I thought enviously.

Should have brought the cognac.

Their group, in turn, were bordered by some pretty raucous, nightclub type celebrations, one playing jazz, one with a thumping disco beat, and a third blasting Top 40 karaoke, while a vamp who ought to know better tried to hold a tune.

Our roof was somewhere in the middle, with a bunch of musicians with colorful *tablah* drums and a dozen female belly dancers in bright yellow and gold spangled outfits. And, okay, what the heck was the rule, I wondered, sizing up the low-cut bras and bare bellies of the dancers. I thought we were being restrained!

But all bets were off tonight, it seemed, because there was some serious shimmying going on.

"It is an interesting art form, is it not?" Louis-Cesare asked, watching one girl's impressive undulations.

She had smooth golden skin, washboard abs, and a belly button piercing. She also had hair, not as much as Maha, but enough to hit the small of her back. And, like a lot of Egyptian women's hair, it was thick, dark, curly and beautiful.

"Yeah, interesting," I said, and pulled him off to what passed for a bar.

The rooftops were open to the stars, although there were numerous wooden pergolas with diaphanous draperies scattered around, as well as some big, square boards that looked like massive T.V.s or small movie screens. They were neither; there were no wires or cables around the bottoms and I didn't see any projectors. But something was being shown on them nonetheless.

"What the—" I stopped to stare at one on the next roof over, which was big enough to be perfectly visible from here.

"Oh, yes. I forgot to mention," Louis-Cesare said, handing me a glass of non-alcoholic punch.

"You forgot to mention what?"

He shrugged. "This is a celebration. They wanted to show people what they had to celebrate."

He drank his own punch, and then frowned at the glass.

"Yes, but—" I stared at the big board some more. It was currently showing me in all of my crispy-fried glory: clothes blackened and half missing, skin burnt, hair—what was left of it—a complete disaster, and mouth open as I thundered across the room on a bright red motorcycle, yelling obscenities at an ancient god.

It was as embarrassing as all hell, and it wasn't the only one. Similar boards were scattered around the rooftops as far as I could see, playing the greatest hits from the day's event. We were all there: Louis-Cesare, climbing up a massive cobra's body with a sword on his back; Hassani, doing his Gandalf routine at the top of the stairs; the vamp squad, carving their way through zombies like they did it every day; and me, trying to shoot a god.

I put my weak-ass punch down and started to look around for a way out of here, but Louis-Cesare knew me. "Not a chance," he said.

And the next second, he'd pulled me into his arms, taken a running leap, and—

"Hey! Some notice next time!" I said breathlessly, as we landed on another roof maybe twenty feet away, but so lightly that Louis-Cesare didn't even spill his drink.

He just laughed and kept going, jumping from rooftop to rooftop all along the block that Hassani owned. In the process, we dodged a trio of dwarves with musical instruments, a line of well-dressed conga dancers, and then almost collided with some more dancers in orange and red fluttery outfits, who streamed across our path without warning. I looked back to see their bodies painting a glittery rainbow across the darkness for a moment before we landed

—

In an all-out bash. This one had party horns and confetti cannons, and dancing boys as well as girls. One of the latter came up and tried to dance with us, despite the fact that Louis-Cesare hadn't put me down yet. He was pretty impressive, with a bare chest glistening with sweaty muscles, dark brown eyes with long, thick lashes, and a blindingly white smile.

His dance moves weren't bad, either.

"You know, I'm starting to see what you meant about art," I told Louis-Cesare, who grimaced and jumped to another roof.

And almost landed in the middle of a troop of six male dancers, who were doing an amazing *tanoura*. The Egyptian folk dance had also been performed at the reception given on our arrival, but that one had been staid and solemn by comparison. These guys were really going for it, with multicolored skirts flinging out like whirling dervishes', and including a huge top skirt that they brought up their bodies and over their heads, manipulating it like a great umbrella to mirror the movements of the skirts below.

And because they were vampires, they were spinning so fast that the sound of their clothes snapping and their feet scraping across the concrete rooftop made almost as much noise as the musicians. They streamed around us, the throbbing beat and flowing colors sweeping us up into the madness for a heady second, and confusing my already spinning head. Then they were gone, whirling off to another part of the roof, leaving Louis-Cesare and I looking at each other, breathless and laughing.

Until I spied the food.

Vampires don't technically need to eat, and the younger ones don't even have working taste buds, meaning that their parties often times don't include food. At best, I'd been hoping for a lackluster buffet with some wilted lettuce and maybe a few pasta salads that hadn't gone off yet. But that . . .

was not what I got.

Hassani's people had devised a street vendor type of set up, the kind sometimes seen at big Indian weddings where there are a ton of people to feed with different preferences. Here that meant happy little booths scattered about everywhere, draped with bunting or shiny fringe or topped by balloons, and each with a different specialty. I guessed the idea was to promote circulation, with people who wanted to eat being encouraged to make the rounds.

I was encouraged.

Especially when the spicy scents from the closest booth drifted over, and my stomach woke up to complain that I'd eaten practically nothing for twenty-four hours. That was a rare event in the life of a dhampir. We have revved up metabolisms that help promote healing and give us added power in fights, but they come with a price: we're hungry all the time, with our stomachs making regular, strident demands. Whatever Maha had done to calm down my system while she healed it had also banished hunger—until right now.

"Put me down," I told Louis-Cesare, my mouth watering. As soon as he complied, I ran to the nearest booth and—yes! I'd thought so.

The vendor was passing out plates of *ta'meya*, an Egyptian version of falafel made with fava beans instead of chickpeas. But that didn't tell the whole story, not by half. Onion, garlic, leek and parsley were added to the mix, giving it a vibrant green color, while coriander, cayenne, cumin and paprika spiced it up before it was made into little balls and fried.

It was always delicious, but after a day with no nourishment, the pillowy soft on the inside, crunchy on the outside, hot and spicy bundles were almost literally heaven.

"Don't fill up," Louis-Cesare warned me. "Look what's next."

He nodded at something further down the roof and, sure

enough, another little booth smelled even better. I hurried over, still stuffing my face with *ta'meya*, and then just stood there in something approaching awe. Because this one had *shawarma*, with a huge tower of lamb and another of chicken, their fat caps sizzling and dripping mouth-watering flavor all down the already highly spiced meat.

I had one of each kind, in two huge stuffed pita breads with tahini and roasted vegetables. And while I was working on those, we passed a *fatteh* vendor giving out plates of an ancient Egyptian feast food. The fried crispy flatbread was piled high with rice, meat, and veggies, and all doused in a sensational buttery, garlicy, vinegary tomato sauce.

"Oh," I said, pointing with a pita.

"I'll get a tray," Louis-Cesare said dryly.

And damned if he didn't find one somewhere. I was too busy jumping to the next roof to see where, because there was a vendor with *bamia* over there, a delicious okra stew with chunks of beef, tomatoes, onions, garlic, and spices. There was also a guy with kofta—spicy meatballs with a yogurt dip—and another with *mahshi*—peppers, zucchini, eggplants and cabbage leaves stuffed with lamb and rice and tomato sauce, and spiced with cinnamon and herbs, which sounds nasty but tastes divine.

"Your tray," Louis-Cesare said, coming up behind me and proffering a shiny brass version, which was good because my hands were full. And we hadn't even made it to the desserts yet.

But they were coming up. I could see a vendor on the next roof with *zalabya*, fried doughballs in sweet syrup, kind of like Egyptian doughnut holes. And another further on who I was pretty sure had *Om Ali*, the best damned dessert in a city of great desserts. It had layers of puff pastry soaked in milk and mixed with nuts, raisins, coconut and sugar. The whole thing was then baked and served with warm cream and garnished with more nuts, usually pistachios and almonds. It was basically Egyptian bread pudding, and was rivalled only by one I'd had in New Orleans once with a caramel whisky sauce.

"Oh," I said, my eyes getting wide. I started that way, but was too late. Hassani wanted to speak to us as well, it seemed, and he'd sent a delegation to find us.

I only knew that because Louis-Cesare shouted it at me as we were swept up by a laughing, chattering, and carousing throng. I found myself grabbed under the arms and taken on a wild ride across a number of rooftops, so quickly that I barely had a chance to realize what was going on. And when we hit down, I suddenly had a bunch of people I didn't know hugging me and laughing and taking selfies.

Whatever reservations Hassani's court had had about us, they appeared to have disappeared. Somebody put a new drink into my hand, and somebody else plopped a flower crown onto my head, a popular accessory tonight as half the crowd seemed to be wearing them. I supposed it was a nod to the ancient Egyptian practice at festivals, or maybe it was just because.

There was a lot of just because going on.

And not only with the locals. I stared around, dizzy and wondering where my food was. But before I could ask, Louis-Cesare was borne away by a troop of guys dressed in harem pants and tasseled vests.

"Wait," I said.

The crowd did not wait.

Instead, I was borne over to a bier with a table and a pergola, with some yellow draperies fluttering overhead which were so narrow that they basically just striped the stars. Hassani was reclining on a chaise, this time in a more comfortable looking outfit of a *galabeya* in unbleached cotton, with a pale blue caftan over the top. His only concession to the festivities was a flower crown, which had fallen to a jaunty angle over one ear, and a goblet of something in his hand.

He waved me up and up I went, mourning my lost tray,

only to find it deposited on a low table in front of our chaises before I even sat down. My mood perked up. The consul saw and laughed.

"Eat, eat," he said with the usual generous Egyptian hospitality.

I took him up on the offer. A young vamp who looked a lot like Lantern Boy but wasn't kept my glass filled with the local version of lemonade. It was called *limoon* and didn't have any alcohol, but went really well with the spicy food.

And some of the offerings needed something to cut the heat, although not the ones on my tray. But they were only half the story, because Hassani kept urging me to also try this hors d'oeuvre and that drink from a seemingly endless stream of passing waiters. *Mezze* is the Egyptian version of *tapas*, enjoyed at cafes and dining tables all across Egypt. And Hassani's chefs had done him proud.

So, in addition to everything on my plate, I ended up consuming pieces of fennel-marinated-feta with olives on skewers; *baba ghanoush*—the spicy roasted eggplant dish— with flatbread; huge dates stuffed with nuts and honey; *dukka*—a roasted leek spread—on tiny potato pancakes; *salata baladi*, a salad made from chopped tomatoes, cucumber, onion, pepper and spicy rocket; lamb and chicken kebobs with the crunchy burnt bits perfectly paired with a lime yogurt sauce; and roast pigeon stuffed with onions, tomatoes and rice.

The result was a captive audience for whatever the hell Hassani wanted to talk about, because I honestly didn't think I could move. Like ever again. Seriously, if anyone wanted to restrain a person without the need for cuffs, this would do it.

He eyed up my massive pile of small, empty plates with apparent approval, but then summoned a boy with coffee, served Turkish style in tiny cups that was rich and dark and syrupy sweet. I drank one anyway, because it smelled divine, and made no apologies. I was basically in a food coma by that point, and not responsible for my actions. I reclined and watched the latest group of dancers through rheumy eyes full of spice-induced tears.

They'd been there a while, shimmying and shaking and managing some pretty impressive feats of acrobatics while I ate, but I hadn't really given them my full attention. I still didn't, being too busy feeling grateful that I'd worn what was essentially a muumuu, rather than one of Radu's skin tight numbers, or I'd have split the seams by now. And then I almost did anyway, although for a different reason.

Because Louis-Cesare was one of the dancers.

I did a double take, but it was definitely him. He'd lost the top half of the tux, including the shirt, had acquired a tasseled vest, and was strutting with the locals. I looked down at my cup in concern, wondering what the hell they'd put in there. And then I was pulled up to join the festivities, which no, no, no, not right now!

Luckily, Hassani intervened, shooing off the boys and allowing me to retake my seat and just watch while they and my husband put on a show.

And a damned show it was. I don't know if it was my appreciation of the other dancer that had prompted it, or if everyone's joy was infectious, but Louis-Cesare was cutting a rug. He was watching the others, who had slowed down their gyrations to something approaching human speeds, and copied their steps pretty well.

Or their shimmy, I guess I should say. Because male belly dancers seemed to have many of the same moves as the women. Meaning that there was a lot of hip gyrating and undulating going on, along with something that looked a lot like twerking to my uneducated eyes.

They moved freely around the big open space, turning and twisting and shaking that ass, at least Louis-Cesare did. He wasn't so great at some of the more complex movements, but he had this sinuous quiver down pat that was, uh, memorable. It was the fencing, I thought, staring at my husband's shapely form more than was probably diplomatic.

But . . . dat ass.

He finally decided that I'd had enough time to digest, which was highly debatable in my opinion, but Hassani was talking to some courtier on his other side and wasn't available to rescue me. So, I ended up dancing, too. Or something that vaguely passed for it, and I didn't even have alcohol to blame it on.

It was probably going to end up on the local version of a jumbotron, I thought in horror, just any minute now.

Fortunately, I had a reprieve when a group of plate spinners showed up for the next act. I'd glimpsed them on one of the rooftops as we sped past, but hadn't had a chance to stop and check them out. And now I didn't have to. Hassani didn't travel to the performances, they travelled to him, so we had a front row seat.

If it hadn't come with more *mezze*, it would have been perfect.

I let Louis-Cesare take the hit this time, who worked his way through a dinner he didn't technically need but seemed to enjoy, while the plate spinners did their thing. They were followed by some sword dancers, which was impressive until you considered that they were vamps; some fire jugglers that were impressive *because* they were vamps; and a woman oud player, with an instrument that looked like a lute and sounded like a Greek guitar, who sang some hauntingly beautiful songs whose words I didn't understand.

Or maybe part of me did.

Louis-Cesare had reclined behind me and his body was a line of heat up my spine, countering the chill in the air. The night sky was beautiful, with Hassani's amazing shields able to bring the Milky Way startlingly close and clear. And the torches surrounding our little bier were starting to burn low, giving everything a dreamy, dim, golden glow that wrapped me in the same sense of warmth as Louis-Cesare's arms.

I'd remember today, I thought. Not the pain; I rarely remembered that kind of thing, having had so much of it through the years that it was meaningless, just the background noise of my life. But days like this one . . . yeah. This was burned into my brain.

And then Hassani ensured it.

"Are you enjoying the party?" he asked, leaning over, and keeping his voice low so as not to interrupt the singer's performance.

"Very much." I hoped I didn't sound as sleepy as I felt.

"That is good. I wanted to talk to you earlier, but were told that you were indisposed."

"I don't heal as fast as a vamp," I said. "Not even with help."

"Really?" A dark eyebrow went up. "That makes your actions over the last few days even more commendable."

I didn't know what to do with that, especially coming from him. "Thank you."

"It is I who should be thanking you—both of you. My court owes you a debt we can never repay."

I tried to summon up some brain power, in order to respond appropriately, but most of the available blood was being bogarted by my stomach. "That's, uh, I mean, you don't have to—"

"That is kind of you," Louis-Cesare said smoothly, rescuing me. "Anything that strengthens our alliance is of mutual benefit, not only to us, but to the war effort."

Hassani smiled at him politely for a moment, and then his eyes slid back to me. "But perhaps I can make at least a small down payment."

"A down payment?" I echoed, confused.

"Yes, indeed." He leaned closer, almost enough to whisper in my ear. "I think I know what the fey want with your sister."

CHAPTER SEVENTEEN

Dorina, Faerie

As it turns out, fey shields do have limits, if very, very high ones. Half an hour later, Ray and I finally managed to fight our way out of the waterlogged sphere, which had become trapped behind some large rocks at the bottom of the waterfall, and drag ourselves onto solid land again. That left us inside a cavern behind the falls, but I did not feel like complaining.

Judging by the way Raymond collapsed face down onto the wet sand and just stayed there, neither did he.

I wasn't sure if his position was because vampires do not have to breathe, or because he simply did not want to see any more of Faerie. In spite of everything, I found this place to be fascinating. He did not appear to agree.

For a while, we simply lay there, him face down and me face up, enjoying the view.

And, as I was beginning to expect from Faerie, it was spectacular.

Right above me, imbedded into the ceiling of the cave, was some kind of ancient fossil. I couldn't name it, as I couldn't name anything here, and I only had bones to go on in any case. But it looked like a winged dinosaur.

Not a dragon, although it had a similar body, albeit far smaller and slimmer. But the head was wrong, being too streamlined, and the tail was different. But it was the wings where the real difference lay, because they were *feathered*. I knew this, not because any feathers had survived who knew how many centuries, but because their outlines had been filled in . . .

With opal.

At least, it looked like opal. I could not be certain, as this was an alien world. But when I rolled my head slightly, back and forth, the bright blue and green colors shifted in a familiar way, sparkling down at me from the surrounding dull brown rocks like a piece of stained glass.

The feathers must have lasted a long time, giving the stone time to work its magic. It had ignored the bones— a dull, yellowish skull, a cage of ribs, a tail mostly sunk in rock—but had spilled delicate colors down each plume. The picture was so complete that I could see the individual barbs, the tiny feathers within a feather that grew out of the shaft.

They splayed out exuberantly, with one wing mostly hidden by the creature's body, but the other looking like it was still in flight. I stared up at it for a long time. I did not understand why it was so bright, but perhaps it was the angle of the sun, spearing through gaps in the falls crashing to my right.

The sunlight didn't penetrate very far. The waterfall was large, and the volume of liquid spilling over the top of it astonishing. It created a thick, white curtain, which contrasted nicely with the black soil inside the cave and the greenish hue of the pool of water beneath the falls. Every so often, I would see a brief flash of sky or of the rocky slopes of the riverbank outside, but for the most part, the view was opaque.

But some light did make it in, and reminded me of the ley lines, being striations of color that bled onto everything else. It striped the rocks inside the cave, the damp sand, and a few crystalline structures in the stone. It was really quite lovely, if less spectacular than the formation above.

But then, that seemed to be true of all of Faerie.

It was lovely. . . right up until it tried to kill you.

I slowly got back to my feet.

Raymond lay where he was, and for now, I thought that was best. I needed to check the cave, to make sure that nothing dangerous lay within, while he needed to rest. People often thought that vampires were like wind-up toys: give them enough blood and they just kept going and going. But it wasn't true. They had more stamina than humans, but they could get tired, too, and he had been through a good deal.

I left him where he was and set off to explore.

The cave was surprisingly big, with quite a few stalagmite and stalactite formations spearing up from the floor and down from the ceiling as I left the relatively open, sandy area near the falls. It was mostly composed of the same brownish stone I'd seen near the mouth, except for the formations, which were a mottled brownish/gray. The sand underfoot was mostly brown as well, except for the black soil near the entrance. I supposed that it must have been carried downstream by the water and deposited there. It looked to come from a different region.

There was enough light to illuminate more of the beautiful fossils that studded the cave here and there. I saw a flash of color underfoot and pushed away some sand to find myself looking at the remains of a beaver-like animal. It had a broad, flat tail that had been filled in with a sheet of bright yellow opal in one stunning, unbroken piece. Like with the feathered creature, the body only had a few spots of color among the bones, but the tail was magnificent.

Even better was a clutch of eggs I discovered in a corner. I did not know if they came from a lizard or a bird, but they were three times as large as a chicken's. Protected inside the cave, the shells had survived, but had cracked at some point through the millennia. And inside had formed perfectly egg-shaped opals, one the same blue-green as the creature near the entrance, one a deep, rich red, and one solid black with flecks of seemingly every color in the rainbow.

I looked at them for a long time before finally moving on.

The light dimmed as I went deeper, becoming murky. Especially once I found a narrow area, like a tunnel, branching off from the main cave. But that was easily remedied.

I switched to night vision, and everything abruptly brightened.

Now I could see glints of crystal throughout the stone, white bits that sparkled like ice. And small, furry creatures, looking more like voles than rats, which scurried into their hiding places as I passed, only to peer out at me with bright, black eyes. There was also a surprising amount of driftwood, with its smooth, silvery fingers stretching toward the ceiling in a great mound.

There were no more spectacular, opal-like fossils. In fact, I almost turned back, because there did not appear to be anything of interest down here at all. It was more like a cave I would have expected to find on Earth, with a faint smell of mildew, a fainter odor of mineral water, and the distant but sharp reek of guano, or something very like it.

The voles weren't the only things that lived in this cave, it seemed.

But something kept me going. Perhaps it was just the contrast: the outer cave so flamboyant and interesting, almost as if designed to make this little detour seem drab by comparison. I'd seen spells on Earth that functioned in much the same way, wards created to hide something, not by making it invisible, but by making it seem so boring that people automatically turned away.

There was no magic here, or if there was, it was of a kind I could not detect.

But my instincts told me there was something.

I pressed on.

It was another few minutes before I saw anything of

interest, and even then, I wasn't sure what it was. It was more than half buried in the dirt, but what I could see looked man made. Fey-made, I corrected myself, and squatted down to dig it up.

It wasn't easy. It separated from the ground reluctantly, as if it had been there for a while, with limestone-like secretions having all but glued it in place. But it finally came free, and after brushing off the sand and knocking away the limestone by smacking it on a rock, I found myself holding something strangely familiar.

It was a wrench.

I frowned in puzzlement at it. It looked a little different than Earth wrenches, being longer and heavier, I supposed to fit the feys' bigger hands. But it was recognizable nonetheless.

I liked the heft of it. It would make a good cudgel. I decided to keep it.

And then I wondered the obvious question.

Why was there a wrench in the cave?

There were a few other items scattered about that could have been flotsam, washed here during a flood: part of an old wooden bucket, fuzzy with black mold and serving as a house for a vole; a tattered bit of cloth that might once have been part of a sail; and some bones that could have come in on a flood or been brought here, still struggling, by a predator. But they were lighter in weight. I did not see how—

I had managed to miss that, I thought, staring at something right in front of my face.

I had been pushing through the enormous pile of driftwood, to see if there were any more potential weapons to be found, moving slowly and looking at the ground more than ahead. Which was why my new find surprised me. If it had been a fey—

Well, if it had been a fey, I would have bashed in his skull with my wrench.

But it was not.

I did not know what it was.

I moved some of the driftwood, which was beginning to look like it had been piled up deliberately. There was a great deal of it, and it was woven thickly together, so it took a while. In the process, I ended up knocking much of the surrounding dirt away from the object, enough to see a gleam of metal.

With patience, more of the crusty covering came off. It was odd, because it looked like it had been there for years, perhaps centuries, until the accumulated dust of ages turned into a good facsimile to stone. But the more I chipped away, the more perfect, gleaming metal met my eyes. Until I finally found myself looking at . . .

Well.

I stood there for a moment, doubting myself. I had been through a good deal recently, and I did not have Dory to help ground me anymore. Perhaps I was having some sort of episode?

Either that, or I had to explain why what looked like a spaceship was sitting in a cave in Faerie.

Or part of a space ship. It reminded me of the capsules that astronauts used to splash down in. It was big enough to hold perhaps four people, had metal sides, and had some sort of writing on the side that I couldn't—

It lit up.

I stepped back abruptly, which turned out to be a good thing. Not only had a circle of lights suddenly flashed to life all the way around it, but part of the side had fallen outward. I just stood there for a moment, nonplussed.

Then I cautiously peered within.

There was a central pole, going up to the top of the structure. There were padded benches covered with a silvery looking fabric surrounding the pole, which almost matched the tunic I was wearing. There were squarish windows in the remaining sides that were bigger at the bottom than the top to accommodate the shape of the capsule. They had metal shutters covering them on the outside, which had raised up slightly when the door came down, but were prevented from going any farther by the thicket of driftwood. There was even something that looked like a spy glass affixed to the pole, standing out from the strangely modern looking interior by the fact that it was in a leather pouch.

I had started forward to see if my guess was right, when someone grabbed my arm. I spun, brandishing my weapon, then stopped partway through the swing. All of an inch from Raymond's forehead.

His eyes crossed, staring up at it.

"Oh." I lowered the wrench. "You startled me."

"I startled *you*? What the *fuck*?"

"I'm sorry," I said, because he looked genuinely frightened. I patted his shoulder, which did not seem to help, so I stopped. "I found something."

"Of course, you found something! I can't leave you alone for five minutes without—" he stopped, finally looking past me. "What the hell is *that*?"

"What I found."

"Shit!" Raymond went into a crouch. "Where are the fey?"

"What fey?"

"The fey from the thing!" he gestured at it.

"There are no fey in the thing."

"Are you being sarcastic again?"

I looked into the small space. There was nowhere for a fey to hide that I could see. The benches would never have accommodated anyone so tall, even assuming they opened up.

"No?"

"Then why is it all lit up like that?" He gestured at the lights shining down from near the top of the capsule, and at intervals around the outside. They appeared to be some kind of liquid suspended under domes of glass, so I wasn't sure how they turned on.

Until I stepped closer, and they abruptly became even

brighter.

"Okay, what did you do?" Ray demanded.

"Nothing—"

"Don't give me that!" He appeared a bit stressed, which was understandable. But no one was attacking us, and there didn't seem to be any reason for concern.

Until more lights suddenly lit us up—from behind.

These lights were coming from outside the cave, but they didn't stay that way. Ray and I crept up to the shadow of a large, protruding rock near the entrance to the tunnel, and watched them slowly get closer, like the eyes of some fell beast. And then breech the watery curtain, pushing through as if thousands of gallons weren't pelting down on top of them.

Neither of us said anything, because neither of us understood what we were seeing. We just pulled farther back into shadow as something streaming with water came into the cave, stopping beside the remains of our shield.

There was no way that the wreckage could have been seen from the outside. The rocks that had trapped it were the only things that extended beyond the falls, and then only barely. The shield itself, now cracked like a giant egg, bounced back and forth behind them as it slowly filled with water.

They *did* have some way of tracking it, I thought, as Ray's grip on my shoulder became painful.

I pried his fingers loose before he cracked a bone, and he shot me a startled look. "Sorry," he mouthed.

I nodded, and went back to staring at the intruder.

Now that the water had mostly streamed away, I could see that it was similar in design to the craft we'd just found, with a slightly rounded top and a capsule-like body. But this one was made entirely out of polished wood, although it otherwise copied the metal version exactly. Right down to the wooden "rivets" in the sides and the indistinct, foreign words on the door.

Only this one was floating through the air.

It slowly rotated, the bluish lights on the sides strobing the rocks and sand, but missing us when we drew back behind the ledge of stone.

The flood of light reached past us, extending halfway down the little tunnel. But the craft didn't seem to find the tunnel very interesting, either. After a moment, it withdrew, and when I checked again, peering out from near the bottom of the rock where the shadows were the thickest, I saw that it had settled onto the wet sand near the shield. The door lowered, and a contingent of silver haired fey poured out, their boots splashing on the waterlogged sand.

"What now?" Ray mouthed.

That was a good question, I thought, watching the fey. They looked eerie in the strange blue light, even more so than normal. It striped their faces and tinted their hair. But they seemed to see just fine, as some of them were already stripping off and wading over to the empty shell of the shield.

They appeared to be having trouble seeing the bottom, as it was partly flooded and the churning action of the falls was keeping it moving. They could probably tell that there were bodies in there, but not how many or what kind. But that would not last long.

Their craft was larger than the one we'd found, and there were a lot of fey. I counted fifteen, and there could be more inside. And unlike the ones who had taken me, these were well armed. While all Ray and I had was a knife I'd taken off of one of our attackers, a broken, tourist-grade scimitar, and a wrench.

"We shoulda taken that shin bone," he whispered, and I silently agreed.

And then my eyes widened.

"Look," I whispered to Ray, and pointed.

"What? I don't—oh. Oh, shit."

I seconded the comment. Because our footsteps were

clearly visible on the wet sand, tracking first up the beach and then across the cavern. They would have been even more so, but the black color of the sand blended them into the shadows somewhat, and there were patches of rock here and there that broke them up. The fey had also landed on top of some of them, putting down on the biggest section of sandy soil.

But any moment now, they were going to be noticed. They had filled up with water, and the bluish light coming off the fey's craft was highlighting them perfectly from this angle. That would likely be true from other vantage points as well.

As soon as one of the fey noticed, we were going to have to fight.

I tensed up, preparing—and then another capsule breeched the falls. It was as big as the last, and its shutters were down, exposing the interior and allowing it to immediately begin spewing forth fey. They leapt from the windows before it had even landed, calling out to their fellow warriors, although whether instructions or questions, I didn't know.

I weighed my options. I had a stun ability that theoretically could take on this many, leaving them defenseless. But the fey were really spread out, and I needed them bunched into a relatively small area for it to work. And it only lasted about a minute. I could kill this many in that amount of time, but what if there were more?

The stun tended to wipe me out, leaving me at a disadvantage in any fight that might follow. I usually reserved it for emergencies as a result: for when enemy backup arrived unexpectedly and I found myself outnumbered, or when I ended up surrounded and needed to escape. It was a good defensive weapon, in other words, but not particularly well suited for offense.

And, of course, there was an even better defense, if we hadn't yet been spotted.

"Well, hell," Ray said. "That's only fifteen, maybe twenty guys a piece."

I looked at him. "Do you think you can take fifteen or twenty well-armed fey warriors?"

He rolled his eyes. "You do know there's these things called jokes, right?"

Yes, but this did not seem like the time.

But perhaps it would help to ease the tension.

"I think we should make like a tree," I said.

"What?"

"Leave."

He stared at me for a moment, in what appeared to be concern. But he must have agreed. "Come on," he said. "Let's get outta here."

CHAPTER EIGHTEEN

Dorina, Faerie

There was only one other direction to go, so we hurried back down the tunnel toward the smaller capsule. It was still lit up, with the silvery blue color splashing the driftwood pile and throwing claw like shadows onto the walls. It resembled a bonfire burning with blue flame.

Ray shook his head in disgust. "That's not gonna work. We gotta find a way to turn that shit off—"

The lights suddenly extinguished.

He and I looked at each other.

"Maybe . . . it's on a timer?" he said.

I had not seen a timer, or anything else that looked like technology, unless you counted the ship itself. But he knew Faerie better than I did. "Have you encountered such things before?" I whispered, as we skirted the thicket of driftwood.

"Other than for the one we hit, you mean?"

I paused. "You mean with the shield?"

He nodded.

"That was one like this?"

"Yeah, only bigger. And made outta wood, like the ones back there." He hiked a thumb at the fey. And then he glanced at me. "Looks like somebody wants you bad."

"We should probably hurry, then."

We hurried.

I was afraid that the cave would come to a dead end, which might have had a double meaning in our case. But instead, the opposite proved to be true. The rocky floor stopped abruptly a hundred yards or so past the thicket, but in a cliff, not a wall.

It overlooked a much larger cavern complex that spread out below our feet. I could not see an end to it, as there was a forest of stalactites and stalagmites in the way, but not like the ones behind us. These were huge, spearing up from the darkness or knifing down from above, and looked as if they had been growing there for centuries. They reminded me of a great mouth filled with jagged teeth, which I did not find to be a happy reference.

I switched to several different types of vision, but they did not tell me much more, and neither did my nose. The air was cool, almost cold, with a clammy breeze that was surprisingly fresh, with just a hint of guano. I thought I heard water rushing somewhere, but it was so faint that it could have been an echo of the falls behind us. There did not appear to be a way down.

Or if there was, we did not have time to find it.

A fey voice yelled, far back in the cave, and was quickly echoed by several others. I did not need to understand their words to know the cause: our footsteps had been spotted. Our enemy was coming.

"Okay, okay. You got a plan, right?" Ray said, bouncing on his toes.

I looked at him. "I do?"

"You're supposed to have a plan! Dory always has a plan!"

I did not doubt that. My twin was very resourceful. Unfortunately, I had always been strong enough to fight my way out of most predicaments, and thus never needed to develop her skill set. And now we were in a land where my physical advantage was diminished.

It was a problem.

"Well?" Ray whispered.

"I am thinking," I said.

This did not appear to reassure him.

It did not reassure me, either, but I did not see—

Anything, I thought, as a sudden blaze of light from behind all but blinded me.

"What the—?" Ray yelled, as we were both knocked off our feet.

I didn't answer. I landed on what felt like cold metal, flipped over, and jumped back to my feet. To find myself standing in the middle of the small capsule we had found. It had scooped us up and darted off into the void, I was not sure why.

Even worse, I was not sure who was driving it.

But that was less of a problem than the line of rapidly diminishing fey on the cliffside. There were at least twenty of them, shooting bolts of some kind of energy at us out of what looked like spears. One of the bolts hit a stalactite and shattered it in a blinding explosion of sharp-edged pieces.

They did not hit us, though.

Because our small craft suddenly dove.

Fast.

"*What the fuck!*" Ray screeched. "*What the fuck did you do?*"

I didn't answer, because I was clinging to the floor in front of the small doorway, trying not to fall out as we abruptly plummeted what felt like thirty stories through the enormous cavern. And because I didn't know. All I knew was that I wanted it to stop!

It did so—quite abruptly. Ray and I hit the underside of the roof, then fell back against the floor. It was very hard.

"Oh," Ray whimpered. "Oh, God. Oh, God, I think I broke."

"Broke what?"

"Everything."

I felt similarly, but the fey had vessels, too, and they would undoubtedly follow us. I rolled to my hands and knees and peered outside the door. But all I saw was darkness.

I switched to night vision, and made out a forest of massive stalactites daggering down from above, the smallest of which was as tall as a redwood, and the largest may as well have been an inverted mountain. I looked down, and still could not see the bottom of the chasm, but there were a few places where a stalagmite had shot up high enough to connect with a stalactite, forming giant pillars in the darkness.

Comparatively, we looked like a gnat next to an elephant, or maybe a mammoth, because the chamber had a very lost world feel to it.

No, not a lost world, I thought.

Just an alien one.

"The damned fey!" That was Ray, struggling back to his feet and grabbing the central pole for balance. That did not help as it rotated when he touched it, slinging him about.

And when it moved, so did we.

The entire little craft spun like a top, throwing me into the door frame and almost outside. It stopped after a moment, leaving me dizzy and Ray clinging to the floor as if waiting for the next shock to the system. But I did not think that this one had been random.

I noticed some small flanges sticking out of the central pole. I staggered over and grabbed one and pushed it very slightly to the right. The capsule turned right. I pushed it down, and the capsule went forward a few yards. Huh.

"Ray," I began. "I think—"

"Yeah, yeah, I got it," he said, jumping up and staring at something past my shoulder. "I'll drive. You do something about them!"

I did not know what he meant, but then I turned around to see another stalactite detonate in front of us. It was a huge one, and watching it crack and slowly slide away was like observing a glacier calve. Fully half of it dropped off, disappearing into the darkness below.

It concerned me how long it took before I heard it hit down.

But by then, we were already speeding ahead, with

Ray cursing and staring at something else, this time above us. I followed his gaze and saw what appeared to be fireworks, but which I realized after a second were more exploding stalactites. The fey were coming, dodging the huge impediments and simply blowing the smaller out of the way with their energy weapons.

"Dorina!" Ray said urgently.

"I'm still thinking."

At least there was only one ship, not two. Perhaps the other was waiting at the cliffside, to make sure that we didn't double back? It seemed plausible, which meant that we might only have to deal with one.

"Think faster!" Ray yelled, staring around. "How do we close the damned windows?"

I assumed he meant the shutters, but I didn't know. What I did know was that a fey was leaning off the side of his capsule, targeting us with one of those energy spears. I threw the wrench, hoping for the best but not expecting much. Hitting a moving target when you are also moving is not easy.

But a second later, he was picked off and went sailing into the gloom.

The others did not go back for him. They did not even pause. What they did do was to send a barrage of energy bolts, exploding enough of the cave formations around us that it looked like we'd been caught in a blizzard. I hit the floor to avoid the stony shrapnel bursting through every window, but Ray was not as quick. I heard him scream in pain, and the sound sent what felt like an electric current through me.

How dare they hurt him, for no more than the crime of helping me?

How *dare* they?

The fey craft appeared out of the fake blizzard, screaming toward us, and I screamed back and jumped for it. They did not seem to have expected that, and abruptly veered off.

But not before I landed on their ship, pulled three of them overboard, sliced another's throat with my tiny knife, and plunged my broken sword into a fifth's abdomen.

That did not stop him, however. Armor must not have fit under the Anubis costumes, as those fey had not been wearing any. But these had on full plate. They also had swords, maces and knives in addition to the energy weapons, although I did not see why.

Those were more than sufficient.

I discovered the truth of that when one was jammed against the bottom of my spine and activated. I assumed they must have had different settings, or the entire lower half of my body would have been blown away. As it was, it just felt as if it had.

My legs gave way and I collapsed to the floor, a leering, too-white face above me, which did not leer for long. I cracked his neck, saw his eyes turn up in death, and started to kick him off of me. Only to discover that nothing below my waist still worked.

I had no way of knowing if that would be permanent, but right then, it didn't matter. Right then, all that mattered was killing fey. And the one who had collapsed on top of me had a spear in his hand.

There was nothing to show me how the energy weapons functioned, but it had a wickedly sharp tip so I shoved it through another fey's eye. The rest had not seemed to realize that I was still conscious until then, but at that point, they all started piling on top of me. I suppose the idea was to immobilize me with the weight of their bodies.

Their armor covered bodies.

I tested a theory and pressed down a little flange on the side of the spear, which looked something like the steering mechanism on the capsule. And, oh, yes, that worked, I thought, as what felt like a lightning bolt tore through me. But it tore through them first, starting with the one on top of the pile that I had targeted and spreading downwards.

And I was not wearing a metal suit.

I must have upped the voltage when I played with the flange, or else dhampirs were partly immune. Because some of them were screaming and some were flopping and some had gone limp. I started to smell the unmistakable stench of burning flesh, which would have been more gratifying had I been sure that it wasn't mine. I tried to let go of the trigger, but my fingers were no longer following my commands. Nothing was. My head had rolled to the side, my tongue had begun to loll, and even my eyes were determinedly staring into those of a dead fey instead of at anything useful.

This . . . might not have been my best plan.

I finally felt the spear be ripped away from me, yet the removal of the problem did not help much. My teeth were chattering as if I was cold, my heart felt like it was skipping every other beat, and my body was trembling except for my legs, which had never even moved.

But my eyes were back under my control, and when I told my hand to flex, it actually worked. Even better, there was a sword coming within reach, as one of the fey clawed his way out of the pile. I managed to grab it from its scabbard and shove it at him. It missed by a mile: my aim was terribly off, but there were so many other fey close by that it hardly mattered. I stabbed another in the arm pit, and the wickedly sharp blade pierced his chain mail.

He screamed, and the fey whose sword I had taken turned around and tried to belt me in the face. But he seemed as rattled as I was and also missed, although the action brought him close enough to kiss. Or to bite through his jugular, so I did, feeling his death throes above me while his warm, wet blood cascaded over my face and breast and hair.

I laughed; I didn't know why. I had meant to roar instead, hoping to disorient my attackers further, and buy myself a few more seconds. But what came out instead was wild, almost hysterical laughter.

But it seemed to do the trick.

The fey who could still function began getting off of me. They began getting off of me quickly. But, ironically, that left me more vulnerable than before, as those who had not been injured started poking at the diminishing pile with swords and spears, trying to skewer me.

They hit their friends half the time instead, but the other half they hit me, resulting in both of my legs taking wounds. I did not feel them, but they were there, and there are plenty of arteries in the legs. I needed to retreat before I bled out, but . . .

I did not know how.

I tried my stun scream, but it did not work, possibly because my brain was still jittering around in my cranium. It left me wailing like a banshee for no apparent reason, on an enemy vessel surrounded by foes who did not seem to recall that they were not supposed to kill me. To make matters worse, there was nothing close enough to jump to, even had I been able; my spirit form persistently refused to manifest; and I was having difficulty thinking straight, which made formulating a plan virtually impossible.

But then something strange happened.

"Augggghhhhh!!! Motherfuckers! Come at me, bra!"

I looked up at the sound of a familiar voice. It was distant, yet rapidly getting closer. The still conscious fey looked up, too, seemingly confused.

And then Raymond kamikazed their ship.

The smaller vessel did not have the heft of this one, but he was going full out when he hit. The crash sent us slamming into a massive stalactite, and suddenly, I wasn't sure where one vessel started and the other ended. But I was sure of one thing.

I had until the fey recovered to get off of this ship.

So, I did, slithering out from under the remaining pile, many of whom had been helpfully thrown into their friends by the crash.

"Hurry up!" Ray yelled. "What are you doing?"

"My legs no longer work," I said thickly, although my elbows were pulling me along pretty quickly.

That was just as well, because my words seemed to utterly incense Ray. "Sons of bitches!" he screamed, and suddenly, the whole capsule was filled with jumping, blue white fire.

I had just rolled back onto ours, which was looking a little worse for the wear, with black impact marks on the metal and a missing shutter. But it was not dented, surprisingly. Although the interior was alarmingly full of rocks.

And so was the side of Ray's face.

He had clearly taken the brunt of the last barrage, but he was a vampire. He remained on his feet, furious and functional. And he looked better than most of those on the now fiery hulk beside us.

"What did you do?" I asked Ray, as the fey screamed and burned, some of them jumping into the darkness, others leaping for us—

And missing, because Ray was backing us up, and backing fast.

"Found these," he panted, pointing down at a trio of nodules sticking out of a panel below the door. They looked like the ends of the fey's spears, only blunted. I supposed because they weren't intended to stick into anything. Instead

—

"Oh, you want some more?" Ray screeched at the fey ship, which was now pursuing us. "You want some more? All right, have some more!"

The darkness lit up with a triple blaze of blue white energy, which smacked into the fey's craft like a fist. I doubted that it would make much of a difference, as the vessel was already burning. I was wrong.

The fey's craft *exploded*, like a brilliant supernova in the darkness, sending fiery shards and smoldering bodies everywhere. It was so bright that it lit up a huge swath of the cave, causing reflected flames to leap on walls of what looked like ice, but were probably just coated in more limestone. Because the stalactites looked like they were boiling, too.

The fey's craft plunged into darkness, dragging flames behind it, and was soon swallowed up, leaving us all alone in the big, echoing, empty space. Only not entirely empty. There was something . . .

"What is that?" I asked Ray, peering into the darkness.

His eyes narrowed, but they probably had the same problem with leaping aftereffects that mine did.

"I dunno. Gimme a sec." He did something to one of the flanges, which abruptly caused all of our lights to go out.

And made those in the distance, approaching from all sides, seem that much brighter as a result. They looked like car headlights, getting closer. Because that's essentially what they were, I realized. Only instead of cars, they were affixed to the sides of the feys' strange crafts—what looked like dozens of them.

All of which were converging on our location.

"Well, fuck," Ray said.

CHAPTER NINETEEN

Dorina, Faerie

Our second waterfall was green. Or perhaps that was a trick of the light. There wasn't much of it, even to my eyes. But some crystals in the side of the cliff where we'd taken refuge shed a faint, emerald glow.

I almost wished they hadn't, as it allowed me to see Ray's pinched and worried face as he examined me.

Outside of the curtain of water, which was less dense than the one in our first cave, I could see the fey vessels patrolling. They knew we were here, as we had not had enough time to escape. They just didn't know where.

But they were searching.

We had slipped behind the waterfall, into a slight depression in the rock, before they arrived, not having any other choice. It made us hard to see with our own lights extinguished, but hard was not impossible, and the fey seemed to have realized that we must be hiding nearby. Their lights had swept past us once already, but the falling water seemed to have confused them. I didn't know how much longer it would do so, however, and I could not walk, much less fight.

This . . . was not how I had envisioned my end.

"It's not your end," Ray said harshly, reading my thoughts. "Stop it with that shit, okay?"

"I did not mean to distress you."

"I'm not distressed!" he snapped, which might have been

more believable if I couldn't see his expression.

He scowled, which dislodged a pebble from beside his mouth. It wasn't the only one. The fey's blast had peppered him with bits of limestone, to the point that he resembled a rock more than a man. That was why he'd taken a few moments to rescue me; he'd been all but immobilized by the sheer amount of the weight that he'd suddenly taken into his body.

His system was still expelling pieces of it as he healed, leading to occasional *plink, plonk* sounds as his flesh pushed out yet another pebble, before closing up again behind it. He still had a way to go, however, leaving him looking like he'd been dragged along a gravel-filled road for a few miles. It upset me to see it, but I looked no better.

We made quite a pair.

"There's nothing wrong with my expression!" he informed me. "It's exactly what it should be seeing as how I'm stuck in Faerie, got a fuck ton of murderous fey on my ass, and—"

"And are partnered with a cripple."

His head came up at that. He'd been bandaging my wounds, using pieces of a blanket he'd found under one of the seats, but now I had his full attention. And he did not look pleased.

"Okay, first of all, nobody uses that term anymore—"

"Partnered?"

"Crippled! It's not PC, okay? It's not even accurate. Just 'cause part of your body don't work anymore—"

"Ray."

"—doesn't mean you can't be useful. You can pilot this thing while I fight them, for instance—"

"Ray."

"—'cause I'm not so bad at it myself, you know? You think Dory would have promoted me if I couldn't throw down? I can throw down!"

"I'm sure you can. But there are so many of them—"

"So, what? We've had bad odds before."

"Not this bad." I looked at him seriously. "I have counted at least eight ships. If there are twenty warriors per ship—"

"There ain't eight ships. You counted some of them twice—"

"There are eight. And possibly more on the way. You must leave me—"

"Bull*shit*—"

"Listen." I caught one of his hands. "I am lame. My hands have stopped shaking, but my legs are useless. I have no idea if this is permanent, but it doesn't matter. It is the case right now, and that means I will only be a drag—"

"Damn it, Dorina!"

"—on you and your chances of escape. But we have one advantage: the fey want me, not you. If they capture me, they won't look for you. You can get away, possibly even get back to Earth. But if we stay together—"

"What?" It sounded like a challenge.

"Then they will get both of us. And they have no orders to keep you alive."

Ray just looked at me for a moment. What I could see of his face looked gaunt and hollow in the strange lighting. It made him look older than his usual youthful appearance, highlighting planes and angles that were not normally visible.

"Cause I'm not young," he said, reading my mind again. "I got four hundred years under my belt, okay? So how about you stop treating me like some kid you need to protect?"

"I would never do that," I told him seriously. Disrespecting a warrior who had fought at my side was unthinkable. "But if the choice is between one of us getting away, and neither—"

"Okay, how about you listen, for once?" he said, cutting me off with a furious whisper. "It's always me listening and following orders, but you know what? I ain't some flunky, some errand boy. I'm a master vamp and I'm your Second.

And you know what a Second does when his master is injured and exhausted and talking crazy?"

"I am not—"

"If you're talking about me leaving you to those murderous things, then yeah, you're talking crazy!" His voice had gotten a little loud, so I put a hand over his mouth. He left it there for a moment, his eyes glimmering at me angrily over the top. Then he removed it, hesitated, and then kissed the back of it defiantly. "This is me taking over, all right?"

I blinked at him, more than a little nonplussed. But the truth was, I had no other ideas. I did not know how to get us out of this.

I nodded.

"Good." Ray went back to fussing with the bandages.

I did not know if the fey had bad aim, or if a few of them had still been trying to wound instead of kill. But no major arteries had been severed in my legs. That was good in the sense that I would not bleed to death, but it did not help with the fact that I remained paralyzed. I concentrated everything I had on trying to move something, even just a toe, for a long moment.

It did not work.

I felt frustration and fear rising in my throat, and tried to tamp them down. But it was not easy. When I became angry, I tended to lash out at whatever was hurting me, but I could not do that here. As weak as I was, even had I been able to manifest my spirit form, I could not have held it for long. I could not do anything!

Meanwhile, Ray's plan seemed to be to wait our enemies out, but I did not think that the fey were going anywhere. Whatever they wanted from me, it seemed important to them. They had the reckless yet tenacious attitudes of men who had been told to return with their shields or on them.

I did not think that going home without me was an option.

"Okay, that's about as good as I can do with a crappy

blanket," Ray said. "Now, you stay here—"

"Where are you going?" I caught his arm.

He pried it off. "I'm gonna go check out this cliff face."

"They'll see you!"

"I used to be a smuggler," he reminded me. "I know how to slip around all subtle like. They won't see me."

"But . . . what do you hope to find?"

"Another way out." It was grim. He glanced at the fey lights, now less like the running variety and more like search lights, that were strobing the cavern. "These guys don't look like they plan on leaving anytime soon. We need a back door, and water erodes. There could be a passage to another chamber or even to the outside hidden in these rocks. And if there is, I'm gonna find it."

With that he was gone, before I had a chance to protest. I stared after him, feeling off balance again. I was not used to being the one left behind, the weak one, the one with nothing to do. It was disconcerting and highly unpleasant. I sat there for a moment, frowning at nothing.

Then I started searching the cabin, looking for anything useful.

The bench seats opened up to allow storage underneath, but there wasn't much there. And what I did find reinforced my impression that this capsule had been used recently, despite its initial appearance. There were no weapons, but there was dried food—still edible—a container of what I assumed to be water, and another blanket.

I pulled the latter over myself, not that it helped much. The depression we were in was shallow, to the point that we'd basically become part of the falls. The entire interior of the craft was wet and I had water beading on my skin and dripping off of my nose.

After a moment, I took the blanket back off and used it as a bag instead, loading it down with the rest of the supplies. I emptied the two bench seats closest to me, then crawled awkwardly around to the other side of the pole to see what else I could find. I was hoping for a map, as our side in the war had allies in Faerie as well as enemies. If we knew where we were, perhaps we could reach some of them.

But there was no map. One of the remaining seats had nothing underneath it, and the last had a coil of rope, some fire making supplies, and a mirror. I took the mirror, which was small and probably also intended for use in making fire. It was a little larger than my palm, and showed me back a face that was pale, splattered with blood, and tired looking. I frowned and turned it on my body instead.

I wanted to see the injury to my spine, but it was difficult, and not just because of the location. But because it was so dark in here. Night vision was good for some things, but the constantly moving shadows from the running water was obscuring my vision. I twisted this way and that, but it didn't help. I needed better light—

And, suddenly, I had it.

A light lit up on the floor beside me, splashing my face with pale blue luminescence. It caused me to suck in a breath and throw the blanket and then my body over it. I froze in place, waiting to see if I had been spotted.

And waited.

And waited.

After what felt like an hour but was probably only a few minutes, I relaxed slightly. Perhaps the fey had not seen me, after all. Or perhaps they had, and were merely mustering their forces.

I waited some more.

But no one came. I eventually breathed a little easier, but wondered what I was supposed to do now. What if more of those lights came on? I couldn't hide them all. What if this one refused to go out, leaving me—

The light went out.

I blinked at it, but it was definitely out. The blanket was soldier grade material, with a rough feel and a loose weave. I could see through it well enough, especially at this distance, and the only lights at the moment were faint aftereffects jumping in front of my vision.

For a moment, I just sat there, wondering why there was a little frisson in my mind. It was a small sensation, hardly there at all, like a tiny fingernail scratching or a dim indicator light. As if something was waiting . . .

I thought, "Light."

And there was light.

"Out." I whispered quickly.

And there was none.

Huh.

I remembered how, when I first found the little craft, I had wanted to see it better, and the next moment, it had lit up. And later, at the top of the cliff in the first cave, I had heard the approaching Svarestri and wished for a way out. And the next thing I knew, Ray and I had been scooped up . . . and taken out.

As strange as it seemed, it appeared that the vessel could read my desires, and respond to them. I did not understand how this was possible. I did understand that this was useful.

Possibly very useful.

Another fey ship approached, with a sweeping blue light that was creeping over the rocks and crevasses of the cliff face, coming this way.

"Out," I thought, as hard as I could, and their light went out.

I smiled.

The fey were unhappy. I could hear them from here, chattering to each other in a strange, guttural language. Odd; I had always heard that their languages were beautiful. Each to their own, I thought, and spun them around.

I actually laughed that time, as their craft slung about, hard enough that several of them almost fell out. But they didn't, catching themselves at the last minute, which annoyed me. They had hurt Ray, had torn him limb from limb, had peppered him with stones. They were still looking for both of us, and would likely kill him if they found us, and take me off for possibly an even nastier fate.

Torture, I thought. They will want to know our plans for the war. I smiled again, and even without the mirror, I knew it was not a nice one. Let me show you my plans, I thought, and sent their craft rocketing across the void—

Straight into another.

The two crashed, then backed up and did it again. And again. And again, until very few of the boards remained intact and even fewer of the fey remained on board. And those who did were screaming.

They must have been yelling for help, because the other vessels came zipping over from every direction, and I learned a new thing: I could not control them all. One was easy; two was possible with simple commands, such as ram each other repeatedly. But no more. Whenever I tried to add a third, it jerked slightly, and seemed to stall out for a moment, but then tore away from my mental grasp.

Fair enough, I thought, and ordered one of the new arrivals to start firing those blue energy beams at all the rest.

"What the hell is going on?" Ray demanded, sliding back inside our ship.

"I am creating a distraction."

"What?"

I sent the wildly firing vessel straight at two more, which sprang out of the way just in time. But they weren't able to avoid getting strafed by those weapons. The sizzling blue beams mostly missed one craft, just sheering off a bit of the top, but the other was sliced clean in two.

Unfortunately, most of the fey appeared to have ducked. Fortunately, that did not help them much, as their craft was now tilting and whirling and acting crazy. It started firing randomly, too, although I had not told it to, which caused the others to scatter.

And gave us a chance.

"Let's get out of here," I said to Ray, who was staring at

me.

"Wait—*you* did that?"

"These things seem to respond to thoughts."

"Since when?"

"Since always?"

He scrunched up his face, then looked around. "Doesn't work for me."

"But it does for me, and we need to *go*."

"Not out there," he argued, checking out the wildly slinging weapons' fire. "We could get hit as easy as them."

"Then what's your plan?"

He thought for a second. "You can control this thing?"

I nodded.

"Then send it back where it came from—after we get off."

"Get off? But—"

"Trust me. Just do it! Do it now!"

I didn't understand the urgency in his tone until I looked up. And noticed that all of the remaining vessels were charging back in, weapons blazing. A consensus had obviously been reached to sacrifice the rogue ship, despite the fact that some of their compatriots were still on it.

Which was a better distraction than anything I'd been able to come up with, I thought, as the cave lit up.

Ray threw me over his shoulder, and as soon as we cleared the ship, I sent the little vessel zipping back across the cavern. That led to mass confusion, as several of the fey crafts continued with the attack, while the rest broke off and tried to follow our speeding bullet. Ray didn't hesitate; he started climbing up the rocks beside the falls, while I hung over his back and tried to keep the chaos going.

It was getting harder. I managed to cause another vessel's weapons to fire briefly, which set a second on fire. I also caused the lead vessel fleeing after ours to stutter and falter for a moment, and almost get run into by another. But then I lost the connection, and it tore away into the darkness.

And when I tried a new command, all that happened was

that I felt dizzy and unwell.

I didn't think we'd be getting any more help. But then, perhaps we didn't need it. Ray had indeed found a backdoor: a tiny crevasse in the rock that we could barely fit through, with the dark, wet stone close on both sides. At one point, he had to put me down, turn sideways, and drag me through an especially narrow area, but I didn't mind.

Particularly when I saw what was on the other side.

"What is it?" I asked, hearing the awe in my voice.

He stared upwards. "I think . . . it's a river."

"It can't be a river. There's nothing holding it up."

Ray didn't answer that time. He just started climbing, taking us higher and higher and closer and closer. The not-a-river continued to sparkle like a vein of pure emerald, cutting across the ceiling of the cavern like another huge piece of stained glass. Only this glass moved.

Sunlight speared down through it as it shifted, dappling our faces as well as the rest of the cave we approached, until we came close enough that I could have reached out and touched it.

I looked at Ray, who had put me down on a protruding rock for a moment so that he could rest. He either read my mind or saw the wish on my face. He shrugged.

"Might as well. We gotta get out of here somehow."

I held up a hand.

Pure, clear water trickled through my fingers, crisp and cold and causing me to laugh with delight. It was a river, a river held up by nothing at all. I splashed us simply by pulling my hand down swiftly.

"Green fey," Ray said, cracking a slight grin himself. "Gotta be. They pull this shit all the time."

"You've seen something like this before?"

He shook his head. "Heard about it. Didn't believe it, though." He looked at me, and there was challenge in it. "Feel like a swim?"

CHAPTER TWENTY

Dorina, Faerie

We took a swim. Ray leapt upwards, into the suspended river, giving me the strange view of his body floating over nothing at all. For a moment, it looked like I was sitting under a swimming pool with a glass bottom, looking up at the sun's rays filtering through onto my face. It was amazing.

And that was before an arm reached down, grasped my hand, and pulled me up alongside him.

The water was cold enough to be a shock, although less of one than the view. I looked down through shifting waters at the massive cavern below us, and something between excitement and fear coursed through me. Cascading sunlight picked out glints in the rocks, gleamed off a forest of limestone formations, and highlighted bats, thousands upon thousands of them, flocking like birds far below.

It was a mind-bending sight that I knew I'd never forget. But it was almost equaled when we burst out of the other side of the stream, and for a moment, I didn't know which way was up. A wave of disorientation hit, giving me the strangest feeling that the world had flipped, and I was about to fall into the huge, blue bowl of the sky.

Then I blinked and everything righted itself, leaving me looking at a truly beautiful spot. The river murmured over clutches of rocks, the wind sighed through the treetops of an enormous forest, the sun streamed down out of a cloudless sky, and a bird sang a brief trill. Even better, the entire stretch of riverbank was deserted, without a threat in sight.

We were out!

Ray and I looked at each other, and despite everything, we laughed. And kept on doing so when he tossed his head, spraying me with water, and I splashed him back. We floated there, having a water fight like a couple of children for a moment, just grateful to be alive.

We eventually started moving, but not toward dry land as I'd expected. The shoreline wasn't far, a brief rocky and then grassy expanse before the tree line, but Ray avoided it. I tried to ask why, but he just shook his head.

"In a minute."

In a minute we ended up by a flat shelf of rock that extended outward from the embankment. Ray scooped me up and deposited me on a dry area out of the waterline. The rock looked like shale and had been washed by the river for so long that it was as smooth as silk under my fingertips. The sun had warmed it, in between sections of a rocky overhang, making it a comfortable enough spot.

Yet I didn't understand why we had stopped here.

Ray squatted down beside me, his face earnest. "Look. You gotta remember three things about Faerie, okay?"

I nodded.

"One, assume that everything is trying to kill you, all the time, because it probably is. Two, never—and I mean never —go into a forest unless you got a fey guide. Seriously. The damned thing will eat you, and that is not a metaphor."

I nodded again.

"And three, try to get out as fast as you can. If you remember those three things, you got maybe a fifty-fifty chance."

I did not like those odds. "But how do we get out? I didn't find a map—"

He waved it away. "Portals won't be on a map, unless they're the official ones we'd never get near anyway. But I got contacts. Soon as we figure out where we are, I'll get us outta here, okay?"

I nodded. I was grateful for Ray's former occupation, which had involved a fair amount of smuggling into the fey lands. If I had to be stuck here with anyone, I was glad it was him.

He smiled as if he'd heard that, which perhaps he had. "Look, I'm gonna go get a fish and some firewood. You want anything else?"

I frowned. "Shouldn't we move on before making camp? Put some distance between us and the fey?"

Ray shook his head. "It's gonna be dark before long. That's rule number four: never travel in Faerie at night. It's dangerous enough in the daytime."

I absorbed that, and my stomach growled, as if placing an order. "Another fish, then?"

"Another fish it is." He arched an eyebrow. "Don't wander off."

I gazed after him, wondering if that had been a joke.

Ray sloshed back into the stream, but the area nearby was rocky and the water turbulent. He eventually ventured further away, where a bend in the river and some trees mostly hid him from sight. I would have been more concerned about that, but he was a master vampire. He could take care of himself as well as hear me if I called out.

And I could hear him cursing in between dives, which made me smile.

After a while, I started looking through the waterlogged blanket of items that I had taken out of the capsule. I opened up the soggy knots and spread the fabric out to dry. I put the contents on the other side of me and took stock.

There were the four blood bags, which had surprisingly remained intact. There was the mirror, which had not, but I had the flint and striker so that did not matter. There was a small bundle of kindling, which seemed odd with how heavily forested this area was—until I remembered Ray's comment about the trees.

I gazed at the ones across the river, but they were so thick that I could not tell if anyone, or anything, gazed back. They had huge, old, wizened trunks, like the last stretch of woodland I'd seen, most of them topped by massive canopies of dark green leaves. There was a scattering of yellow tops among the group as well, one that was violently red, and another that was vividly purple.

The more colorful ones explained the varicolored leaves that floated gently downstream, and had collected near the waterline. They were all different sizes and shapes, some spotted and speckled with age, others still bright and vibrant. I couldn't name all of the species, but some were oak and a few looked like maple.

If there was anything odd about the trees, other than their size, I couldn't tell. Although occasionally one would shiver slightly as if in a breeze, while the surrounding forest stayed still. I slowly laid the sticks out to dry, still watching them, and wondered if it would be taken as an offense if we actually built a fire.

And then wondered at finding myself in a place where that was a reasonable question to have.

I went back to exploring our cache.

There was the small bag of emergency food, which was nuts and some orange colored, dried fruit. There was the canteen-like container of something that was definitely not water, as I had first assumed. I sniffed it, and then tried a minute drop on the end of my tongue.

Fey wine.

And it was fresh. Like everything else in the cache, it had been put there relatively recently. As if someone else had discovered the capsule and did their best to hide it, but also used it on occasion, for what I did not know.

But I did not think that it had been the Svarestri, who had seemed as surprised by it as we were.

I put the canteen aside.

There was also the knife that I had managed to hang onto somehow, although Ray had taken it "fishing." And a few strips of the first blanket, which he had ripped up for bandages. And that was all. That was everything we had to help us survive in the hostile environment of an alien world.

Fifty-fifty, I thought.

I put the blanket aside and started massaging my legs, trying to get them working again, but had to stop when the pressure opened one of the wounds. I frowned at myself— I should have expected that—and rebandaged it with some more blanket strips. The wounds were deep, as if the fey had been attempting to hamstring me, but not dangerous, and they did not impede my movement as my legs were nonfunctioning anyway. But it felt strange, not being able to feel my fingers moving over my flesh.

There was no pain, even when I washed the seeping wound in fey wine to disinfect it. Dhampirs do not suffer from infections, but that was on Earth. Who knew how it worked here?

I thought about that, then unwrapped the other wound and disinfected it, too, just to be safe. Again, there was no discomfort. It was almost as if my legs were not there at all, which was . . . disturbing.

I tried telling myself that it would be fine, that I would return to Earth, reunite with Dory, and that our body would be whole again. Only, what if this was our body? I had assumed that the original had stayed with her, simply because I was used to thinking about it as hers more than mine. But what if she had the duplicate?

What if I returned to her, and paralyzed us both?

I pushed that thought away—hard—because it made the cold water beading on my skin feel like it reached all the way to my heart. I shivered anyway, probably because my tunic was wet. I pulled it off and laid it in the sun, and even found a small patch of warmth for myself while it dried.

The rocks overhead looked a bit like an open hand, I

decided, with four fingers of stone sticking out, and the thumb being the stony protrusion behind me. It showed me the sky in pieces, but provided a little shelter in case it rained. Assuming that it did that here.

I didn't know because I didn't know the rules of this place. Not any of them. It made me uneasy, like the thought that I might not be able to fight off an attack if it came.

But there was nothing obviously threatening at the moment, and I had started to relax by the time Ray returned, with four large fish, a crab-like creature, and a sliced-up nose. And a slightly horrified expression when he caught sight of me. "Oh, hey! Hey, yeah. Um—"

"Is something wrong?" I asked, because he'd looked away. And then almost turned his back on me.

"No, no, hell no. Not a thing. It's just . . . it gets cold here, at night. You, uh, should probably put that tunic back on."

I reached over and felt of it. And to my surprise, it was dry. The strange material had wicked away the water and the sun had warmed it. I pulled it over my head and Ray was right. I did feel better.

"What is it you have there?" I asked.

He glanced over his shoulder, and looked faintly relieved for some reason. Then he looked down at his catch. "Oh. Crab," he explained, shaking the obviously dead creature. "I'm gonna enjoy cooking this bitch up. It almost took my nose off."

"*Can* we cook?" I asked, as he squatted down by the river to clean his catch. The sun, or what passed for it here, was getting lower. It would be dark soon, and a fire would show our location all too well.

And that was assuming that the trees didn't get us first.

Ray shrugged. "May as well. We have to have a fire anyway." He thought about it. "That's rule number five. Never sleep without a fire, especially not at water's edge."

"But if we light one, somebody might see us."

"And if we don't, something might *eat* us."

"There seems to be a lot of that going on," I pointed out.

He started to say something, but then looked up and saw my face. Or perhaps he read my mind, and picked up on some of the strange feeling I was having. Not fear exactly, but something approaching it. Anxiety? Was that the word?

"That's the word," Ray said. "And if you didn't have any around here, you'd be either stupid or crazy."

"All right," I said.

"In Faerie, you gotta pick your battles," he added, working on the fish. "Look, I'm not gonna lie to you and promise that we're going to make it out of here, okay? I'm not gonna do that. But I will promise that tonight, *we'll* do the eating."

I felt my face crack, and then smile. Ray had a way with words. It wasn't a conventional way, but it was a way.

"I'll make the fire," I said.

* * *

The meal was simple but good. Hunger is the best sauce, as someone once said, and I was very hungry. I ate all four of the fish, some of the dried fruit, and most of Ray's crab. It had almost taken his nose off in an epic battle, so he had eaten some as a point of honor.

He had also drunk another pint of blood, reducing our stash to three, which told me how much healing he'd had to do earlier. A master shouldn't have needed another feed so soon. Especially not with a family back on Earth to draw from.

"Can your family not supply you?" I asked, as I handed it over.

He rolled his eyes, which I was beginning to see as a favorite gesture, and poked our fire with a stick. He'd found some driftwood along the banks, so we had a good blaze. It was chilly now with the sun down, but the fire warmed not only us but the rock behind us. I thought we'd sleep comfortably enough.

"You seen my family, right?" he said, after a moment.

"Yes."

"So, what do you think?"

I ate a fish eye. "I think they are too weak to help you, and that it is my fault."

He looked up, the firelight splashing his face. "Why would it be your fault?"

"I am not a proper master. Neither is Dory. Your old master could give you power through the blood bond, but we cannot. As a result, your people draw from you, but you have no one to draw from in return. It weakens you."

Ray picked at the mostly empty crab shell. "That's one way of looking at it."

"Is that not how you look at it?"

He shot me a look. "No."

For a while, nothing else was said. The wood popped, the wind rustled through the treetops, and the water murmured over the stones. I looked up, and the rocky fingers seemed as if they were reaching out to clutch the sky. There were stars visible, but no moon. I wondered if Faerie even had one, and felt a strange quiver at the thought that I didn't know.

"I look back," Ray finally said, "at four hundred years of slavery. You know when Dory cut off my head that time?"

I nodded.

"We were nothing to each other then; never even met. I was just some loser she'd been sent after, just a paycheck. Yet she was more polite to my decapitated corpse than my old master ever was to the whole man. That fucking prick."

I blinked.

"So, you gotta weigh it out. On the one hand, sure, I don't get any power boosts, but that miserly bastard never gave up much anyway. And on average, I'd rather have some goddamned respect than all the power in the world. You know?"

"No," I said honestly. "I have never met a vampire who did

not crave power."

"Didn't say I didn't crave it," Ray corrected. "Right now, I crave the heck out of it. I just crave something else more. You spend four hundred years being treated like nothing, just nothing at all, and maybe you'd understand."

This time, I was the one who was silent.

"I did," I finally said, and saw him blush.

Or maybe that was the fire. It was sending a cheerful glow over the flat stone beneath us, the rocks behind us, and the fingers above. It had also given Ray back his youthful appearance. There was no gray in the shock of black hair, and the blue eyes, so startling against the tanned skin, were unlined. At a guess, I would have said that he was Changed young, no more than early twenties.

"Nineteen," he said roughly, and looked away. But a moment later, those blue eyes were back and staring at me challengingly. "What about you?"

"I am not a vampire," I pointed out. "I was not Changed."

The eyeroll was back. "No, I meant what do you want? You asked me, so it's only fair."

I agreed that it was fair. It was also difficult to answer. I decided to take my time, as he had, and lay back against the warm stone to look at the stars.

Like everything else here, they were both familiar and not. The small, pinpricks of light were the same, but there were no familiar constellations. Orion, the Big Dipper, the Pleiades . . . they simply were not there.

Of course, they wouldn't be, would they? I had heard that Faerie was in a completely different universe, connected to our own solely by a small breach in space-time. It was on the "heavenly" side, whereas Earth was part of the "hells", although those terms did not have the same connotations that I had been taught as a child. They simply denoted the rules under which the two universes operated, acknowledging that their magic, and possibly even their physics, worked differently.

"They got constellations," Ray suddenly said. "They're just different from ours. See that line of four stars in a row, with three more curving up from it?"

I followed the line of his pointing finger, and nodded.

"That's Gangleri, the Wanderer. Said to be the ship the gods came here in. The story is that they were like space Vikings, poor adventurer types searching for wealth, lands, people they could conquer—basically anything. They traveled all over their galaxy, plundering the shit outta everybody who didn't beat them up first—"

"Beat them up? When they were so strong?"

He settled onto his back and put his hands behind his head. "Well, that's the point. They weren't that strong then. They were only overpowered when they came here, where the rules are different. They discovered that in our universe they were like, well, like gods. They could beat up anybody."

"But they weren't in our universe," I pointed out. "Faerie is in theirs."

"Yeah, but it's the closest world to the rift on their side, like Earth is on ours. Both worlds are a little weird, 'cause things bleed over. That's how the gods found us; we're not that far away, you know?"

I shook my head. I didn't know. I had never heard this before.

"How did you come to know so much?" I asked.

He shrugged. "The fey. If you wanna do business, you gotta have a meal, drink some wine, smoke some herb. And while you're doing that, you talk, so they can decide what kind of person you are. They been ripped off before, but it don't happen often 'cause they've been trading a long time. They're pretty good at sizing a guy up. But anyway, eventually they talk back, usually telling stories."

"What kind of stories?"

"Any kind. Every kind." Ray grinned. "Bullshit, mostly: heroes and villains, epic journeys and daring deeds, damsels needing rescuing from ugly ogres . . . unless it's the ogres telling the story. In which case it's usually about light fey trespassers getting what's coming to 'em. And about roasting pretty fey princes over a spit until the juices run clear."

I blinked. "You traded with the dark fey, too?"

"Sure, why not? They have portals. They also got stories, but they're not so nice. The light fey were the ones the gods interbred with. The dark fey were the ones they experimented on. Guess who was treated better?"

I did not have to guess. Dory had dark fey friends who had fled to Earth, where they were thought of as monsters. Yet they had better lives there.

I looked up at the glimmering constellation, sailing across the heavens. It resembled a Viking ship, with a long body and a raised prow. But judging by what I'd seen today, I doubted it had looked like that at all. Probably a case of the fey interpreting the idea of a ship in a way that made sense to them.

Was that all the gods were? I wondered. Just space vagabonds looking for an opportunity, and finding it because of a happenstance of physics? Like a human walking on the moon could suddenly jump higher because of the difference in gravity.

"What if God was one of us," Ray suddenly sang. "Just a slob like one of us?"

I laughed; I couldn't help it. He always seemed to know what to say.

"And then Great Artemis' spell banished the gods and blocked the breech behind them, preventing their return," I said. "But it had to encompass Faerie as well, since the ley lines connected it to Earth. Thus, cutting Faerie off from the rest of the heavens."

"Pretty much," Ray agreed.

I watched the stars wheel above us. There were so many here, and so close. Maybe it was just the lack of light pollution, but it looked as if someone had pitched a great, glittery tent in the heavens.

One the fey could no longer reach.

I wondered what they thought, looking up at a sky cut off from them forever. At worlds they'd never visit, at a universe they would never explore. I couldn't imagine what that must have felt like, to be suddenly so alone.

Or perhaps I could.

"I don't know what I want," I said to Ray.

CHAPTER TWENTY-ONE

Dorina, Faerie

"That's a cop out," Ray said.

I frowned. Slang sometimes threw me. It was what came from having very few conversations over the years. "What does that mean?"

"It means that you don't wanna tell me, so you're evading the question."

"I am not evading."

"Look, I get it. You just don't wanna talk about it. It's okay —"

"I do not mind talking."

Talking was strange after a lifetime filled with silence, but nice. I had discovered that I quite liked talking. It was so much easier to gather information that way, than by merely observing.

And yet it required putting into words concepts that did not always seem to fit.

"Then do it however you like," Ray said. "We're pretty simpatico mentally. Just send me the images."

Yes, but of what? I thought. There was so much . . .

"I got nothing but time," he pointed out.

I nodded, but then just lay there for a while longer, saying nothing. Pondering how to explain the thoughts and feelings I'd been having over the last few months. It felt odd to have someone ask.

It felt odder to want to answer.

"My life . . . isn't mine," I said slowly. "I live in the house of Dory's friend. I do not have a house; I have never had one. I grew up in my father's house, and since then, my sister has decided where we live."

"But I thought you liked—"

"Shhh."

I put a hand on Ray's arm and he quieted.

"It is not my house," I repeated. "And the people who live in it are not my friends. I see the fey sometimes—the honor guard to the princess?"

He nodded. It was a strange fact that my twin's best friend had married a fey prince, and was thus a princess, but we had both grown used to it. What I had not grown used to was her bodyguards. Her father-in-law, the fey king Caedmon, had supplied them, and they did not like me.

"They like you," Ray protested.

"They like Dory," I corrected. "Not at first, but I think they have changed their minds. Yet they watch her, nonetheless, or rather, they watch *for* me. To see if the monster is going to emerge."

"You are not a monster."

"No, but I am an unknown, with power they cannot always counter, and thus a threat. I do not blame them; it is their job. But the fact remains, they are not my friends."

"*I'm* your friend."

I rolled my head over to look at him. "I would like to think so. But if so, you will be the first in a very long time."

I heard childish laughter, from long ago, and it was so real that I started slightly. I remembered too much, and too well; it was both a blessing and a curse. I wondered which this was, as faces appeared in my mental eye that I had not thought about in years, but who had lived on the same street in Venice with me when I was a girl.

There was pudgy Luysio, who used to distract the candy

vendors, so that I could steal a morsel for us both; here was pretty Gerita, with her flashing dark eyes and bouncing curls, who was such a good dancer that people would pay to watch her; over there was Rigi with his wooden sword, who had learned how to fight from a great uncle and then taught the whole street; here was tiny blonde Coletta, who liked to feed the birds . . .

"Whoa, who are they?" Ray asked, because he could see them, too. I could have closed my mind to him, but I didn't. I did the opposite, because I wanted him to understand.

And, suddenly, we were back there, my memory perfectly recreating the scene: red bricks and crumbling stucco buildings bordering dusty streets with narrow walkways, because you had to make room for the canals; pigeons nesting in ancient statue's crowns, dripping droppings down the proud features of some Very Important Person who nobody remembered the name of anymore; heat shimmering off of the marble facades of the wealthy, the shiny black paint on the gondolas, and the awed, sweaty faces of the tourists, and darkening the clothes of the beggars with lame legs who got up and walked home at the end of the day.

"Shit!" Ray said, gazing around.

I supposed this wasn't what he'd meant by images.

"No, it's just—I just—wow," he said, and I smiled.

Venice was indeed overwhelming. There were the scents: spices and dirt, unwashed bodies and exotic perfumes, but most of all the ever-present smell of the sea and the things that came from it, the latter of which the city's fleet of fishing boats brought back every day to sizzle in peddler's carts and drive the street dogs wild. There were the people, from literally every corner of the Earth: glittering ladies tottering about on platform shoes, their attendants following them like a flock of twittering birds; harried men, grasping at their hips for swords they weren't allowed to wear here; foreign merchants with their robes and turbans and troops of slaves; dirty, olive-skinned children running underfoot in droves and pickpocketing you if you weren't careful. And, finally, there were the colors: a city of white sails and blue-green water and black smoke from the kilns at Murano, and huge skies in a whole palette of shades, and towering mountains of clouds that painters came from all over Europe to set down for posterity, but that we saw every day.

"Wow," Ray said again, sounding awed.

"You were never here?" I asked.

"No, and I kinda think I missed out."

I smiled, glad to be able to show him this.

"What is this, exactly?" he asked.

"We are on the way to one of the *battagliola*, one of the street battles fought with sticks," I informed him. "There were few chivalric tournaments in Venice, there being little room for the horses, so street fights took their place. Even better, you did not have to be a knight or some wealthy man's son to take part. There was no armor to buy, just wooden weapons and leather shields, which almost anyone could afford. Whole neighborhoods used to join in, or all the members of a single guild. It was like a sport, you see?"

Ray nodded, perhaps because he *was* seeing it, through my eyes.

"We found a spot with a good view," I continued, taking him to where I'd been that day, high above the teeming street.

We suddenly reappeared on a rooftop—perhaps a little too close to the edge. He abruptly stepped back. "Hey! A little warning next time!"

"Sorry." I grinned at him, and he shook his head.

"Everybody in this damn family is crazy," he muttered, but he did return to the edge after a moment, to gaze downward.

"There are so many people," he said, sounding surprised. "There's gotta be half the city down there!"

"Not quite. But some of the bigger fights could draw thousands, sometimes tens of thousands. It was free entertainment."

"But with so many fighting at once, it looks like a battle down there!"

"Most of those are onlookers," I said, amused, because the battle hadn't even started yet. "They were merely jostling for a good spot."

I peered down alongside him for a while, at people crowding the streets and balconies, at hawkers selling sweet fritters and sausages and veal liver fried in olive oil, at old ladies clutching handkerchiefs, ready to wave them furiously at their favorites, and at men holding rotten vegetables and rooftiles, with which to pelt the cowardly.

"You did have a good spot," Ray said, watching Coletta come up alongside us, to toss scraps to the pigeons. It caused a mini battle in the skies, with the faster birds catching her offerings mid-air, swooping and diving at fantastic speeds, and making her laugh delightedly.

Then the main event began, while the birds still cawed and circled overhead. The teams were from different neighborhoods: ours, who were mostly fishermen, and one from close by the Arsenal shipyard, who were mostly shipwrights. There were only fifty or sixty combatants per group, unlike the hundreds who sometimes participated in later centuries. But their taunting cries filled the air nonetheless, stirring up the crowd, who were already rowdy enough.

"The locals are missing out," Ray said.

"How so?"

"Everybody's getting buffeted around down there, and the fight hasn't even started. I bet it gets worse later."

"Frequently," I agreed.

"Well, if it had been me, I'da set up a stall selling wooden shields with the different faction's symbols on 'em. Protect yourself on the day and keep them as a souvenir for later." He shook his head. "These people got no idea how to merchandize."

I grinned. "They became better at it in later years. They

started holding the battles on bridges, allowing spectators to watch from their gondolas, which was marginally safer."

"Marginally?"

"People did tend to get tossed off the bridges."

Ray laughed. "Godddamn!"

"The gondolas were so closely packed that vendors could walk from boat to boat, hawking their wares. But we always watched from the top of a local church."

"Wasn't that considered sacrilegious?"

"Of course." I smiled. "That's why no one else was up here."

I turned around to show him our little group. We'd spread out a blanket on the flat roof of the church to hold our feast. Zilio's father was a fisherman so he'd provided the spiced anchovies; Gerita and her little sister Maria had brought cheese stuffed eggs; Rigi had not been there, having come down with the pox, but his brother Gallo had brought a custard tart. Luysio and I had arrived last, having stolen some honey spiced walnuts from a vendor. We'd shown up breathless and pink cheeked, just before the fighting started.

There was a shout on the street, and we turned back to the fight, with Ray batting at long dead pigeons in order to see better, and me laughing when it didn't work.

The captains gave the command and the two sides rushed together, each group running from a different end of the street, waving canes and cudgels and knocking over any observers who got in the way.

"Shit!" Ray yelled, as the two groups came together, with a clash of arms and a roar of approval from the crowd. An all-out melee immediately resulted.

The weapons being used were wood, but they still struck a good blow, and so did fists and feet and sheer momentum. One man dual wielded a couple of pointed canes, clearing a space all around him; another had a shield that he was using less for protection and more as a cudgel to batter his enemies; yet another lost his shield, but stole a cloak from a bystander to wrap around his arm instead. That gave him some protection, but also inadvertently brought another foe into the fight when the furious bystander waded in to the fray, determined to retrieve his outerwear.

Eyes were blackened, faces were bloodied, and tender areas received rough treatment. There weren't a lot of rules to the fracas, and bystanders were not above tripping or even punching members of the opposing team, to help out their favorites. It was a crazy, sweaty, chaotic good time, unlike anything I'd seen in the modern world.

"They fought for the honor of their neighborhoods," I told Ray, as he laughed at a group who staggered off the main road and into a peddler, who saved his great dish of sardines in saor, a popular sweet and sour sauce, by holding it high above his head. "But they or their families often also had bets on the outcome."

"So bragging rights and money, same as today," he said, grinning.

I nodded, and we watched the fight for a while, because I found that I didn't want to leave. I could feel that long-ago sun baking into my skin and see it sparkling on the distant water, could hear my friends' laughter from behind us, could smell the food and the salt and the sweat and the blood. It had been a savage time, but I had loved it here, in this strange city in the sea.

I had never thought to feel at home again, after father took me from the dense forests of Wallachia, the only world I'd ever known. But I had been wrong. I had grown attached to our little sagging house on stilts, where you could sit in the open back door off the kitchen and dabble your toes in the surf. Had enjoyed getting up early to help Horatio, our old servant, fix breakfast, and to greet my father when he came home from a long night of gambling, having tricked the humans into providing our bread. Had loved . . .

Him.

Ray yelled and slapped the edge of the roofline excitedly,

probably because the blue shirts of the fishermen had regrouped and were charging again, their numbers reduced but their courage undaunted. The black shirted Arsenal cluster had been distracted, fighting with some local boys who had decided to throw rocks. They turned just in time to see a wall of blue descending onto them.

But I was no longer paying much attention, letting the memory play out for Ray while I toyed with another. It wasn't one I usually allowed myself to see. There was no point anymore.

But something about today was different, as if there was magic in the air. Or perhaps seeing Venice once more, another memory I rarely looked at, alive and bright with Ray's shared joy, had triggered it. Either way, I was suddenly back there again, seeing my father coming home on a winter's night, knocking snow off his great cloak.

I knew immediately that he'd had success at the tables.

It was in his step, light and joyful; in the way he picked me up and spun me around, as if I weighed nothing; in the smile on his face and the set of his shoulders, straight and unbowed, as if, for once, he had been able to lay down his burdens.

He had so many of them, that it was a rare sight. Many vampires who came to Venice, seeking the minimal security it offered to the masterless, could not even manage to provide for themselves. They fell prey to dark mages, to charlatans, to unscrupulous masters who preyed on the weak and helpless, dangling the idea of a family in front of their noses to get them to do all manner of illegal deeds, while never intending to pay up.

They found those poor unfortunates all the time, or what was left of them: bleached bones on the beaches, the only remains of so-called immortals, who had never even made it past a normal human life span. They could not handle the stress of facing the world alone, but Mircea had had to do that as well as to provide for two dependents: me, and his old tutor and friend Horatiu, who was aging and no longer able to earn his bread.

If Mircea didn't care for us, no one would, and the knowledge gnawed at him.

Yet it had been nowhere that night.

"Look what I brought you," he said, sitting down on a stool by the fire, and pulling me into his lap.

The firelight was kind to the rich, mahogany of his hair and to the dark eyes that were so much like mine. It was less so to the strained face, the features as handsome as always, but drawn and tired looking as well. Vampires were often seen as superhuman and invincible, but Mircea was a very new vampire with no family to draw on. And these nightly forays, into a dangerous city filled with vastly stronger predators than he, were draining.

But his expression was nonetheless happy and even proud. He brought something out from under his cloak, and for a moment, I was afraid. Because it was a gift, a large, square box done up in brown paper with a string knotted into a bow on top.

I sat with it in my hands for a moment, steeling myself, because Horatiu had gotten me a gift that day, as well. My birthday was coming up soon, only nobody really knew when, for there was no one to ask. But father had assigned me a day to celebrate, we'd had better food than usual for the last week, and Horatiu had surprised me this morning with . . . a doll.

It had been exquisitely made; I had seen that at once. The body was carved out of bone and had articulated joints, moving almost like a real person. The hair was carved, too, but painted a glossy black, and the eyes were a deep, rich brown. It had carved shoes on its feet and a pretty, real cloth dress made out of a scrap of blue fabric. There was even a miniature necklace of tiny seed pearls around its long, aristocratic neck.

I knew immediately that Horatiu had not bought it. Such things would have been far outside our means, no matter how much he had scrimped from the household budget. He had made it, perhaps getting a little help with the finer features from Mircea or the woodcarver down the street, as his old eyes were failing.

But he had made it, nonetheless, for me, and I could not even imagine all the long hours that must have gone into it. I had seen him hiding something whenever I rose early or came home unexpectedly from play. I hadn't thought much about it, but now I knew: all his spare time, for months and months, had gone into this.

I'd had no choice but to love it.

And I had, because I loved him, but I did not want a doll. They were the pretty playthings of the wealthy, for girls who did not have a whole city to explore. I did not want to sit inside and play with a doll when there were so many more interesting things to do. But I would; I knew that as soon as I saw Horatiu's proud and happy face. He was so pleased that he'd managed to get me something that belonged to a girl of my station, as he insisted on calling it, despite the fact that none of us had a station anymore.

We were exiles from a throne I'd never known, and which my father had never wanted. It was now occupied by someone else, who I wasn't sure as it changed often, but not us. And it would never be us again.

But Horatiu saw me as a little princess, and now his princess had a doll. I had hugged his neck and told him how much it meant to me. That, at least, had not been a lie. But I had been dismayed to think that I was to be stuck inside with it, while my friends stole candy and played pranks and watched ships come in at the docks, carrying untold wonders from faraway lands.

And now I had two dolls.

I smiled anyway and unwrapped my gift, and then just sat there for the longest time, staring.

It was not a doll.

"Do you like it?" Mircea asked, his face growing concerned. Probably because I had immediately thanked Horatiu this morning, whereas now, I couldn't seem to speak.

It was a small copy of Mircea's own artist's box, the one he used to paint the pictures that supplemented our income. It had a plain wooden cover concealing wonder after wonder. There was a sheaf of finely made brushes, half vair hair, from the squirrels whose bluish gray fur often lined gowns in winter, and half pig bristle; a wooden palette fitted for a small hand, and complete with a flask of linseed oil, already reduced in the sun and perfect for mixing paints; a bunch of willow twigs made into charcoal for sketching; some costly rag paper, which could also be used for sketching or could be coated in linseed oil and made semi-transparent, for tracing.

But as astonishing as all of those were, they paled in comparison with the pigments, so wonderful and so many! There were the two mainstays of lead white and lamp black, the latter made from the soot collected from oil lamps. There were the arsenic-derived hues of orpiment and realgar, the first of which was a bright, lemon yellow, and the second a vivid orange, and which mixed together made a color reminiscent of gold. There were the clays: the beautiful reddish-brown of sienna, the softer, yellowish brown of umber, and the rich, dark brown of burnt umber. There were the blues: the deep sapphire of indigo, the sparkling, blue-green of azurite, and the purplish red of madder root. Even the rich crimson of vermilion had been included, and the costly but brilliant green of malachite.

But they weren't in solid form, as I'd expected. Instead, finely ground powders resided in small, square wooden cells that took up fully half of the larger box. I had never seen anything like it.

"I ground them for you," Mircea explained. "Some of the pigments can be dangerous. This way, you don't have to touch them."

"No," I whispered.

"And no licking the end of your brush. We've talked about that."

"No," I promised. It was all I could seem to say.

I had wanted to paint for as long as I could remember, and had watched him doing so longingly. But the most he would let me do was to sketch with charcoal on some of the cheap brown wrapping paper he brought home, the kind that sweets were sold in. He had said that I could paint when I was older, but I had thought to use a few of his scraps, not . . . not anything like this.

"Do you like it?" Mircea asked, when I continued to sit there silently.

I found that I still couldn't say anything. I just looked up at him mutely. But when Horatiu, who had come in at some point, tried to take the paint box, my hands refused to let it go.

"I think she likes it," the old man said, and ruffled my hair.

"Dorina. Dorina."

I blinked and the second memory faded, leaving me with just the first. Which I realized had stopped, like a movie that had run to its end. It had stalled around Ray, with Colette's birds paused in the air above his head, reaching for the last scraps of bread; with the door to the bell tower opening behind him, and an angry priest halfway out, his black cassock looking hot and uncomfortable in the summer sun; and with a bunch of guilty appearing kids looking up, halfway through their feast.

"I'm getting tired," I explained. "It becomes harder to project."

"Then don't," Ray said. "That was incredible. I've seen stuff in other people's heads before, but nothing like that."

I nodded absently, still half lost in memory. "There wasn't much more. The priest came to run us off. I think he had promised the view to some of his chief donors."

"Figures," Ray said cynically. "Everything's sacrilegious 'till it involves moolah. By the way, who won? I got my money on the fishermen."

"You would lose. The shipwrights won. I had a bet with Luysio. He owed me pistachios and sweetened rice cakes . . ."

"Did he ever pay up?" Ray asked, leaning over the roof for a final view of the fight, which he didn't get because child-me had turned to look at the priest.

"No."

"Welcher," he said, smiling.

I shook my head. "It wasn't his fault. I had a fit that night, my third in a month. And father decided it was enough."

"Enough?"

"He separated Dory and me, and after that, she was in control." I looked around, feeling strangely lost suddenly. "This was my last memory as . . . me."

CHAPTER TWENTY-TWO

Dorina, Faerie

The sun-drenched scene of old Venice faded, to show me Ray's face splashed by firelight. He looked confused, as people often did when surfacing from another's mind, but also troubled. He didn't look like he knew what to say, which was fair, I supposed.

Neither did I.

"Was it . . . painful?" he finally asked.

I shook my head. "Not the separation, no. But I did not understand what had happened. It felt like being in a prison cell, a dark, echoing space from which I could not escape. I thought I had gone mad for the longest time. And when I finally understood—"

"Wait. It took *years*?" He sounded appalled, having seen the truth in my mind.

"It . . . came in pieces, over time. I began to see things, slowly, here and there. I was conscious when Dory was not, but I did not know that at first—"

Ray frowned. "How could you not know you were conscious?"

I blinked at him. "Her eyes were closed."

He swore and took a drink.

He had apparently decided that there were better uses for the wine than the one I had found, and I agreed. He handed me the canteen and I had a small sip. Fey wine smelled like herbs and burned like flame, but I found that I did not mind so much tonight.

"But during the in between times, when the mind is neither asleep nor awake, I began to get glimpses," I explained. "Enough to understand that I was somehow still moving about, was living in the same house, in the same room. There were sketches on the walls that came and went, which I did not recognize, but that looked like my work. And, eventually, a fine oil painting of a dog chewing up his master's slipper. I recognized the brushstrokes, yet I had not done them . . ."

"Jesus."

I nodded, remembering the surreal feeling of being an exile in my own body. "I slowly began to understand that my power grew at night. When the body I no longer controlled slept, I would awaken, although for a long time, I didn't understand that I could go anywhere. I looked at things from under her lashes for weeks, perhaps months, before I learned that I could move about spiritually."

"How'd you find out?"

"By accident. Horatiu came to rouse Dory one morning and startled me. I sat up but my body did not. Before I could figure out what had happened, Dory was awake and I lost consciousness. But the next night—"

"Freedom," Ray guessed, his expression lightening.

"Not . . . quite."

I gazed out at the water. The fire was sending orange ripples over the dark waves and gilding the rocks. It looked the way the Grand Canal had the next evening, when I'd gone exploring in my spirit form. I had been left shaking and amazed at the sights of handsome people laughing from gondolas, light splashing out of the fronts of palazzos, torches blowing in the wind. It had been the most beautiful thing I'd ever seen, and the most confusing.

It was only when I tried to speak to someone that I

realized: they couldn't see me. I didn't know why that had so surprised me; I had flown over the city like a great black bird, seeing it from a completely new angle. Had I really thought that a creature who could do that would be visible? Or that people would react well to it if it was?

My only excuse was that I didn't think. I had been so alone for so long that I was giddy with all the sights and sounds, the smells and colors . . . I felt almost drunk on them. Until I realized: I could look, but nothing more. I couldn't interact with anyone.

No one heard me when I spoke or saw me when I passed by. It was like being a ghost, yet I hadn't died! I went back home and there I was, asleep in my bed. I was perfectly fine—

"Except you weren't," Ray said, following the conversation I was having in my head.

"Except I wasn't." I hesitated, not sure that I wanted to share this next part, but nothing would make sense without it. "The following night, I tried to talk to Mircea."

"Not that night? Because I'da wanted some goddamned answers!"

I shook my head. "Free flight—what I do outside of a body —cannot be sustained for long. It drains me terribly, to the point that I almost did not make it back to the house. I was panicked and exhausted, and could not think properly when I returned. But later . . . I thought he would help."

"Let me guess," Ray said cynically, and took the canteen.

"He did not hear me, either, when I spoke, but we share mental gifts. I thought I would talk to him that way, mind to mind, but . . . it did not go well."

"How bad is not well?"

I didn't answer.

I had entered father's mind, expecting a reaction, but . . . not the one I received. He had thrown me out, as viciously as if I was a demon he was trying to exorcise. And when I stubbornly returned, he tore up the front room of the house, yelling and throwing things, and waking everyone—

including Dory.

That had put me back to sleep, and the next night, I hadn't dared to try again. But I had gone exploring. And had slowly discovered through trial and error what I could do.

Not everyone reacted like Mircea. I learned that the vampires often did, seeing me as an invading spirit, but the humans scarcely seemed to notice my presence at all. I found that I could suggest things to them, and they often took my suggestions. I could go anywhere . . .

Just not as myself.

But being inside a body, any body, renewed my strength. And allowed me to move about the city once again, as I had once done. Although only when the person I was starting to think of as a separate person from me, as a sister, slept.

Ray drank fey wine and scowled. "Okay, so, what you're telling me is that your father didn't explain anything to you before the separation? He didn't tell you what he was trying to do or ask you what you thought or *anything*?"

I shook my head. "I was asleep and then I was alone."

"Motherfucker!"

"He was afraid that I would fight him, if he gave me any warning. I wasn't as strong then, but neither was he. And it was an experiment, a last-ditch effort to spare his daughter's life—"

"His *daughters'*. He has two daughters," Ray said angrily.

"He does not see it that way." My mind went to another memory, a far more recent one, before I could stop it.

"What? He wanted to lock you away *again*?"

I shifted uncomfortably. I had not intended to show him that. "He did not plan for the barrier he put in our mind to fall," I said awkwardly. "He always refused to remove it, afraid that I would take over completely and that he would lose Dory. She is all he has left of our mother—"

"She is not all he has left! He has *you*!"

I did not answer immediately, wondering how to explain my and Dory's childhood, the bright, sunny days and the screaming, terror-filled nights. The nights were when the fits had come that had threatened to tear our mind apart, and when Mircea had fought battles with me for his daughter's sanity, for her very life. I did not have the words.

Just as I did not have them to explain what came after.

"Ten of the sardele," *Mircea said, surveying the afternoon's catch. "The same of the* moeche. And . . ."

He paused and I saw him eye the mackerel, their black and steel blue stripes gleaming in the last rays of the afternoon sun. Their basket took pride of place on the slanted table top that showed off the fishmonger's wares. More baskets sat around, although many were empty. It was nearing the end of day.

He decided against the mackerel. "Do you have any mussels?"

"No, but some nice eels came in today." The rotund little stall owner gestured at another table with an arm full of cheap bangles. "Make a fine bisato su l'are."

Mircea shook his head. He was not fond of eels. I had known that, and had suggested them deliberately, trying to buy time.

It wasn't helping.

He walked to another table, scrutinizing the available offerings. He was dressed in a conservative, dark blue brocade that set off his shoulder length, dark brown hair and piercing dark eyes. It was understated, yet almost screamed quality, as did the sapphire signet ring set in heavy gold on his right hand. Anywhere else in the world, he would have looked a little odd perusing a table full of fish.

But this was Venice, where the men of the house typically did the shopping, including for groceries. Even wealthy men, including senators, could be seen in the marketplace, trailed by servants who were there only as human pack animals, to take the foodstuffs selected by their masters back home. Trade was the heartbeat of the city, and it could not be left in servants' hands— or in women's. Only men, it was thought, could judge quality.

Of course, Mircea flouted conventions regularly, but he had learned to enjoy picking out his own dinner when he was poorer, and often still did so. And Dory had taken a late afternoon nap, knowing that we were having guests tonight, and that she might be up late. I had been waiting for just such a chance for a very long time.

And yet, here I was, ruining it!

"Canocie?" *he asked, talking about the sweet little shrimp that went so well in so many dishes.*

"What you see is what we have . . . Mircea."

Father's head came up at that, startled. He had come here before, but there was no reason for the vendor to know his name. They had spoken about fish, nothing more.

I waited patiently as his eyes went over the body I was using.

She was a sweet old woman, with sixteen grandchildren, a half gray topknot perched precariously on her head, and a pleasant, wrinkled face. She wore a black shawl around her shoulders, knitted by one of her many granddaughters, far too much cheap jewelry, and a pair of red Moroccan slippers. She was a puzzle, and I saw Mircea's brow knit.

"The octopus, then. Two of the larger ones—with the ink, grasie."

I packaged up his fish.

He handed me the coins, and I slipped them into a pocket in the old woman's dress. I gave him his purchase, but held onto it until he looked up, and our eyes met. "I need to talk to you."

"About?" *It was courteous. He still didn't understand.*

"About . . ." *I stopped, all of my carefully prepared speeches leaving my mind, all at once.* "About Dory," *I blurted out.* "I never meant—I wasn't trying to hurt her. I didn't know—"

I stopped again, but this time, it was because he did understand. He'd always been quick, and a second later the package was gone and so was he. I stared at the empty spot where he'd been, then threw my mind outward, leaving the old woman behind, a little befuddled, but unharmed. And took flight.

I spotted him near the water's edge, about to take a gondola. I waited until they had pushed off, then settled onto the gondolier. He was distracted; he had problems with his woman, who he suspected of cheating. It was easy to redirect his thoughts while I borrowed his tongue for a time.

"Mircea—"

"Is this what you do now?" he demanded furiously, looking up from his seat. "Take over the lives of others—"

"You left me none of my own! Why do you not release me?"

"You do this and you ask why?"

"I'm not dangerous—"

"You're the most dangerous creature I know!"

And with that, he was gone again, leaping to the embankment before I could stop him, not that I knew how. I only knew how to follow, so I did, flying up into the sky, searching the crowds while a pink and orange sunset made the whole city blush. It was busy; it was always busy. But I caught up with him again nonetheless, in a narrow street notorious for its prostitutes.

Here it was already as dark as night, with the overhanging upper floors of the houses forming a long, dim corridor. Only the rectangular doorways of the brothels provided any light at all, throwing elongated yellow squares over the cobblestones. A matrone sat on a stool beside one of them, calling out to passersby, telling them that her girls were the best: young, clean, and enthusiastic. She did not call to Mircea, nor see him. He was a shadow, having gone dim to try to elude me.

I did not know why. Did he think I didn't know about the fine house he had now, in a fashionable part of town? I lived there! But I wanted to do this away from prying ears, so that he could speak freely. Why would he not talk to me?

The girl I chose looked young, but she was not clean and definitely not enthusiastic. Pale, dyed blonde tresses fell in greasy clumps around her face, and pox scars marred one side of her face. But she was different from the others on this street, and when her hands latched onto him and pulled him out of shadow, he found her grip to be like steel.

"You see?" he demanded, glaring at me. "You can take a vampire. How long can you hold her? What can you make her do?"

"Nothing, I just want to talk," I said, and smelled the stale blood on her breath that had him rearing back, looking revolted.

She needed to feed. She had come here to do so easily and quickly. But her hunger left her vulnerable, and I had taken her.

But Mircea was a master now, and no longer caught off guard. He threw us against the brick wall and left, his power sparking off the walls, as if a thunderstorm had been trapped inside. I let him go.

Hours later, I tried again. But this time, it was at his stylish home. Dory's rooms were down the hall, a beautifully appointed suite suitable for a wealthy young lady. Our uncle Radu lived on the floor below, in a bright yellow apartment that hurt the eyes. But Mircea's own chambers were here, a quiet oasis away from the hustle and bustle of a sleepless city, full of dark woods, plush green fabrics, and fine oil paintings, many of which were his own.

He was sitting by the window, a glass of red wine in his hand. I could only identify it by the smell, as I could barely see. I had acquired another body, but this time, it wasn't stolen. This time, I had been invited in.

"I know it's you," Mircea said, when I approached. He slurred his words slightly, as if drunk. I knew he couldn't be, but his eyes were bleary when he turned them up to me. "What do you want?"

"To understand."

I lowered Horatiu's body, vampire now, but badly made, into a chair. Mircea had almost waited too long to perform the Change, and the old man would never be right. Horatiu had waffled back and forth, one day resolute, the next unsure again, and only made the commitment on his death bed. I was surprised that the transformation had taken at all.

Mircea swallowed the rest of the contents of his glass and let it fall to the floor. It was heavy; it did not break. Horatiu picked it up of his own volition, and put it on a table, quietly judging his old charge as he did so.

Mircea laughed, suddenly. "You have better things to judge me for, old man."

"As does she."

Horatiu had let me borrow his body; he had never said he was going to be quiet.

"I am not a monster," I said, and Mircea's head came up.

"Then what are you?"

"A dhampir, like Dory—"

"You are nothing like her!"

"I am exactly *like her. We are the same person; you know that better than anyone—"*

"No!" And, suddenly, he was in my face.

For a long moment, he searched the rheumy old eyes. I only had Horatiu's sight to work with, but Mircea was so close that I could clearly make out the handsome features. The ones that suddenly looked like they smelled something bad.

"I've met dhampirs," he told me harshly. "And spoken to others who met more, as I searched for a way to save her. They go mad, I was told. Their human and vampire natures rip themselves apart, I was told.

"I was never told about you."

I stared at him, uncomprehending. It did not last long. I had asked for the truth, and I was getting it, but every word felt like a heart blow.

"I do not know what you are, but you are not dhampir. Dory is, and she has and will suffer for it, all her life. But you—I fought you. I was an adult and a vampire, already rising in power, yet I barely overcame you. You almost killed me, as well as her. You invaded my mind, as easily as you do that of all your puppets. You used advanced mental combat techniques against me, and you supposedly just a child. A child!"

He laughed, and slumped back into his seat.

"No child of mine."

CHAPTER TWENTY-THREE

Dorina, Faerie

"Fuck," Ray whispered, because I supposed he had seen.

I didn't say anything. The golden glow that the wine had given me was gone, and instead I felt something like I had that night: cold, frozen, disbelieving. Had I been in my body during that conversation, I might have fainted. As it was, I had just sat there, dizzy and blank, while Horatiu berated his old charge.

"As he damned well should have!" I looked up to see Ray incandescent. "What the *hell*?"

"Mircea saw—sees—me as a threat," I said. "A demon or worse—"

"*Why?*"

I waved a helpless hand. "Dory was growing, as all children do, but that tortured me. It is why dhampirs go mad. Vampires are supposed to be immutable, always the same. But she was human and ever changing, ripping my mind apart whenever a growth spurt hit."

"Damn."

"I lashed out in pain, in terror, not understanding what was happening. I wanted to be in charge, in order to stop the changes, to end the suffering. But had I succeeded, I would have killed us both, as children cannot simply stop growing

—"

"You were a child, too! You didn't understand!"

"And neither did Mircea. He only understood that I was threatening his daughter, and that I must be contained."

"*You* were his daughter," Ray repeated stubbornly.

"No."

I left Horatiu, still arguing. I couldn't listen anymore. I fled down the hallway to Dory's rooms, stunned, confused, and heartbroken.

And then I stopped and stared about, wondering why I'd come. I looked with blank eyes at the prettily appointed rooms, blue and white and soft gold. Serene, like a Venetian morning.

Like her, when I was gone.

She was asleep, her long, dark hair spreading over a pillow and dropping off the side of the bed. It flowed below her waist whenever she stood, a smooth, silky fall that her maid would insist on doing up in one of the intricate styles that Venetian ladies loved and Dory hated whenever we had company. There were still a few small braids in place, weaving through the unbound mass, ones she'd been too impatient to undo before bed.

I sat on the edge of the coverlet, my spirit form not even denting the fabric, but boiling up blackly around the posts. It looked like smoke. It looked like the demon spirit Mircea thought me to be. I sat there for a moment, staring at it, finding it hard to think.

Was he right? Was there something . . . wrong . . . with me? I did not know. Unlike him, I had never met another dhampir. Except for Dory . . .

I had always assumed that her abilities were limited because of her human nature. That she carried more of our mother's blood and me more of our father's. But Mircea was right about one thing: even he could not do some of the things that I could.

What was I?

I didn't know, and there was no one to ask. No one who knew anything about dhampirs, or . . . whatever I was. I wanted to do something, but . . . there was nothing to be done. Nothing at all.

My eyes finally focused elsewhere, on the dress Dory had worn tonight. A paler blue than Mircea's brocade, it fell over a nearby chair like water. The dinner party that had necessitated the postponement of my plans had required formal dress, although it was only a small gathering of friends—humans, of course.

Mircea was hiding his secret from the vampire community, lest his dhampir daughter be used against him. He had enemies, as all masters did. Kidnapping her could put pressure on him; killing her would hurt him. There were those who would like to do both.

Thus, discretion was needed, despite the fact that he had received permission for her to grow up. Dhampirs were supposed to be killed on sight, but he had traded another life for hers. A woman had tried to usurp the consul's position, and failed, thanks to him. That and helping his superior to obtain the consulship in the first place had made him a rising star in the vampire world.

But even stars had to obey the law.

And time was running out.

I rose and went to the window, needing to move. I also needed to return to our body; I was draining myself this way. But I was reluctant.

It wasn't my body.

It wasn't my life.

I looked for my reflection in the window, but of course, it wasn't there. I stared out at the empty street, feeling unreal, imaginary. Like the ghost that I sometimes wondered if I was turning into.

Perhaps I should. I could fly into the sky and just keep going, until my power gave out and my essence dissipated on the wind. That might be better for everyone, in the end.

Only it wouldn't be. Because the consul's forbearance was at an end. Mircea had kept doing her favors, working tirelessly to shore up her government, and in return, had obtained extension

KAREN CHANCE

after extension on the initial pardon. But she had informed him last month that there would be no more. Dory was an adult now, and a danger to the vampire community. At the end of this year, he had to kill her or release her—which the consul assumed would amount to the same thing.

It was probably why he had exploded on me the way that he had. Even through the pain, I could see that. He had formulated a plan to keep her safe, to erase her memories and to plant in her mind—and thus in the minds of any vampires who read her thoughts—the idea that the two of them had long been estranged. That he didn't care about her, that she was nothing more than a mild embarrassment, and that killing her would avail them nothing.

But while that might keep his enemies off her back, plenty of dhampirs died who were not well connected. And the more people he had watching her, trying to protect her, the more likely he was to lead his enemies straight to her. Or to alert the consul that he was defying her orders, and have the senate itself put a bounty on her head.

Mircea was in agony, not knowing what to do, and I had just made it worse.

I moved back to the bed.

I put a hand out to touch the shining fall of hair. She stirred slightly, as if she had felt me. Perhaps she had.

Mircea had blocked us from each other, made it impossible for us to communicate, even though we shared a mind. I could have circumvented that, had I wished. Could have taken another body to speak with her, could have written her a note . . .

And say what? I thought angrily. Draw her into my world, and cause her even more pain? This wasn't her fault, any more than it was mine. But she would blame herself, I knew she would. There was no solution to our problem, and I was tired of bringing her only sorrow.

I slipped back inside our skin, and felt her shiver a little at the sensation. She absently pulled up the coverlet, as if that was the cause. And then, still half asleep, she paused, looking at her

258

reflection in the window glass.

But, this time, it was my face that looked back.

We stared at each other for a long time. She looked like a child still, with pink cheeks, tumbled hair and sleep filled eyes. His child, with the same high cheekbones, finely arched brows and expressive mouth. They were so alike . . .

I did not know what she was thinking, but I flashed to an image of Mircea as he had been when he entered our mind that last time: a lone warrior determined to battle a monster for his daughter's life. He had been grim and resolute, but fearful, too. Fearful of me.

But not for himself. He had been afraid that he would fail Dory, as he had failed our mother. He had not known what I was, but he would face me, nonetheless, even if it meant his life, because she had no one else.

Only he was wrong, I decided.

She had me.

Ray made a slight sound, and brought my thoughts back to the present. Venice faded away and I was glad to see it go. I wanted no more of it tonight.

"You stayed alive to save her?" Ray asked, as if unsure of what he'd seen. Or perhaps of whether it was all right to ask.

I nodded in reply to both. "It gave me something to live for, to fight for. I stayed alive to save her, but in giving me a purpose, she also saved me. I do not think I would have made it, otherwise."

"But . . . how did you always know when she was in trouble? If you two were on opposite schedules—"

I took a drink from the fast-depleting canteen. "I discovered that I could take over when Dory was frightened or overwhelmed or excessively tired. Pain, panic and exhaustion shut down her brain enough that I could slip through the cracks, and take over."

"And throw down."

"Yes." I put a hand to my head. This had been cathartic,

but more overwhelming than I had expected. I had never thought that talking could be as tiring as fighting, but it appeared so.

Ray pulled the blanket around me, and tucked it in. I looked at him strangely. He looked back, a little embarrassed, but defiant.

"Everybody needs taking care of, once in a while."

I did not know what to say to that, so I said nothing at all.

"And now that you've succeeded?" he asked, sitting back again. "Now that Dory is not only safe but a bigshot in the vampire world? What now?"

"I don't know."

"You don't know?" He looked like that hadn't made sense, although it was rather the point of all this.

"You asked me what I wanted," I reminded him. "I told you the truth: I don't know. I've lived for one thing and one thing only for centuries, and now . . ."

I let it trail off.

I didn't have any answers for him, or for myself. I wasn't even sure I knew the right questions. I had been alone for so long, that I didn't know where to start to build a life, or how or even if I should. What if Mircea had been right, and I was some kind of monster? He was a gifted mentalist. What had he seen, exactly, that had frightened him so?

And even if he was wrong, and I was merely a dhampir and Dory's other half, did it matter? After so long, was I not broken beyond repair? Could I ever really hope to—

"You're not broken! And Mircea can go fuck himself."

I had started to take another drink, but Ray's voice was hard enough to have me lower the canteen instead, and look at him in surprise. Nobody talked about father that way. "You sound angry."

"And you're not? You ought to be furious with him!"

"I was, for a while."

"Well, why the hell did you stop?"

Horatiu was banging pots around the kitchen, loudly enough to be heard throughout the house. They crashed like cymbals in my ears, making me wince. The kitchens were often on the upper floors in Venice, in case of floods, and a moment later, what sounded like every pot we had was flung down the stairs.

Horatiu was a vampire; he could not disobey his master's wishes.

He could, however, make his feelings known.

Mircea did not comment about the noise as he came back into the house.

He had been giving final instructions to the large group of dark clad men outside. They looked so different from the usual sort one saw in the city, where the men were as fashion conscious as the women, and often outbid them on the finest jewels and most sumptuous materials. I had seen a popinjay of a boatman pass by, just this morning. His varicolored hose had been black and white diamond patterned on one leg and bright red on the other, while his doublet was a brilliant green. He had worn a black hat, but it had been crowned with a scarlet feather.

But these men were different. Their clothing was dark—rough browns, grays and blacks—and cut from coarse, long wearing fabrics. Their faces were weathered, and some of them had beards, something also out of fashion in Venice. But it was their expressions that really gave them away, or would have, had Dory been awake to see the hard, solemn, no-nonsense countenances of the finest mercenaries that money could buy.

But it was early morn, with the sun just beginning to peek over the horizon. She was still asleep, and under a spell to keep her that way. She went to bed last night, the petted, pampered daughter of a wealthy Venetian gentleman. She would wake somewhere, and as someone, far different.

I was still conscious, however, and watchful. Mircea knew, but he did not care. Today, he did not care about much of anything.

He had just come in, but he turned around and went back

out again, having thought of another proviso for the mercenary squad. They were mages, half of them, and strong enough that their magic peppered the air, even from this far away. The other half were vampires, powerful day walkers who had been hired to protect their precious cargo at night, but who could be active in daytime as well, if needed.

I watched father through a window, haranguing the men in tones few would have dared to use with them. Yet they did not flinch, much less object. Perhaps it was because they were being paid a king's ransom for this, but I thought there might have been another reason, at least for some.

They were men who had seen almost everything, yet still there were glimpses, here and there, of compassion on those hardened features. Or maybe that was merely me, projecting what I felt onto them. I looked at Mircea's agitated gestures, his dead white face, and the wildness in his eyes, and I both loved and hated him.

But mostly, I hurt for him.

This was killing him.

He came back in and slammed the door, in another uncharacteristic gesture. And then just stood there for a moment, breathing hard. He didn't need the air, but there were times when emotion took over, making demands that the body didn't require, but that the mind did. His power was also flinging about all over the place, a tendril knocking a vase off a mantle, another sending papers scattering in the office across the hall, like doves taking flight.

Finally, he looked at me.

"You are going to take care of her."

"Yes."

"It is your life, too. If she dies—"

"She won't. All will be well."

"Nothing will be well after today! But she will live. Swear it to me!"

He was suddenly in front of me, gripping my upper arms hard enough that Dory would have bruises the next day. I would *need to come up with a story for those, I thought. Something for the men to tell her—*

Mircea shook me.

I looked up at him solemnly. "I swear it."

He let me go.

The men outside were beginning to shift slightly around the fleet of gondolas bobbing at the quay, there to take us out to the large galley in the harbor. I was already dressed in the plain blue dress and brown cloak I was to use for traveling. By the door, a crossbody bag in sturdy woolen cloth, waxed to keep out the weather, waited with a change of clothing and some money.

Upstairs, the great trunks packed with the finest of linens, with silks and velvets and costly brocades, were closed, unneeded, unused. They would only serve to mark us for attention in our new life. They and the jewel casks and the artists supplies, a whole room full of the latter, with scattered easels and half-finished works, would remain behind.

Horatiu told me, much later, that Mircea burnt it all. That he couldn't bear to look at it. That he had retreated into his chamber afterwards and had not come out for weeks, not feeding, not speaking to anyone. Not even Radu, who Mircea had sent away on an errand yesterday, not wanting anyone around who might interfere, who might talk him out of this.

I had not known that, then, but it is what I would have expected, looking into his face as his hands settled on either side of my temples.

It was time.

I stayed very still; this was a difficult task he had set for himself. Not only to erase a lifetime's worth of memories, but to rebuild new ones in their place. There would be gaps, even large ones. There was no way to avoid that. But dhampirs were said to be mad, and it was hoped that she would blame it on that.

But it would be hard and she would be alone, which was probably why Mircea's hands shook at first against my skin. But then his eyes flashed gold, and the Basarab strength boiled to the surface. It had allowed him to claw his way out of his own grave once; had spurred him to flee his homeland, his wife, and everyone he knew, lest he hurt them; had let him start over in a dangerous new world that he had already started to conquer.

Yet I saw the thought in his mind before he could hide it: what did it matter anymore, when he had done it all for her?

And then there was silence, and a blinding whiteness, and the sensation of falling.

And it was done.

CHAPTER TWENTY-FOUR

Dorina, Faerie

"I'm gonna need another drink," Ray said, and took back the canteen.

I let him have it. I had the impression that I had had enough in any case. My tongue felt numb and the rock underneath me had started to feel oddly floaty, as if it was rising and falling along with the waves.

Yet I felt good, too, and strangely lighter for having finally told someone my story. I had never given Dory most of the details that Ray now knew. I wasn't sure why; perhaps because it seemed like a burden that she shouldn't have to bear. Ray blamed Mircea; Dory had a tendency to blame herself. In reality, it wasn't anyone's fault.

It simply was.

Mircea could have let the dhampir nature rip our minds apart, and we would both be dead now. Or, he could have done what he did, and saved us. It was all he knew how to do; I could not fault him for that. I did fault him for not releasing me later, once Dory and I were both adults and the reason for the fits had passed. But if he really believed me to be a malevolent spirit . . .

Would I have taken that chance, in his place?

I honestly did not know.

There was one thing I would ask him, if I thought there

was any chance of a reply: why had he left the memories with me? He had erased them from her side of the mind, but hadn't touched them on mine. Why?

Had he wanted her to have those sun-drenched days again? Those happy, laughing faces, those friends, those *firsts*? Otherwise, her first glimpse of Venice—gone. Her first birthday celebration—gone. Her first new clothes, her first taste of candy, her first kiss—from a flirtatious boy who had worked in the pigment shop where we bought our colors, when she was fifteen . . .

Could he not bear to erase them all, with no hope of redemption? Did he think that I could protect them? That no one would be able to find them in my mind, as it was no longer the dominant one?

Or had he been afraid to battle me again, after I was older? Long decades had passed since our last confrontation. Was he worried that another clash might undo his previous work, and release me?

Or perhaps, just perhaps, did he think that, one day, there might be a way for Dory and me to be whole again?

"Then why did he try to persuade her to lock you away a second time?" Ray asked, his voice slurring slightly.

I frowned at him. His face was slightly flushed and his eyes were glassy. He looked half asleep, yet he clearly was not.

"How are you able to read me so easily?"

"Maybe 'cause we're both drunk." He turned the bottle over and I watched a couple of droplets splash onto the stone. It appeared that we had consumed the whole thing. I blinked at it in surprise.

"What?" he asked.

"I have never been drunk before."

He cocked his head. "Whaddya think?"

"I think I like it."

"Wait until tomorrow," he said ominously.

He tossed the empty onto our supplies and added the remaining driftwood to the fire, turning the undersides of the stone fingers above us a bright gold with reflected light. It actually became quite warm in our small camp after a time, a little too warm. I pulled off the blanket, yet still was not comfortable.

A moment later, I realized why.

"Perhaps you could help me down to the river?" I asked Ray.

"We're already by the river."

"I meant . . . further off?"

"Why? It's cold away from the fire and—" He stopped. "Oh. Sure."

He scooped me up and carried me to an outcropping of rocks a few dozen yards upstream from our camp, but fairly near to the shoreline. Then he walked off, to give me some privacy, I supposed. The rocks kept me out of the stream, except for my feet and lower legs, which didn't feel it anyway.

And while the wind was cold, the view was worth it.

There *was* a moon, a huge thing, orange as flame, rising up behind the trees. I hadn't seen it as it had been behind us, and now appeared perfectly balanced in the palm of the hand of stone. Our firelight was almost the same color, making it look as if the moon was melting and dripping down through the fingers to puddle below. While behind it, the dark treetops met the thickly, star strewn sky.

Faerie never failed to impress, I thought, just staring for a moment.

Then I did my business, washed off, and waited for Ray to come back.

There was a surprising amount of wildlife for the middle of the night. There were a few birds, brown or gray and vaguely owl-like, swooping about, chasing small animals or darting after fish. They had huge eyes that reflected the moon when the angle was just right, making them flash orange from time to time, like feathered fireflies.

The water was as active as the air. Once in a while, a silver fishtail would emerge to splash the surface before disappearing again. A large turtle slid off of the embankment and into the current, like a slow-moving rock. And a small, green frog with long, red toes jumped into the spray from a nearby perch, evading one of the birds.

But nothing jumped at me.

For the first time, it felt peaceful here, in this strange new world. I realized that I did not have many memories of peace that were not also lonely. Dory needed sleep, so I could not be active for the whole of the night, and when I was awake, there was no one to talk to. Horatiu and I had had chats from time to time, but they made him feel bad. Reminded him of things he did not agree with, but could not change. I had gradually let them fall off over the years, like with so many things . . .

But I did not feel lonely here. I had talked and talked. And Ray had listened, and seemed interested, or at least entertained. It had felt strange, to open up to someone like that, like so much lately. It was exciting, almost dizzily so. I could not remember the last time I had looked at the future and not had any idea what it might hold.

That was why, as frightening as Faerie was, it was thrilling, too. And without Dory to worry about, I could . . . I could do anything. Just anything at all!

Well, anything that my body would allow. But even worry over my legs did not weigh me down that much. For the first time in memory, I felt free.

I almost did not want to sleep for the joy of it.

The wind picked up, and gooseflesh prickled my arms. I felt myself shiver, and drew further into my thick tunic, which was remarkably warm. I saw Ray start back this way, ostentatiously looking at the sky, giving me a chance to notice him.

"Dorina," he called out. "Are you ready to—"

His voice cut off abruptly, I did not know why. Then a cascade of mental images hit me, too many and too fast to even try to process, like bubbles foaming up from the surf.

And something huge stirred in the depths of the water.

Oh, I thought blankly.

That was why.

And then Ray started to run.

He was coming this way, and coming fast, or so it would have appeared to anyone looking at a photo of him. His feet were digging into the soft sand near the shoreline, his arms were in the classic running pose, and his face was snarling enough to show fang. But despite the fact that vampire speed should have had him beside me in an instant, he was barely moving.

I did not think that was his fault, however.

The disturbance in the water became more pronounced, and for a moment, I thought that the fey had found us. That one of their wooden ships was pushing up through the waves, and that we were caught or soon to be. But if it was one of their vessels, it was larger than any I had yet seen.

Quite a bit larger.

Ray was still running, but had yet to complete a single stride. Whatever was boiling toward the surface, however, was moving quickly. It broke through the waves a moment later, in a furious surge of water and a mass of spray worthy of a Yellowstone geyser.

I sank back against the rocks, hoping that they would hide me. They weren't that much darker than the gray tunic I was wearing, especially now that it was wet again. Perhaps, if I was very still, the Svarestri would pass on by and—

That was not the Svarestri.

The water had fountained up, far into the sky, and was now coming back down again, raining hard on me and half the river. But not so much so that I could not make out what sat in the middle of the stream, threatening to turn my mind inside out. I looked at it for a moment in consternation, because that . . . could not be what I thought it was.

Yet it continued to sit there, disturbing the currents. And displacing enough water that a tide had washed up, soaking our camp and the riverbank in both directions. It was as if a ship the size of a submarine had somehow surfaced in the middle of our quiet mountain stream, only it wasn't a submarine.

It was . . . a seahorse.

It was bluish-gray, with great, translucent fins crowning its head and wafting along its sides, and a long, delicate snout. It had jewel-like scales that caught and reflected the moonlight, giving it what appeared to be an orange racing stripe down its side. I stared at it for a moment longer, and then I frowned.

Like the tide, the racing stripe was quite advanced for an illusion, which often ignored the lighting in an area entirely. It was one of the easiest ways of spotting a cheap spell, in fact, if distortions around the edges didn't already give it away. But this had no such distortions. It was simply a huge, ridiculously pretty seahorse that my mind persisted in telling me was real when it quite obviously wasn't.

After all, we were in fresh water here, not salt, and in any case, seahorses were not the size of school buses!

And then it spoke.

"Here! You, girl. What are you?"

The question was in English, which was also absurd, as there would be no way for any randomly passing seahorse to know what language I used. I started to say something to that effect, and about the fact that illusions didn't work on me and that I was going to see through this one any minute. But I didn't.

Instead, I just stopped and stared again, because the seahorse hadn't been the one speaking, after all. Its rider had. And this illusion was even better than the last. This illusion was—

"Beautiful," I whispered.

It was a completely inadequate word. Completely. It wasn't even accurate because beauty was supposed to delight and please the senses, but this beauty . . .

Hurt.

It was so overwhelming that it bent the mind, resulting in a sensation very much like pain. I gasped at the creature who had just leaned over the side of the great beast, feeling as if I had been struck in the solar plexus and left breathless and disarmed. And enchanted, possibly literally, although I wasn't sure that I cared any more.

The rider was a woman, but not like any I had ever seen. She was framed against the huge, orange moon as if haloed by it, but she didn't need the help. The moon paled into insignificance in comparison.

Virtually anything would have.

Her thick, dark hair, which appeared to be as long or longer than her body, seemed to have a life of its own. It spread out wildly, blocking half of the moon's light, like the branches of a very strange tree. It appeared to move on the wind the way hair usually does in water, wafting about as if on unseen currents.

Her face was almost too beautiful to look upon. Her eyes were a turbulent blue-gray that nearly matched the color of her strange steed, and her lips appeared to be greenish-blue as did the blush on her cheeks. Although perhaps that was due to cosmetics or to the strange light she seemed to give off.

She was wearing some kind of diaphanous, blue-gray-green robes that boiled around her like chiffon or, more accurately, like waves of seafoam. Only I had never seen anyone wear seafoam before. I did not know that I was seeing it now, but I was no longer annoyed.

I was grateful to see this, even as an illusion.

I was grateful.

"What?" she called down. "Speak up!"

"I said that you are beautiful!" I shouted, wondering if I had gone mad.

"Yes, I know." She sounded peevish. "That is not what I asked."

And, suddenly, without warning, I found myself rising off of the rocks, but not under my own power. And not to my feet. My useless legs dangled beneath me as my dripping form was levitated into the air, until I was roughly even with the astounding creature sitting on a coral saddle.

It appeared to have grown organically around the seahorses' giant belly, then upward, before smoothing out to provide her with a delicate orange perch. There were no reins, but then, I doubted that she needed them. Her mount seemed perfectly in tune with the wishes of its mistress, moving one of its great fins aside so that her power could bring me closer, for inspection.

"What are you?" she demanded again, as I stared into the loveliest face I had ever seen.

"I . . . am Dorina," I whispered.

"And what is that?"

"It is . . . my name?"

This answer did not seem to satisfy her. "I did not ask for your name; I asked what you are." But, this time, she did not give me a chance to answer. Her beautiful brow knit. "Not human, although you speak their tongue. Not fey, not demon —"

"I am not a demon?" I asked hopefully.

The beautiful eyes narrowed. "You do not *know*?"

I shook my head.

"Well, you are not," she said, frowning. "I know their stench, and it is not upon you."

My body began slowly rotating, giving me a view of the flooded embankment and of Ray's frozen, screaming face. I hoped that she would not remember him, as I did not yet know if she was a threat or not, and she did not seem to. Instead, she was glaring at me when I came back around again.

"You are in my waters—"

"I am very sorry—"

"Do not interrupt me!"

"I'm sorry—"

"That is an interruption!"

I closed my mouth.

"You have come here without permission, invading my lands, you and that vampire of yours!"

She looked at me challengingly.

I looked back. She was truly amazing to gaze upon. There appeared to be tiny, jeweled crabs in her hair that caught the light, twinkling like orange diamonds.

One moved slightly, adjusting its grip on a tendril.

Jewel-like, I corrected myself.

"Well?" she demanded. "Do you have nothing to say for yourself?"

"I . . . did not wish to interrupt."

The waves around us became agitated enough to wet my feet again. "Do you mock me?"

"No, I—" I stopped myself, because this was not going well. Possibly because I couldn't seem to think and look at her at the same time. "I beg forgiveness," I said, and bowed my head.

"Hmmph." And then something reached out and poked my dangling legs. It was almost without color, although prismatic, flashing with fire like a giant diamond.

Perhaps, I realized slowly, because it had been carved from a giant diamond.

I blinked at it.

"Do you want a fish tail?" the creature asked.

I looked up. I did not know how to respond to that. "I . . . have had dinner?"

She stared at me. It lasted a long time. Then, very slowly and very deliberately, she poked my legs again. "Would you . . ."

She paused and waited. "Yes?" I finally asked.

"Like to have . . ." she poked my legs again.

"Yes?"

"A fish's tail."

Poke.

I looked down. I looked up. "No?"

She frowned. "Are you sure? These things," she prodded my legs again, "do not appear to function."

"I . . . not at present, no."

"The present is all we have! You could be dead by tomorrow!"

"Yes, but . . . I would still prefer to have all of my original parts."

She did not seem to think much of that answer, but at least she did not poke me again.

"I do not know how you think to live through what awaits you with half a body," she said.

"What awaits me?"

She ignored that. "But if you are what I think, you will manage. And if not . . . then you should not have come here at all, should you?"

"I did not trespass willingly," I said. "I was brought by—"

"I know who brought you." She smiled suddenly, but it was not very nice. There were some . . . very unusual teeth in that lovely mouth. "Yes, I know. Make them pay for it."

Then she was gone.

CHAPTER TWENTY-FIVE

Dorina, Faerie

"That was interesting," I said, back at camp.

I was wrapped in the blanket, which was the only dry thing we had. Ray had found me sprawled on the rocks, soaking wet, which was how I knew that what I'd experienced had not been an illusion. Or if it had, something had wet me, the shore and our camp, leaving everything soaked except for the blanket I had thrown off earlier, which had landed just outside of the tideline.

My tunic had been laid flat to dry once more, although that would likely take a while as our fire was also out. Ray was attempting to get it going, with the little dry wood he'd been able to find, and I was talking some more. Not for any real reason; it almost seemed as if my brain was trying to make up for five hundred years of silence, or perhaps it simply needed to babble for a while to process what I'd seen.

Ray did not seem to mind, or even appear to be listening. He was cursing under his breath, although whether that was at the new kindling, which did not seem to want to light, or at fate, or at . . . I realized that I did not even know her name.

"Nimue," he said, scowling.

I propped myself up on my elbows. "Do you really think so?"

He paused to look at me over his shoulder. "Really?"

I decided he had a point.

"So that is the Lady of the Lake," I mused. It seemed that the Arthurian legends had failed to do her justice. Had *completely* failed.

"She looks different on Earth," Ray said, and then paused to blow on a spark. It went out. He snarled at it.

"Oh?" I asked. "How?"

"More toned down. So people don't get overwhelmed," he added, shooting me a look.

I failed to blush. "She is overwhelming," I agreed, and snuggled further into the blanket as a chill wind swept over us.

The material was scratchy against my skin, but I didn't mind. I would not have minded a flail in order to have seen that. "She is very beautiful," I said, only to have Ray pause again and glare at me over his shoulder.

"She's a goddamned menace, that's what she is, and possibly nuts! The fact that she knows we're here is Not Good, okay? The idea was to stay under the radar!"

I did not point out that we had not been doing so well at that before, because he seemed tense.

"She did not appear hostile," I said instead.

"Oh, she's hostile." It was grim. "The villagers avoid her like the plague 'cause she keeps stealing their babies, always wanting more soldiers for her stupid wars—"

"What wars?"

He shrugged and started over with the fire, having assembled some more moss. "Take your pick; she fights with everybody. Aeslinn, 'cause he keeps raiding and taking her lands. Caedmon, 'cause they used to be married and there's a lot of bad blood there. The dark fey, 'cause she keeps trying to steal lands from them, every time Aeslinn does it to her, which means she's basically fighting all the time. Or she was, anyway."

"She was?"

He nodded. "She up and disappeared a decade or so

ago, just noped right out of her job, her capitol, all her responsibilities. Left her armies in the field with no leadership, her nobles with no idea when or if she was coming back, and enemies all around. It caused chaos, but did she care? But that's a demigod for you."

"She is a demigod?"

That won me another look. "You sound surprised."

"I am." I thought back to the amazing creature I had been privileged to see. "I would have thought that she was the real thing."

He gave a short bark of a laugh. "She'd like you. From everything I ever heard, she's vain as hell. But no, she's only half."

I thought about that. It made me wonder how we mortals were supposed to fight beings sired by the gods. Even space vagabond gods. It did not seem fair.

But Ray would not have an answer to that any more than I did.

"Why did she leave her court?" I asked, instead.

"No clue." His face was focused, as he was trying to light the moss without lighting himself. "Nobody has one. Least not the villagers, who started buying in bulk from people like me because, all of a sudden, the rules changed. And not the courtiers who—

"Ow, shit!"

A spark had hit his thumb, and despite the fact that it went out almost immediately, it left an inch-long wound. I frowned at it, even as it began to close up. "Let me," I said, and took the flint and striker.

He made a be-my-guest gesture and I rolled onto my stomach and inched up to the little mound of moss. It was damp, which was why he was having so much trouble. I pushed it aside and substituted some small, dried twigs instead, one of which I crumbled almost into powder.

"What were you saying?" I asked.

"Just that her courtiers are fighting each other over the

throne, 'cause there's no direct heir. Her loyal people are busy trying to keep the treasury from being plundered, and her armies are scattered. Some of the troops are with her, wherever she is; some are with her nobles—half of which went over to Aeslinn's side after she left, although what they're doing now is anyone's guess; and some just fucked off and started raiding the common folk—"

"Hence the need to buy weapons from smugglers," I said, concentrating.

Ray nodded. "The dark fey have started a surge, too, from what I hear, using the chance to get back some of their stolen lands. They've been raiding light fey villages, who have been raiding back, and the whole thing is devolving into a free for all. And what's Nimue doing?"

"I have no idea," I said, before blowing lightly on a promising spark.

"Nobody has any idea, that's the problem."

"Have you told the senate about this?" I asked, looking at him over my shoulder, because he had backed up, out of the spark zone.

Ray barked out a laugh. "The senate don't seem real interested in my opinion."

"But . . . it's important information, isn't it? They're always saying that the war is hampered by the fact that they know so little about Faerie, yet you seem well informed—"

"About the common folk," he said sardonically. "They don't care about the common folk. Some villagers' problems don't mean a damn to the high and mighty senate."

"But Dory—"

"I told Dory. And she tried to inform them, but nobody cares. If it's not about the nobles or the court, they're not interested." His mouth twisted. "It's another thing our worlds got in common."

I thought about that. It seemed shortsighted on the part of the senate, but maybe it was simply that they found Faerie overwhelming, too. There was so much we didn't know, and what we did seemed so fantastic . . . perhaps it was easier, focusing on the actions of a few people at court, rather than the masses beyond.

"Simpler ain't smarter," Ray said, and then he paused and pointed. "Ha! Ha, ha, ha!"

I looked back at the would-be fire to find a small flame flickering in the middle of the kindling. I held my breath, waiting to see if it would last, and another gust of wind threatened it. But I hunched my hands around it and the small fire held. Ray came over and slowly added larger and larger sticks, until he had a teepee of them, burning merrily.

Then he sat back and sighed in relief. "I hate camping."

I thought it was rather fascinating, so far.

He just shook his head. "You ain't done it enough. You might feel differently by the time we get out of here."

I thought that entirely possible. Although I also thought that he might feel differently, too, had he seen her. But he had seen only the fluttering of images in his mind.

They had blocked him from interfering in my and Nimue's conversation, and essentially stunned him. Of course, we had traded memories since, but I was too tired to do a proper job of it. Yet what he'd shown me had been wonderful, just wonderful!

He had seen deep, underwater caves filled with almost no light, except for massive, bioluminescent fish. He had seen waves crashing onto distant shores above shallow lagoons, where the spears of sunlight from above made the coral reefs almost as bright as day. He had seen enormous flooded castles filled with treasures beyond imagining, guarded by people with the same fish tails that she had offered to me.

He had also seen other things that had made no sense, and which he'd only glimpsed: shipwrecks and storms and a mass of people with air bubbles magically affixed over their heads, holding those same energy spears that we knew so well. They had been swimming downward, and swimming hard. But a kelp forest, as vast and dark as anything on land, had suddenly engulfed the scene, hiding them from view.

"Do you think Nimue was attacked?" I asked. "That perhaps that is why she left?"

But Ray only laughed.

"In water? Not unless somebody's got a death wish!"

"Or help," I pointed out. "You said her courtiers are fighting over her throne—"

"Yeah, because she's AWOL. They toed the line as long as she was there, believe me."

"But perhaps they resented it?"

He rolled his eyes. "You want this to be some epic story, like the ones the fey tell, but the truth is usually simpler and grubbier."

"Such as?"

"Such as an already unstable queen goes nuts and fucks off to play with seashells." He had laid down, and now he moved around, as if trying to get comfortable on the bare rocks. It did not seem to be working.

"Instead of a fishtail, she coulda offered you a damned tent!" he said.

"We have shelter," I pointed out, looking up at the fingers, which were starting to glow once more. But he shook his head.

"I didn't mean a regular tent. Fey nobles, when they travel, use a special kind."

"How special?"

"Very. It seems tiny, just a regular old thing on the outside, but when you go in . . ."

"Yes?"

He grinned, probably because he knew he had me. I was quickly becoming fascinated with Faerie. I wanted to know about everything, even their tents.

"It's like back at Dory's house. You ever been in one of those little two-man things the fey parked in the garden? The ones they act like such martyrs over—oh, no, how could anybody be so cruel as to make us sleep outside?"

I shook my head. I assumed he was talking about Claire's fey bodyguards, who had indeed been banished to the garden, because the house did not have room for them and they were messy. They had pitched small tents back there, bivouacking in the backyard.

"Well, I have," Ray said. "Not that I needed to; I recognized the type. I knew this orc chieftain once, and he'd taken one off some Green Fey idiot who'd ventured into his lands. The boy had a bet with some friends that he'd bring back an ogre's tusks. Instead, he didn't come back at all and the ogre ended up with his tent. I was there to trade and I guess the chief wanted to impress me, so I got the grand tour."

"What was it like?" I asked eagerly.

"It was freaking awesome," Ray said, his eyes shining in the firelight. "First, 'cause they're not really tents at all. They're the entrances to portals—"

"That go where?"

"Nowhere. That's the point. They fold back on themselves, creating a stable little pocket in non-space. The same kind that supernatural Hong Kong exists in, you know? They phased that thing so they could park it in the same space as regular old Hong Kong. But the two never touch— well, almost never—cause one is in real space and one in non-space, like the ley lines."

"Or Louis-Cesare's Veil."

"Yeah. Or a fey tent."

"So, what do they put in there?" I asked curiously, lying down beside him.

"Anything they want. Most of the time, its just to give 'em more space, like a lot more. But some really slut 'em up. The ogre had lucked out and ended up with a mansion with a couple dozen rooms, all of them filled with gorgeous fabrics, finely made furniture, crystal stemware, and opulent dishes . . . you name it. He even got the kid's wardrobe. Of course, none of it fit . . ."

I laughed.

"But he paraded around in it anyway, until the predictable happened."

"His trousers split?" I asked.

Ray turned his head to blink at me. For a moment, his expression reminded me of Nimue. "No."

"Oh."

"Well, I mean, they probably did, but that's not the point. A portal is like any other spell: it needs magic to keep running. I guess it had some kind of talisman powering it, but those are just long-term batteries. They can soak up magic from the natural world, to extend their lives, but sooner or later, you gotta replace 'em or they stop working."

"What happens if they stop working?"

"Nobody knows, 'cause nobody that it happened to ever came back to tell anyone. But most think that it's one of two things: either the whole thing collapses and you're compacted into a tiny, tiny speck of dust, or . . ."

"Or?"

"Or the portal closes up, but the room inside remains in a bubble of non-space, only with no way out. Leaving whoever is in there trapped and floating around forever. Or, you know, until the air runs out."

I thought about it. "I think I would like a fey tent."

"And take the risk?"

"I would remember to change the battery."

Ray laughed. And then his expression faded to something more serious. "I thought you didn't want things."

I looked up at the fingers. They were glowing gold again, giving our tiny encampment a cozy feel. The fire seemed to banish the winds, enveloping us in warmth. It made me sleepy, something I could hear in my voice when I replied.

"I did once, when I was young."

"Young as in, before the split, or . . ."

"Both. Before the split I mostly wanted food. Venice had all sorts of wonderful food, but we couldn't always afford the better cuts of meat, or all the candy I would have liked.

Which was just as well, or I'd have no teeth left."

"And after?"

"Freedom. Being able to go where I chose, when I chose. I wanted to see so many things, but I could only go where Dory did."

"But you were in control sometimes, too, right?"

"Yes, but never for long. Only when she was in serious danger, and her grip over her mind and emotions weakened. Panic was a conduit for me, and fear. But that meant that there was always a fight waiting when I emerged." I rolled my head over to look at him. "I do not mind fights, but there were times . . ."

"Yeah?"

It was embarrassing. But he had been honest with me. "There were times when I wanted . . . to go shopping."

Ray blinked at me. "What?"

I nodded. "Or to a café. We were in Paris once, long ago, and I saw this café. It was so beautiful, with a wisteria vine growing all over it. The vine was as big as a tree, as if it had been there for centuries. I remember wanting to sit at one of the tables and drink coffee and watch the people go by."

"Why couldn't you? Didn't Dory ever do that?"

"Perhaps, but I was asleep then. I'd woken up that night because she was fighting a group of mages who had been stealing magic and making the deaths look like revenant attacks. They thought no one would notice that their victims had died from being drained of all their magic, if their corpses were also savaged. If you are missing much of your torso, people do not look far for another cause of death."

"Yeah, I guess not."

"Dory, who specialized in revenants, had been brought in by the French authorities to investigate and find the killer," I added. "She had done so, and the mages did not like that. They ganged up on us and we were surrounded. I woke up in time to fight them off, but it's strange. I don't remember much of the fight at all. I was killing mages, but I was looking at that little café. It was closed, it being the middle of the night, but I was imagining myself in a pretty dress, sitting in the sunlight, drinking coffee . . ."

I trailed off. Ray didn't say anything for a long time. That was all right. I found that I enjoyed his company even without speech. I did not entirely understand it, since he screamed and cursed a great deal, yet I found his presence soothing.

"And now?" he finally said. "Now that all this has happened. The fey and Faerie and—" he waved a hand around. "This. What do you want now?"

I stared at the flames for a minute. It did not help. "That is difficult to answer. I have not thought about it in so long, that it doesn't even feel like the right question anymore."

"What is the right question?"

I remembered what Mircea had asked, all those years ago, what I had once wondered and what Nimue had demanded tonight. Perhaps that was the question I should have been asking all along. Only I didn't know the answer to that one, either.

"What am I?"

CHAPTER TWENTY-SIX

Dory, Cairo

We withdrew to Hassani's personal chambers, to speak in private. And, despite his reputation, they were definitely the rooms of a scholar more than a warrior. The outer section was clearly an office, with a simple wooden desk at the far end and several chairs. But it was large enough and stuffed with enough antiquities to qualify as a small museum.

There were two large glass display cases with numerous shelves in the middle of the space, which acted as a sort of room divider. Hassani picked up a blue faience item from one of them and handed it to me. It was a shawabti, one of the thousands of small, human-shaped figurines that used to be buried with the pharaohs to serve as servants in the afterlife. I'd seen plenty of them in the Cairo Museum when we'd visited the day after our arrival.

But none so fine as these.

I found them fascinating, or I would have, if I hadn't been so anxious to hear what the consul had to say about Dorina. But I knew old vamps, and pushing them rarely resulted in anything good. I had about a thousand questions for Hassani, but ironically, the fastest way to get them answered was to bite my tongue and smile.

It wasn't as hard as it might have been, because the

figurines really were interesting, and not only for the artistry that went into them. But because they reminded me of some modern-day versions I'd seen at Aswan. The market there had had tiny clay statues of vegetable sellers, basket weavers, potters, spice vendors and fishermen, with some clearly modelled on local residents. One little guy had even had one of the famous crocodiles draped over his shoulders, the beast gazing smugly at potential buyers as if to say, "Why yes, this is my due."

That one had been my favorite, but they were all exquisitely detailed, and painted in bright, happy colors. The tomatoes in front of one vendor were a cheerful red, the leaves in another's basket were a brilliant green, and the spices another was hawking were a delicious-looking saffron yellow. But other than for the vivid hues and modern clothes of the Aswan figures, the two groups might have been made by the same craftsman.

Different artists, thousands of years apart, but they'd both captured perfectly a slice of Egyptian life. The ancient version had tiny bakers rolling out dough; tiny cow herders leading their spotted charges; and tiny beer brewers leaning over pots half as big as they were, checking on the quality of the item that was so vital to the Egyptian diet that it was often used in place of currency. There were a surprising number of women depicted, too, with one playing a lute that didn't look so different from the oud player upstairs, and another with a harp. There was even a female artisan painting a figurine of a goddess.

"Women played an important part in ancient Egyptian life," Hassani informed me, seeing the direction of my gaze. He indicated the figurine he'd just given me. It was of a weaver at her loom, with a smaller figure, perhaps her daughter, kneeling beside her, as if helping or learning.

"Yeah, doing the hard work," I pointed out cynically.

He smiled. "Yes, but most work was hard then, and they were well compensated. They wove the linen, you see." He took me over to a wall, where a piece of ancient fabric resided under a slab of glass.

It had yellowed slightly over the years and, by modern standards, was a little clunky, with some of the strands slightly wider than the others. But it was also very sheer, surprisingly so. I'd have easily been able to see my hand through it had I been able to touch it. As it was, I could see the pattern of the wood on the shelf below.

"The ancients described this type of fabric as royal linen," Hassani informed me. "The very finest kind. Well, other than that made for the pharaoh himself, which would have had gold threads woven through it."

"It's. . . very nice," I said, trying to think of something to say about a piece of old fabric.

But, of course, that only encouraged him.

"Fine linen was a luxury item that brought huge prices, both inside and outside of Egypt," he continued. "In fact, it sold for so much, that the women weavers sometimes out earned their husbands."

"That must have been awkward."

"Not at all. Their earning potential was valued, and made Egyptian women powerful. Alone among the ancient civilizations, women in Egypt were considered equal to men under the law. They owned their own property, could conduct business the same as any man, could testify in court, could even sue for divorce if they wished, advantages that women in the West would not have until the last several hundred years. Some noble women were even educated and held important government positions, becoming viziers or priests. Did you know, the first female physician in recorded history was an Egyptian?"

I shook my head.

"It is true. Lady Peseshets, who lived in 2500 B.C. Egypt understood the power of women, all those years ago. Ironic when you consider that the modern world still often overlooks it. If I wanted to hide a weapon . . ."

"What?" I asked, because that had seemed a strange segue.

But Hassani only smiled.

I'd have liked to look through the whole collection, which took up both of the mid-room display units. Or to have examined the beautiful painted pottery, much of it intact instead of in shards like in the museums, that was scattered around. Or the gorgeous gold and carnelian jewelry on several plinths, as well as an entire overdress made out of delicate beading that a model was wearing.

But we weren't here for that.

Fortunately, Louis-Cesare changed the subject.

"You managed to recapture the artifacts," he said, from the other side of the room.

I carefully returned the shawabti to its place and Hassani and I walked over to some shelving along a wall, where the fey items we'd brought had been displayed. Well, most of them. One large basket-like thing was on the ground, with a strange blue light shining from under the lid that I didn't remember having been there before.

Considering what had happened the last time a fey artifact lit up, I gave it a wide berth.

"Yes," Hassani agreed, gazing at the shelves. "Most of the attempted thieves were apprehended on site, and the rest were tracked down shortly afterward." He reached up and took down a small object. "We also recovered this from the location of your attack."

I hadn't seen what it was, because it had been sitting behind something else. He handed it to me, but this time, it wasn't a cute little statue. This time—

"Shit!" I dropped the wicked thing, which still reminded me of a stone hockey puck: small, round and flat, with a crusty, whitish gray color and strange cracks scrawling across the surface.

"What is it?" Louis-Cesare asked, pulling me back slightly.

"That thing! That *fucking thing*—"

I started to kick it away, but Hassani moved faster, scooping it up.

"My apologies," he said, and he sounded genuinely disturbed. "I had not thought—but of course, it would be traumatic for you."

"What is it?" Louis-Cesare demanded, and this time, there was no courtesy in his tone.

"The thing that separated Dorina and me," I said, panting slightly. The damned thing was just lying there in Hassani's hand, but it was about to give me a panic attack. "You should have destroyed it!"

"That is, of course, up to you," the consul said, looking grave. "However, I would caution against rash action. You may need it, after all."

"Need it? For *what*?"

He cocked his head. "Why, to put you two back together again."

I stared at him, still half panicked, with my pulse fluttering in my throat. But after a moment, I realized that he was right. I didn't know what had happened to me in that alley, and the only people who did were probably fey, who weren't likely to tell me.

Even if I found Dorina, it wouldn't do much good if I couldn't put us back together.

"Thank you," I said roughly. "For retrieving it."

Hassani inclined his head graciously. "It is yours, of course. I only wish I could tell you how it functions. I had my people examine it, but even my best mages had no idea."

"Our senate has additional resources," Louis-Cesare said, taking the horrible thing so I didn't have to touch it. "An entire research department has been set up to study fey artifacts taken in the war. We'll have them look at it."

"I wish you success," Hassani said, bowing slightly. And I guessed he decided that we'd seen enough exhibits for one day, because he led us through the mini museum into a finely appointed sitting room that branched off to the right.

It was down three steps, like a sunken living room, and had the usual tan and cream color scheme that I had come to associate with Hassani's court. It also had some more of the expansive windows. These were long and curved, to follow the rounded wall of the medieval tower that comprised part of his suite. But outside wasn't the night view of the city that I'd been expecting, or even a glimpse of the ongoing party. For a moment, I didn't know what I was seeing.

"The sound and light show at the pyramids," Hassani explained, as we sat down on a large, half-moon sofa positioned so as to take in the view. "We couldn't have fireworks inside the city, but we thought it would do to bring some color to the festivities."

I guess, I thought, remembering how close his shields had made the pyramids look once before. He settled onto a small sofa opposite us, leaving him silhouetted against all that vivid color—electric blue and green, bright pink and purple, brilliant yellow and blazing white, that flowed across the ancient monuments. I assumed there was a story that went along with the visuals, because occasionally a diagram or a pharaoh's head appeared, including one that was superimposed over the sphinx briefly. But I couldn't hear anything.

I couldn't even hear the sound of the party, still going on above. It didn't surprise me that Hassani's chambers were soundproofed: when you lived among hundreds of beings with supernatural hearing, it was probably a requirement. But it made for a faintly eerie ambiance: the dim, almost dark room, allowing us to appreciate the spectacle outside; the vivid colors flowing over the furniture and splashing our faces; the dark silhouette of the consul, his back to the light show, his face in shadow.

A strange ripple went across my skin, like a moving wave of goosebumps. I suddenly wasn't sure that I wanted to hear what he had to say, after all. But it was too late; he'd already begun to speak.

"I have become a bit of a history buff, as you see," he said, gesturing back at the outer room. "It was always an interest, but it became something of an obsession over the years as I searched to find some chink in my former master's armor."

"Your master? You mean—" I paused wondering how to phrase it politely. I gave up. "That thing downstairs made you, too?"

"No." He shook his head, a brief jerky movement unlike his usual elegance. It wasn't quite a shudder, but it told me how much he liked that idea. "It's ironic, in fact. His blood flows through the veins of every consul on Earth save two: the Chinese Empress and me."

"Yet you called him master," Louis-Cesare pointed out.

Hassani nodded. "It was an unusual situation, I admit. The consul before me was a despicable man who started life as a Canaanite mercenary in the Amarna period by the name of Dalilu. He ingratiated himself with Setep-en-Ra by his willingness to do literally anything his pharaoh asked. I will . . . spare you the details."

"Thank you," I said fervently.

"I hated him for his depredations, his dissolute behavior, and the harshness of his rule. It was only once I took his place that I realized: he had never really ruled at all."

"Setep-en-Ra did," Louis-Cesare guessed.

Hassani inclined his head. "Of course. As he always had. He had followed the trade routes west to Rome, and taken the consulate there, as well. But to him, that wasn't abdicating a throne, but simply adding another land to the ranks of his worshippers. The "consul" he left behind was merely his deputy, ruling in his stead while he was away. He considered himself to be the rightful ruler of the world, you see; he simply hadn't officially claimed the more far-flung lands as yet."

"Some of those lands might have had something to say about that," Louis-Cesare said dryly.

"Indeed." Hassani looked thoughtful. "Although whether they would have triumphed, had it come to a contest, is an open question. I think he was a bit mad, even then, but madmen often succeed. They take chances that saner ones will not."

"They get themselves assassinated, too," I pointed out.

I should know; I'd killed a few.

"Sometimes," Hassani agreed, "although it was not so easy, in his case. Many tried before anyone succeeded, and even then, had he been in his right mind, had he not underestimated his opponents, had your father not been there, to assist at just the right moment . . . he might rule still."

"But he doesn't. So, what were you saying about Dorina?"

Hassani glanced sharply at me, probably because that had been less than diplomatic. But I couldn't wait any more. I didn't see what any of this had to do with her, and it had been almost a day since she was taken. I wanted to chase something; I wanted to kill something. Not sit here looking at pretty colors and talking ancient history!

Fortunately, he was too well mannered to point out my rudeness.

"Do you know of my master's power?" he said instead.

"No," I lied. Most vamps liked to keep that kind of thing under wraps, in case they needed to use it in a duel, and that was especially true of consuls.

He smiled slightly, but didn't call me on it. "I see truly," he said, "and clearer than most. As with many masters, I can also see through the eyes of my Children—and share it."

And I guessed my impatience might have annoyed him, after all. Because that was all the warning I received before I was suddenly back there, dumped abruptly into the crazy streets of the Khan-el-Khalili, with multicolored lamps swinging, people screaming, and shops exploding. Only this time, I was watching myself from afar. And jumping over the gap in between buildings, trying to catch up with a crazed cartoon carpet and the two mad types riding it.

"Get her!" I heard myself yell. The phrase was in Arabic, but I somehow understood, maybe because I was borrowing someone else's brain.

Another vamp looked at me, his eyes wild. "You get her! I can barely keep up!"

My vampire—one of Hassani's men, I assumed, since I was seeing through his eyes—cursed, and then cursed again as a jackal-headed fey sprang from a higher rooftop, right down on top of us. But the new arrival didn't attack. He was too busy throwing himself off the roof at Dorina, who was zipping past down below.

And, damn. I knew what had happened, of course; I'd been there. But it looked a little different from this angle. She was standing, perfectly balanced, on a tiny scrap of carpet, despite the fact that Ray was slinging it all over the damned street. And while one of her hands was clenched white knuckled around the graffiti gun, the other was slicing and dicing fey almost casually—

And there were a *lot* of fey.

I remembered maybe half a dozen or so jumping at us, which were the only ones who'd gotten close enough to snag my vision. But there were so many others that I hadn't seen. And while the handful of Hassani's people following us had taken out a few, the vast majority—maybe three or four dozen fey warriors in all—had been dealt with—

By Dorina.

I blinked, but no, I wasn't seeing things. Or, rather, I was, and through the eyes of a vamp as nonplussed as me. It was all happening so fast, and he was busy leaping and occasionally fighting his way through it, so he might have missed something. But what he saw was plenty good enough.

In short succession, Dorina grabbed a passing line of bare light bulbs, held it long enough to stretch it out, then released it to spring back and knock a trio of fey off our backs; shoved another fey away hard enough to impale him on a piece of wood sticking off of a roofline; then grabbed a poster advertising a museum exhibit on Nefertiti and—*shit.*

"Did you *see* that?" I asked Hassani, because she'd just created the world's worst paper cut, slitting a fey's throat with a *poster.*

"I saw," he said, his voice drifting across the scene. He courteously didn't remind me that of course he'd seen it, or I wouldn't be able to. But I didn't care about details right now.

Dorina had just hit her groove.

She performed a double decapitation with the sword, ducked under the two arcs of blood, and threw her scimitar ahead of her, piercing a falling fey partway through his jump. She grabbed a passing pole or a long piece of wood off a shop —I didn't have time to see which—and a second later, it had two fey impaled on it. Then she pulled her scimitar out of the *still falling fey*, gutted another attacker, dodged his spilling entrails and used the tip of the sword to pluck a brass platter off a display. Which she then slammed into yet another fey's face hard enough to leave an impression of his features in the metal.

And she did it all one handed.

But while that was as impressive as hell, it was nothing compared to the second act.

I couldn't see anything of my actual surroundings, or feel except for a vague impression of Louis-Cesare's body beside mine. But I sat up anyway at what my vamp was now seeing. "What the—"

"You did not know she had this power?" Hassani's voice asked, as a great black specter rose out of Dorina, the cheerful lights of the marketplace still visible through the ends of its tattered form, but the eyes—

Were solid red and burning.

CHAPTER TWENTY-SEVEN

Dory, Cairo

"Shit," I said softly, staring as the inky black specter launched itself at a group of maybe a dozen fey, who had been about to end this whole affair with a massive drop from both sides of the street. Instead, they didn't even have time to shit their pants before—

"Allah preserve us," Hassani said softly, while I just sat there, staring.

The vamp whose eyes I was seeing through had had much the same reaction. He skidded to a halt at the edge of a gutter while a hail of body parts rattled down on the rooftops, street, and crowd of screaming, running humans below. Right before getting splashed in the face with a huge gout of blood from a savaged torso.

It smacked down at his feet, pale and naked and looking like a wild animal had been at it. A really big animal. Vamps are not squeamish for obvious reasons, but I felt this one's diaphragm give a slight lurch of sympathy.

Because she'd torn them apart, literally ripping the contingent of fey limb from limb, and so fast that my eyes couldn't track it, because the vamp's couldn't. He stared down at the modern-art-like splatter of white skin, yellow fat, and red blood and veins and meat that was all that was left of a being possibly older than the pyramids. Then he looked up, a little dizzily, giving me a diminishing view of the mad cavalcade as it disappeared down the street.

I saw Dorina flow back into our body, hacking and slashing without missing a beat. I saw Ray fling us around the alley as if he was born to it. I saw myself . . . well, honestly, I didn't remember what I'd been doing. All of this crazy shit had been happening around me, yet I'd noticed very little of it.

Which made no damned sense at all!

Was Hassani doctoring the images he was sharing for some reason? Because I wasn't that oblivious and Dorina . . . couldn't do any of that. My brain skidded off the topic of the specter, as if unwilling to deal with it right now, and concentrated instead on the swiftness of the attack. She had the liquid speed of all masters, but she wasn't that fast—I *knew* she wasn't.

Louis-Cesare had been faster than her when we'd fought while he was possessed. Not by a lot, but enough that I'd lost a leg to that damned blade of his! Mircea had managed to reattach it, but I still had the scar. It was only a fine line now, barely even noticeable, just a shade lighter than the rest of my skin. But still. If she'd been able to do what I just saw, I wouldn't have a mark on me.

And Louis-Cesare would be dead.

Of course, I'd been holding her back, fighting with everything I had, because my lover was not in his right mind and I didn't want her to gut him. Whereas, last night, I had been helping her. Had my contribution really made so much difference?

Or had she merely been learning new skills since then, spreading her wings now that she could, becoming what she was meant to be all along? Instead of helping her, had I been holding her back all these years? I had no idea.

I looked up and saw Hassani's eyes on me through the hazy street scene he was still projecting, probably because he was waiting for an answer to his question. I licked my lips.

"I . . . never saw her . . . like that."

"And now that you have?"

I refocused my eyes and stared at the bloody mess scattered across the souk. The consul's vamps were doing the same, appearing a little shell shocked. But they had a job to do, and to give them credit, they didn't hesitate for long.

They began dropping off of buildings, with most grabbing passersby and wiping their memories, as well as any phone or other recording device they could find. Others began cleaning up, piling pieces of once formidable adversaries into whatever receptacles were available. There were plenty to choose from, everything from baskets to brass platters, since the shopkeepers had all fled.

Not a single vamp went after Dorina.

I didn't blame them.

"I got nothing," I told Hassani honestly.

"Well, perhaps I do."

The vision faded, bringing his features more clearly into view, or maybe that was the brilliant white light of the laser spectacle behind him. I spread my hands. "Go for it."

"I *have* seen something like that once," he said. "Long ago. I saw one who could fight in spirit as well as in body, and lay waste to hundreds, all on his own. I saw one who moved faster than eyes could track, even our eyes. I saw an army in the guise of a single man, and I never forgot it."

It took me a minute, because my mind was mostly still back at the souk, trying to reconcile the two versions of events, mine and Hassani's. And then I still wasn't sure that I understood him. Because he seemed to be implying . . . no. No!

"You think Dorina is . . . like that thing downstairs?" I said slowly. My skin crawled at the very thought. It crawled *hard*.

"You misunderstand—"

"I damned well hope so! She doesn't—she isn't—I *damned well* hope so!"

"I only meant," Hassani began, but I wasn't done yet.

"That thing didn't fight like her! He wasn't a spirit, or whatever the hell. He was a *snake*—"

"Which is rather the point," the consul said mildly. "He could take many shapes, but not hold two different ones at the same time. We had deprived him of his greatest power by burying him so far underground, away from the sun. He therefore chose his next favorite form—"

"Bullshit! This is bullshit! They are not the same!"

"I never meant to imply—"

"Then what the hell did you mean?"

"I would like to hear that myself," Louis-Cesare said, his jaw tight. He looked disturbed. Yeah, no shit!

Hassani sighed, and ran a hand through his hair. It was dark brown and lay in perfect waves, because he was using a glamourie. I'd seen him without it and it had been half gray and wiry, and his face had been lined as it wasn't now. But the natural elegance of the man wasn't fake.

Yet his movements at the moment were abrupt and lacking grace, and his face was showing too much emotion for one usually so poised. It occurred to me to wonder if there was a reason why he had been beating around the bush so much. He didn't know how to talk about this, either.

"I am explaining this badly," he finally said. "Let me go back to the beginning. To what we were discussing in the temple earlier today."

I realized that I'd stood up at some point without even noticing it. I wanted to keep on going, to walk right out. I'd been so sure that Hassani had something useful, something that would lead me to Dorina or at least to Jonathan, and this was it? Some crazy shit about—

God, I was pissed!

I should have left as soon as I woke up this evening, just grabbed Louis-Cesare and gone. He'd seen what was in the morgue, before it tried to kill us. If there were any clues, he had them, and I had people—

Hell, I was a *senator* now. I didn't even need my old

contacts, although I had them, I had plenty of them! But I could also call on the Hounds the senate employed. Their vamps could track a fly in a hurricane. I didn't need this—

Louis-Cesare took my hand. Immediately, I felt calmer, more grounded, more in control. I resented it, because I didn't want to be calm right now, but I acknowledged that I needed it. Because, yes, I could do all of that. But if Jonathan had taken a portal what good did it do me? He could be anywhere by now, and Hassani's people were the only ones who might have seen something useful.

I was going to have to be a freaking diplomat if it killed me.

I sat back down. "All right."

Hassani looked like he was about to say something, then changed his mind and just got on with it. "The gods became aggressive toward each other after a time on Earth," he said, "unable to decide how to allocate its resources and those of the hell regions beyond. Yet they were too well matched for one group to triumph over another, and thus tried to create themselves armies to tip the scales in their favor. But humans were not strong enough for the purpose, and thus experiments were made to improve them."

I bit my tongue to keep from pointing out that I knew all this. Some I'd heard from the Irin, and the rest from the countless senate sessions we'd had lately about the war. How all the gods had been vying with each other, trying to come up with some kind of advantage over the rest. Then one, Artemis, realized that she already had it. While everyone else was struggling to build armies, she was building up *herself*, using her unique ability to traverse the hells to hunt the juiciest prey: age-old demon lords with millennia of accumulated power, all of which she'd absorbed after killing them.

It had made her into an army all on her own, which had eventually allowed her to kick the other gods off of Earth and to slam a metaphysical door—in the form of a powerful spell

—behind them. But Artemis had since died, and the old gods were now pounding on the door trying to get back in. And to make matters worse, they had supporters on this side of the barrier, including the fey king Aeslinn, who had donated all those warriors last night.

We were attempting to hunt him down before he succeeded in finding a way to throw open that door, leading to the ass kicking of the century for our side. So far, it had been going better than expected, mainly because we had a demigod in the ranks, the child that Artemis had had before her death. And despite the Pythia's questionable taste in jewelry, she had been able to pull victory after victory out of her ass.

Problem was, it only took one defeat, one thing that we didn't see or account for, for the tide to turn. Once the gods were back, they were back, and we had no way to fight them. Aeslinn's capitol currently lay in ruins, his people scattered, his army decimated. But he was still out there, he had a fighting force, and he was plotting.

The question was, what was he doing?

"But this did not work out quite as planned," Hassani said, watching me. "The gods' experiments resulted in some of the greatest heroes—and monsters—of our mythological past, but the disciplined armies they hoped for did not materialize."

"We don't know that," I pointed out tersely.

"Oh, but we do. Not from records, I grant you. Few have survived from that era, and none from the gods themselves. But we can extrapolate from the changes they made in the prototypes."

I frowned. "You mean the dusting away in the sunlight, stake through the heart stuff?"

He nodded. "And the instability of weres around the time of the full moon. If an army is loyal to you, you have no reason to reduce its effectiveness in such ways."

"And an army that goes insane once a month is

vulnerable," Louis-Cesare added. "As is one that burns up when the sun shines."

I looked back at him. I had no idea what he thought about what we'd just seen, but he hadn't pulled away from me, and there was no revulsion on his features. Just concentration, as if he wanted to understand this.

I just wanted Hassani to get to the point already!

The consul nodded. "Such a force can still be used against your enemies, who do not know of the safeguards that you have built in. But should your army rise against you, you can easily wipe them out."

"Okay," I said. "But what does any of this have to do with Dorina? She wasn't tinkered with by the gods; she wasn't even born then!"

"No, she was not," Hassani agreed. "And we also know when your father was born . . ."

He trailed off, waiting.

I just looked at him. If he wanted to play little games, he'd picked the wrong woman and definitely the wrong night. He began to look slightly uncomfortable after a moment, but he didn't say anything else.

"He is speaking of your mother," Louis-Cesare finally told me, and I suddenly understood the consul's silence. He'd wanted my husband to say those words, because if it had been him—

We'd have had a diplomatic incident on our hands.

"I'm done here," I said, and got up.

But Louis-Cesare obviously wasn't and he still had hold of my hand.

"Dory."

"This is *bullshit*. You know it is."

"Dory—"

"First, he insults my sister, comparing her to that evil . . . thing . . . we killed, and now my *mother*?" I looked at the consul, who was still just sitting there. "You don't know the first damned thing about my mother!"

"And neither do you," Louis-Cesare said, causing me to look down at him, confused and hurt.

He took my other hand as well. I wasn't sure if that was supposed to be for added comfort, or if he was trying to make certain that I didn't put a fist through Hassani's face. But it made me feel trapped and that . . . was a mistake.

"Let me go." It was flat and completely uninflected.

Louis-Cesare let me go.

I started for the door, got halfway there, then spun around, so angry I could barely see. "My mother was a Romanian peasant girl! She died almost six hundred years ago!"

"So I understand," Hassani said, leaning forward and finally speaking quickly, as if he didn't know how much time he had. "The question is, when was she born? Was she the last of the godly prototypes, one more powerful than all the rest? Was she the reason Artemis acted when she did, and drained herself so badly fighting an entire pantheon on her own? Would she have preferred to wait, to accumulate even more power, but couldn't, with a new army on the way that could tip the scales—"

"This is *ridiculous*!"

"It is speculation," he admitted. "It may have been the fey who engineered your mother instead, using the knowledge they'd gained from the gods. But, either way—"

"Consul," that was Louis-Cesare, his voice sharp. "A moment."

Hassani stopped talking.

I stared blindly past his fucking head at the light show outside, which was apparently coming to an end. The colors were rapidly changing and lasers were flinging everywhere, as if the age-old monuments had stumbled into a disco. They strobed the room, bright enough to hurt the eyes, but I stared at them blindly for a moment anyway, before finally looking at Hassani.

And for once, I didn't give a shit what was on my face.

"Then tell me this," I rasped. "If she was so powerful, how did Vlad the bitch Tepes manage to kill her? He staked her to death, left her writhing on a pole for hours. I thought she'd died when her village burned, but I later found out—"

I stopped and shuddered all over. Louis-Cesare got up, but I waved him off. I didn't like to think about what had happened, even after so long, didn't like to face how she must have suffered.

But I was going to, because I wanted a goddamned answer!

"If she was some demigod super soldier, then how in the *hell*—"

"She was likely not a demigod," Hassani said, his voice low, slow and non-threatening. For some reason, that made me even angrier. Louis-Cesare got up and moved in between us. I stared at him, and then almost laughed.

Even for me, the last twenty-four hours had been hell. I was exhausted—mentally, physically, and emotionally. What the fuck did he think I was going to do to a consul?

And then I realized what he thought.

I stared at him. "You think I'm a monster."

"Dory, no—"

"You do! You think—you believe him. *You believe him*! You think I'm like that—that hideous—that—that—" I cut off, not being able to breathe, and a second later, his arms were around me. I was furious, but I didn't even struggle. It hit me, all at once: losing Dorina, fighting all day, yet not being one step closer to getting her back, Hassani's lies, my *mother*—

I sank to my knees, gasping for air, and suddenly the lights all cut out.

I thought for a second that I was about to pass out, then I realized—the damned light show had just ended. I faintly heard clapping from somewhere; the party I assumed. Glad someone was having a good time.

And then Maha was there, kneeling by my other side. Hassani must have summoned her, and was probably regretting it, I thought vaguely, as her eyes flashed at the two men. "What happened?"

"She became upset," Louis-Cesare said.

"And why did she become upset? What did you say to her?"

"It was more what I said," Hassani admitted, causing his Child to whirl around. "I am sorry, my dear. It seems I am losing my touch."

Maha started to say something, then bit her lip. "Whatever it was, it can wait. She needs sleep—"

"I slept most of the afternoon," I said, a little breathlessly. But I was feeling better—a lot better. Her touch was goddamned magic.

"You were sedated most of the afternoon," she corrected. "You need natural sleep in order to heal."

"I'm well enough," I said, trying to push her off so I could stand.

"You are not!" It was snapped and it was loud. All three of us stopped to look at her.

Maha had struck me as the type who was usually cool, calm, and peaceful. A soothing presence for her patients and an overall kindhearted person. She wasn't looking so kindhearted right now.

"You are going to sleep," she told me furiously. "Right now. As for the two of you—"

And at least I got this much, I thought, watching two first-level masters, one a consul and one who could have been had he wanted to try and salvage Antony's wreck of a court, shrink in on themselves, one might almost say cower, before a pissed off woman.

Maybe we did have power, after all, I thought dizzily. But I never got a chance to find out what she told them. Because her hand slid onto my shoulder again, and this time—

"Well, crap," I said, and passed out.

CHAPTER TWENTY-EIGHT

Dory, Cairo

I awoke to sunlight streaming through diaphanous white curtains, which were ruffling in a breeze coming across a balcony. The wind smelled like butterscotch, which confused me. Until I realized who was sprawled across me, like a big, sweaty blanket.

Well, in fairness, Louis-Cesare didn't sweat, but he was warm enough to make me do so. Not to mention that Cairo in November still gets into the upper seventies during the day. During the day, I thought, blinking at the sunlight, and wondering why that phrase—

I sat up. "Damn it!"

"It's all right," Louis-Cesare said.

"How the hell is it all right? We've lost even more time and—what are you doing?" I demanded, as he scooped me up into his arms.

"Bath time."

"Bath time my ass! Put me down!"

And he did—in the big sandstone pool that was masquerading as a bathtub.

I started to get out for any number of reasons, the first of which was that I was still dressed. Someone—hopefully my husband—had put me into one of the filmy nightgowns I'd brought along because this was supposed to be my honeymoon. But because it was my honeymoon, I hadn't actually worn any of them for more than five minutes.

And this proved to be no exception.

"Give that back!" I said, and grabbed for the swath of silk that a supercilious bastard had just pulled over my head.

I missed.

"After you've bathed," the bastard said, and started the faucets running.

That wouldn't have been so bad except that the pool had a rain shower built into the ceiling that wasn't so much a shower head as a waterfall. It had to be three-foot square and it started bucketing down, resulting in my slipping and falling onto my still bruised ass. It hurt, but when I started to complain about it, all I got was a mouthful of water.

Louis-Cesare got in beside me, not having had to waste time stripping because he never wore anything to bed anyway, and started soaping up my back. He didn't use the loofa on a stick, which would have been rough on my still healing skin, but rather his hands. Which somehow managed to be both incredibly strong and completely gentle at the same time. I groaned and leaned my cheek on the cool stone side of the tub, just for a minute.

"That's not fair," I mumbled. "That's cheating."

He didn't reply. He also didn't stop. Not until my muscles were putty and my spine was liquid and I was about to slip under the water because I was so relaxed. Which I shouldn't be; I had things to do, important things, and—

"The jet is fueling up as we speak."

I looked over my shoulder. "The jet?"

"The senate's airplane." An auburn eyebrow went north. "The one we came here in?"

I tried to think, which wasn't easy with the rhythmic kneading going on. "Where is it going?"

"We."

"What?"

"Where are we going," Louis-Cesare corrected, then got

up briefly to drip across the floor and grab something out of his clothes. As usual, he'd flung them down beside the bed, because there was supposed to be a servant to pick them up. There weren't any; the egalitarianism that was a hallmark of Hassani's court ensured that the rooms were cleaned, but anything we threw down stayed where we'd dropped it.

That had left me acting as a substitute valet all week, if I didn't want people to think we were complete slobs, but I didn't mind so much at the moment. Didn't mind at all, I thought, checking out the shift and play of sleek muscles in what had been called the best butt in history. Of course, it had been called that by me, but still. It had been called that.

The view was impressive, and that was before he turned around to walk back over and hand me something. He got back in the tub while I looked it over. And maybe it was because I had just woken up, but I didn't get it. "Did I leave this downstairs?"

It was his turn to look puzzled. "*Quoi*?"

"After the fight. I thought Hassani's people had returned them all, but . . ." I trailed off, frowning. Come to think of it, this didn't look like one of mine. It was a small golden charm, of the type that looked like a tat on the body, but I couldn't remember grabbing one depicting a Chinese character from the senate's armory.

"Ones like it were found on the body of the thieves," Louis-Cesare said. "All of them. As far as Hassani's people can tell, it's a key—it opens a warded door."

"A warded door where?"

"We don't know. But the consul has agreed to allow us to take this one."

I didn't ask "take it where." I already knew. I'd seen a couple of the thieves up close, and with this . . .

Son of a bitch.

I started to get up again, but he pulled me back down. "The plane will wait."

"For what?"

"For us. We need to talk."

I turned around, because side eye wasn't going to work for this. "About?"

Blue eyes met mine unflinchingly. "I think you know."

I would have gotten out of the tub again, but he'd just follow me. That look said this was happening, one way or the other, and I wasn't a coward. I was a resentful little lump with greasy hair, however—until Louis-Cesare started shampooing it.

"Stop." I caught his wrist.

"Stop what?"

"It's not—I mean, I can do that."

That won me another look. "But I am already doing it, you see?" He held up soapy hands.

I went back to resentful lump status, because it was either that or explain that I didn't want him touching my ugly head. Somebody had removed Maha's elegant solution, and hopefully put it somewhere safe, so it was just the bumpy skin up there.

Thanks to her, it was no longer red and there was actual epidermis covering the burn, but it wasn't back to normal. Like everything lately. Like the whole world, which was suddenly uncomfortable and upsetting and strange.

"Hassani made a tape for you," Louis-Cesare said.

I looked up, and had to blink to keep suds out of my eyes. "What?"

"A videotape. Well, actually, I think it is a computer file—"

"Why would he do that?"

"I believe he thought it was the best way to have a conversation. We can pause it when you become—" He saw my expression. "We can pause it when you like."

Which, of course, basically ensured that I wouldn't, which he very well knew. He wanted me to see the damned thing for some reason. I wanted to pull on some jeans, strap on a fuck ton of weapons, and go murder something.

But then he started it, and I was stuck.

A T.V. screen that I hadn't noticed flickered to life on the opposite wall, showing Hassani wearing his serious face. He had on the same outfit as last night, so I assumed this had been made shortly after I left the party. I sighed.

Louis-Cesare pulled me in front of him and continued shampooing and then massaging my ugly head while I prepared to listen to a load of bull crap. He reached my neck, and the wire tight muscles there, and I leaned into it. But I did it resentfully.

"My dear Dory," Hassani said, as if starting a letter. He paused. "I hope I may call you that after everything we have been through together this week. It feels as though we have known each other for far longer, does it not?"

"An eternity," I muttered, and felt Louis-Cesare's chest vibrate slightly behind me.

"I consider you and Louis-Cesare to be friends of my court, and as such, would feel remiss if I did not finish our discussion, however uncomfortable it might seem at the present."

"Uncomfortable for who?" I said sourly, but he was already moving on.

"As I said, I do not think that your sister, as you call her, is a monster—or a demigod, either. The gods seem to have begun their experiments by crossbreeding themselves with humans, as well as with demons and fey, and fairly indiscriminately at that. But the results were . . . a mixed bag. Some of the children they sired were mad, if the ancient myths are anything to go on, and the rest were either too weak or too disobedient to be useful. They frequently caused as many problems as they solved."

"Iphemedia," Louis-Cesare said. "She was a human woman who gave birth to the Aloadae giants by Poseidon. They were so powerful that they kidnapped Ares and required both Apollo and Artemis to take them down."

I looked at him over my shoulder. "Hassani told you that," I accused.

He looked hurt. "I read."

"You read Barbara Cartland."

"Shh," he said, because Hassani was continuing.

"The gods did not want rivals," the consul said. "But rather loyal and capable armies. Indeed, looked at through the right lens, that is what most of the old legends are about. The story of Lycaon, King of Arcadia, for instance, who was transformed along with fifty of his sons into the first werewolves by Zeus. Or the centaurs, who may have been a failed attempt at another shapeshifting army by Zeus, but which stalled halfway. Or the Spartoi, who were said to be Earth born warriors who sprang from the teeth of a dragon. We now assume "teeth" to mean DNA, which is often found in the roots of teeth, and which Ares crossed with the human genome to make another fey-human hybrid."

"Can we fast forward?" I asked Louis-Cesare.

"He's coming to the point," he assured me, and then dunked me into the waterfall to rinse my hair.

When I emerged, I discovered that that had been a lie, because Hassani was still going strong.

"—Amazons, who were described as the daughters of Ares and a wood nymph, but nymphs in the Greek tradition are almost always fey of one type or another, and most of the Amazons do not appear to have been strong enough to have been demigods. This may indicate a fey-human hybrid which was facilitated by Ares—"

"Oh, God, make it stop!" I said.

"—but I digress," Hassani went on, as if he'd heard. "The point is that the gods seemed to have replaced their early efforts at having children to assist them in their wars with attempts to make armies by hybridizing "lesser creatures", possibly infused with a small amount of godly DNA to bump up their effectiveness. Which brings me to your sister."

I sat up.

"The gods must have learned a great deal from their experiments, information they left with their fey allies, who continued their work. We both saw the results of some of the fey's experiments, which were loosed on us at your consul's court. They were supposedly the failures, and yet they were formidable."

"Damn," I said, and Louis-Cesare reached over and stopped Hassani mid-word, giving me a moment.

I needed it, because the consul was right about that much —the fey *had* been experimenting. I'd been running across some of their rejects for a while, including my adopted son and the misbegotten monsters the fey had thrown at us as cannon fodder. I just hadn't thought that I might be one of them.

I scowled. Only I wasn't, and neither was Dorina. This was—I didn't know what this was, but it didn't prove anything.

"You don't believe him," Louis-Cesare said, watching me. "Do you?"

"I don't know. But it would explain a great deal—"

"It explains nothing! My mother *died.*" I didn't know why nobody seemed to get that simple point. "If she was some super soldier, she might still be here. She certainly wouldn't have met her end screaming on the end of a pike!"

Louis-Cesare didn't say anything, but I could tell that he wanted to.

"What?"

"Merely that, when your parents met, two lines of godly experimentation came together for the first time. Vampire from your father, and . . . whatever your mother may have been. Neither of the two strains may have been completely satisfactory on their own, but together . . . they created something new."

I frowned at him, because that had actually made a weird sort of sense. Except for the obvious. "Then why the hell was she in Romania, living like a peasant?"

"I don't know." He shook his head. "But she blended in well enough to fool even your father. Perhaps that was one of her gifts: camouflage. Perhaps she escaped from the fey, made her way to Earth, and went to ground, in the most out of the way place she could think of. Perhaps she thought she'd be safer in a peasant's cottage than somewhere more prominent—"

"So she dates a prince?"

"People do fall in love, and she did not live with him in the castle. Perhaps—"

"Perhaps, perhaps, perhaps! This is all speculation!"

"Yes, it is. But what else can we do? She is not here to ask."

"No." I hugged myself. The water suddenly felt cold. "She isn't."

Louis-Cesare pulled me back against him. He didn't say anything, and for a long time, neither did I, but not because I was processing. I should have been, but all this was too much to take in, and it brought up too many memories.

My mother's house, snow covered and burnt out, like a reproachful corpse. The wind high in the tree tops, seeming to whisper: "Too late." Mircea, giving me a sketchbook that he'd made, with her image caught a thousand different ways, so he'd remember even as the centuries piled up.

Dorina, sitting on the slant of a roofline, outside my window. Showing herself to me for the first time as a transparent, spirit-like being. Not like the specter tonight, but softer, sweeter, speaking of hope and new starts and a better life for both of us.

Where was that life now?

"How do the fey even know about her?" I demanded harshly. "*I* didn't even know until recently."

"You mean Dorina?"

I nodded.

"Efridis," Louis-Cesare said, his own voice tight. Probably because she was the fey queen who had ordered his possession. "She fought you herself, and had plenty of time to receive reports from others who had done so. She may have even seen the experiments that created your mother. As

Aeslinn's wife, she surely knew about them."

"But she's dead—"

"Yet plenty of her people aren't, and she had time to tell any number of them about her suspicions."

I didn't like it, but it fit. Dorina had helped me to defeat a queen of the light fey, but had she outed herself in the process? I shifted uncomfortably.

"There is one thing that does seem certain," he murmured. "The fey wanted her very badly. They traded a great many warriors' lives for her, something Aeslinn can ill afford at this juncture."

That was another point, much as I hated to admit it. I didn't know how many fey Aeslinn had lost in the assault on his capitol, but it had been a lot. And his people had a really low birthrate, meaning that he couldn't easily replace them. Yet he'd just risked something like a hundred soldiers to do a snatch and grab on Dorina?

My frown turned into a scowl as I contemplated the obvious reason why.

Louis-Cesare seemed to think the same. "The fey may not be able to recreate the events that led to Dorina's birth, but they do have thousands of years of godly experimentation to draw on. If they have a living example to hand—"

"They could extract her DNA, study it, and make thousands of Dorinas," I finished for him. "Or people just like her."

"Not just like her. Ones loyal to them, brought up to be their obedient servants—"

"Not if they're like Dorina!"

"But they won't be," he said gently. "However uncomfortable your early years may have been, you complemented each other perfectly. You acted as camouflage for her, while she kept you safe through your travails. Giving both of you time to make up your minds about the people you wished to be. The children brought up by the fey will have no such advantage."

"And the fey timeline often runs faster than Earth's," I realized. "If they hit a patch like that—"

"They will have an army in no time." He moved around to see my face, and his own was serious. "How old were you before you were deadly?"

I thought back, which wasn't easy with the blood freezing in my veins. "I don't remember."

"Your first kill then."

"I could walk," I said slowly. "I remember toddling over to a wolf, which was trying to steal some of our stew. The Romani group I was with had gotten drunk that night and forgotten to put it away. It was winter; the beast was probably just hungry. But so were we . . ."

"You killed it."

I nodded, remembering the warmth of its blood on my hands, the softness of its fur, the sadness I had felt at its death. "One of the women made me a coat out of its pelt," I said quietly. "They called me Little Wolf for the longest time . . ."

Louis-Cesare sighed. "I do not think there is time to waste, then."

No, but I'd been wasting plenty of it! "I need to talk to Hassani," I said angrily. "I need to talk to him now!"

That was easier than I expected, as it was a smart T.V. that could connect to the computer in his office. I'd gotten out, dried off, and put on a robe by the time Louis-Cesare managed to get him online. But Hassani still looked a bit shocked.

Like I gave a damn.

"Yesterday morning, you were trying to ship me off to Whatshername's temple without a word."

"Hatshepsut's Temple," he agreed.

"With all this happening? With time running *out*?"

"As I believe I said, it would have reassured my people to see us carrying on as normal whilst the investigation was made."

"But that's not what you did. You took me downstairs—"

"Yes. After you made it clear that you intended to follow your lover—excuse me, your husband—and find your sister. It occurred to me that you might be the only one who can."

"But your people must have seen something. They were all over that bazaar—"

"And I have shown you what they saw. I have held nothing back."

"I need to talk to them, everyone who was there—"

"Lady Basarab—"

"—and I need to see the bodies. I know they've been gone over, but I want to see them again—"

"Lady Basarab—"

"—along with anything they were wearing, and that includes—"

"*Dory!*"

I paused, because the volume had just missed a shout. But he was looking a lot less prim and proper, suddenly. For the first time since I arrived, he looked like the man I'd seen at our senate. For the first time, he looked like the assassin instead of the teacher.

I immediately liked him better.

"Do you know why I help you?" he demanded.

"Because we're friends of the court?" I deadpanned.

His eyes flashed dangerously, and Louis-Cesare tightened the hand he'd placed on my arm. I didn't need the warning. I could almost feel the consul's power, his anger, from here, and he was in his office almost a block away.

But I didn't think the anger was for me, something he confirmed a second later.

"I lost ten Children in the assault on this court, killed not in combat, which would at least have been an honorable end, but by a coward's weapon, a missile that tore through my shields and incinerated them where they stood. I lost six more in the fight that followed, chasing thieves and murderers through the streets, and another seven in the temple below us, battling the ancient curse they unleashed upon me. *Twenty-three*, young one. Twenty-three who drank of my blood, who shared my trials, who lived in my heart. Twenty-three whom I shall never see again.

"Someone will pay for that.

"Someone will *bleed* for that."

"Fuck, yeah," I whispered.

"But these are enemies I do not understand, who come from a land I do not know. I have only one card against them, and I am playing it. Find them for me. You know all that we do, and you know Dorina better than any of us. And she knows you. You are two halves of one soul, yearning to be reunited. You will find her.

"And you will call me when you do."

"I'll call you," I said. "If she's left any of them alive."

And for the first time, Hassani and I shared a look of perfect understanding.

CHAPTER TWENTY-NINE

Dory, Hong Kong

Supernatural Hong Kong was looking a little worse for the wear these days, having been through a major battle recently. And by worse, I mean half tumbled down skyscrapers with mostly missing windows, other buildings blackened and burnt out, and large swathes of land chewed up as if a gigantic mole had been tunneling. It honestly didn't look that much better than it had during the battle itself, except that the fires had been put out.

Largely put out, I corrected, noticing flickering red light staining the inside of an already charred hulk. Of course, that could have been somebody making dinner. Housing was at a premium these days, and squatting was rampant in anything that was remotely structurally sound.

Although some people had been more creative than that.

"What the—what is *that*?"

Bahram, the big, bearded vamp from Hassani's court, grabbed my shoulder and pointed at something off to the left. I had no idea what, because I was driving, which in Hong Kong meant piloting a repurposed rickshaw around the skies. And because the skies were so full, he could have been pointing at anything.

"Don't grab me," I said, shrugging off his hand.

He turned in his seat to stare at something behind us, and

Rashid, the big, bald vamp on the other side of the backseat, frowned. "Shouldn't Louis-Cesare be driving?"

"Why?"

A crazy-ass vehicle comprised of a couple smallish fans and someone's living room sofa dipped down almost on top of us. Once upon a time, that would have been illegal. You couldn't merely slap a levitation charm on something and call it a day. There were rules; there were laws; there were standards.

Right up until the city got the crap blown out of it, along with half of its vehicles. Now, it seemed that anything worked, only it didn't. It didn't at all! I grabbed a broom stick off the floorboard and beat on the bottom of the couch.

"Mm goi jeh jeh!"

A small child's face appeared over the back of the sofa, and stared down at me curiously, before someone who I assumed to be her grandmother pulled her back so she could stare at me instead.

"Mm goi jeh jeh!" I repeated. Which was the polite way of saying "move your ass" in Cantonese. At least, I assumed so, since it had been yelled at me a few dozen times now.

It seemed to work. A moment later, the fan on the left-hand arm of the sofa was turned to the right, causing the whole contraption to veer in that direction. And almost collide with a floating Pot Noodle Shop in the process.

"That is why," Rashid said dryly.

"I do not know how to drive one of these," Louis-Cesare informed him, just before we were bumped by a careening taxi, which resulted in us scraping along a levitating sidewalk for half a block before I could get the sticky control mechanism to put us back into what passed for a road.

"Neither does she," Rashid replied, holding on white knuckled to the side of the rickshaw.

He said something else to Bahram, but I didn't understand since it was in Arabic. That was probably just as well. My backseat driver had been kibitzing ever since we left the rent-a-rickshaw place, and I was getting tired of it.

I didn't clap back, however, because I was busy keeping us alive. The rickshaws were kept in the air by standard levitation charms, but that was the only thing about them that was standard. They were powered by huge fans in the back, like the ones on airboats, and they were dangerous as hell.

Ours had a safety cage over the wildly whirling blades, but plenty of those around us did not, and there weren't a lot of road rules in Hong Kong. That had always been true, but it was especially so now, as the usual land arteries had been mostly severed by damage from the battle, and people had been forced to take to the skies. That had resulted in a much more crowded airspace than I had seen before.

And the damned pirates didn't help.

"Not today," Louis-Cesare said, and brought up an arm, knocking a would-be thief back onto his flying rattletrap.

It was a casual gesture, but it must have been damaging, because it really pissed off the thief. He was a vampire, if a very stupid one, who didn't bother to check out the power signature of the guy he was attacking. The rattletrap swerved away, and then abruptly swerved back, and the bastards actually tried to board us!

Bahram and Louis-Cesare made quick work of them, which was good as I was busy accepting the fact that we were lost.

"God damn it," I muttered, and fished the map out of my jeans again.

I'd had the guy at the rickshaw place print it out for me, because my phone's tiny screen was hard to read, but it didn't help much. Especially not here. I stared around, looking for a reading light, and wondering where all the animated ads had gone.

Once upon a time, the skies would have been full of transparent fish swimming across the darkness, their glowing sides advertising sushi bars and sashimi places, or if said fish was also wearing a monocle, possibly fish and chips shops. There would have been cuties in miniskirts waving from the sides of buildings, trying to lure people into clubs and karaoke bars; fake, neon rain pattering down for half a block, only to have a swirl of branded umbrellas come flying to the rescue; and actual, physical ads jumping off their billboards to harangue passersby.

You haven't really lived until you've been chased down a sidewalk by a human-sized bowl of noodles that is brandishing chopsticks menacingly.

But there was nothing like that now. There were still billboards scattered around, what looked like hundreds of them. But most contained script only, without an image in sight. And many were completely empty, with just a few, ragged pieces of paper fluttering in the breeze.

It made me wonder why anybody would bother to remove old ads in a time of war, but there was no one to ask, at least not until we figured out where we were going.

I finally parked us by a huge, neon yellow sign advertising beer. It was a human-style LED variety, of the type that was still spotting the darkness here and there. But while it was bright, it kept switching things up every minute or so, sending alternately yellow, blue, pink and aqua tinted light dancing over the car, and making the map almost impossible to read. And that was before a passing rickshaw clipped us and sent us spinning into the stream of traffic again.

Rashid gave a sharp little scream when I abruptly dropped us the hell out of there and looked for another bolt hole. That wasn't easy as my requirements were: no crumbling buildings, no neon, and no pirates, which left out eighty percent of the city. But I finally located one under a levitating restaurant with festoons of lights draped along the balcony, and got my map out again.

The problem was that nothing in this city was fixed anymore. The damaged buildings had left plenty of people homeless, and that had only been exacerbated by the fact that the battle had done a number on the shield that kept this place safely wedged in non-space. The fighting had torn holes in it in places and weakened others, leading people to worry about their block suddenly being consumed by a new fissure.

As a result, thousands had fled their homes for the skies, living above the city rather than in it. That wasn't as unusual here as it would have been most places, as supernatural Hong Kong had always been a city of bridges. Forced to grow up instead of out due to the constraints of the shield, it had long had the habit of parking shops, eateries, and even housing on the thousands of bridges that connected many of the buildings.

I guessed it wasn't much of a stretch to go from living on a bridge over a big drop to just living over the drop, but it was damned inconvenient for us. It meant that, not only were there crazy, repurposed vehicles flying around, but also repurposed *housing*. Not that most of the houses were flying, but they were definitely in the way.

"There's another one," Rashid said, excitedly pointing off to the right. "That's what I saw before. Are people really living there?"

"Looks like it."

I could kind of understand his surprise. Floating off to our left was a group of old, rusted out buses that had been gutted and turned into makeshift apartments. They had curtains, window boxes, and somebody's deck chair on a roof, and were surrounded by a bulwark of worn-out tires. They were linked together by some walkways made out of wooden siding and the whole thing had been tethered to a burnt-out skyscraper so, I assumed, that it wouldn't float away.

The sky was full of similar rough-and-ready living spaces that hadn't been there when my map was written. To make matters worse, where people went, others had followed to cater to them. Meaning that I also had to dodge floating restaurants, bars and snack shops.

Some of those were fairly compact, with just a counter in front where you flew up to get your order. Others boasted stools affixed to the bottoms of the counters, leaving the patrons' feet dangling over nothing at all. And a few were taking alfresco dining to a whole new level, by parking levitating platforms out from their cookshops for those who wanted a better view and a shorter lifespan.

Yet there were people eating at them, and more ordering take-out, with vehicles of all descriptions buzzing about like flies, probably because most of the makeshift apartments didn't have stove tops.

Louis-Cesare waved one of the returning take out guys over and got a menu. He perused it while I tried to read the damned useless map by the light of a swag of bare bulbs hanging off the diner's balcony. It didn't go well.

"Is there a problem?" Rashid asked, his voice making it clear that he already knew the answer.

"No," I said, not needing help from the backseat driver, who I hadn't planned to bring along anyway.

That had been Hassani's idea, probably to protect his interests. And since we were currently such good friends, I didn't see how I could turn him down. Especially since the Middle Eastern Mr. Clean back there and his bearded buddy hadn't exactly asked. They'd shown up on the tarmac with bags packed.

So they could damned well keep their opinions to themselves!

"Then why did we stop?" he asked, tempting fate.

"I'm hungry." It was true; dhampir metabolisms were a bitch.

Of course, it was also true that I didn't know where to find a floating whorehouse in all this, despite the fact that I'd read the map right. It was supposed to be right here! But there was nothing of the kind in view, at least not as far as I could tell.

"Give me the map," Rashid demanded.

"Get your own."

"You are obviously lost—"

"I'm not lost. The damned brothel is lost—"

"We are going to a brothel?" That was Bahram, suddenly acquiring an interest.

"Not anytime soon," Rashid said, under his breath.

"I'll find it, okay?" I said, and snatched back the map that he'd tried to steal.

"Why are we going to a brothel?" Bahram inquired, as Louis-Cesare held up a hand.

I was about to answer when one of the guys at a nearby dim sum shop opened a door on the side and kicked out a set of wooden stairs. They'd been folded up under the door, out of the way. But now they spread-out and down, allowing me to see that they were held together by sturdy metal hinges on the side of each step.

Rotating hinges, I realized, as the thing snaked around the skies for a moment, until the waiter pushed it in our direction. It reached all the way to the rickshaw and then some, falling another half story below us. And allowing the man in his fresh white apron to run down and stop by our side.

He took out a small note pad and looked at us inquiringly.

"*Char Siu Bao*," Louis-Cesare said. He held up a thumb and two fingers. "Three, yes?"

The waiter guy nodded and wrote on the pad.

"Beer," I said. "And we're gonna need more of those barbeque buns."

"I just ordered three," Louis-Cesare protested.

"But I'm going to eat two orders myself."

"I, too, would like barbeque buns," Bahram said, leaning forward.

Louis-Cesare looked over his shoulder at Rashid, and cocked an eyebrow enquiringly.

"I would like to get where we are going!" Rashid said, and stole my map.

I decided to let him have it, because I couldn't figure it out and eat at the same time.

"*Char Siu Bao.* Four," Louis-Cesare corrected, holding up a thumb and three fingers.

"Six," Bahram corrected. I looked at him. He shrugged. "I have an appetite."

"Not for those," Rashid said, his eyes searching the map.

"Why not?"

"They have pork." He looked up at Louis-Cesare. "They do, yes?"

"Usually." Louis-Cesare looked back at the menu. "*Har Gow*—shrimp dumplings?" He looked at Bahram.

"They are *mukhruh*," Bahram said sadly. "Not forbidden, but—"

"Not encouraged?" Louis-Cesare guessed.

Bahram nodded.

Louis-Cesare went back to perusing the menu. I leaned over the seat to look at the map. It was upside down, which gave me a new perspective, not that it helped.

I got out my phone.

Phone connections had been restored with the reopening of the city's portals, allowing me to get a signal. I texted a friend: *Your map sucks.* And waited.

"Curried fishballs?" Louis-Cesare suggested.

Bahram made a face.

"*Fung Zao?*"

"What is that?"

"Chicken feet. They are deep fried, then marinated, then steamed. They come with a black bean and chili sauce."

"They eat the feet?" Bahram looked shocked.

"They're quite good."

He appeared dubious about that. But then he shrugged. "I will try."

"*Fung Zao*, two," Louis-Cesare told the waiter, who

nodded.

"And beer," I added, glancing in the back. "Unless—"

"Tea," Rashid said, still frowning at the map.

Bahram frowned. "I will have—"

"Tea," Rashid said firmly.

Bahram sighed. "Tea."

The waiter nodded, turned around, and tripped lightly up the stairs.

My phone dinged.

Where you at, short stuff? I read.

Underneath the *Little Pig Mongolian Hot Pot.*

"Are you sure that is the name?"

That was, of course, Rashid, reading over my shoulder.

"Why don't you go up and check?" I asked, smiling.

Rashid stood up, grabbed hold of the edge of the restaurant and levered himself up.

"Are you hoping he'll fall off?" Louis-Cesare mouthed.

I looked back innocently.

But, of course, he was a vamp. He didn't fall off. He did surprise a diner at a table by the railing, however, who screamed and dropped a beer.

Bahram caught it and drank it quickly, before his friend got back.

Sending some guys, my phone informed me.

What will they look like?

You'll know them when you see them.

But how will they know me?

Babe.

That was it. That was all I got. I frowned at it.

Then I shrugged and put my phone away.

Rashid rejoined us. "It is called 'Little Pig Mongolian Hot Pot' he informed Louis-Cesare, who ignored him both because he didn't care, and because our food had arrived.

It looked like the dim sum place was doing a bang-up business, and was churning the food out. They must have already had everything made; they'd just needed to dish it up. Which they'd done in traditional white to-go boxes, which Louis-Cesare handed around.

"What is this?" Rashid asked, holding up something from one of Bahram's boxes.

"*Fung Zao*," I said, my mouth full of barbequed pork.

"And that is what?"

"Good!" Bahram said, looking surprised. And dug into his feet.

A large, shiny, floating limo glided toward us, not bothering to dodge anything as we, and everyone else in the skies, had been doing. But then, it didn't need to, as everybody gave it an extra wide berth. It reminded me of a shark cutting through the ocean and fish suddenly remembering somewhere else they needed to be.

Only it wasn't a shark that decorated the face of the man who looked out of the back window, after it silently lowered.

I didn't know him, but I knew that tat. A beautifully rendered tiger prowled across the cheek of a handsome Chinese guy in an expensive suit. The tat matched the one I'd put on before we landed, because Kitty was not only security in these parts; she was my calling card.

I held up an arm, and my own tiger growled a little at his, before the two recognized each other and settled down.

"Dorina Basarab," the man said, and bowed his head slightly. "If you will come with me?"

The door was opened and a hand extended. I grabbed my buns and happily scuttled over. Louis-Cesare followed, despite not being asked, and got away with it because he always did; it was a talent.

But Rashid found the door closed in his face.

"What—we are with them!" he said indignantly.

My new guide popped an eyebrow worthy of Mircea. "I was told to pick up two senators. Are you a senator?"

"I—no, but—"

"Then you can follow us."

"But—but—we don't know how to drive this thing!"

"You were just saying you could do better," Bahram said, around a mouthful of feet.

"I did not!"

"Yes, you did, just a minute ago—"

"Be quiet!" he was told.

He may have been told other things, as well, but I didn't hear them. Because our ride was smoothly gliding across the skies, which seemed much less chaotic with tinted windows and soft music tinkling in the background. And champagne on offer.

"I left my beer," I realized.

"Bahram will no doubt handle it," Louis-Cesare said, accepting a glass of bubbles for us both.

I smiled and ate pork buns.

I could get used to this.

CHAPTER THIRTY

Dory, Hong Kong

"Okay, how did I miss this?" I asked, after Louis-Cesare helped me out of the limo.

It looked like there was already stratification taking place in the new, floating city. The rusted-out buses we'd passed earlier were nowhere to be seen, nor were there any tire buffer zones. Instead, the limo pulled smoothly into a berth beside what reminded me of a dockside village, only there was no water. It floated on air instead, high above the ruined cityscape, like a man-made island complete with greenery and a central fountain.

The buildings were wood, I guessed because it was lighter and quicker to build, but they weren't houses. The ones I could see from the outskirts looked like nightclubs, bars and restaurants, with a few shops littered in between. There was a movie theatre, a couple of dueling karaoke bars blasting waves of sound back and forth, and even a miniature night market down the center.

It was a floating entertainment complex, I realized, and appeared to have a large clientele.

The limo was secured by a little gate in back of the berth, and we exited straight onto one of the wooden sidewalks that connected the buildings. They were broad and a little bouncy, but perfectly walkable. On either side, there were shrubs in pots and squares of grass in planters, on what, now that I looked at it more closely, did seem to be a base of old tires. But they were covered by the sidewalks and greenery and thus almost invisible.

"How do you keep from floating off?" I asked our guide, whose name—I shit you not—was Elvis.

"Engines underneath. Enough to move us about, when we need to."

"Why would you need to do that?"

"Hot spots," he said, which didn't tell me anything, and he strode away toward a large building before I could ask.

It was nothing special on the outside, not that any of the buildings were. There hadn't been a lot of time for decoration, I guessed, or even painting. The bare wood had mostly been left the way it was, except for a few signs and some ads rippling across the surface of the boards.

In this case, the ads had gotten an upgrade, with the two scantily clad, cartoon cuties who hedged the door encased in large gold frames with solid backgrounds, giving them the look of paintings. Except that these paintings moved: dancing, gyrating and blowing kisses, I guess to entice visitors. Fun, I thought—right before one spotted Louis-Cesare.

A 2-D leg immediately emerged from the wall, stepping down onto the sidewalk in a six-inch, bright red, platform heel. A wiggle and a grunt later, and the rest of the body followed, clad in a red, floral-patterned cheongsam, which barely managed to contain the unlikely curves within. The body was still 2-D for a second, but then she shivered all over and fluffed out to full size.

And full-sized was no joke, because she wasn't Chinese, but rather a svelte blonde Valkyrie type who latched onto Louis-Cesare's arm with a hand tipped in two-inch long, bright red nails.

"Back on the wall, Svetlana," Elvis said, sounding annoyed.

Svetlana ignored him. "Aren't you a handsome one?" she purred at my hubby. "And so tall. I love a tall man—"

"Did I stutter?" Elvis demanded.

She pouted at him. "I'm bored! All I ever get to do out here is wave at people. I want to go back inside—"

"You can go back inside when it's your turn."

"Hey, cutie." A pair of jet-black nails latched onto Louis-Cesare's other arm. "Well, aren't you the one?"

I did a double take, both because the voice was low and husky enough to be a man's, and because—

"Shit!" I said, stepping back a pace. The newbie was a Betty Boop clone, which was not fun in person. Not at *all*.

She'd looked kind of adorable on the wall, where I'd have assumed, if I'd had time to assume anything, that she was advertising some sort of cosplay. But no. The head was hugely oversized, and the eyes were massive and glassy and staring. The body was tiny by comparison, ludicrously so, and completely black and white except for a little gray shading here and there.

"You can ask for me at the desk," she told Louis-Cesare huskily, who was just standing there, appearing vaguely stunned. "They put me out here, but if you ask—"

"Back on the wall!" Elvis said, sounding pissed.

And then he said something else, but I didn't hear him.

"Auuuggghhhh!" I screamed, when something jumped down from the roof and knocked me to the ground. I was back on my feet in a second, and pulling a gun—

On a giant pair of tits.

I stared at them for a moment, speechless. The tits had legs, encased in black fishnets and ending in red stilettos. They did not have anything else. They were just a fully realistic, hugely oversized, pair of boobs that had just pushed me back to the ground and were now trying to motorboat me.

Or maybe that was the other way around. I didn't know, because it's kind of hard to think straight when you're about to be crushed by the Grand Tetons up there. Louis-Cesare pulled me out from under before my brain completely broke, and all of us ran into the vestibule of the building, with Elvis slamming the door behind us and calling for back up on a radio.

I didn't know what he was saying, but a couple of mages hauled ass past us a moment later, one of them throwing a spell before the door was even fully open. I hugged the wall and stared at Louis-Cesare, who stared back. After a moment, I cleared my throat.

"Gonna ask for her at the desk?"

"You think you're funny . . ." he said, looking shaken.

"Not at the moment," I said fervently. "What the f—"

"Sorry about that," Elvis said, as what sounded like a battle started up outside. "They get like that sometimes. Too much magic floating about."

He waved a hand around his head.

I just looked at him.

"This way," he said, after an awkward silence.

We went that way. And discovered that the vestibule let out into a smoky club with a split personality. Like, really split.

On the one hand, the club's basic features were surprisingly upscale. There were discreet, red leather booths around dimly lit tables, a modernistic chandelier, and an extensive bar, where tuxedo clad waiters were getting drinks for the well-dressed clientele. It looked like a cross between an upscale gentleman's club and an expensive restaurant.

On the other hand, there was the artwork, in big, golden frames stuck anywhere that had enough wall space. The cuties in here were as active as the ones outside, dancing, gyrating and posing inside their frames, until somebody expressed an interest. And then the "art" stepped out of its painting, and walked off with a customer.

But at least, other than for a few anime types, they looked pretty much like real women, if real women had been designed by the Mattel Company. But that did not make it any better. If anything, it was somehow worse, only I wasn't exactly sure how. But I was feeling less than comfortable as we were led across the room to a booth in the far corner, where a friend was waiting.

"Hey, short stuff." A Chinese vamp who threatened to make Louis-Cesare look petite grinned up at me with a cutie pie on either knee. "I'd rise, but as you can see . . ."

What I could see was that the girls were either more fakes, or else they'd gotten extensive plastic surgery with Jessica Rabbit in mind. Or maybe one of the anime girls, since they were both Chinese. They could have been twins, except that one had a blue cheongsam and a short, blonde bob, and the other a slinky silver cocktail dress that Radu would have loved and a fall of long, straight black hair.

"Is that a gun in your hand, or are you just happy to see me?" Zheng asked, apparently reading my mind.

I looked down to see that I was still clutching my .44. I put it away but didn't apologize. "You're lucky I didn't shoot the tits," I told him.

"That would be a shame," he agreed. "They're our mascot."

And then he did get up, dumping the cuties and hugging me. "How the fuck you been, anyway?"

"Weird."

He pulled back and grinned. "Know the feeling." His eyes went to my receding hair line. "New style?"

"Decided to punk out."

"It suits you." He shook Louis-Cesare's hand, and gestured at the booth. "Sit down, sit down. These two were just leaving."

The girls took the hint, slinking off to charm some other table, and we slid into their place. "What the hell?" I asked, looking after them.

Zheng grinned at me some more. He was looking prosperous, in a dark gray suit that managed to camouflage most of the muscles, and was jazzed up by a discreet, paler gray pinstripe. He had a gold watch on one wrist, a matching ring on the other hand, and a tie tack with a ruby the size of my thumbnail.

Unlike his city, he seemed to be doing okay these days.

His attire, which matched the swanky clothing of the rest of the room, made me feel slightly out of place in my black jeans, matching T-shirt and leather jacket. But at least Louis-Cesare looked nice. He wasn't dressed up—he rarely was if not at court—and only had on a dark blue button up with equally dark jeans. But, somehow, on him it matched any suit in the room, bringing out the red in his hair and the sapphire in his eyes.

Or maybe that was just me.

"Got a nice set up, Lily does," Zheng was saying, when I tore my attention away from my husband. "And she thought it up all by herself, I'm ashamed to say. Can't believe I missed that one."

"Lily?"

"The proprietor. She'll be along eventually."

"And what set up, exactly, does she have?" Louis-Cesare asked, because he seemed as confused as me.

"Exactly what it looks like." Zheng took a drink from the heavy crystal glass in front of him, then waved it around. "A lot of people vacated the area after the big boom, including most of the girls. Lily, who is—or was—a working girl herself, soon had too much work to handle. So, she got this idea . . ."

"To make herself some help?" Louis-Cesare asked, checking out the completely unbelievable proportions on the cigarette girl who'd just wiggled by.

Zheng nodded. "It started with these cards she had made up, business type things. Used to put them in the phone booths around the city, in shops, anywhere they'd let her. For advertising, you know."

I kicked my husband, who was still watching the cigarette girl. She had a black spangled, Playboy-Club-without-the-ears outfit that did tend to draw the eye, especially from the back. Which was no excuse, damn it!

"I didn't think you were the jealous type," Louis-Cesare murmured, as a waiter came by to take our order.

"I'm not. And if I was, it wouldn't be here. They're not real."

"Oh, they're real enough," Zheng said. "That's the beauty of it."

I eyed the figure on a voluptuous redhead in a glittery gold gown who was slinking our way. "No way in hell."

He laughed. "Oh, I didn't mean flesh and blood real. I meant personality wise. Well, sort of."

"Sort of?"

He nodded. "Those business cards contained a photo of Lily in a provocative pose, to lure in customers. It was animated so it'd gyrate around and catch your eye. But the mage she got to enchant them was a friend, and wanted hers to stand out. When he did the spell for the 'toon, he added a bit more oopmf than strictly necessary, and some of her personality got imbedded along with her looks."

"Fascinating," Louis-Cesare said, now also watching the redhead.

"Oh, that wasn't the fascinating part. One of her cards was caught in the cross fire during the battle, and somehow got transferred to a mage as a temporary tattoo. He and I ended up joining forces—you remember him," he added, looking at me, because I'd crossed paths with the man briefly.

"Typical war mage; completely nuts," I told Louis-Cesare, which wasn't entirely true—the typical part, not the crazy—but I didn't want to get into all of that now.

"He was that," Zheng agreed. "And—well, let's just say that the tattooed version of Lily turned out to be a true asset. Enough that I decided to meet the real woman, and we joined forces."

"Joined forces as in . . ."

He grinned. He seemed to be in a good mood today. "That, too. But mainly, the family needed a new line of work now that we're legit, and she needed protection in these difficult times. And the magic to try out the idea she came up with after I told her how we 'met'."

"And the personalities?" I asked, as the redhead paused by a nearby table to light a man's cigarette.

Zheng shrugged. "She talked a few of her friends into lending their characteristics to the new scheme, in return for a cut of the take. So far, it's been very lucrative."

"How?" Louis-Cesare asked, still watching the redhead.

I really couldn't blame him, this time. The others we'd met had been well into uncanny valley territory, with even the more realistic having improbable curves and weird, glassy eyes. They looked like what they were: sex dolls that could walk around. But this one . . . could have fooled me.

That probably wasn't true for Louis-Cesare, because there was no blood flowing in the veins she didn't have and no heart beating in that ample chest, something that a vampire would detect immediately. But there was a dewy freshness to the skin and a glossiness to the hair, which wasn't the flat, dyed red of several others in the room, but a rich flow with hints of brown and gold. And her eyes—her eyes were perfect.

"Would you like some company?" she asked me, smiling, and bending down enough that I was able to see the striations of yellow and a dot of brown in the otherwise clear blue of her iris. She had a tiny mole on her left temple, like a beauty mark. And thick, dark eyelashes that were a little uneven, like a real person's.

And, suddenly, I wasn't sure anymore.

"Is she?" I asked Louis-Cesare, who was looking at her with concern.

He shook his head.

"No, thanks," I said, and she gracefully moved on to the next table.

"You cannot be making a profit," Louis-Cesare said to Zheng. "The amount of magic such realism must require— the cost would be prohibitive. Especially for so many . . ."

His eyes went around the place, and I could see him getting more and more puzzled, as he did the mental math.

Zheng saw it, too, and his expression changed. "You asking as a friend or . . ."

"Or what?"

"A senator. You are one—"

"As are you."

"—and maybe you'd like to be one after the war, too."

It was Louis-Cesare's expression that changed this time. "Meaning?"

"Meaning that our dear consul is going to want a reason to flush those of us she doesn't like, but needs for the war, once the fighting is done. Especially ones like me, who she doesn't trust anyway."

"You think I would betray you?"

"How should I know?" Zheng sat back, and spread his long arms along the top of the booth. "I don't know you that well. Short stuff here, well, that's a different story. Assuming she's vouching for you?"

"He's not going to say anything," I said, impatiently. "You can trust him like you would me."

"Oh, well, that's different then." Zheng paused. "And as long as we're all friends, I was thinking—"

"Here it comes," I said, and took the glass the waiter brought me. I hadn't ordered anything, but Louis-Cesare knew what I liked, and it was a fine old scotch that went down so smoothly that you barely noticed how much it burned.

"—that we all got something in common."

"Such as?" I asked.

"Such as the fact that the consul doesn't like any of us. You're a dhampir, he screwed up, and I'm an outsider who she thinks may be a spy for the East Asian Court."

"Are you?" Louis-Cesare asked.

It was a little too abrupt for somebody like Zheng, who came from a culture who valued dignity, aka "face", above all.

And who was also a master vamp, none of whom like being challenged, even indirectly. But he didn't take offense.

A suspiciously good mood, I thought, and drank whiskey.

"I was approached," he said. "Too bad our dear empress spent hundreds of years knocking me down to size and treating me like a pariah that wasn't good enough to kiss her little feet—"

"Big feet, according to your old boss," I put in. Lord Cheung was the other would-be member of the East Asian Court who had ended up on ours instead. He was Zheng-zi's old master, although they were equals now, both being senators.

"He would know better than me," Zheng agreed. "At least he got a few trips to court. I was never good enough. And now she's not good enough for me—unless I need to start kissing up?"

"And why would you do that?" Louis-Cesare asked.

He shrugged. "What you think. We work our tails off, risk our necks, and after the war, when we've made plenty of enemies on our dear consul's behalf . . ."

"She cuts us off," I said. It was what I'd been assuming, too.

He nodded. "Possibly literally. Call me paranoid, but I've been feeling the need for some reassurance, lately."

"What kind of reassurance?"

"An alliance with clan Basarab." He shivered suddenly in apparent delight. "Ooh, just the thought makes me all tingly."

"What kind of alliance—" Louis-Cesare began, before I set down my glass—hard.

"No."

"No?" Zheng raised an eyebrow. "You don't even want to hear my proposal?"

"No. Not now, not today. I get my sister back, I get Ray back, then maybe—"

Zheng tilted his head. "Where'd they go?"

I told him.

CHAPTER THIRTY-ONE

Dory, Hong Kong

"That's . . . a lot to take in," Zheng said, and I'd given him the truncated version.

I nodded. "Then you see why we need help —"

"And I need an alliance. With your old man gone, you're head of the clan, so you can make those kinds of—"

"Wait. What?" I looked from him to Louis-Cesare and back again. "What do you mean, gone?"

It was Zheng who answered. "As in away. As in, nobody knows where he is, or they aren't saying. I've been trying to get hold of him for more than a week, but—"

"You've been trying to get in contact with Mircea for a week?" I asked, making sure I understood.

He nodded.

"And it hasn't worked?"

He nodded again.

"Did you know about this?" I asked Louis-Cesare.

"No, but it does not surprise me. I tried to contact him mentally the night that . . . everything happened . . . but could not reach him. I was told that he was unavailable—"

"His daughter was just kidnapped, and he's unavailable?" I stared at him.

"That is what I was told. I then tried his phone, but could

reach only his batman," he said, speaking of the military attaché Mircea had acquired after being promoted to general of the World Senate's combined army.

The promotion had made him more difficult to contact lately, as he was constantly in a meeting or running around, putting out fires. Or actually fighting in Faerie, where the first battle of the conflict had been an overwhelming success, although with significant losses for our side. I hadn't seen him since he'd healed my leg, having first been recovering and then, once I was back on two feet, off on the current, diplomatic whirlwind.

But still. Louis-Cesare was family, not to mention a senator who might have picked up important intel on his travels. Getting in touch shouldn't be this hard!

"What did Gerald have to say?" I asked, referencing the pinched faced batman.

"That 'General Basarab is currently unavailable'."

I frowned. That bastard. He never told anybody anything.

Of course, that was true of somebody else around here.

"And you didn't mention this?" I said. "Why?"

Louis-Cesare didn't even have the grace to look uncomfortable. "I was going to, but you had enough on your plate."

"Don't you think I should have been the one to decide that?"

"Normally, yes—"

"Normally?"

There was some kind of commotion across the club, but I didn't look up. I was too busy looking at my husband. "Team Basarab here." I pointed back and forth between the two of us. "We're supposed to be on the same side—"

"We are on the same side—"

"Until it's inconvenient for you—"

"Inconvenient?" Louis-Cesare's eyes flashed. "Inconvenient?"

"Oh, boy," Zheng said, and sat back.

"You almost died!" Louis-Cesare said. "Am I not allowed to take care of you? To make decisions when you are hurt and in pain?"

"It depends on the decision. Look, I know you're used to deciding for the family—"

"And you are family!"

The commotion was getting louder, but a glance at the door to the foyer revealed nothing, and anyway, I was busy. Zheng needed to keep his damned club in line. "Yes, but not subordinate family! We are partners. Partners talk, they tell each other things—"

"I intended to tell you as soon as there was anything to tell—"

"Again, not your decision. What if Mircea was kidnapped, too? What if all this was some kind of move against the family—"

"He was not kidnapped—"

"You can't know that—"

"He *can* know that," Zheng said, looking apologetic.

"Mircea is a master mentalist," Louis-Cesare reminded me. "The whole family would know the moment such a thing happened—"

"Unless someone . . . got the drop on him," I said, which, okay, wasn't likely, but in that case, where was he? I hadn't thought about it before, because I'd been a little busy, and because Mircea and I didn't live in each other's pockets. But I should have, because this wasn't the sort of thing he'd just ignore.

That would have been true even if we hadn't been drawing closer these last months, which we had. It had been almost like having a normal family for the first time, or as normal as a vampire clan got. And yet . . . Dorina was taken, and he said nothing? Did nothing? Even if just for family pride, he would have had to respond.

"I don't understand this," I said, and Louis-Cesare nodded.

"Neither do I, but Radu does. He was my next call, after Gerald gave me nothing—" I pulled out my phone, but Louis-Cesare just shook his head. "He won't tell you anything, either, except that Mircea is busy."

And that was no doubt true, because Radu doted on his one and only Child. If Louis-Cesare couldn't get anything out of him, it was unlikely that I'd have better luck. But what the hell?

"*Busy*? What could be more important than—" I broke off, because I couldn't hear myself think. "What is going on out there?"

"That's what I'd like to know," Zheng said, getting to his feet.

Which was when a small woman with a big voice came into the room, walking backwards, while yelling at—

"Oh, shit," I said, because I'd forgotten about them.

Bahram and Rashid stumbled into the room, being beaten on by what looked like every toon in the place. Stilettos—of the type that Jimmy Choo makes—were brandished, fists were flung, and purses were slammed upside heads that were cowering under arms, or at least Bahram's were. Rashid was dumb enough or proud enough to lower his guard for a moment, and got nailed by a large Birkin.

"It was justified!" he said, staring around.

I slunk down in my seat.

"Is there perhaps a back door?" Louis-Cesare asked quietly.

But not quietly enough.

"It was justi—there!" Rashid pointed straight at our table, and he and Bahram made a beeline for us, despite being beaten up every step of the way.

Fortunately, the club's patrons seemed to view this as entertainment. Unfortunately, Zheng did not. "What the hell is this?" he demanded, his brows lowering.

"He kill Bertha!" the small woman said, pointing at

Rashid.

She was an attractive, thirtyish, Chinese woman with long black hair and an expensive yellow suit made out of flowered cheongsam silk, but in a Western style. And she was human, something I knew without needing to ask. She lacked the statuesque frame of the fakes, and also their exaggerated charms. But the big giveaway was that she was hopping mad, to the point that veins were standing out on her temples.

Lily, I assumed, although I had no chance to ask.

"You *killed* someone?" I asked Rashid, in disbelief.

"No! I killed—it was an abomination. I do not have words —"

"Find some," Louis-Cesare suggested.

But it was not Rashid who found the words. It was Bahram, and they weren't exactly words. He put his hands well in front of his chest and cupped them in the unmistakable, universal gesture for big boobs.

I felt my spine turn to water.

"Oh, thank God." I sat back against the booth.

"No, no thank God! He killed Bertha!" Lily was clearly out for blood.

Louis-Cesare still looked confused, probably because Bahram was turned away from him, and he hadn't seen the universal gesture.

"He shot the tits," I told Louis-Cesare.

"No! He no shoot," Lily said. "He push, right over the edge!"

"Seriously?" I asked Rashid, whose cheeks were burning.

"It assaulted me. I have the right to defend myself!"

Zheng was still standing there, with an I-don't-believe-this-is-my-life face. "You're gonna have to pay for that," he told Rashid.

"I was attacked!"

"Yeah, by a pair of tits." Zheng looked him over. "You are a vamp, right?"

"He's a master," Bahram said, munching on something. It wasn't chicken feet, so I guessed they'd made a stop.

Rashid's cheeks went puce, a fact that did not stop his mouth from opening. But Lily wasn't finished yet. *"What about poor Bertha?"*

"He'll pay for another one," Zheng assured her.

"I not want another one! I have Bertha long time. I want her." Her eyes suddenly went huge. "What if she not dead? What if she down there, all alone? Hurt and—" Her hand went to her mouth. "What if monsters get her?"

"What monsters?" I said.

Zheng put a hand to his forehead. He stood like that for a few seconds, while Rashid continued to be assaulted. He didn't push anybody else over any ledges, however, so I supposed he'd learned something.

"Alright," Zheng said. "You," he pointed at Rashid. "Pay for the damned tits. You," he pointed to a couple of his guys, who were just standing in the back, watching the show. "Take a car and have a look down below—carefully. You," he pointed at me. "Come this way. I'd like to talk where I can hear myself think."

* * *

We ended up in a dark red corridor with dim lighting, probably to cover the signs of a hasty construction job. Red flocked wall paper hid the plywood walls, and plush red carpet covered the floors. There were a lot of doors all along one side.

The client rooms, I guessed. They must have been soundproofed, because I didn't hear anything as we walked along. But not that well soundproofed, judging by the expressions that crossed Louis-Cesare's face, which ranged from slight amusement, to wincing sympathy, to—

"What? What was that?" I asked, because it had looked a lot like envy.

"Tell you later."

"Well, at least you'll tell me something later."

That did not get a response before we entered a large office at the end of the hall. It was a semicircle with almost a full wall of windows behind the desk. It looked like it had been scavenged from some high-end spa or executive's corner office, which it probably had. The authorities had better things to do these days than police the wreckage, and supernatural Hong Kong had a history of repurposing everything from pirate ships to the ubiquitous rickshaws.

"Can I see the tat?" Zheng asked, before he even sat down.

He looked over the item that Hassani had given us while we took chairs in front of the desk. It was a huge, old-world, dark wood item that Zheng had come up with somewhere, and that looked like it might have been part of one of the aforementioned pirate ships at one time. It had small, carved figureheads for posts—tits out, of course, which actually fit in with the overall ambience around here—and wooden curlicues that almost matched the wallpaper outside.

It was elaborate enough to give the office a feeling of luxury, despite the fact that the plywood walls were still bare.

Well, almost.

There was a set of kinetic armor that I'd seen Zheng wear into battle once, hung on one wall, with occasional arcs of what looked like electricity jumping from one little trefoil decoration to another. There were some weapon's cabinets in the same dark wood as the desk that were hedging the door, where I supposed their contents would be handy. And there was an old, expensive Persian rug on the floor, in blues and yellows and whites, covering most of the unstained boards.

But it was the view that stole the show, with all kinds of strange vehicles filling the skies and several other floating gardens looking like green clouds in the distance. This wasn't an area with a lot of skyscrapers, and the ones that did exist weren't in direct line of sight. Giving me the surreal sight of an entirely floating city, with nothing underneath but air.

It could have kept me occupied for hours, but Zheng didn't need them.

"Shit." He didn't look happy.

"You know what it is," I said, pulling my attention back to the tat.

"I know some things about it." He put it on the desk and looked up, and he had his poker face on. "But I need a guarantee first."

"We're on the same senate—" I began hotly.

"Yes, and I just finished explaining why that doesn't help either of us if we don't align. Look, I get it; you two don't speak for the old man, wherever the old man is. But you do speak for you, and you have influence with him. I want a guarantee of an alliance between us, and an assurance that you'll work on Mircea to get him to at least consider my proposal."

"Which is what?" Louis-Cesare asked warily.

Zheng shrugged. "What I said. The consul isn't fond of us —any of us, and from what I hear, that includes him. The day may come when we'll all need friends. I can be a good friend, to those who're good to me."

"That's damned vague," I pointed out.

The big, handsome face was sober. "When you're talking about this kind of stuff, it's best to be vague. I'll be more direct with your father, if he wants it."

Louis-Cesare frowned. "You ask for a great deal. How do we know that your information is worth it?"

Zheng lit up a cigarette and sat back in his chair, allowing the smoke to wreath his head. "I'm not offering merely information. I can help you. But it's dangerous, and I want to know that it's worthwhile."

"It's worthwhile if we get Dorina back," Louis-Cesare said, "not otherwise."

"Hey—" I began.

"And if she's already dead?" Zheng demanded. "You're

still going to want a pound of somebody's flesh—"

"If she's dead, we'll be taking a great deal more than that," Louis-Cesare said grimly.

"Exactly. And you'll need help—"

"We won't need help with vengeance, I can assure you."

"And I can assure you that you will. You don't know Hong Kong, especially now—"

"Then let us say that any agreement would be contingent upon us finding Dorina—in whatever condition she may be —and upon your information and aid being material to her retrieval. If it doesn't help us, you get nothing—"

"Hey!" I said, a little more forcefully.

"—and, of course, there will be further conditions—"

"Aren't there always?" Zheng asked sardonically.

"—which will have to be negotiated, although that can wait until—"

"Hey!" I slapped the desk, hard enough to rattle the few items on it.

Both men stopped to look at me.

I frowned at Louis-Cesare. "We need to talk."

"Now?"

"Yes, now."

"I'll step outside," Zheng offered.

"We will," Louis-Cesare said, which made Zheng raise a big, black eyebrow. As if offended that we might think his office was bugged. But he didn't object, probably because the whole damned place was.

We stepped out. And immediately wished we hadn't, or at least I did. Because the hallway was already full.

"No, she *better*!" Lily was saying, as I started digging through my purse.

"What are you—" Louis-Cesare began, watching me.

"Just wait a minute." The bag was larger than the one I'd lost, an experimental type that I'd left on the plane when we went to Hassani's, because I was still getting used to the idea. It had come courtesy of the same guy who'd designed the graffiti gun, the father of a war mage friend who loved to tinker with strange magic.

And this was about as strange as it got.

Not that it looked like it. It was almost a clone of my other purse, both big, black leather numbers, although this one had an extra wide opening. It also had an added feature, if I could remember how to turn it on . . .

"That's absurd," Rashid was saying, with a sneer. "These . . . things . . . of yours are not superior to real women."

"Oh, no?" Lily pulled a petite brunette, who had just left a room with a client, into the argument. "You like big bust? Big bust!" she said.

Louis-Cesare made a sound and I looked up. I don't know what Lily had done; I hadn't seen her do anything. But the girl's former A cup was suddenly full and running over, to the point that she popped a couple of buttons on her shirt. One of them hit Bahram, who was eating again, but he didn't seem to mind.

Unlike his friend.

"That!" Rashid said pointing, and appearing outraged. "That is absurd!"

Lily made a disgusted sound. "You not know what you talking about! You like the booty? There you go, big, big booty!"

She held a hand over the area in question, and the brunette's backside suddenly ballooned outward, until a Brazilian supermodel would have been envious. And until I feared for the integrity of her skirt. Fortunately, it stretched.

"Stop that!" Rashid demanded angrily, as the girl flexed one side and then the other, getting used to her new assets. And then twerked a little, because who wouldn't have?

But Lily did not stop. "You like big lips? There you go. Big lips!"

The girl suddenly looked like a Juvéderm ad. Rashid started to say something, which by the look of things would not have been polite. But then Lily looked down the hall and saw us. "Tell me what real girl can do that?" she said proudly.

"The Kardashians?" I offered.

"They not here!"

"Finally!" Rashid said, striding down the hall toward us. "I need to talk to you—"

"Maybe later," I said, grabbed Louis-Cesare by the hand, and ducked into an empty room.

"That won't hold him," Louis-Cesare pointed out, as I slammed the door.

"It doesn't have to. You ready?"

"For what?"

"For this," I said, and pulled him inside—my purse.

CHAPTER THIRTY-TWO

Dory, Hong Kong

It was dark, until I fumbled around in my pocket and found a light. It was only a cigarette lighter, which is a useful item to carry when you regularly fight vamps, even if you don't smoke. I clicked it, and the flame lit up our faces with a dim, golden glow, although the rest of the space remained in darkness.

Louis-Cesare's face was showing a certain amount of surprise, which was valid.

"What is this?" he asked, glancing about.

"Fey tech. I got trapped in one of these once. You remember; you came in to get me."

"You mean the laboratory."

I nodded. "That would be the one. Some dark mages folded over a flap of non-space to make themselves an illegal lab that nobody could find, because it didn't exist in real space. I thought I'd repurpose the idea for something good."

"Repurpose it how?" Louis-Cesare asked. He could probably see more in almost complete darkness than I could, but this deserved better lighting. I fumbled around on the wall until I found the switch and flicked it.

"What . . . did you do?" he asked, his eyes widening, and amazement in his voice.

"That."

I gestured around proudly at what looked like a simple, cement walled room with a concrete floor and no windows. But the bare bones didn't tell the whole story—not by half. Because this room . . . was filled with wonders.

I'd spent half of my convalescence moving things around, getting it just the way I liked. There was a squashy armchair to sit in, for cleaning guns and bandaging wounds and just resting in between bouts. There was a light overhead, just the bare bulb for now, but I was thinking about getting a decorative fixture to spruce things up. There was, of course, a beer fridge, and it was fully stocked, because what am I? An animal?

But the real story was what was scattered around, covering almost every available surface. When I designed this place, I had thought of it as fairly expansive, because I'd assumed that I'd be filling it via the contents of my own, rather thin, bank account. But afterwards, I'd found another solution.

Or, to be more precise, Ray had found it.

"You gotta see this!" he said, taking my hand and all but pulling me down a set of stairs at court.

"See what? And why are we going to the dungeon?"

"It's not a dungeon. What is this? The Middle Ages?"

"No, but this house does belong to the consul," I reminded him. And she'd always kind of struck me as pretty damned medieval.

"Yeah, that's the point," Ray said excitedly, as we all but ran down a narrow set of stairs that I'd never seen before. Of course, that probably had something to do with the fact that they were hidden by a painting, a corridor, another painting, and a set of bookshelves, but trust Ray to suss them out, if there was something valuable to be found.

I just didn't know what yet.

"I mean, I knew they hadda have it somewhere," he was babbling. "But I couldn't find it—"

"Find what?"

"—after all, we're at war. Even if they didn't have one before, they'd have to have put something together—"

"Ray. One what?"

"—and knowing her Stinginess, I didn't figure on her letting it too far outta her sight. So, it had to be here—"

"Ray! What had to be here?"

"That," he said, grinning, and threw open a door—to Ali Baba's cave. Or it may as well have been.

Damn, I thought, staring around. I'm gonna need a bigger room.

And I did, most definitely. But I hadn't had a chance to address that yet, the original one having been pretty damned costly. So, I'd made do.

Which was why the now rather small-looking space was crammed with shelves of guns, ammo, grenades, and a grenade launcher—easily enough to fight a small war. And cabinets of magical charms, potion bombs and spelled objects, sufficient to make a war mage drool. And decorative displays of more old school weapons mounted on the walls, with fans of everything from swords and pikes to knives and axes.

"The senate's armory," I explained, as Louis-Cesare moved forward, appearing as stunned as I had been when Ray had first showed me. "Or as much of it as I could steal, anyway. The room is also soundproofed, so we can talk freely."

But Louis-Cesare wasn't talking. Louis-Cesare was exploring, particularly the rack of swords, rapiers and cutlasses on a nearby wall. They'd just been piled up in dusty chests at the consul's, because nobody really used them anymore, so I'd helped myself. And, of course, I'd taken the pretty ones.

I guessed I must have chosen well, because Louis-Cesare took down one of the rapiers and slashed the air with it a few times. Then looked up at me, his eyes shining.

"I used to have one like this as a boy. It is an antique."

"Have that one if you like. I took it for you." I sat on the chair. "I don't do a lot of fencing."

"I could teach you."

"Maybe someday."

I watched him slash the air some more, and make a few pretty lunges, with his body extended and his form perfect. He never looked so at home as when he had a blade in his hand. It almost didn't even seem like a weapon anymore after he picked it up, but more like an extension of his body.

"This is a work of art," he said admiring the chasing on the knuckle guard that fitted over the grip. "Are there any more like this?"

"I wasn't paying that much attention," I admitted. "You should go take a look for yourself. Haven't you ever been down there?"

"No. But perhaps I should." He made a few rolling motions with his wrist, causing the blade to glimmer and gleam as it slowly wove a pattern in the air.

"You might want to give them some time to restock," I said. "I already took all the good stuff."

"And this place?" he stopped admiring the sword long enough to look at me. "You made yourself an armory—that you could carry about with you?"

I shrugged. "Technically, the armory is in a pocket of non-space, so I'm not really carrying anything but the fixed mouth to a portal. But, sure. It sounds cooler your way."

He just looked at me.

"I got tired of running out of weapons," I explained.

He shook his head, and put the rapier back. And the next moment, I was enveloped in a warm hug. "I do love you," he said, a smile in his voice. "And I am sorry, for not telling you about your father."

"Okay."

Louis-Cesare pulled back after a moment to regard me

more soberly. "It isn't, though, is it? You're upset."

"Yes, I'm upset. About that, and about what just happened with Zheng."

His forehead knitted. "What just happened?"

Damn it, I knew it!

"You were negotiating for me," I explained patiently. Or as patiently as I was able to manage right now. "I was sitting right there, not two feet away from you, yet I couldn't get a word in—"

"I would never do that!"

"—edgewise."

He frowned.

I pinched the top of my nose, because I was getting a headache. I was also getting a heartache, because this was something like the third time that we'd had this conversation, and I wasn't getting through. I was starting to wonder if I was ever going to.

And what if I didn't?

Louis-Cesare was watching me and he seemed to get that this was serious. I supposed that was something. I just didn't know if it would be enough.

"I understand that we're both used to being on our own," I said. "To not having anybody to answer to, to making all our own decisions. But—"

"We're not on our own anymore."

I shook my head.

He sighed and sat down on the floor beside me. He rested his head on my knee, which was cheating, but I decided I'd allow it. The tiny room stuffed with weapons was strangely peaceful after the last few days, a quiet, dimly lit oasis where the outside world couldn't intrude.

We needed to talk, and I fully intended to. But I was willing to postpone it for a few moments. This was nice.

Louis-Cesare's hair had gotten a bit windblown on the ride over, so I undid the clasp at his neck and ran my fingers through it because I didn't have a comb. It was the only drawback to having your purse turned into an armory: you no longer had a purse. I had pockets on the outside, but they were usually stuffed with weapons, too. It was a dilemma . . .

"I don't want you here," Louis-Cesare said abruptly.

My fingers stilled. "That . . . was not what I expected you to say."

"But it is the truth." He looked up at me, and the sapphire eyes were sober. "I want to be the knight in the fairy tales, defending his lady. I want, with all of my being, to know that you are safe, and that whatever happens to me, you will remain so. When I saw you there, in that alley in Cairo, when I realized that Jonathan had hurt you, and that he'd been able to do so because of me—"

"It wasn't because of you. You heard Hassani; the fey were everywhere that night. If I hadn't followed you, they'd have gotten me somewhere else."

"Perhaps; perhaps not. But then to see you in that temple, and to know that your pain was my fault, that I had failed you once again—"

"You didn't fail me," I said, getting exasperated. So much for the warm, cozy feeling of a moment ago. "That had nothing to do with you—"

"But it did! I should have been there! Even after I saw that Jonathan hurt you, that he had targeted you, I gave him the opportunity to do it again—"

"You gave him nothing. I chose to go down there. It was my decision—"

"But if I had been there—"

I got up suddenly, because I couldn't think straight with auburn silk cascading over my legs. And because I needed to move. Louis-Cesare followed me with his eyes, and there was no question in them. He believed, absolutely, in what he was saying.

"You know it's true," he said, echoing my thoughts.

"What I know is that you're acting like a master vamp who let down one of his family."

"Is that not what I am?"

"No." Damn it, I knew it. "I'm your family in that Radu is my uncle and he's your sire. But I'm with you because I choose to be. I chose you; I marked you because I see you as an equal. I always have. But I wouldn't have done that if I'd had any idea that you see me as an inferior—"

"I do nothing of the kind!"

"—who needs protection because she can't handle herself!"

"I want to protect you because I love you!"

"I believe that," I said, working to rein in my temper. Because he had to get this. I had to be able to explain this, or we were through. I loved him—so much—but I wasn't going to live like this. I wasn't going to be the little woman to be cherished and lied to and protected, while her man went out to face the world's terrors alone—

And didn't come back.

That wasn't who I was; wasn't who I could be, even if I'd wanted to. Dhampirs ran on adrenaline and anger and action, needing combat as much as we needed air. Yes, I got beat up sometimes, even a lot of the time, but I came through it; I always had. And even if, someday, I didn't, I'd rather die fighting by my husband's side than sitting at home, wringing my hands, and waiting for news that would kill me anyway.

Not to mention the fact that we were at war. Did he really think I'd be that much safer back home? There was no safety anymore, except for what we provided each other.

I just wished I knew the words to get him to see that.

I walked back over and knelt beside him. I took his hands in mine, stupidly huge things that they were, because this was a last-ditch effort so I might as well go for broke. "I believe that," I told him again. "But I also believe that you see me as someone who you give information to when you feel like it, who you protect whether she likes it or not, and who you make decisions for. That's a problem."

Louis-Cesare didn't say anything for a long moment,

although his eyes searched my face. That was good. I wanted him thinking.

Whether it would do any good, I honestly didn't know.

"I don't know how," he finally said, and then stopped himself and thought some more. I waited. His eyes found the floor and he stared at it for a long time, before finally looking up at me. "I assume that you want complete honesty?"

"Yes."

"Even if you won't like it?"

"Yes."

He nodded. "Very well, then. The truth is, that I don't know how to be the partner you want. I have never been a partner—to anyone. I was a burden to my family; Christine was a burden to me." He paused again, and then continued in a rush. "I try, but I tell you truly, if breaking up with you would keep you safe, if I knew that it would, I would do it. If locking you away would keep you safe, I would do it. If making you hate me was the only way—"

I stopped him with a hand on his cheek, because I already knew all this. His actions lately had made it more than apparent. I just didn't know why.

"Where is all this coming from?"

"You have to ask?" His hand pushed up the bottom of my jeans enough to show the tell-tale scar on my calf. His finger traced it, the touch gentle, barely there. But I felt it down to my bones because of the expression on his face. "I did this to you—"

"You didn't know—"

He quieted me with a look. He meant this, all the way from his soul. "I *did* this. I wasn't strong enough to wrest back control, and keep you safe. Just as I wasn't strong enough in that alley, or in that tomb. I know you say it was not my fault, but it was my hand on the sword, and my negligence the other times. *I did this*."

He put a hand in his hair, pushing it up, looking slightly deranged. I'd known that this had been playing on his mind;

I'd caught glimpses, here and there, and been paying enough attention to interpret half cut off words. But I hadn't realized it was this bad.

He looked up at me, and the blue eyes were tortured. "But I also know that leaving would not keep you safe, either. I do not know what will, and it tears at me."

I put a hand on his shoulder, and felt the strain there. It was like touching steel with a thin veneer of flesh on top. Everything I'd needed to know was in that one touch.

But I still didn't have the words to make it better.

"I've been around a long time," I finally said.

"Yes, as a dhampir assassin nobody knew. You're playing on a different level now. You know this."

"Yes, I know this. I know something else, too."

He looked at me.

I struggled for words, and when they came, they weren't particularly elegant or refined. But they were heartfelt. I meant every word, just as much as he had.

"I was alone for a long time. I didn't know about Dorina, I thought my father hated and was ashamed of me, and the people that I did have relationships with were business contacts and those who wanted something from me. That was it. That was how I lived, year after year after long, lonely, pain-filled year. And, yeah, there were better times, once in a while. But there weren't a hell of a lot of them.

"Some people make it through hard times by telling themselves that things will get better. But after so long, you begin to realize: they never will. That was as good as life got, as good as I thought it would ever get. A desert of pain with a few oases dotted here and there, just enough to keep me going. That was all, and wanting anything else, much less expecting it . . .

"Was a child's foolish dream. Just wishful thinking.

"But then, I met you."

I looked at him, and I still saw it, just as I had on that first day, although I hadn't wanted to admit it to myself: the little girl's dream of prince charming, complete with the stupid hair and the gorgeous body and the even more beautiful soul. And I still didn't have the words. Because what do you say to a dream come true?

But something must have shown on my face, because his hands tightened.

"I don't know what to tell you," I said. "I wish I did. All I can say for sure is this. If some genie had come to me and offered me a trade: a few years of being with someone I truly care about in exchange for all the centuries that I had left like that? Yeah. I'd have made the trade.

"And I still would."

CHAPTER THIRTY-THREE

Dory, Hong Kong

We reentered Zheng's office sometime later, without encountering Hassani's vamps. I didn't know where they were, but was grateful that they were gone. I wasn't even sure what the hell they were doing here in the first place. Did Hassani think I wasn't going to track down my sister's kidnappers? Or that I was going to let them off with a slap on the wrist? And if he did think that, what exactly were two guys going to do about it?

I mean, yeah, they were pretty good in a fight, but still. Two guys. I couldn't really see them taking on a whole contingent of fey on their own.

But damn, if they weren't sticking like glue.

"Tossed your buddies out," Zheng said, answering my unasked question while cradling a phone under his chin. "Lily was getting pissed. They're waiting outside."

"Did anybody find Bertha?" I asked.

He rolled his eyes. "Whoever did probably went screaming down the road. Can you give me a minute?"

We nodded and sat back down.

"Yeah," he told the phone. "All of them, even the creepy mage. Yeah, I know, but he's sneaky. He might have something up his sleeve . . . No, gimme an hour." He eyed us. "I think I'm about to make a deal."

He tossed the phone in a drawer and looked at us.

"What Louis-Cesare said before," I told him, because I hadn't objected to the terms, merely to being excluded from having a say in them. "The alliance is contingent on getting Dorina back, and is defensive only until we see how things go. But that does not mean defending you because you attacked someone and they attacked you back. It means unprovoked."

"I know what defensive means." Zheng took out another cigarette and lit up. "And I got fire power. I don't need more boots on the ground."

"Then what do you need?"

"Information and contacts. I don't know your territory any more than you do mine. You needed help in Hong Kong, and you came to me, which was the smart move. Well, I need help in North America. I got some contacts there, sure, but not at the higher levels. I saw a senate seat go up for grabs, and I grabbed it. It was only afterward that I realized—shit. I might have just put my head in a noose."

"So, we're supposed to keep your head out of the noose," I clarified.

"That would be nice," Zheng said sardonically. "And I'll do the same for you, if I can. But I'd settle for knowing that it's being prepared."

"And you think you wouldn't know?"

He shrugged and sat back with his cigarette. "I keep my eyes open, but they're messing with us newbies at court. Rumors, rumors everywhere, but who knows what to believe? I've been walking around with goose flesh up my back for months now, right over the spot where somebody's probably planning to plant a stake in it. I need information I can believe."

"And Cheung?" Louis-Cesare asked abruptly.

"What about him?"

"Does this deal include him, or are you simply going to inform him of everything we tell you?"

Zheng's eyes flashed dangerously through the smoke. "You got a mouth on you."

"It's a fair question—"

"It's not the question," Zheng said, sitting up. "It's how it's asked!"

Louis-Cesare started to get up, but I put a hand on his arm. "How would you like us to ask it?" I said.

"With some respect!"

"I have respect for you," I told him truthfully.

"Yeah, but does he?" Zheng stabbed his cigarette at Louis-Cesare, who was still bristling. Master vamps did not take a challenge well, even an indirect one. But I didn't think that was what this was.

Zheng hadn't even noticed my hubby's hand going to his shiny new rapier; he was too busy going off.

"Mr. Aristocrat, looking like he smells something bad, just like everyone else at that damned court! I thought it would be different from Ming-de's," he said, talking about the East Asian Consul, who headed up the Chinese version of a senate. "But some things never change. Be part of the wrong family, and no matter how hard you work, you're never—"

There was a knock on the door.

Zheng called out something in Cantonese, and Lily came in backwards pulling a rolling cart. She seemed to be in a better mood, and the cart's contents put me in one. I didn't know what time it was, jet lag having done a number on me, but every time is tea time in China.

Lily bustled in and served everyone their choice of tea and sandwiches and little cakes, which mostly meant serving me because the vamps only took tea. I ate anyway and something about watching me stuff my face seemed to calm Zheng down. "If you want something more substantial, we got a full kitchen," he told me.

"This *is* substantial," I said, around a cucumber and tuna paste sandwich. Lily had brought enough high tea for a family of twelve. "Thank you," I told her.

"Your friends at night market," she said. "They get fed, too."

Well, I hoped they were discreet about it.

She bustled out and everybody sipped tea for a moment, before the conversation resumed.

"I have respect for you, as well," Louis-Cesare said to Zheng. My hubby was quick tempered, but he wasn't stupid, and he wasn't belligerent. If he had time to think, he was a better diplomat than me. "If I indicated otherwise, my apologies. I am merely trying to protect the family interests."

"Yeah, I get that," Zheng said. "But you have to understand that I've spent months getting flak from a bunch of butt-hurt, would-be senators who didn't have the guts to face me in the ring for the seat they wanted, but are happy enough to disrespect me at every turn. Half the time I don't even know when senate meetings are being held, and when I do show up, nobody explains anything. I'm a damned gangster to them, a low life smuggler and an outsider who doesn't deserve what he got. But I bled for my seat, risked my neck for it, like I'll bleed for this alliance—"

"You think you'll have to?" I asked.

He paused, but then he nodded. "Yeah, I think I'll have to." He glanced at Louis-Cesare. "I'm making this agreement for me. Cheung wants in, and he can deal with you separately. Which I'll tell him to his face."

Louis-Cesare looked at me. There wasn't much to talk about, since we'd already agreed before we came back in. I nodded.

"We have a deal," he told Zheng.

Zheng smiled and blew some smoke. And then decided that it deserved more than that, and laughed. "Well, all right, then! Let's go."

"Where?" I asked. I was still eating tuna.

"To meet your squad."

* * *

In a few moments, we were back in the limo again, going where, I wasn't sure. But I had a picnic basket and Zheng was finally talking, so I was happy. And he was talking a lot.

"Look, you have to understand a few things before we get started. Like the fact that there's two different Hong Kongs right now, and I don't mean human vs. supe. There are a few areas around the portals that are okay; there's some stuff in the financial sector that wasn't hit too hard, either. But then there's the stuff you've been seeing since you got here—areas devastated by the battle that are probably going to take years to put back right, and that's after we get all the pillars for the shield back up. And then there's that."

I hadn't been paying much attention to what was happening outside the windows, since the back of the limo made for its own snug little world. But when he nodded to the left, I looked left, and then lowered the tinted glass to get a better view. It didn't help much.

Instead of a neon lit cityscape, I found myself staring at what looked like a tide rolling in—one of thick, white fog. It was so dense that only a few, blackened and burnt tops of buildings broke the cloud cover. Or whatever it was, because I hadn't noticed any fog tonight.

"What *is* that?" I asked.

"A problem," Zheng said. "And why our consul has me stationed here for the time being."

"Why does she care what happens in Hong Kong?" Louis-Cesare asked.

"I'm getting there." Zheng settled back against the expansive seat. "After the battle, life was pretty disrupted for a while. We had the dark mages who'd attacked us, and the traitorous dogs from the East Asian Court who had helped them, to track down. Ming-de and her soldiers were all over the place, ordering people about and contradicting the commands of the local authorities, creating mass confusion. There was looting going on, there were droves of people clogging the portals, trying to get the hell out, and there were mages crawling everywhere, attempting to get the shield stabilized or to collect their dead or to do investigations . . .

"My point is, we were busy."

I nodded.

"Then one day, out of the blue, we woke up to find that a third of the city looked like that." He nodded at the swirling clouds of white. "Whole blocks were taken over by that stuff, and wherever it went, magic went haywire."

"What do you mean, haywire?" Louis-Cesare asked.

"I mean huge clouds of free-floating, unattached magic, with no spells binding it."

"Like wild magic?" I said, talking about the naturally occurring stuff that the world throws out from time to time.

But Zheng shook his head. "If by 'like' you mean in the vague ballpark of, sure. Otherwise, not really. You know how talismans store up power for months, sometimes years, to get enough for a single spell?"

I nodded. Me and my bank account knew all about that. Magic was expensive, which was why most magic workers normally used their own. Any spell you had to buy that was worth a damn cost the Earth, not because the spell itself was that hard to cast, although some were harder than others. But because of the power that went into it.

The amount of charms I'd expended staying alive in Hassani's temple would have cost me . . . I didn't even know. Years of hard work, probably, if I hadn't had the senate's reserve to draw from. And then Zheng said something that had me sitting up and forgetting my picnic.

"Well, there are clouds in there," he gestured at the fog, "that have enough juice to run a major ward for the next thousand years."

"What?"

He nodded. "And the problem is, when one of those connects to a spell—any spell—one of two things happens. Either the spell blows up, overloaded to the point that it can't maintain integrity anymore, or . . ."

"Or what?"

"Or that," Zheng said, looking out of the side of the car again, but not in any particular direction, because it had started circling.

Louis-Cesare leaned over and we both looked down, only at what, I didn't know. It was big, though, maybe the circumference of an oil tanker, and was clogging a small street. It was round like a tanker as well, only not as long. In fact, it kind of looked like—

"A soup can?" I said, noticing a familiar blank spot on a nearby billboard.

We were nearing the edge of the billowing whiteness, but were still well out of the danger zone. Or we should have been. But smallish tendrils were creeping out of the main flow here and there, and one had snagged the billboard, curling around it like a fist.

And, sure enough, what had been a simple, animated ad, suddenly got up from where it had landed in the roadway and ran down the street, ahead of a bunch of mages that tore off after it.

They managed to get lasso spells on it, golden ropes of gleaming power that brought it down, just shy of an apartment block. It didn't look like anybody was living there; in fact, I didn't see anybody in the whole area except for the mages, and the kicking, screaming thing on the ground. Which was now trying to roll over and crush them all.

But it made my heart skip a beat, nonetheless.

"They run out of the dead zones, as we've started calling them, from time to time," Zheng explained. "We've taken down all the magical ads and graffiti we can find out here, but occasionally one slips past us. And inside the fog . . . well, there aren't too many people willing to go inside the fog."

"That's why all the billboards were blank, or text only, on our way here," Louis-Cesare said. Because I guessed he'd noticed, too.

Zheng nodded. "The easy ones are the graffiti," he continued. "Most of them are too weak to survive an infusion of that much magic, and just explode. Or the advertisements that somebody did construct well enough to take it, but which were designed to be fairly benign. They're mostly just a nuisance."

I thought about the gun that Ray and I had devised, which had been based off of magical ads that we'd encountered during the battle for this city, and which we'd overloaded with power to help us out. I'd seen them slow down, and in some cases stop, a troop of war mages, the magical equivalent of tanks. I thought Zheng was kind of underselling the combat potential of animated soup cans.

But he was already going on.

"Others—the more dangerous kind—are protection wards and spells that used to guard bank vaults, weapons' shops, and jewelry stores, places where people were serious about others not getting in. Unlike the ads, those were designed to be mean, and now they got the power to back it up. But the worst of all, the ones that really ruin everybody's good time, are the arsenals."

"What . . . arsenals?" Louis-Cesare asked, looking like he didn't want to know.

"A lot of the triads and such had arsenals in the dead zones. They needed someplace to put all the stuff they . . . creatively acquired . . . on jobs, or that they were planning to sell or use themselves, if the situation warranted it. There are disputes from time to time between rivals, and it's always a good idea to have a reserve. Cheung had a storehouse in there himself, for emergencies, and for wards and weapons he was planning to trade to the fey."

I started to get the picture. "But now, with all this free-floating magic . . ."

"They're running loose. And sometimes the weapons encounter an ad with the arms and legs they lack, and merge with it. Making a hybrid with tons of power and a really bad attitude. The good thing is, they largely stay in the dead zones, 'cause that's where the magic clouds that feed them are located. But you'll notice I said 'largely'."

"The monsters," I said, remembering what Lily had said.

Zheng nodded. "They get out sometimes, and prowl around the streets down there. But most of them can't fly—"

"Most of them?" Louis-Cesare repeated.

"—so elevated real estate has become real popular."

"I bet," I said.

"But what causes all this?" Louis-Cesare demanded. "Wild magic is usually found in minute amounts in nature. It takes a thunderstorm and a witch who knows how to ride its power, or a talisman to make it usable. It doesn't look like that!"

"It's found in minute amounts *on Earth*," Zheng corrected.

He sat back against the seat and poured us some whiskey. I had finished my tea, so I was happy enough for it, but I had a feeling that it was less hospitality and more a leftover from his human days. A here-you'll-need-it kind of thing.

I took it anyway, because I did need it.

I wasn't liking where this conversation was going.

"The shield that protects the city does double duty," Zheng said, and since he didn't sound as if he was changing the subject, I assumed this was relevant. "See, nobody else sits on top of a ley line vortex the way we do. It's considered, well, insane. The thought, before we proved everybody wrong, was that no shield could possibly withstand that kind of constant pressure. That it would buckle for sure."

"Why doesn't it?" Louis-Cesare asked.

"Because it's made up of the energy of the lines. And, yeah, I know, that's supposed to be impossible, too," he said, before Louis-Cesare could object. "That's what everyone was always told: the lines are too powerful; try to tame them and they'll tame you instead, and by tame I mean dust to ashes. But our vortex is different."

"How different?" I asked. "The one here is said to be more powerful than anywhere else, with more lines crossing and crisscrossing than at any other point on Earth—"

"Exactly. It's ironic, but ours is usable because it's so powerful. So many lines run together here that their energy gets jumbled up. Instead of pooling, like in other vortexes, it's more like a volcano erupting, all the time. Only you ever see magma, the kind that floats to the surface of a lava flow?"

"I guess," I said, not really seeing where this was going.

"It's black, right? That's because the crust is cooler than the stuff underneath. The same is true here. The ley line energy piles up, higher and higher, until it forces some of it closer to real space than anywhere else that we've found. And that kind of . . . cools it off . . . over time."

"Cools it off?"

"Okay, technically thins it out might be better, but it wrecks the analogy. The point is, it's like the crust on magma as it encounters the air. Hot and burning underneath, but cooler, and thus less dangerous on the top. That's what we use, the very top most layer, forming part of the energy of the lines themselves into the shield that protects us. The rest goes into the phase that keeps us out of alignment with real space, and able to live without having to hide what we are. And the remainder, a relatively small amount—"

"You skim off for yourself," Louis-Cesare said, looking like something had finally made sense.

CHAPTER THIRTY-FOUR

Dory, Hong Kong

I tensed up, afraid that comment was likely to piss Zheng off again, not because it had been belligerent, but because it was true. No way was a city founded by pirates and gangsters going to miss a chance like that. But he merely shrugged.

"Of course. The gals back at Lily's, for instance, that's how we fuel them. That's also why they get a little aggressive, from time to time. Smaller bits of power get flung off that thing," he gestured with his glass at the wall of ominous whiteness, "that are too thin to see, but when they impact one of the girls . . ."

"But why do they get hostile?" I asked. "You designed them, right?"

"Lily designed the bodies," he corrected. "But the personalities were those of her friends, and some of those ladies have a temper. But mostly, they just get a little willful or catty or whatever. They're not a problem.

"Those are the problem."

I realized that we'd started moving again, and were now approaching some kind of stadium. I couldn't see it too well, as it was on the opposite side of the car, but it looked pretty big. Although not compared to what was floating in cages beside it.

"What is *that*?" I asked, staring at the nearest one.

"What we came to see."

The car swung around, getting into a queue for admission, I guessed. A bunch of guys on bright red rickshaws were patrolling the airspace around the main event, probably to discourage freeloaders. The new position gave me a better view and answered a few questions, although not all of them.

The "stadium" wasn't actually floating, as I'd first thought. Even for a city with magic to burn, that would have been excessive. The base was five skyscrapers built around a small park, and the still functioning bridges connecting them. The roofs of the skyscrapers and the entire length of the bridges were crowded with spectators, but far more people had brought their own seats. Thousands upon thousands were crammed into vehicles of all descriptions, which filled the spaces between the buildings as well as the skies all around.

Some of the flying stadium seats were small, including a ton of two or four-seater rickshaws. At the opposite end of the spectrum were levitating platforms holding hundreds of spectators in nicely slanting rows so that everybody got a view. And in between was every kind of vehicle imaginable.

There were buses with twenty or more people on top, yelling and cheering. There were stretch limos serving as stadium boxes for the rich and well connected. There were people on things that weren't technically vehicles at all, with the sofa I'd almost collided with earlier suddenly making more sense as I spotted dozens more just like it. Some people had even had their makeshift sky houses towed over to the event, so that they could watch in comfort from their balconies.

And then there were the cages, given plenty of space by the crowd, maybe because they were rocking from side to side while the contents screeched and cawed and howled. Even with the limo's obvious soundproofing, the ruckus could be clearly heard. As could the low-level roar of the crowd, the whir of hundreds of fan blades, and some Cantonese being broadcast either through a spell or a hell of a lot of loud speakers.

It must be deafening outside, I thought, wondering how anybody stood it. And then I noticed a guy in a rickshaw with some Chinese writing on it, and a picture of earplugs underneath. Ray would like this place, I thought with a pang. They really knew how to merchandize.

"When the Circle started to pull their people out of here for the war, it left us with a problem," Zheng said. "Local mages and some reinforcements from the mainland had to take over patrolling the dead zones, but most didn't know how. They were wardsmiths and spellbinders, not war mages, and this was not their skill set.

"But there wasn't anybody else, so the Circle started bringing some of the nastier things they captured over here, where the new guys got a chance to learn the techniques they needed to take 'em down. Word got around and people began coming to watch, then somebody figured, hey, why not charge admission to help with the rebuilding . . ."

"And, thus, a new sport was born," Louis-Cesare murmured.

Zheng nodded. "All the usual ground games—football, horse racing and the like—have been cancelled due to the possibility of the participants being attacked. The matches quickly became the only game in town. Now, it's not just new mages learning the ropes. They still have some of that, usually as a warm up. But there's also teams of crazy people who volunteer to take on the worst of the worst."

"And the city allows that?" I asked. "What if they get killed?"

Zheng shrugged. "It's volunteer only, so they know what they're getting into. And mage squads are in place—the trainers and their students—if things get out of hand. But the purses for the victors are pretty substantial, as the better the show the more spectators it draws in." He shrugged.

"The Wild, Wild East," I said.

Zheng laughed. "That it is. At least until we can figure out what the hell went wrong with the system."

"What did go wrong?" Louis-Cesare asked, while I eyed up the creature in the nearest cage.

It looked like an Escher drawing of some type of squid. I couldn't be sure as it kept morphing and twisting in totally impossible ways that hurt the brain and crossed the eyes, while flashing in changing, neon colors that didn't help. Graffiti, I thought, looking away before I was mesmerized. Guess not all of it exploded. And now some kid's idea of cool had turned into something that could possibly eat your brain after it finished frying it.

"That's why I'm here," Zheng said, answering Louis-Cesare. "Our consul isn't too happy about a boat load of free-floating magic in the middle of a war. She wants me to find out why the system that worked for hundreds of years is suddenly bubbling over with extra power, and what can be done to stop it."

"And have you?"

He snorted. "Do I look like a mage to you? I lived here most of my life, but that doesn't mean I'm an expert on how everything works. Fortunately, I do know a few. They've been working with the Circle's men to fix things, and their theory is simple: get the damned pillars back up."

"The pagodas that were destroyed when the city fell," I explained to Louis-Cesare, who hadn't been here. "They served as waystations for channeling the power of the lines into the phase."

"And they channeled a lot," Zheng added. "They absorbed a ton of power, even though most of them were redundant. As we found out the hard way, one pillar can support the phase alone if required, but the designers put in multiple redundancies because if the damned thing fails, the city falls back into real space, taking out human Hong Kong along with it."

Louis-Cesare nodded. We'd been briefed about this in the senate, although judging from his expression, being here made it much more real. Try being in the battle, I thought, remembering.

"But now that most of these pillars are down," Louis-Cesare said. "That power is going where?"

Zheng gestured at the white fog again, boiling maybe ten or so blocks away. "In there. It's just floating around, like overflow from a faucet that nobody remembers how to turn off, because everybody who designed this city is dead. People know how to run the system, but not how to restrict it to a trickle until we get the rest of the pillars back up."

"Then what are you doing about it?" I asked.

He shrugged. "Living with it. The theory is that the excess magic will become less and less of a problem as each pillar comes back online. They'll be sucking up most of the overflow like sponges, just like before, and what little is left over will be grabbed by the government or hijacked by people like me." He grinned. "Until then, we're stuck dealing with the consequences—and so are you."

"Us?" Louis-Cesare said sharply. "Why us?"

Zheng took out the little golden charm that we'd brought from Hassani's and weaved it in and out of his fingers. "This is the Chinese symbol for eternity. It's also the calling card of a new triad that started up recently. Nobody knows much about them, except that they operate in there," he nodded at the cloud again, "and that they deal in stolen power. The consul worries that they're maybe selling it to the wrong people."

"Are they?" I asked.

"Hard to say. If so, they're keeping it quiet. None of my contacts have seen massive new amounts coming onto the market—"

"But if they're selling it to the other side in the war, you wouldn't," Louis-Cesare pointed out.

Zheng nodded, looking vaguely surprised that there was a mind inside that pretty head. "Yeah, that's the worry. But they could also just be stockpiling it, waiting for the price to go up as the war progresses. Like I said, it's hard to say. Everybody skims some; it's almost expected. But if they're trying to turn it into a big-time operation . . ."

"Is there any evidence of that?" I asked.

"Not . . . directly, no, or we'd have already moved against them. Well, if they ever come out of there, anyway." He grimaced, looking at the fog. "But one of the new pillars was sabotaged the other day, and some think that these guys may have been behind it. Like they weren't happy about the pillars going back up and ruining their business—"

He broke off as a two-seater rickshaw drew up alongside us. A window went down, but the expected blast of sound did not follow. The silence spell wasn't linked to the windows, it seemed.

A bored looking official poked his head in. And then he saw Zheng and his eyes blew wide. He started bowing excessively, almost hitting the window frame in the process, and talking a mile a minute. I didn't know what he said, but a moment later, we were being ushered to one of the inner circles of hovering vehicles, with an excellent view of the ring.

"I know one of the show runners," Zheng explained. "He owed me a favor."

"Meaning we get a good view?" I asked, as Louis-Cesare and I rearranged things, so that we could both see.

"No, we get the order changed."

"The order of what?"

"Who fights the 'monsters'. I want you to see the squad I've been using to poke around inside the dead zones. They're one of only three groups crazy enough to go in there, and they've managed to narrow down the location of the Eternity gang's headquarters to within a couple of blocks. They'd probably have found it outright by now, but they waste part of their time on this shit."

He shook his head in apparent disgust.

"Can't you use one of the other groups instead?" I asked. "To finish the job?"

Zheng made a moue. "Could if they weren't all dead or in traction. Anyway, if you want to check out Eternity, these are your guides."

The crowd gave a sudden roar that was so loud it rattled the limo, sending us rocking a bit in the air. I held on and watched as, down below, a small group of people emerged from under a covered walkway. It connected to one of the skyscrapers, where I guessed the green room was located for waiting fighters.

There were four of them, none of whom I could see very well from up here. But then, I didn't have to, as a couple of large billboards suddenly flashed with their faces. Electronic confetti and fireworks went off behind them, as if they were sports figures being introduced, which was fair, I guessed.

They kind of were.

A woman was shown first, who looked vaguely Asian with slanting hazel eyes and long, straight dark hair. But she also looked partly something else, possibly European, with olive skin and a Roman nose that was a little too large for her face. She was pretty, though, and knew it, with the brilliant smile of someone comfortable in her own skin.

She had on a leather catsuit, which I thought a bad choice for combat, but the crowd seemed to like it. She blew them a kiss and they went wild again, sloshing us around on the sound waves until Zheng knocked on the partition to the front and said something to the driver. We stabilized, right around the time that the second face came up.

This one looked like a male version of the girl—black hair, warm brown eyes, and tall, maybe a few inches over six feet. He was dressed more casually, in jeans and a hoody, but with enough firepower draped over his person to count as a platoon all on his own. I smiled approvingly. This was a guy who brought a knife to a gun fight—and some throwing stars, and a bazooka, and a dozen more guns.

He was also the kind of guy who walked out alive from a gun fight.

The next couple of faces weren't so nice, not that the crowd seemed to mind. A tall, gaunt man with deep set eyes and a sallow complexion was next, with greasy black hair that matched the color of his worn and potion-stained robes. If he'd had "dark mage" tattooed on his forehead, it couldn't have been any more obvious. I was surprised that he hadn't been rounded up with the others, but maybe he'd been smart enough to see which way the wind was blowing and join the right side.

Didn't make him any less creepy, though.

His buddy was a bit more of a mystery, reading as magical human to me, but as something else, too, something other. If I'd encountered him in a fight, I'd have kept my eyes on him above any of the others, although it wouldn't have been a fun experience. He had the face of a pugilist who'd been hit one too many times, knocking things out of whack to the point that they couldn't be set right anymore. There wasn't a feature on his face that wasn't skewed, and he also had some pretty impressive scars, as if something had gotten claws into him at some point.

Interestedly, he hadn't bothered to cover anything up with a glamourie. Maybe he liked looking like a tough guy. The crowd certainly seemed to approve, roaring in support when his face was shown.

But their biggest roar of all, the one that had us rocking again and Zheng cursing, was for the fifth member of the group, who had just emerged from under the walkway. Only, in his case, I wasn't sure whether the cheering was for his fighting prowess or his good looks. He could have been the lead on a telenovela: cheekbones high and sharp enough to cut you with, only you'd take it smiling because they were paired with golden skin, short, well-styled, dark hair, and movie star good looks. Not to mention a lithe, muscular body that filled out the jeans and casual black button up he was wearing to perfection.

He was the kind of guy who turned heads. He turned mine, but not for the usual reasons. I tensed up, with every dhampir sense I had suddenly blaring away.

In contrast to the other guy, he didn't have a weapon on him, but that didn't surprise me. What did surprise me was that a first-level master vampire was hanging out with a bunch of pit fighters, because that was undoubtedly what he was. The flood of his power was unmistakable even this far away, making my skin crawl with the energy he was sending off.

And I wasn't the only one to notice. Louis-Cesare had been watching casually from beside me, drinking his whisky and chatting with Zheng. But he was suddenly sitting up, was staring out the window, was *opening the car door*—

"What are you doing?" Zheng and I asked, simultaneously.

I doubted that Louis-Cesare heard the question, even with vampire hearing. Because cracking the door did what the window going down had not, and cancelled the silence spell. A wash of pure sound blasted over us, so loud that it was like being struck by a fist. I actually felt my head go back for a second, which is how I saw Zheng echoing my own question. And then I grabbed hold of the back of Louis-Cesare's trousers, because a fall from that height could kill even a master.

He turned around, detaching my hand. "I have to go down there."

I saw the words, rather than heard them, but either way, they made no sense. "What are you talking about?

He said something, but I still didn't hear, and my lip-reading capability is limited.

"*What?*"

"I said, I have to go down there!"

"I got that much! What I didn't get was why!"

He said something else, but I didn't catch it. But I decided that that was beside the point at the moment. "Do you remember what happened the last time you went running off?" I demanded.

"You don't understand! It's—"

The crowd roared, drowning him out.

"What?"

Louis-Cesare repeated himself once more, but the crowd was still going crazy, and I didn't hear.

"Did you say Jonathan?" I asked, and grabbed my purse.

He shook his head. "No! I said—"

Another roar, goddamnit!

"He said Tomas," the attractive pit fighter said, appearing out of nowhere, and clinging to the side of the car like Spider Man.

He grabbed my husband, threw him off the car, and leapt into open air after him, while Zheng and I just stared. "Don't!" Zheng said, grasping for my arm.

But he missed, because I was already throwing myself into the void.

CHAPTER THIRTY-FIVE

Dory, Hong Kong

I didn't make it far, but not because I slammed into the ground. I hit a party barge instead, landing near a crowded bar and causing a bunch of beautiful people to pull back and slosh drinks everywhere. There probably would have been more of a reaction, but Zheng smacked down beside me a second later, and people tended to give him a wide berth.

And because I didn't stay put.

"Dory! Damn it!" I heard Zheng yell, but I was already running and then leaping to the next vehicle in line, a large platform which I tore across in record time, because Louis-Cesare and his one-time captive were battling on the other end of it.

But vamp reflexes are as good or, in the case of these two, better than mine, meaning that they were gone again by the time I skidded to a stop at the edge of the platform, and looked around frantically.

I spied them after a moment, impossibly far away, leaping and fighting their way across the stadium. That would have been less terrifying if the "stadium" hadn't had huge gaps between sections. And if the vehicles comprising much of it hadn't been constantly moving, jockeying for position, and making the spot I was trying to jump to suddenly not there anymore.

I managed to snag a bright red rickshaw before I plummeted to my death, being driven by one of the stadium ticket enforcers who I pushed off onto a bus. That made following the guys easier, or it would have if two hundred and fifty pounds of master vamp hadn't suddenly landed on the back of my ride, sending us spinning out of control. I managed to compensate after a moment, swerving around a floating house and ducking under a sashimi place. But it meant that I'd lost Louis-Cesare again.

Damn it!

"What are you doing?" I demanded, looking over my shoulder at Zheng.

"I could ask the same of you. What the hell?"

"Tomas, the guy with your guide group?"

"What about him?"

"He was Louis-Cesare's prisoner for something like a century."

"What?"

"It's a long story. All you need to know is that Tomas hates him and is probably trying to stake him!"

"And you're going to do what about that?" Zheng demanded.

"Stake Tomas first!"

I spotted the two battling masters on the opposite side of the arena, and decided to take a short cut across the large open space. Which . . . probably wasn't the best plan I ever had. Zheng yelled a warning, half a second before a four-story-tall, bright crimson devil, complete with horns and a pointed tail, leapt out in front of us—

And grabbed the squid monster in a headlock before they both fell into the ring.

I didn't know what had happened for a second, and then realized that Louis-Cesare and Tomas had been fighting near the devil's cage. They must have damaged it enough to release him, just about the time that the squid thing was let out for the match that was supposed to be taking place right now. It wasn't, because something better was happening instead.

The crowd roared approval, louder than ever, as two titans faced off. I guessed they didn't usually see the monsters fighting each other. And for good reason, I thought, because things almost immediately got out of hand.

"Shit!" I yelled, as a flashing aqua, green and bright orange tentacle slashed through the air, barely missing us. And then another one clipped us, sending our ride spiraling toward the dirt, before the devil's tail punched through the back of us. And we suddenly found ourselves being used like a brick to pummel the squid.

"Every time!" Zheng was yelling. "Every goddamned time —"

I had no idea what he was talking about, and cared less. I felt my fingers slipping; felt an arm the size of a tree trunk go around my waist. And then we were leaping, straight at a man in a smaller, one-person rickshaw.

It was the only vehicle close enough, as everyone else was rocketing away from the fight. But the man—the mage, as it turned out—didn't want company. He saw us coming, cursed, and got a lasso on us. And, holy shit!

For the record, magical lassos are not fun when you are the recipient. It hurt like hell, burning whatever skin it touched, but it didn't touch us for long. Because he whipped us over to the side of the great space, onto a grassy bit of land. And as soon as we hit down, he went buzzing away again, to join a dozen more who were attempting to regain control of the situation.

Only that . . . wasn't going so well. And neither was this, I thought, as Zheng got me into a headlock while the squid screeched loudly enough to threaten my eardrums, and the devil laughed, a great, sonic boom type of thing that made hearing impossible. Except for a master vamp yelling in my ear.

"—not happening! Do not stake my damned team!"

"I'm not staking your team," I said, thrashing, and really putting my all into it. "Just one."

"Yeah, but he's the best one!"

"That's what I'm afraid of!"

I had been playing fair, which was why I wasn't going anywhere. I decide to remedy that, and elbowed Zheng considerably below the belt. He didn't let go—gotta give the guy credit—but he did loosen his grip slightly as well as snarl. "You're going to pay for that."

"Maybe, but not now," I said, and stuck my head into my purse.

The mouth of the portal grabbed me, sucking me inside, and leaving Zheng literally holding the bag. Until I re-emerged with a warded tab of the type that I'd used on Hassani, and slapped it onto his torso. "What the—"

I grabbed my bag and sprang away, and Zheng went into Asian Ken doll mode, trapped in his little warded cell. Or maybe not Ken, I thought, seeing the frozen snarl on his face, which was showing a lot of fang. The tab would probably hold him about as long as it had Hassani, but I hadn't had a whole lot of non-lethal alternatives.

I took off, knowing that I had seconds at best.

Make that a second, I thought, as he tackled me.

Son of a bitch!

I flipped over, about to give him a piece of my mind, and found myself looking at Tomas instead.

"You're really . . . pretty," I gasped, surprised.

He blinked. "Thank you?"

"You're welcome," I said, and tried for a repeat of the trick with Zheng, but the damned vamp was in the way. So, I sucked him into my purse, instead.

I stood up, feeling dizzy and slightly unwell, because my stomach and brain had no idea where we were right now, and were arguing about it. Zheng and Louis-Cesare showed up a second later, and stared at me. "Where is Tomas?" they

QUEEN'S GAMBIT

demanded.

I still couldn't talk properly, and just held up the bag.

"You put him in *there*?" Louis-Cesare asked, in disbelief.

"What?" Zheng looked from me to the large expanse of black leather. "Wait. You have a master vamp in your *purse*?"

"Yeah?" I didn't know what they were complaining about. He was contained.

"How?"

"Why?" Louis-Cesare demanded.

"Because I didn't have . . . a lot of options?" Talk about gratitude!

"Dory. The *armory* is in your purse!"

Oh.

Yeah.

And then Tomas was back, having figured out how this worked in record time. He was also loaded for bear. "Shit," I said.

He smiled.

And then, just as fast, he was gone, plucked off the earth and into the jaws of the giant squid.

"What the—" I said.

"They're attracted to power!" Zheng yelled. And then he frowned. "I think I've been insulted!"

Louis-Cesare grabbed me, jumping us out of the way of a snarl of huge tentacles headed this way. Zheng ran in the other direction; I didn't know why. We landed behind a small building that looked like a closed shrine of some kind, and wasn't very sturdy, but one of the skyscrapers wasn't far off. We could take shelter there, find a rickshaw, and then get the hell out of here!

I wasn't the only one to have that idea. The ground was suddenly streaming with headlights, as hundreds of vehicles took off, getting away from the now completely out of control fight. The mages were doing their best, but they had obviously not planned on this, and I wasn't sure what was going to happen.

383

Except that Tomas was about to get eaten.

The massive squid had a huge tentacle wrapped around the arm of the devil, and a smaller one squeezing its neck. But its mouth was full of vampire, with the fang-rimmed hole only being kept from closing by a master's strength. But I doubted that that would work for long.

Graffitied monsters didn't get tired, but master vamps did.

Tomas was toast.

Until his four crazy-ass partners decided to get busy, and help their friend. I saw Zheng over by the group, gesturing and pointing. They'd been hanging back until now, probably thinking that this was above their pay grade. And that prize money is no good if you're not alive to spend it.

But it looked like their buddy being taken had changed things, and they were moving in. The dark mage did something that caused a plume of smoke to engulf one of the flailing tentacles, which slowly started to lose color as its strength was sapped. But the main body of the creature did not seem affected, nor did the other arms, and I didn't think he had time to take it piece by piece.

The ugly bruiser with the torn-up face opted for a more direct approach. He ran and then launched himself at one of the flailing arms, using its momentum to send him soaring at the bulbous head. Where he landed and proceeded to attack with what looked like a large hatchet or possibly a battle ax.

That would have worked fine on a real animal, which might have broken off its attack at a threat to its head. But this thing didn't appear to notice or care if it did. Maybe because it didn't run on blood like the rest of us, but on pure magic, which it still had plenty of. The bruiser could probably cave in the whole head, and the tentacles would still function.

I didn't know if he had enough brain power to figure that out, but somebody else did. The girl stepped forward and raised an arm. The guy, who I was assuming was her brother based on looks, was firing everything he had at the squid. That included a rocket that exploded a mass of blue-green slime out of the thing's body when it detonated, covering a third of the ring.

The girl just continued to stand there.

For a moment, nothing happened. And then slowly, from far beneath the ground, a rumble could be heard. I didn't know what was happening, but assumed it wasn't good. Because the mage squad suddenly dropped their lassos and fled, and the sort of orderly—for Hong Kong, anyway— exodus became an all-out rout.

People screamed, vehicles bolted, even the ponderous platforms, which handled like a semi with all the tires flat, started to move away. Why, I wasn't sure, although something was definitely happening now. Something bad, I thought, as the ground swelled, as pipes broke and spewed water everywhere, and as bridges rocked wildly even as hundreds tried to get off.

And as a tiny finger of blue light speared up from below, tearing a hole in the devil and causing him to roar and fall back a step.

"Stop her!" Louis-Cesare said, grabbing my arm. "She'll rupture the shield!"

"The—shit!" I said, and finally realized what I was seeing. That the crazy woman was trying to use the power of the lines to fight her battles for her, and was going to kill us all in the process. "How in the *hell*—"

"She's a jinx. Don't let her so much as look at you."

Great.

"And what are you going to do?" I demanded.

He kissed me briefly, but fiercely. "Save Tomas."

Shit.

But he was gone before I could stop him, because of course he was. The damned man had just tried to kill him, but letting someone he'd once been responsible for get eaten wasn't in Louis-Cesare's nature. It was in mine, but nobody had asked me.

I said a bad word and ran straight for the girl.

It was harder than it looked. The ground was streaming with shadows and colors, because some of the crazy cavalcade up there had multicolored lights hanging off of their buses or draped around their balconies. A few even had strobes on their party barges, which sent wildly waving disco lights across the remains of the park, and flashed blindingly bright in my eyes.

They were confusing, although not as much as the waves of dirt being flung upwards by the tentacles, or the massive feet of the demon, which were slamming down here, there, and everywhere, threatening to pound me into the ground. Or the water blasts from the ruptured pipes, which were trying to drown me in the gigantic mud puddle forming under my feet.

Or under my knees, since it was already that deep in places, causing me to flail, and making each step a hard, sucking slog. I wasn't getting anywhere this way, I thought, watching the tentacles waving about everywhere. And then reaching up and grabbing one going in the right direction, which ripped me out of the mud and launched me at the bitch causing all of this.

I didn't make it all the way there, as I had to let go when the tentacle started to head back up. But I hit a mostly solid piece of ground and was up and throwing myself at her a second later. And I wasn't in the mood to be gentle.

She went down and then out when I belted her upside the jaw, possibly hard enough to break it. I threw some magical cuffs on her and kicked her into my purse, because I couldn't carry her through all this otherwise. Then I took off, running and leaping and occasionally falling through the chaos, heading for the side of the ring and the shadow of a now deserted broadcasting booth.

The two announcers had long since fled, although the

nearby Jumbotron was still running with images. I didn't try to figure them out; I was far too close. And the same was true when I turned back to the fight, which was so high above my head that I couldn't see anything.

But nobody had turned off the second Jumbotron across the park, which gave me a perfect view of Louis-Cesare stabbing his sword hilt-deep into a giant squid eye. And unlike with the side of its head, which the creature hadn't seemed to give a shit about, it was Not Happy with this latest attack. Probably because a blind animal is very soon a dead animal.

It sent out another of those skull-piercing shrieks, echoing off the buildings and pulling a collective groan from the remaining crowd. It also thrashed wildly, trying to find this dangerous new threat—and in the process dropped the old one. Tomas went tumbling out of the beast's mouth, Louis-Cesare reached for him and missed, and the now tiny looking body plummeted straight for the ground—

Before a slashing tentacle smacked him my way.

I started slightly as he hit the Jumbotron, causing all of the colors and images to scatter wildly for a moment. And then to stabilize, when he peeled off and fell limply to the ground, face first. He just lay there, as if dead, but he wasn't dead. He was a first level master and while that probably hadn't done him any good, he'd recover.

I glanced around.

Nobody was in the area, unless you counted the fight going on overhead, which looked like it was winding down. The thrashing had caused the tentacle around the devil's arm to loosen, and he'd seized his chance. He'd grabbed the squid thing, trying to rip it apart, giving Louis-Cesare a chance to escape.

And me a chance to assemble my crew.

I ran over to the not-moving vamp, crawled inside my purse for a second, and came up with another Spider's Bite. I threw it on the bastard, watched it web him up, and dragged him inside. Fucker.

Then I moved over to the bottom of the now wrecked cage that the devil had been in, with its huge door hanging off its hinges and the metal bars twisted or broken. Another slumped figure lay beside it, having been tossed there at some point in the fight. I checked his meaty neck for a pulse, and it beat strong and steady. He might not be smart, but he was tough. He was also starting to come around.

I threw a couple of pairs of cuffs on the bruiser, hands and feet, then added a third to connect them in back and hogtie him, just to be safe. Then into the purse he went. Okay; that was three.

Where was number four?

Surprisingly, four was still in it, spraying both of the creatures above him with bullets, apparently not realizing that his friend was no longer in need of rescue. That was good. It kept his attention elsewhere.

And in all this, it wasn't like he could hear me sneaking up on him, was it?

A moment later, number four was secured, leaving only one.

But the dark mage was wilier, and very much aware of what had just happened. He had simply been too far away to stop it. But now he was running at me, both hands consumed by black, oily-looking clouds, which based on what had happened to the squid, were intended to drain me of magic and/or life as soon as they touched me.

Great.

To make matters worse, Louis-Cesare, who should have been down by now, had become stuck—literally. The blue gel that the squid's body had thrown out was apparently harmless, but very sticky. Which meant that it wasn't harmless since it had glued my hubby in place, stuck to what was left of the squid's body as it and the devil reached crunch time.

I reached back into my bag of tricks, grabbed a grappling

hook, and slung it at a passing rickshaw. It caught the back seat, jerking me up and over the dark mage's head before he could grab me, which was good. But it was traveling in the wrong direction, which was not. The maneuver also seemed to really piss off the mage, who dropped the power sucking spell in favor of a lasso, and a moment later, he was in my face.

So, I put a fist in his, something he hadn't seemed to expect, because mages never do. They're so used to finding magical solutions to problems that they sometimes forget that the old fashioned, bare knuckles type works, too. In fact, it worked a little too well, because the bastard let go of the lasso and started to slip and fall away.

I caught him. I almost tore my shoulder out of joint in the process, but I caught him. And got my legs around him a moment later, because he was dead weight and I was holding us both up one-handed while being jerked across the damned sky!

Even worse, the lasso spell hadn't faded away yet. It was lashing me like a burning rope every time the damned rickshaw driver changed direction, which was often because the mages were back. They had regrouped and were heading into the fray, seeing an opportunity to finish this.

And in the process, they were freaking out my driver, who encountered grim war mages everywhere he turned, who were not happy to see him. One of them plucked him out of the driver's seat and yelled something at me; what I didn't know because I was busy, damn it! And I don't speak Cantonese.

But I'd managed to get my free hand into the bag and felt around. I needed something to hold the mage, but it would have to be something special. Something he wouldn't immediately know how to counter, something that would take him by surprise—

Something like that, I thought, as the pissed off war mage got tired of talking and threw a cuff at us, which latched onto the mage's ankle. It quickly started climbing his body, spewing out chains with locks every few inches. And, knowing war mages, each one of them probably required a different spell to release.

That'll do, I thought, and stuffed my purse over his head.

A second later, he was gone, and that made five.

The team was assembled, although they hadn't impressed me much so far. But at least they knew where Eternity was, which was more than I did. Now I just had to get out of here.

Another cuff was thrown at me, but missed because I was launching myself into the now empty driver's seat. A second after that, I was peeling away from the war mage's rickshaw, back toward the fight. Right alongside a phalanx of other vehicles, because the mages were diving as one.

I dove faster. Louis-Cesare was tiny compared to the creatures they were fighting, and I didn't know if they'd see him or not. And the kind of combined spells they could throw might not be survivable, even for a master. So, I floored it, heedless of thrashing tentacles, battling giants, and pursuing mages. But spells travel faster than people, and they were gearing up to throw, and—

And they had to abort, sending colorful spells shooting off into the night, because a huge limo was suddenly rocketing into the scene, like a shiny black bullet.

Several spells hit the side, which had thrown itself between Louis-Cesare and the mages. I expected to see it go up like a fireball, but it must have been warded. Because, instead, all I heard was—

"Short stuff! *Grab him!*"

I grabbed him.

Not that I had to do much. Louis-Cesare had almost freed himself already, and jumped into the seat beside me as soon as I got close enough. I didn't have to stop or even pause as a result, just took off in a new direction, trying to get as far from the fight as possible before—

That, I thought, as a tentacle caught us a massive blow.

It was the biggest one of them all, which had been wrapped around the devil's arm this whole time. But he was being targeted by the mages now, maybe because he was in better shape than his beleaguered, half blind, and battered opponent, allowing the tentacle to spring free. And the squid's full strength to hit us broadside.

Louis-Cesare grabbed me as our vehicle went flying in a great inverted parabola, high over the city. He held on as it broke in two, falling away as we reached the apex of the arc. He stared at me, his face terrible for a long instant.

And then we fell.

CHAPTER THIRTY-SIX

Dorina, Faerie

R ay was up before I was the next morning. In fact, I wasn't entirely certain that he had been to sleep at all. Because he had made something.

"Is it . . . a raft?" I asked, sitting up.

He was standing down by the water, with the hem of his tunic wet and his hair damp and sticking out everywhere, as if he had shaken it dry. He put his hands on his hips. "Why you gotta sound like that?"

I yawned. "Like what?"

"Like you're not sure if that's the right word."

In truth, I wasn't. The item was floating—for the moment—but I did not know how much longer that would hold true. He appeared to have used the fey rope to tie together a great mass of driftwood, but not to lie it flat, as you might expect. Instead, it was literally a pile of sticks that I assumed we were meant to straddle, as that appeared to be the only option.

"It is a very nice raft," I lied, because he had probably worked hard on it.

"It's a piece of crap," Ray said grinning, instantly changing his demeanor. "But there's a method to the madness."

I blinked, trying to keep up with what I assumed was another joke. Humor was difficult. But he seemed to find the situation amusing, and was now patting the raft fondly.

"This baby is gonna get us so far away from here, that the damned Svarestri will never find us."

I looked at it again. I decided to attempt some humor. "Do you wish to bet on that?"

Ray frowned and sloshed up the bank. "I know it don't look like much, but you gotta understand how things work here."

"All right." I did not try humor again. I did not think I had gotten it right.

"The forests are impassable—at least to us. They're right out." He picked through our supplies and handed me the fey version of trail mix.

"Thank you."

"The roads are no better," he added, sitting beside me. "The Svarestri are hunting you, so they're probably watching 'em all. Plus, there could be bandits and God knows what lurking around, 'cause I don't even know where the hell we are. Judging by the whole ancient demigoddess visit/river flowing over nothing thing, I'd guess somewhere along the border of Nimue's lands. But that don't narrow it down much."

"The river was . . . enchanting," I said, remembering.

He snorted. "Yeah, that's one way of putting it."

I cocked my head. "How would you put it?"

"That it's enchant*ed*. It ain't about being pretty. It acts like fortress walls, all around her realm. From what I hear, if anybody tries to invade, she just—" he made a strange sort of jerking gesture.

"She does what?" I asked, because I hadn't understood that.

"Pulls the rug out from under 'em, or in this case, the river. She's said to be able to do almost anything with it: make it flood and wash their whole army away; make it seep evil smells that confuse man and beast alike, until they drown in only a few feet of water; use it to carry illusions of massive armies that don't exist; or cause it to vanish completely, dropping the invaders hundreds of feet onto all of those waiting stalagmites . . ."

I realized that I had leaned forward as he spoke, eating my trail mix like a child in a movie theatre absently munching on popcorn while being engrossed with the story on screen. I sat back up and attempted to act as if I was unmoved. I do not think I succeeded, as Ray grinned at me.

"Or that could all be a load of crap. The fey love stories, and the more exaggerated, the better. Best not to pay too much attention to what they say."

"But even exaggerated stories often contain truth," I pointed out. "And after what happened last night . . . perhaps it would be best to avoid her lands."

"Yeah, only that would be kind of a trick. Nimue's realm lies in the middle of everything, bordering Aeslinn's kingdom, the dark fey, *and* the Blarestri."

"The Blarestri are on our side, are they not?" I asked, remembering Caedmon, the odd creature who was their king. I had not known what to make of him, but I hadn't trusted him. He had tried to make a claim on Dory, declaring that she was part fey and thus belonged to him. He had made it sound like he was doing her a favor, but there had been an acquisitive look in his eyes. And then the fey had come to kidnap us . . .

But his fey were golden haired for the most part, with bright blue eyes instead of the pewter ones of the Svarestri. And he had seemed more the type to try to seduce his way to what he wanted, rather than take it by force. But then, seduction had not worked . . .

I frowned. I did not know who to trust in this strange land, but I did not think it was him. And it appeared that Ray agreed.

"The fey are on their own side," he said cynically. "Never forget that. If Caedmon wasn't making out like a bandit in this war, he wouldn't be helping us. But his old rival just got run out of his kingdom, leaving Caedmon in charge of two now. Don't be surprised if he's not too quick to change that."

I nodded slowly. "It seems that you were right. Some things are not so different from our world."

"Now you're getting it. Anyway, the river is our best bet. We wanna avoid the la-di-da type of fey and hit up the villages, and most of them are built along the rivers." He frowned and took one of my nuts. "I just wish we had something to trade."

"Like what?"

"Like a lot of things. The regular fey, they're not opposed to some smuggled Earth luxuries, now and again."

"What kind of luxuries?"

"All kinds. Our biggest sellers, though, the stuff that really got good value . . ."

"Yes?"

He shook his head. "You won't believe me. Nobody does, not until they come with, and see for themselves."

"I'll believe you."

"Okay, but I'm not talking nobles here. They're a different breed. But the regular Joes . . . liked Little Debbies."

I blinked at him. "What?"

He nodded. "Hand to God."

"Why?"

"Think about it. This ain't the kinda climate that supports sugarcane. Honey is what they use for a sweetener here, and it's hard to come by. So, anything sweet is a big deal."

"But . . . Little Debbies?"

"The highly spiced ones. Spices are expensive, too. So, sugar and spice together—that's a luxury item right there. They mostly wanted the pecan cinnamon rolls, honey buns, and those pumpkin spice things you see around Halloween. I used to get the guys to take a van around and load up."

I tried to picture that, to wrap my head around the image of a bunch of vampires driving a van full of snack cakes, or standing in line at the supermarket with two or three shopping carts' worth of them . . . and failed.

"Did anyone ever ask why?" I said.

He nodded. "Told 'em the truth. Gonna trade it to some faeries for fey wine and potion supplies."

I laughed. "You did not."

"Well, I was drunk at the time. Hadda check the wine when it came in, you know, make sure it was a good batch."

I copied one of his favorite gestures and rolled my eyes at him. I also gave him back the remains of the trail mix. I was still hungry, but I might need a quick energy boost later.

Ray packed it up in the blanket along with our other supplies, and stowed it in back of the raft. Then he carried me down to the waterline. Our new vessel did not look any better close up, but I decided not to mention that.

However, there were some things that I hadn't seen from a distance. Ray had made two indentations in the pile of sticks that I assumed were supposed to be seats. They actually worked pretty well, I discovered, after he lifted me onto the one in back. The sticks had been piled up high, giving me some support. They also curved slightly around me, like a half cage, so that I wouldn't fall out, I supposed.

He checked it anyway, rocking me back and forth to see if I'd shake loose. Only when he was satisfied did he get in the front "seat," settling himself and causing the contraption to sag somewhat. That left my legs in water almost up to my knees, and to my surprise, it felt a bit cold. I could actually feel the chill of the current, which was more than I'd been able to do yesterday.

I felt myself getting excited at the idea that perhaps my legs weren't completely dead, after all. But I quickly tamped it back down. Dhampirs usually healed quickly, vanishing minor wounds within a day, and major ones within a week or so. But a week was a very long time in Faerie.

Still, I decided to take it as a good sign. And then Ray reached back and pulled my feet up, tucking them into the briar patch of a raft and out of the stream, and I thought I felt that, too. Or maybe it was just wishful thinking.

"What was that for?" I asked.

"Same as this," he said, and leaned over the side to pick up what looked like another pile of sticks, which had been floating in the water.

I'd assumed that it was merely additional driftwood that had not been needed, or perhaps a trash pile that had accumulated against the rocks. It contained leaves as well as sticks, a few clumps of grass, and some fish carcasses, the latter of which I recognized as the remains of our meal from last night. Even the crab shell was there, perched on top like a weather vane on a house.

And then perched on top of us, when Ray dragged the whole thing over our heads.

"Ray!"

"This is how we used to smuggle stuff," he explained, working to arrange the thing, so that it formed a type of canopy. I could now see that it wasn't flat bottomed, as I'd thought, but hollow, with the trash carefully woven across an archway of sticks.

It was dim in here, but I could still see, especially when facing forward. The trash was thinner there, probably so that Ray could see to navigate. But there were also places along the sides where the riverbank was clearly visible.

"Like I said," he continued. "Getting around Faerie is dangerous, even when people aren't chasing you. And when they think you're smuggling, they usually are."

"But you were smuggling snack cakes—"

"Well, they were more of a sweetener—ha!" he added, seeming pleased with himself over the pun.

"You are good with humor," I said truthfully.

He glanced back at me and grinned. "Thanks. Anyway, food is always appreciated, 'specially when it's something you don't get every day. I'd add a crate or two of honey buns or something to the delivery to get a better price. You'd be surprised how quickly people change their tune when you're waving their favorite treat under their nose. I always used to suggest we have a sample with our tea, while we negotiated."

"Negotiated for what?" I asked, because it didn't sound like Little Debbies formed the majority of his inventory.

He shrugged and pushed us off from the bank with a driftwood paddle. "Weapons mostly, like we talked about last night, and wards—"

"Wards?"

"Yeah, 'specially any big enough to hide a barn so that an enemy couldn't burn it down. Or to camouflage a safe house stuck somewhere out in the woods, where a family could retreat if needed. Wards were a big seller."

"But I thought Earth magic didn't work in Faerie."

"Oh, it works," he said, aiming us toward mid-stream, where the current was swiftest. "Just not for long. Earth talismans can't gather magic from Faerie—"

"You could use a fey talisman," I pointed out, but he shook his head.

"Yeah, but then the magic it collects will be fey, too, and that only runs fey spells. When the whole point of buying from me, or other human smugglers, was to get something different. Something their enemies wouldn't know and might overlook. Or that might blow them away because they never seen it before."

"I see."

"I made out better than most 'cause my stuff lasted. I got some coven witches to do the spells, and coven magic is basically a cross between human and fey. So, their talismans will work here, only not as well. But a little help is better than none at all."

"Yes," I agreed and looked down, to where some small fish were attempting to nibble at my toes. They were silver bright and shining in the sun dappled water, and followed us for a minute before realizing that they couldn't quite reach the tempting morsels. They gave up, darting after easier prey, as our speed increased.

This world was so beautiful, I thought, looking around. Like Earth in many places, but an untouched Earth, with clean water and old growth forests. Yet, just like back home, all anybody seemed to want to do was fight.

"It is a shame that the fey only wanted weapons," I said.

"Yeah, well, you prioritize, don't you?" Ray asked. "They might like other stuff, but they need things to keep them and their families safe. This place has been deteriorating for a while."

The current caught us a moment later and we took off, the few leafy branches on our strange canopy flapping in the breeze above our heads. The cover worked surprisingly well structurally, with its weight supported by some of the larger limbs that stuck up from the main body of the raft. It probably worked as camouflage, too. Unless someone looked very closely, we could easily appear to be nothing more than a shaggy patch of trash that had collected and was floating downstream.

And I didn't think that anybody was likely to look that close. The river flowed roughly as fast as a person could run, ensuring that we made good time. Even better, it required very little effort on our part. Ray had to occasionally use the paddle he'd made to push our craft off of some stones, or to steer us clear of the shallows. But for the most part, the current did the work.

After a while, I began to enjoy myself.

The forests, deadly though they might be, were also beautiful. The high, rocky banks often covered them from view, but at times they would drop to show huge, verdant swaths of trees, mostly still green but some with brilliant yellow or red tops. Some of the closest of these had roots as big around as old oaks back home, which dipped down into the water or scrawled along the bank in wild tangles, while their branches shed early autumn leaves on us, like multicolored rain.

As we proceeded, the river started to move a little

faster, heading downhill and gushing over miniature falls, anything from a few inches to a foot or so in height. The bed slanted enough to show long stretches of waterway, with blue gray mountains receding into the distance, while in between the trees I occasionally caught glimpses of windswept grasslands or mysterious caves. There were also some furry creatures that looked somewhat like large squirrels, but had flat, beaver-like tails. They ran through the trees with ease and chittered at us from overhanging branches.

"Don't let 'em get too close. The little bastards bite," Ray warned.

"Good thing we have the canopy then."

He grinned at me over his shoulder. "It's an added feature."

We traveled a bit more, but while the current was loud in places, especially when gurgling over stones, it was easily quiet enough to talk. So, I did. I had many questions.

"You said that the villagers were different from the nobles—"

"Oh, yeah."

"How are they different?"

Ray glanced over his shoulder. "Why you want to talk about that?"

I shrugged. "We fought some fey nobles yesterday. We are being stalked by others. I would like to know more about my enemies."

He thought about it. "Okay, but this is gonna sound stupid. Mostly because it is really, really stupid. But maybe it'll help."

I nodded.

"There are two kinds of fey. Unless you wanna count the dark fey. But they're a lot more like the villagers, the light fey common folk, than anybody would like to admit. So, basically, you got two kinds of fey: the nobles and everybody else."

I nodded again.

"Normal fey want comfort, ease of living, security. They want to dangle a grandbaby on their knee before they die, maybe leave something to the kids. Have somebody shed a tear when they go."

"Like people everywhere," I said.

"Yeah. But the nobles . . . they already have all that, or can easily get it. It don't mean the same."

"What do they want?"

He shrugged. "Adventure, challenge, adrenaline. See, their mythology is really messed up, but it has some stuff in common with the old Greek way of thinking. Maybe that's even where the Greeks got it."

"Got what?"

"The hero myth. The idea that you're a hero, or you're nothing. That the only life worth living is one that gets songs sung about your deeds long after you're gone, that has kids looking up to you, women wanting to f—uh, date you, and guys wanting to be you."

"What about women heroes?"

He shot me a look over his shoulder. "I don't think the Svarestri have women heroes."

I frowned.

"Anyway, it all goes back to their myths," he continued. "The Greeks thought only heroes ended up in the Elysium Fields after death—their version of Heaven. Everybody else either went to Tartarus, if they were really bad, or the Asphodel Meadows if they were just meh. Neither was a good time. The old Scandinavians thought the same. Heroes went to Valhalla or that other hall, the one Odin's wife had." He snapped his fingers a couple of times. "I forget. But, anyway, the ticket to ride was always the same: big deeds. Hero stuff. Kind of good didn't cut it."

"And the fey nobles feel the same?"

He nodded. "Only more so. They think their future reincarnation depends on their actions now. Be legendary and you come back as a king or a noble. Be courageous and maybe you get to be a warrior. Be basic and you'll be grubbing in the dirt for eternity, which is why they don't think much of the common folk. Be a coward and, well, you might not come back at all."

"So that is why Aeslinn fights? I heard it was for more . . . present rewards."

"Oh, well, it's different for him. He's already a king. There's not much higher he can go. Except the obvious, I guess."

"The obvious?"

"Well, Hercules became a god, didn't he?"

"But he was already a demigod."

"Well, what do you think Aeslinn is?"

I blinked. "Really?"

The dark head nodded. "According to rumor, all three of the leaders of the great princely houses are children that the gods had with fey nobility: Nimue was the daughter of Poseidon, or Neptune or Njǫrd, whatever name you wanna call him. Caedmon was the son of Zeus—or Jupiter or Odin— the original sky god."

"Zeus?"

"Yeah, he's fighting against his own father, again according to rumor."

"And Aeslinn?"

"Hades."

I supposed that made sense, in a way. "So, the three divine brothers of the Greek pantheon are still battling it out, only by proxy."

"Yeah, only they didn't win, did they? Artemis did. The underdog defeated them all, just like we're gonna do."

I smiled.

CHAPTER THIRTY-SEVEN

Dorina, Faerie

The river became wider after an hour or so, and faster, with the little drop offs not quite so little anymore. But landing anywhere wasn't possible. The woods grew thick and close to the waterline here, hedging the flow so tightly that it almost looked like the trees were wading out to meet us.

"I been in spots like this before," Ray said, raising his voice to be heard over the sound of rushing water. "They usually don't last long."

I nodded, and then continued to do so as we juddered over some rocks, hard enough to make my head bobble. But the occasional glimpses I had ahead, as the river snaked through the trees, was less the smooth green ribbon we had been traversing and more a mass of leaping white water. It was not encouraging.

And neither was that, I thought, as a bird cried high overhead.

My eyes turned upward, but for a moment, I couldn't see anything. I squinted and focused on a black dot silhouetted against the sun. It was so high and so small that it would have been easy to overlook had its call not sounded like an alarm.

And had it not been fluttering in my face a moment later.

It was just outside the cage of branches, its wings moving almost as fast as a hummingbird's, although it was much larger. But it had the same bright coloring, with a crimson head, a blue-green neck, and an iridescent green body. And a pair of intelligent black eyes.

Too intelligent.

Shit, as Dory would say.

"We're going to have company," I told Ray, as the bird's wings battered against our camouflage.

"What?" It was another yell, because the white water I'd glimpsed through the trees was almost upon us now, and deafening.

"Company! We've been spotted!"

The bird soared away, far into the sky, its mission accomplished. Some of the light fey had the ability to see through the eyes of animals, including birds. They called it farseeing, as it was often used to spy on places that they could not go themselves. Or to cover a large area, as had probably been the case here.

The fey had not known of the hidden crevasse that Ray and I had used to escape them, or how we had managed to ditch our vehicle and exit the cave. But they had known that we must still be in the area. So, they'd sent their creatures to find us.

And they'd chosen one with far sharper eyes than they had themselves.

"We have to get off this river," I told Ray. "We have to get off it now."

"Not good timing!" he yelled back, gesturing at the high banks and thick forest cover beyond them.

"It is going to be worse in a moment," I said, and once more, I tried to launch my spirit form.

There was a chance, I thought, that my recent difficulties lay in attempting to use the combat version of my ability, which had manifested only recently. But there was the other, much less taxing type of projection, the one that was more mental than physical. The same type that the fey had just used.

I threw my mind outward, trying to find a bird of my own, or any creature whose body I might borrow for a moment. I wanted to see how much time we had, and the direction of the coming attack. It wasn't much, but it was the only way I could help Ray, who was battling to keep us upright as we approached true whitewater.

I latched onto one of the beaver-like creatures, intending to send it scurrying for the higher treetops, and give me a view over the forest. But something went wrong—very wrong. I had it for a moment, looking down through its eyes at our paw, and the fat grub we had just fished out of a tree. The insect was squirming, but we were gripping it determinedly, feeling satisfied and anticipatory, all at once.

But then something happened, and instead of one pair of eyes, I was suddenly looking through dozens, maybe hundreds.

Furry things were waddling through tunnels or nursing tangles of bright-eyed babies in burrows. Others were chewing through acres of wood, sending fresh smelling chips flying. Still more were running along the high branches of trees, their tails *thwap thwap thwapping* along the bark behind them, the ground dizzyingly far below as they leapt from limb to distant limb.

And all of it was happening at the same time.

I tried to rein it in, but instead, my vision shattered into a kaleidoscope with far, far too many facets to even try to process. There were whiskers in my face, a furry snuffling; there were claws, as one of the creatures wrestled another for a female's affection; there was a furious chase around and around a huge, old trunk by a trio of youngsters, their claws gripping the wood as easily as human feet would run across sand. There was a sudden plunge under water, with furry bodies twisting and turning and racing after gleaming fish—

I exerted all my strength and finally managed to pull

back, my heart pounding, my mind stuttering, my breath catching in confusion in my throat. For a moment, I was unsure whether I was in the river below or in the canopy above or far beneath the ground. I stared about, trying to will my eyes to focus on the here and now.

And snapped back to churning water and the back of Ray's dark head.

I let my breath out in a trickle as reality returned.

I did not think I would try that again.

No, I did not think that at all.

Not that it would probably have worked if I had. Farseeing required concentration, and we had just hit the rapids—hard. I came fully back to myself to find waves crashing over the raft in a stinging spray, our little vessel shaking hard enough to send pieces of it boiling away over the water, and Ray digging his makeshift paddle deep, trying to keep us upright.

And then we plummeted over a six-foot waterfall.

It was tiny compared to the others we had encountered in this world, but it immediately led to four more in quick succession. It felt like we were bouncing down a giant staircase, except that we went under every time we splashed down, leaving water cascading off the canopy when we emerged, making it hard to see. And most of what I could make out was blurred by the prismatic effect of the sun through all those droplets.

Ray started trying to steer us toward shore, as the battering we were taking was not sustainable. I worked to tighten the ropes, and to keep the rest of his creation from falling to pieces around us. But that was made challenging by the rocks, which scraped across the bottom and slammed into the sides, flinging us this way and that. And by the current, which felt considerably faster, bringing more obstacles along every moment. And by the spray, which was constant now, and hitting us from seemingly all sides at once.

And by Ray suddenly flipping us over in the water.

I did not understand why, but it had been deliberate. He'd headed straight for some rocks beside a mighty swirl of white water, then pushed off of them, throwing his strength and body weight into the roll. As a result, instead of landing in the calmer waters near the shore, where we had been heading a moment ago, we went straight into the heart—

Of a raging vortex.

Water closed over my head, bubbling madly in every direction, and cutting off what little vision I'd had. Even worse, the high sides of the raft, which had once helped to support me, now served as a cage. My legs were useless and my arms couldn't seem to push past the thicket-like canopy, which was making our vessel seem less like a raft suddenly and more like a wooden coffin.

I thrashed uselessly, before finally managing to throw off the camouflaged top, but it didn't help much. I continued to be sucked down a twisting, churning, water-filled passage, while the raging currents tried to decide whether they wanted to beat me to death or drown me. And I still couldn't see!

The water was murkier than I'd expected and swirling madly all around me, leaving me so disorientated that I had no idea which way was up. I forced myself to release some air, intending to follow the bubbles to the surface, but they didn't go anywhere. They stayed clustered around my face, as if they were confused, too.

But a moment later I abruptly hit air again, although it was less like surfacing and more like being vomited up by some great sea creature. It felt like my body partly left the water, then smacked back down again, but I couldn't tell for sure. I was too busy gasping and coughing and retching, my starved lungs struggling to drag in breath after breath. I did not think I was doing too well.

"Dorina!"

I heard Ray's voice, but couldn't answer.

"Dorina!"

"I'm okay," I finally managed to croak, although in truth, I wasn't sure about that. Spots danced in front of my eyes and the world had gone dark. Or perhaps it had already been that way, I thought, finally blinking enough water out of my eyes that I could see.

Only what I saw didn't make sense.

And then I realized what I was looking at, and it still didn't.

"A cave?" I gasped, staring dizzily down at a seemingly never-ending drop. One that I was suspended over by nothing more than the water churning around me. The raft, which had floated a little way off, looked like a twiggy chandelier hung over the vast, echoing space. Even stranger, a waterfall flowed up some nearby rocks, spraying like a fountain into the air.

Even having been in a similar situation recently, I found it . . . mind altering.

"The underside of the river!" Ray corrected, his voice loud to compensate for the sound of the falls. He must have been thrown clear of the raft at some point, and had ended up a few dozen yards away. He spotted me and started to swim over.

"Why . . . did you bring us . . . here?" I gasped. "And how? Wood is . . . buoyant."

"Yeah, well, I had some help!"

His voice echoed strangely, as did my own. It did not improve my dizziness any. "What kind of . . . help?"

"The legends about Nimue's powers, the ones that talk about the river. She's said to have made escape hatches for her people, in case they got surrounded—"

"That was an escape hatch?" I did not bother to keep the incredulity out of my voice.

He grinned from a little way off, having snagged what was left of the raft, which he started towing over. "It's all relative! Her people travel across water the way we do land.

Some say they can even walk on it—"

That claim would have sounded absurd to me a mere day ago, but that was before I had been to Faerie.

"—for them, what we just slid down would probably be a piece of cake."

"A what?"

He shook his head. "I forgot; you don't do slang. I just meant—" he broke off, and his eyes blew wide. "Get back on the raft!"

I looked for the threat that his reaction had told me was close, but did not see anything. Until he pointed at something in the water. I saw glimmering emerald depths with a crashing sea of sunlit white above—or below, depending on how you wanted to look at it. And dark figures moving against all that light, coming this way.

Fey, I thought sickly. They must have arrived in time to see where we went. Which meant—

"That we're fucked, if you don't get on!" Ray yelled.

I did not understand what he was talking about, since the river was upside down. It was in the cave ceiling, not running through the darkness below. There was nothing to get "on" to.

Yet he was clinging to the raft, nonetheless, gripping it with his legs and holding out an urgent hand to me. I took it because I did not know what else to do, and he gave a heave, dragging me up behind him. And as soon as he did—

The strangest thing happened.

I had been bobbing upside down, my head and arms sticking out of the water like a human stalactite. But when Ray hauled me onto the raft, it was as if the world suddenly flipped. I found myself right side up, clinging to his waist in an underground river that ran along the bottom of a large cavern.

Suddenly, everything made sense. The waterfall crashed over rocks that looked darker where it flowed, and sprayed out at the bottom as gravity demanded. The huge echoing space was now above us where it belonged, with the witchy fingers of limestone hanging downwards instead of spearing up. A few bats also hung properly down from their perches, instead of looking as if they'd gone to sleep standing upright.

I nonetheless stayed where I was for a moment, my head against Ray's back, my mind spinning as it slowly adjusted to this new reality. He started to paddle, hard, and we began to move down what appeared to be a perfectly normal river. Well, perfectly normal if you ignored the sunlight sparkling below us, and the dark silhouettes swimming upward toward us.

And gaining.

These might not be water fey, but they almost moved like it, bulleting towards us at speeds that almost looked enhanced, as if a human-like body could not attain them unaided. But we were moving, too, with a motivated master vampire leaning into every stroke. The raft was in no way aerodynamic, but it almost seemed like it for the moment, shooting ahead as if we, too, had a motor.

In front of us, maybe a few hundred yards away, I saw another vortex. It was churning in the middle of the stream, but with nothing around it to explain why. The rest of the water on this side of the river could best be described as gentle fluctuations, or at most small wavelets. They did not even crest, yet the furious, white-edged mouth of the vortex started dragging us forward.

I looked behind us again, and the number of fey had grown. Where there had been only a few before, now there were dozens, a continuous line of divers heading toward the surface. I saw the first break through the water and sweep long, wet, silver hair out of his eyes, and thought that he would take a moment to reorient himself as I had done.

But I'd hardly had the thought when he began swimming after us. The strokes were worthy of an Olympic athlete, digging hard into the water, the light from below gleaming off his hair and water-slick muscles. And that was despite the fact that, to him, it must feel like he was swimming upside down.

But the vortex's current had a firm hold on us now, and we were speeding ahead, so quickly that Ray no longer bothered to paddle. He glanced back at me, his face flushed and wet and strangely savage. "You don't talk much!"

"What would you like me to say?"

"Most people would be yelling at me for an explanation!"

I thought about it. "I assume we are going back up top, because the fey are down here now?"

He laughed, and oddly considering the circumstances, it sounded genuine. "Right in one!"

And then we were falling.

The trip through the second watery escape hatch was no easier than the first, and I came no less close to drowning. But when we popped up in a deserted stream, I felt the same slightly mad smile stretch my face that had been on Ray's. We had made it!

The world was upside down again, and despite the fact that I had expected it this time, it was still bizarre to see blue sky below us and trees above. The whitewater rush tossed us about and sounded loud in my ears. The warmth of the sun played over my face. And then the world flipped and I laughed, because Ray's ruse had worked!

The fey had been left behind!

Well, most of them.

I spied several dark figures slinging around the vortex below us. But vampire stamina rivalled that of any fey, not to mention vampire strength. Ray started paddling and our little craft took off, almost flying down the rapids.

And this time, I knew what to look for.

"There!" I yelled, clinging to his waist with one arm, while pointing with the other. "Right there!"

"I see it!" he yelled back, looking at the tell-tale whirlpool almost hidden among the crashing waves. He made for it, just as I felt something whiz past my ear. A fey arrow quivered out of a piece of driftwood where none had been a second ago, and then a barrage followed.

I looked about, confused as to how they had gotten here so fast, and how they had shot waterlogged weapons when they did so. But then I glimpsed a fey with dry clothes on the bank, with a foot looped under a root to allow him to lean out and fire arrow after arrow at our wildly bobbing vessel. Most of the arrows missed, but several ended up tangled in the thicket around us, and one slammed into Ray's thigh.

"Fuckers!" he yelled.

And then we were plunging down another watery conduit.

I did not know how we were supposed to get ahead of our pursuers if they were on both sides of the river now. I assumed that Ray had been right: these tunnels had to be easier for Nimue's people to navigate. Perhaps they used them like slides, giving them a speed boost and leaving their enemies floundering in their wake. But we were not Green Fey.

We were, however, on the ride of a lifetime, because this vortex seemed stronger than the last two, or perhaps we had just entered it going at a greater speed. All I knew was that we shot out of the water on the other side of the river, sticks flying, Ray cursing, and me clinging to him with an iron grip. And trying to tell myself that we were not about to plunge to our deaths as we sailed straight into the huge open space below us.

It was still a shock when we slammed into the water again, upside down. And even more of one when the mind wrenching feeling of having the world reorient itself hit again, so abruptly that I wondered if this sort of thing led to brain damage if done often enough. I did not have time to wonder long, however.

The current was stronger here, grabbing us like a closing fist, ripping us out of the area around the vortex and all but throwing us down the river. But I did not feel like complaining. Because the fey were back, or, more likely, had never left.

I did not know if some had stayed behind deliberately, or if they had simply not made the transition fast enough, but dark shadows were already leaping along the "banks" behind us, finding toe holds in the almost perpendicular rock, and making themselves a pathway where none existed.

So that they could send another barrage our way.

"Damn it, get in front of me!" Ray yelled, as arrows hit the water on both sides of us.

"No! Ray—"

"I can take a few arrows; you can't!"

"That's more than a few!"

He turned around and grabbed me by the front of my tunic. "Look at me. I am the captain now, all right? Now get the hell in front!"

But as it happened, I didn't have to.

The current whirled us around a second later, leaving us facing the wrong way, and Ray gasping as three arrows slammed into his back, almost at the same time.

"Fuckers," he yelled again, although it sounded more like a wheeze, his lungs having just been shredded.

"I need a weapon," I gritted out, furious.

But I didn't have one. Our pack was long since gone, lost along with everything we owned in the raging rapids. But then a fey dropped down on top of us from the slick side of a stalactite, and it turned out that I had everything I needed, after all.

I snatched him out of the air before he could grab Ray, who had slumped over. I wasn't sure how much leverage I had with my useless legs, but for once, luck was on my side. They had become entangled with the wreckage of our raft, giving me enough control to punch the fey repeatedly in the face, throwing all my weight and rage behind it.

I felt teeth shatter and tear the skin of my knuckles. I felt bones break—his, I was pretty sure, although at that moment

I didn't care. I felt his nose cave in and something that might have been an eyeball squash against my hand, before popping like a grape. My arm shuddered and my shoulder muscles cried out at the sheer amount of force I was demanding of them; my face was splattered with blood and my throat was sore from screams I hadn't even realized I had been making. Yet I continued—

Until a hand grabbed my wrist.

"I think . . . he's dead," Ray gasped.

I looked down at what I was holding.

Yes, I thought; yes, he was.

I looked up, and saw half a dozen fey, the only ones close enough to have witnessed the fight, clinging to rocks and limestone formations, staring. I bared my blood covered teeth at them. Yes, I thought. You understood that, didn't you? Then understand *this*, and I tore the fey's head off, ripping the sinew and muscle from the bones, and tossing it to one side of the craft while the body slipped away on the other.

Then we fell down another vortex.

CHAPTER THIRTY-EIGHT

Dorina, Faerie

I hadn't realized that the vortex was so close and I wasn't prepared. And perhaps it was because I was exhausted, but the currents seemed harsher this time. They felt like they were going to tear us apart before the fey had a chance.

I barely noticed when we surfaced again, didn't even feel the rotation when the world flipped and righted itself. I vaguely understood that someone was hitting my back, but didn't know who. But the blows were hard, shuddering my ribcage, and forcing water up and out of my throat.

"Damn it, breathe!"

It was Ray. He sounded upset. I frowned, because I couldn't remember . . .

Oh, yes. He had four fey arrows sticking out of him. Three in his chest and one in his thigh. And something about that thought did what nothing else could, and roused me.

I came back to myself, only to find that I was sprawled over the raft, face down and puking my guts out into the river. I still couldn't half breathe, but Ray was rhythmically beating on my back, which seemed to help. Every time he did it, more water and phlegm came up, or perhaps that was the remains of breakfast. Didn't know; didn't care.

And then my eyes were crossing at a neatly fletched arrow that was sticking out of my shoulder, a bright shock of pain.

"You bastards!" Ray sounded like he was sobbing.

I looked back at him and my thoughts, my heart, and quite possibly the blood in my veins halted, all at once. I stared at him for what felt like an hour, because I had been wrong. There were not four arrows.

The fey had riddled his body with them while I had been out, to the point that his skin ran with rivulets of blood, blood we could no longer replace. There were twenty or thirty shafts; I didn't know. Couldn't count. They had literally ripped him apart and he had allowed them to do so, in order to shield me.

Another shaft slammed into him a second later, forcing out a small cry that had me trying to surge to my feet, forgetting that I couldn't. I collapsed back against the raft, and almost fell out. Only my unwounded hand caught me.

"This is the great warrior we've been told so much about?" A fey appeared on the river bank, flanked by several others. One of them had a bow in his hand with another arrow already nocked, but the leader put out an arm, stopping him. "I have to say, I'm disappointed."

I didn't bother replying. It had been years since a taunt had been able to anger me, and certainly not one from a murderous thug. My eyes scanned the banks, only to see more and more fey revealing themselves. I could not count them all; the tree line hid them too well, with only flickers of silver among the sun dappled leaves. But the ones I could see
—

Were too many.

Had I been home, on familiar ground; had I been well, and properly equipped; had I been rested—perhaps. But here . . . no. I could not take so many, if I could take any at all. I needed another solution.

I threw my consciousness outward, as far as it would go, searching for any possible advantage.

I had not tried summoning our little capsule before, as

the fey knew where it was and might be watching it. It would have been useful, without my legs, but I had been afraid that it might lead them right to us. But now that they were already here, I found that I could not reach it, after all, the little frisson I remembered being completely absent.

Perhaps the fey had damaged it, or perhaps it was too far away to hear my call. I tried to contact one of their vessels instead, but the same thing happened. I could not reach them. I could not reach . . .

Anything.

"Nothing to say?" the fey tried again. He was tall as they all were, and dressed in the same silver-gray tunic and leggings as the rest. He had the same long, silver-white hair, too, unbound and blowing slightly in a fair breeze. It seemed to be a hallmark of the Svarestri, making them look like brothers or clones. At this distance, it was difficult to see much variation.

"I will talk, then," he informed me, sitting on a large rock and resting his bow on his knee. "I was sent to retrieve you—alive. I find myself suddenly less interested in doing so."

"Then why not . . . kill me already?" I panted. "You had . . . the opportunity."

"Ah, so it can talk." He smiled. "I wanted you awake for this. Not an easy death, not a quick slipping away into darkness—no. This will not be easy, and I assure you, that it will take a very long time."

I ripped open my tunic, spilling out my breasts—and the handprint between them. It was a burn, one Dory had long concealed with a glamourie, lest her lover go mad and try to hunt down a fey prince. But I had no such ruse, and no need for it here.

Quite the contrary, in fact.

"Your prince marked me . . . as his prey, and his alone. You cannot touch me."

The leader smiled again. "Ah, yes. I seem to recall something of the kind." He looked around at the river and spread a hand. "But as you can see, he is not here."

"You would fail in your mission then . . . to return with me?"

"It is a dilemma," he agreed. "Succeed, and win myself rewards and accolades. Fail, and suffer a harsh punishment. It would seem an easy choice."

"But you do not find it so."

"I did, until you killed eight of my men during your escape, and mutilated their corpses. I did, until you burned thirty more in those caves, turning our own weapons against us. I did, until you murdered my cousin, ripping his head from his shoulders and tossing his body away like filth, oh yes, I *did*.

"I find myself of a different mind now."

He raised his own weapon, and leveled it at me. To my surprise, a fey beside him knocked his arm down, and began arguing sharply with him. I did not know their language, but judging by the gestures the other fey made at me and the heat in his voice, he was not so sure about disregarding his prince's orders.

I expanded my call, put everything I had left into it, searching through heaven and earth for anything, anything that might serve. Not as a weapon; I did not know this world well enough for that. But as a distraction, something to allow us at least the chance of escape.

In my desperation, I even called on Nimue, my consciousness running through the deep caverns and liquid arteries of her lands. It boomed down tunnels, rippled over streams, echoed off ancient cavern walls, all the way to the very heart of the earth. But she did not answer. She had wanted to see what I could do, and I had shown her.

And as Ray had said, the gods had no reward for the weak.

"You aren't weak!"

Ray hadn't spoken aloud, possibly because I would not have heard. Our raft had hung up on some rocks, and the crash of the churning waters was loud in my ears. But more likely because he could not. The last arrow had taken him through the throat, and probably severed his vocal cords.

But then, vampires do not have to speak to communicate.

"*Run,*" he urged me, the thought echoing loudly in my mind. "*Dive off and swim for the next vortex. The current will help carry you—*"

"No."

"*—and you can hide in the caves. They're so vast that—*"

"No."

"*—the fey might never find you!*"

"*They would find me. And I would not face my end that way.*"

"*Why?*" the voice in my head raged. "*You have to try! You know you can't win if you stay—*"

"*This isn't about winning.*"

"*Then what the hell is it about?*"

I cupped his cheek, and felt his blood slide under my fingers, warm and wet and precious. "Pain."

He looked at me, uncomprehendingly. But something else heard, and finally understood. From somewhere, far underground, there came a distant rumble.

My calls had not raised the goddess I'd sought, and they had been ignored by the only other ears there were to hear. Something in the caverns had listened, but not comprehended. What did they care for honor, a concept both foreign and trivial? What did they need of revenge? These were not words they knew, or cries they answered.

But, by chance, I had stumbled across one they did.

The cry of my heart had reached them as the call of my mind had not. Because yes, pain was a concept they knew. They had felt the red burn of it in the flesh—their own or a mate's or a child's taken too young; they had heard the sweet sound of it in an enemy's cry, savaged in tender places, never to threaten them again; they had tasted it, thick and warm and meaty in their throats.

Yes, they understood pain, in all its permutations, as I did.

And now, they listened.

Come to me, I whispered, my mental voice fading along with my strength, but still echoing in the vast chambers below. Come to me and I will give you all that you seek, and more.

Come to me . . .

The argument on shore was a short one. The leader knocked the argumentative fey to the ground, who swept his feet out from under him and pulled a knife. But two more fey stepped forward before he could use it, holding him at spearpoint. And another kicked him savagely in the head, bouncing it off the large rock.

It seemed that the leader's take on events was popular.

But I needed more time.

"Let the vampire go, and I will come with you," I offered. "Quietly."

"The time for negotiation is past!" the leader snarled, jumping back to his feet. "The only thing I want from you is blood!"

The rumble was louder now, enough that several of the fey had noticed. They turned their heads toward the skies, as if they thought a thundercloud approached. Not quite, I thought, and strengthened my call, putting every ounce of my energy I had left into it as the leader raised his weapon again.

The fey on the ground was now either unconscious or dead, unable to help. And none of the others seemed remotely interested. But something else wasn't under the leader's command, and it had heard me.

And it had decided.

Only no, I thought, as the ground shook and the fey stared about and some of the smaller rocks on the hillside tumbled down toward the water, that wasn't exactly right. Not 'it'. They.

And as in the case of the small, furry things, where my power had cascaded across the entire group, giving me a hundred eyes at once, it overflowed this time as well. Only this time, there weren't hundreds. There weren't even thousands. This time . . . there were millions.

A living, breathing cloud of blackness that burst out of caves in the banks, out of tunnels in the rocks, and from crevasses so small that you would not have thought an insect could have fit through them, much less an army. Yet an army is what came forth.

They erupted like black geysers all along the riverbank: bats of every type and description, from tiny things barely the size of my hand, to huge, fanged beasts half as big as me, with wing spans that looked more like a pterodactyl's than anything from the modern world. And everything in between. Whole colonies of them had answered my call. I had always had trouble holding a single animal on Earth. But here—

It was different.

I could not fight, could barely even remain upright. My legs did not work, my shoulder throbbed and bled, my hand had already swollen to twice its normal size, beaten almost as badly as the fey it had pulverized. No, I could not fight at all.

But they could fight for me.

And fight they did.

Some late arriving Svarestri broke through the water, looking a little disoriented after the rage of the vortex, and never had a chance to adjust. The humongous cloud descended on them as soon as they breeched the water, pelting them like missiles, ripping at them with feet and claws and teeth, and screeching so loudly that the echoes alone were pain. They drowned out the river and bounced off the thick packed trees, almost as well as they had off the cave walls below.

The echoes were *awful*.

Someone screamed at the reverberation of all those screeches against the great wooden walls, piling up on each other, higher and higher and over and over, until it felt like being in hell's kettle drum. I thought my ears would burst. I thought I might go mad. And then the almost machine gun sound of all those tiny bodies hitting the water, the screams of the fey as they were ripped apart, and Ray's curses were added to the mix, and I knew I was.

I started laughing, possibly hysterically, but I didn't know because I couldn't hear it. I couldn't hear anything. I couldn't see anything but fluttering, half crazed bodies. I couldn't smell or taste or feel anything but water and the ammonia reek of bats and the coppery tang of blood, although whose I didn't know.

And then the wave parted, as if unzipping down the middle, leaving the stream almost clear as they rose up in the air. The great plume wasn't all of them; I could see the trees rustling, could see bright flashes of red when another fey was torn apart, could hear voices screaming at each other, and then being suddenly silenced. But it was enough.

Then they dove, spearing down toward the small group around the leader, like the fist I could no longer wield. He saw it coming, saw death in flight, and to give him credit, when he ran, it was not away. It was toward me, taking off across the water along with three of his men, who must have had a little Green Fey blood in their veins.

Because they were not swimming.

They ran instead, their feet barely denting the waves, their swords out and slashing, battling to reach me through a thickness of fur and teeth and fangs. The leader was the quickest, surging across the stream with great strokes, crossing the churning waves in seconds, his eyes burning, his face terrible.

He almost made it.

"Fuck me," Ray's mental voice said quietly.

The bats must have been the flesh-eating variety, because the fey were eaten alive while still moving, stripped of every ounce of flesh on their bones as quickly as if they had swum into a group of piranhas. But piranhas don't levitate their prey into the air, don't eat the faces of their victims while they are still screaming, don't drench bystanders in a wash of blood that had Ray cursing in my head and me just lying there, watching bones splash down into the current and be swept away.

The leader was left until last. I did not consciously request it, but perhaps subconsciously, I had wanted this. *The only thing I want from you is blood!*

Yes, that sounded right.

What was left of him finally slipped below the waves, all of a yard from his goal. There was blood, enough to turn the waves pink and frothy as they carried him downstream. I stared at it as if entranced, marking his journey by the color he left behind, and only realized how exhausted I was when my eyes started to lose focus.

There were still bats above us, as well as all along the river, a great mass of them turning and twisting and battering each other as they fought over scraps of flesh. But I could barely see them. The world went dim and swimmy, and I would have slipped off the raft had Ray not caught me.

"Dorina! Dorina!"

He was somehow still functional, in spite of everything. I did not understand how. But I understood one thing.

"Get us out of here," I slurred. "I can't . . . hold them . . ."

Ray said something back, but I did not hear it. Blood was rushing in my ears, my vision was blurring, and my heart was threatening to pound out of my chest. I had only ever held one animal at a time before, and had found that to be difficult. I did not know how I was doing this at all, and was desperately afraid that I wouldn't be for much longer.

And when I wasn't, would they turn on us?

Would they do to us what they had just done to the fey?

"Hold on," Ray said, as water splashed us and the rain of blood from above doused us, and the remains of countless fey went rushing downstream pursued by screeching black clouds, still feeding. I watched them, feeling my control slipping away.

Then it snapped, my hold over the murderous colony above us completely gone. I watched them through bleary eyes as they spiraled up into the sky, almost as one, just as I had seen them do right before they attacked the fey. And then they dove—

Straight for the caves and crevasses from which they'd come, desperate to get away from this awful, lighted world and back into the cool dampness of home.

I watched them go, half disbelieving. And then exhaled a shaky breath, and sagged against Ray. He sagged back, having freed the raft but being too exhausted to paddle.

We let the river carry us downstream.

CHAPTER THIRTY-NINE

Dory, Hong Kong

"Wʜat the—where are we?" Louis-Cesare asked, his voice strained.

I flipped the light switch, showing the bare cement blocks and shiny weapons of my armory. He stared around for a second, his eyes wide, a pulse pounding madly in his throat. As if he'd expected a very different view, like maybe of the afterlife.

Finally, he looked at me. "You brought us back *here*?"

"Was there a choice?"

I sat down in the chair, feeling a little dizzy. The squashy old thing had come from a thrift shop, bought because it was the right size and shape to fit the space I had left, and because it was comfortable. I hadn't actually noticed until this moment that it had a print on it, composed mainly of pastel yellow pineapples on a faded pink background. I looked away.

I did not want my last glimpse of the world to be polyester kitsch.

Unfortunately, that left me looking at my captives, some of whom were awake and unhappy. They were going to be a lot unhappier if this didn't work. Or possibly even if it did, since we'd been over the dead zones when we fell.

But I didn't have to think up a speech, because Louis-Cesare grabbed me. "We are falling to our deaths!"

And, okay, if I'd wanted a phrase to get everyone's attention, I couldn't have done any better. Eyes widened, breaths caught, and yet nobody spoke. They just looked at me.

I didn't respond or explain, because I didn't know what you said to that. And because it didn't matter anymore. I just pulled my husband's face close and kissed him, because that was what I wanted my last sight to be.

For a moment, it was perfect: the slight scrape of bristles along his jaw, the warm fullness of his lips, the silk of his hair falling all around us, and the hardness of the chest under my hand—

Until he pulled back and shook me, which, yeah.

Not really part of the fantasy.

"Did you hear me?" His face was wild and his hair was everywhere, probably because I'd forgotten to put the clip back in place earlier. I absently looked around for it, and the shaking recommenced. "Dory!"

"I heard you. But it's kind of taking a long time, don't you think?"

Louis-Cesare stared at me some more. Then he did exactly what I should have expected from my impetuous husband and threw open the door, poking his head out of the portal. That wasn't exactly recommended operating procedure, and on a regular portal would have had the effect of sending his head somewhere very far from the rest of his body, while spaghettifying his neck.

However, this was a fixed portal, so he came back in after a moment, looking shaken and deathly pale, but otherwise fine.

"Is there a problem?" I asked.

He nodded.

Together, we looked back outside, which . . . yeah. Still not recommended, I thought, as it left us sticking out of the top of my wide-mouthed purse like two disembodied heads. That was bad, but charging down a foggy street at about fifty miles an hour was worse. Not as worse as it could have been, but still . . .

I didn't understand what had happened until I looked up. And then I still didn't, although there was a large, golden horn sticking through the purse's handles. We'd obviously gotten snagged on something when we fell, but what, I wasn't sure.

Then the bag shifted a little as we skidded around a corner, showing me a brief glimpse of a wall eye, a large rump and a sparkly mane. There were cartoon flowers in the mane, and also on the body that I saw when I turned around. It looked like Rambo's daughter had designed a unicorn: white body, pink flowers, golden hooves, and big, butch muscles.

For a long moment, neither of us said anything.

"Did you know this would happen?" Louis-Cesare asked.

"This exact scenario?"

He looked at me.

"The room isn't inside the purse," I reminded him, as the breeze blew what hair I had around. "In fact, nothing is inside the purse, as the purse isn't a purse, it's a portal entrance. So, as long as it maintains integrity—"

"We can still get in and out."

I nodded.

We went back inside.

The dark mage was kind of impressing me, as he was about two thirds of the way out of the war mage's cuffs already. That put him ahead of everybody else, including Tomas, who apparently wasn't as smart as he was pretty. Because he currently resembled a white tumbleweed.

A large one.

That was a problem since we had a limited amount of space in here. "Don't struggle!" I yelled, to get through all the layers of webbing. "They pull power from you; they only get stronger if you struggle!"

I couldn't tell if he heard me or not.

I sat back down.

The girl had found her voice, and she glared at me from her cuffs. "What the hell is this?"

"On the plus side," I told her. "We didn't all die from plummeting about sixty stories. I guess purses have decent wind resistance. On the negative . . ." I trailed off, looking at Louis-Cesare, who had started attacking the tumbleweed. "What are you doing?"

"Freeing Tomas!"

"Any particular reason why?"

"We'll need him."

"We'll need him if he's going to play nice," I pointed out. "Otherwise, we have enough problems."

Like the fact that the mage had just freed himself. But, surprisingly, he didn't attack. He just walked over and stuck his head out of the door, AKA the top of the purse. He was there for a while.

"What are you talking about?" the girl demanded. "What negative side? And what did you do to my brother?"

"Standard knock out potion. He's fine—"

Her face flushed angrily. "What gives you the right—"

"You did, when you decided to tear the city a new butthole. Seriously, what the hell?"

She looked as belligerent as someone in handcuffs can, which as it turned out, was pretty damned belligerent. Then she looked at the cuffs, and something about that gaze had all the hair standing up on the back of my neck. I remembered what Louis-Cesare had said about not letting her look at me.

Probably because of that, I thought, as my brand-new handcuffs fritzed out, despite the fact that they were guaranteed.

Against anything but a jinx, it seemed.

"If you don't want that to happen to you, I'd better get some damned answers," she said, getting in my face.

Or trying to. The mage was back, striding in between us, and heading for . . . the beer fridge. He grabbed a six pack and took it off to an empty piece of wall, where he squatted down and proceeded to chug like a freshman in a frat house.

"Hey!" I said.

"You have beer?" The bruiser asked, sounding hopeful.

I hadn't noticed him coming around, but he was watching the mage enviously while still hog-tied on the floor. His buddy hadn't bothered to free him, and he didn't offer any beer. I sighed and started sorting through the remains of my stash, calling out the names of various crap beers, because I am not picky.

"Anything," the bruiser rasped. "I'm parched."

"You want something?" I asked my hubby, who was currently shoulder deep in tumbleweed.

"No." Louis-Cesare's voice was muffled. It was also pissy. He was having a moment.

I left him to it.

"How about you?" I asked the girl.

"How about I get some answers?" she snapped, and then apparently decided the heck with it, walked over and threw open the door.

Unlike the mage, she was not out there for long.

"What the fuck?"

She came back in, slammed the door behind her, and plastered herself against it, her eyes huge.

"Okay, the short version," I told her. "This is my girl cave. I brought us in here because—well, in your case, I was rounding up my squad—"

"Your squad? What the—"

"Shut up?" I suggested.

And I guessed she really did want answers, because she shut up.

"I was rounding you guys up, got interrupted by the fight, and the squid kindly sent us flying over the city in a destroyed rickshaw that was about to plunge Louis-Cesare —this is Louis-Cesare, by the way," I added, introducing my husband's ass, because that was all that was sticking out of the tumbleweed at the moment.

"Hello," the bruiser told it.

I decided to let him loose so he could drink his beer, which he did very politely.

"Anyway," I continued, "we were about to plunge to our deaths, so I shoved us both in here, figuring that it gave us the best chance to survive—"

"And where's here?" the girl interrupted.

"A stationary portal in non-space, kind of like the phase that allows this city to exist, only much smaller. I had a mage put the doorway in my purse—"

"You carry a phased arsenal around in your *purse*?"

"You'd get answers faster if you didn't keep interrupting me," I pointed out.

"Then get on with it!"

"I'm trying." I was also trying to hold onto my temper, because we needed them. But she wasn't making it easy.

"Anyway, we survived the fall, obviously, so here's the deal. Louis-Cesare and I were at the fights hoping to meet you. Zheng-zi said you might be able to help us out—"

"When are you going to get to the point?" she practically shrieked.

I paused. "And which point would that be?"

"Why we're in what looks like the goddamned dead zones on the horn of some monster, that's what!"

I looked at her in confusion. "That's where the purse landed?"

"Auggghhhh!"

She actually said that. And then pulled at her hair with both fists in a way that had me wondering if she was deranged. Since her next move was to round on the dark mage, who had already downed three of the beers and was popping the top on number four, I was pretty sure the answer was yes.

"You said this wouldn't happen!"

He looked at her over the top of his beer can. "Sorry?" It was sarcastic as hell.

Despite myself, I was warming to the guy.

The girl, on the other hand, clearly was not.

"Auggghhhh!" she said again, and proceeded to do some more hair pulling.

I watched her enviously.

Must be nice.

"Is there a problem?" I asked, looking at the mage, who seemed the most clear-headed. "Because we were told that you guys are experts on—"

The girl laughed. It was not a nice sound. "We're all going to die," she announced. And then she, too, raided my fridge.

This is why I stock crap beer, I thought. People always drink it all anyway, so why keep the good stuff? She came out with a can, looked for a place to sit down, didn't find one and plopped back onto the floor where she'd been.

I eyed her warily.

"See," I began.

"We aren't experts in anything," the dark mage said, starting beer number five. "It's all bullshit."

"Excuse me?" I blinked at him politely.

"It's a living," the bruiser agreed.

"What . . . is a living?"

"He had this thing," the girl said, her voice tragic. She suddenly looked like she sounded, with her long, dark hair everywhere and her eyes huge and staring. She drank beer, and wiped the back of her hand over her mouth. "Zheng-zi, I mean. A tattoo, one of the magical kind, you know?"

I nodded.

"Well, Ranbir had seen one like it before—"

"Who's Ranbir?"

The dark mage lifted his beer can.

"That's him," the girl confirmed. "That's my brother Jason," she added, indicating the still unconscious dude on the floor. "I'm Sarah and that's Ev. I mean, Evelyn."

"Your name . . . is Evelyn?" I asked the bruiser, because I assumed that I'd misheard.

He sighed. "I get that a lot. It's British. My mum was British."

"Okay."

"It's usually pronounced Eev-lin," he added helpfully. "Sarah keeps forgetting, because she usually just calls me Ev."

"Uh huh."

"You know, it used to be given more to boys than girls. It's from the seventeenth century and means 'desirable one.' But I guess people thought that better fit a woman, and after a while—"

"I'll give you a beer if you stop talking," Ranbir offered.

Evelyn considered it.

He took the beer.

"Anyway," Sarah said, eyeing them. "Zheng didn't understand what he had. I was sort of surprised, as he's triad —or he was, I don't know about now—"

"He's still triad," Ranbir said. "It's a lifelong thing."

"Well, anyway, the triads all have tats, don't they?" she asked, pushing messy hair out of her face. "So, I thought he'd know, but it was obvious that he didn't."

"Know what?" I asked.

"How the tat worked. This Eternity thing—"

"What Eternity thing? You mean the symbol they all wear?"

She nodded and pulled a small, golden charm, just like the one I'd given Zheng, out of her shirt. It was on a necklace, but she took it off and handed it to me. "That's it. He found it on one of their boys, after a fight. He was going to interrogate him, but somebody activated another tat the guy was wearing, and blew him up. I suppose his group realized that he'd been taken, and didn't want him talking."

Sounded about right. The same might have happened to the guys at Hassani's, except that they'd all been killed, and that Jonathan had been able to use them as his little puppets. Only I still didn't understand what that had been about.

Jonathan was obsessed with Louis-Cesare. He wanted

him back under his control; he didn't want to kill him. And even assuming that he'd turned into one of those "if I can't have you, nobody can" types, that whole attack seemed a bit . . . excessive. As for me, I couldn't imagine why he would care about me at all, since they already had Dorina.

Unless he was afraid that I'd come after him, which, yeah.

Should have gotten me the first time, I thought.

"Anyway, Zheng still wanted to find out more about them," Sarah said. "But nobody knew anything, and nobody would go inside the dead zones. He kept offering more and more money, and . . . well . . ."

"And well *what?*"

She took the tat back and pressed it, not to her skin as I'd expected, but like a fob for a car. A grid popped out into the air, in bright red lines like a hologram. It looked like a map of some kind, although I found it hard to read as it kept moving and changing.

"Why is it doing that?" I asked.

"Doing what?"

"Moving around?"

"Because we are," Ranbir said.

Sarah nodded. "It'll stabilize if we ever do. It needs a fixed point—"

"For what?"

She looked at me like I might be slow, for not having already figured this out. "It's a homing beacon. We think that, because of how unstable the zones can be, Eternity has to move around a lot. So, they equipped each of their members with one of these, so they can always find their way back to base."

I frowned at it. "But you found the base already, or narrowed it down. Zheng said—"

I stopped, finally getting a clue. As well as a sinking feeling in my stomach—a bad one. It felt like falling from a height, all over again.

"You didn't find it," I said.

"It was a lot of money," Sarah told me, suddenly earnest. "The kind that could be life changing. And get us permanently out of those penny ante gigs we used to—"

"You're telling me that you didn't go into the zones?" I interrupted. "That you just sold Zheng a load of crap?"

"It wasn't crap!" She had the gall to look indignant. "He got what he paid for. The homing beacon did give the location of their base. We just stretched things out, feeding him a little more info each week, so it would be believable—"

"But you fought in the ring! You were going to fight tonight!"

She nodded. "We acquired a reputation, after a while. There were only three groups in the whole city that would go into the dead zones, and we were the best known, because we never got hurt—"

"I gave myself a black eye once," Ev said. "To be more, uh, authentic . . ." he saw my expression, and went back to drinking beer.

"—never got hurt bad," Sarah corrected. "And people started to ask us about the fights. We couldn't keep saying no, or it might have looked suspicious."

"Then you *do* know how to kill the monsters."

She shook her head. "We went out there to put on a show, but it was mostly theater. Tomas is a first level master vamp, and he protected us. We made it look good for a while, then the mages took over. We gave them a kickback from the purses, a decent percentage. They weren't allowed in the ring, you see, and this way . . . everybody was . . . happy . . ."

I looked at her. She gazed back miserably. "You're telling me—" I stopped, needing a moment. "How many times have you guys actually been in the dead zones?"

"We . . . haven't ever . . . actually . . ." she trailed off.

I stared at her.

"One," Ranbir said, tossing his last empty onto the little pile he'd made. "The number you're looking for is one. *This* one."

CHAPTER FORTY

Dory, Hong Kong

Half an hour later, things had not improved.

Well, that wasn't entirely true. Jason, the girl's brother, had woken up with a typical potion's headache, and was nursing it with the last of my beer. Louis-Cesare had finally managed to free Tomas, and taken a right hook for his trouble. They were currently glaring at each other, or at least, I assumed so. That's how they'd been when I left, as persuading Tomas to help out wasn't going well.

Of course, neither was this.

"You're going to spook him," Ranbir said. "You need to get the blindfold on him first."

I paused, partway out of the purse, to glare down at him.

"He'll see me and bolt."

"If you do it fast enough, he won't see anything. That's rather the point."

"You want to come do this?" I whispered.

"No."

"Then shut up."

He shut up, but his expression was eloquent.

I ignored him and concentrated on the task at hand. Problem number one was that the horn was really long, and right between the beast's eyes. The purse had therefore been messing with its vision and bopping its muzzle whenever it moved, much less galloped. That had panicked it, because horses were not the brightest of animals, and the sparkly unicorn version was no better.

Problem number two was that, if I emerged too far from the purse, I'd get caught by the portal. That was how portals worked; you were either in or you were out, and if I fell out, this thing was going to go ballistic. But right now, I was no heavier than the purse itself, still technically being in non-space, and the unicorn was ignoring me. Even better, it had stopped to explore something on the side of the road, meaning that the horn was almost horizontal.

The idea was for me to jump, jump, jump in little motions, until the straps hopped off the end of the horn . . .

Without doing that, I thought, as one strap broke free while the other stayed put, tipping me too far out, and causing the portal to grab me—

And dump me right in front of a pissed off unicorn.

Shit, I thought, as it reared up on two legs, bright gold hooves waving.

I rolled out of the way—fast—but this unicorn had a 'tude and followed. I dodged behind an abandoned minibus, which was promptly a very holey minibus, as the horn went to work trying to skewer me. It appeared to be made of some diamond-hard substance that treated the minivan's metal sides like they were made out of aluminum . . . foil.

Shit, I thought, as glass shattered, seats were slashed, and metal separations were ripped through as if they were nothing. I need a sword made out of that stuff, I thought, as three heads popped out of the purse. And were slammed into the bus's remaining windows, more than once.

Ranbir, Louis-Cesare, and Tomas glared at me.

"Do you want that blindfold now?" Ranbir asked.

"Just snap the straps," Tomas said, and reached for them.

"No!" Three of us said, simultaneously.

"Why the hell not?"

"This isn't a purse; it's a portal," the mage said, more patiently than I would have. "Interfering with its integrity could collapse the whole—"

Tomas wasn't listening. He was reaching out again, before Louis-Cesare knocked his hand away. So, Tomas punched him, and the two disappeared, probably wrecking more of my girl cave in the process.

I sighed.

Ranbir was then joined by Ev—I couldn't bring myself to call him Evelyn—who appeared to be trying to get out.

"Let her handle this," Ranbir said.

"She is so small," Ev protested, eyeing me.

"She'll be fine."

"How do you know?"

Ranbir cocked an eyebrow. "I've seen her fight."

Well, great. Now I had something to live up to. But there were no convenient flying rickshaws at the moment, because sensible people stayed the hell out of here.

Of course, there was another option.

"Give me the blindfold," I said and Ranbir passed it over.

I ripped off one of the bus's windshield wipers and tucked it through my belt. I backed up, giving myself a little room and a few seconds for a pep talk. Then I took a running leap, got a foot on the bus's fender, catapulted up to the indentation for the wipers, and finally hit the roof. Before throwing myself off—

Onto the unicorn's broad back.

It.

Was.

Pissed.

Fortunately, I'd expected that, and held on like a limpet, burying my arms up to the shoulders in the huge, sparkly white mane.

I stared at the pink, cartoon flowers while the beast bucked like a bronco on steroids. And then took off down the street, slamming itself into parked cars and, when that didn't work, running onto sidewalks, trying to scrape me off on the sides of buildings. That was fun.

But it didn't work, although less because of any great

ability on my part and more because sheer terror had locked my hands in that mane. I didn't think I could have let go if I'd wanted to, and I didn't want to. Did I mention that it was a very large unicorn? It stood the height of a Clydesdale if not taller, and was built like a brick shit-house.

I was not going to tire this thing out, I realized. I was going to have to put the damned blindfold on. Of course, that would be easier without the kibitzing.

"I'm coming out." That was Louis-Cesare, in his stubborn voice.

"Do not come out."

"We talked about this!"

"Yes, we did. We agreed that I was smaller and less likely to be noticed—"

"I think it has noticed!"

"Do not come out," I said, through gritted teeth. "I've got this."

"I'm coming out!"

Shit.

But the conversation did give me the impetus to finish the job, edging up and throwing the blindfold in the form of Jason's hoodie over the beast's face.

For a moment, nothing happened, unless you counted a wildly whipping head as the creature tried to sling off what I was determinedly holding in place. But when that didn't work, it started to slow down, not liking the idea of pelting forward without being able to see. Finally, it stopped altogether.

For a moment, both of us just stayed there, breathing hard. Or, at least, I was. Slowly, slowly, slowly, I crawled forward, stretched out an arm with the windshield wiper clutched in it, and snared the final purse handle—

And pushed it off the horn.

It landed in a gutter, splashing Louis-Cesare's jeans when he suddenly appeared beside it. I hopped off the unicorn's back, dragging the hoodie along with me, and preparing for a fight. But it bolted instead, glittering off into the night, the gilded hooves galloping down the road in what sounded like relief.

Or maybe that was me. I sagged back against my hubby, whose arms went around me. "You make me crazy," he whispered, and kissed the top of my head.

"Next one's on you," I promised, shakily.

"Yes, it is." It was grim.

And then our brief moment of privacy was over, and we were standing in a crowd. One by one, the other members of our team appeared, scattered around the street and sidewalk. Only, they weren't our team.

Not even close.

I guessed that was what everyone had been discussing while I was busy.

"Well, I'm staying with them." That, surprisingly, came from Ranbir.

"What the hell?" Sarah demanded.

He took the charm from her and activated it again. He had been right: now that we were stationary, the map was a lot easier to read. There was also a new feature, or one I hadn't noticed before.

The streets were demarcated with a 3-D outline, but also featured dots—some large, some small, some huge—moving along them. I was pretty sure that I knew what the dots were, which was not good news. There were a crap ton of them.

"This is us," Ranbir confirmed, pointing at a small group of dots. "This," he pointed at an area way the hell off to the side, "is the closest point outside the fog. In between, you'll notice that there are fifteen streets?"

"Streets filled with monsters," Ev added helpfully.

"We'll take a rickshaw," Sarah said stubbornly. "There has to be one around here somewhere."

"Yes, I'm sure there is," Ranbir agreed. "I am also certain that it will eat your face."

"Why . . . why eat?" I asked.

He shrugged. "For the same reason that the monster in the ring went after Tomas. These creatures need magic the way we need food. Any magic they come across, they will try to absorb—including us. And the stronger you are, the tastier."

He looked pointedly at the two vampires.

"I'll take my chances," Tomas snarled, and started off.

Ranbir shrugged, and went back to scrutinizing the map.

"Wait," the girl said. And ran after Tomas.

"You can't tell me that every magical device in this area has been . . . affected," Louis-Cesare said, his brow knitting, probably because he couldn't find the right word.

"Monsterfied," I offered, and the mage suddenly laughed.

"Monsterfied; I like that," he said, rolling it around on his tongue. "And, yes, you're absolutely right. Many of them aren't a problem anymore. They've already been cannibalized."

"How do you know that?" I challenged. "You just said, you've never been in here."

"I haven't. But I've talked to those who have, to get details to make our story believable. What they told me convinced me that I never wanted to find out for myself."

"Yet you seem in an awfully good mood."

"I'm just thinking about the reward Zheng is going to cough up, once we hand him Eternity's ass. That is the plan, yes?" he tilted his head.

"That's the plan," I agreed.

"And if you two are who I think you are, you have no need for money, yes?"

"You can keep the reward, if there is one," I said. "But there's reason to think that my sister may be in there. We get her out alive. That's job one."

"And what does she look like?"

"Me. We're twins."

He nodded, as if making a mental note. He didn't have any hair on his face, even eyebrows, but a patch of skin in the appropriate spot went up. "And since we're helping you, I assume there's no question of mentioning our little ruse to the senator?"

"As long as you *do* help."

He smiled broadly, showing a lot of misshapen and yellowed teeth. "I believe you have a team, Miss—"

"Dory. Just Dory."

"She does not have a team!" That, of course, was Tomas, striding back over from where he and Sarah had been talking. I was starting to find him less pretty.

Ranbir turned to look at him. "I thought you'd left."

"You aren't coming?" Tomas demanded.

"No, I believe I mentioned that."

"I, too, am staying," Ev said staunchly.

Tomas looked at him like he was crazy. "She kidnapped you, put you in chains, and dragged you into the dead zones! Why on earth would you help her?"

Ev looked at him placidly. "She gave me beer."

Tomas threw up his hands.

"And Ranbir is right. This will make us lots of money."

"If you survive!"

"I will survive. And I like money."

"It's closer than the way out," Sarah said, biting her lip. "And we have better odds with a group—"

"Until you arrive at your destination," Tomas snapped. "And the unknown number of triad members who await you! Has everyone suddenly gone mad?"

"Perhaps they are simply not cowards," Louis-Cesare commented.

"Are they always like this?" Sarah asked, as Tomas launched himself at my husband, and the two rolled into the street, kicking and fighting.

I sighed.

It was starting to look like it.

"You've got a hell of a storehouse down there," Jason said, emerging from the portal.

I hadn't seen him go back inside, but he must have, and not just to look. The kid believed in being loaded for bear, and was practically bristling with weapons, most of them mine. If we had to haul ass, he was going to have a problem in all of that hardware.

"I hope this was okay," he added, noticing my expression. "But we don't know what we'll find here, and I like to be prepared."

"Doesn't hurt," I agreed, as a screech echoed through the air.

We looked up to see a flock of birds overhead, which I couldn't see too well because of the fog. But their shadows rippled over the street, human-sized and oddly pointy, with strange angles. I looked for a parting of the clouds, to get a better view.

Only it seemed that something wanted a better view of me, too.

I had a split-second impression of something mottled yellow with a triangular head, appearing out of the fog, and then I was hitting the dirt. And so was everyone else—with one exception. Jason opened up with a brief explosion of machine gun fire, whether intentional or as a reflex, I didn't know. But it was enough.

The creature cried out, a haunting, almost human sound, and the next moment, the entire flock was diving.

"Get under cover!" That was Louis-Cesare.

"No magic!" Ranbir yelled. "No magic!"

I dove behind what was left of the minibus, not understanding what he meant. But I pulled a .44 instead of anything magical, because he was a mage. He was supposed to know this kind of stuff.

But bullets simply bounced off these things, whatever they were, and that's when you could hit one at all. I could barely track them, and my eyesight is considerably better than human average. To Jason and his sister, they must have been just orange streaks in the night, which was probably why they panicked.

It all happened in a second: one of the things dove at Louis-Cesare, who dodged with liquid speed, so the creature grabbed Jason instead. It sank talons deep into his shoulders and back, causing Sarah to scream and throw something. I didn't see what it was, but Ranbir obviously did.

"No! Get away! Get away now!"

But Jason couldn't get away, and then I understood everything the mage had been saying, all at once. Because the creature was suddenly enveloped in a mass of blue smoke: a standard knock-out potion, very similar to what I'd hit Jason with. It should have been safe, and it should have dropped both man and beast.

But this was the magical Twilight Zone, and nothing was safe here.

Instead of dropping the creature, it fed it, and when these things were fed, they got bigger. Ranbir yelled something I didn't hear, because I didn't need to. The creature that had started life as some kind of origami crane and been maybe six feet long from tip to tail, was now double that and growing.

And while it had been able to hurt its prey before, now it could do worse.

Sarah screamed as the massive bird flapped its greatly expanded wings, sending trash spiraling and my remaining hair whipping, as it prepared to escape—and take Jason along with it.

There was a burst of gunfire, but as I'd already discovered, that didn't work on these things. Tomas leapt for it, but three more of the flock targeted him, and the remainder were dive bombing the rest of us. One slammed into the already weakened top of the minivan and burst through to the inside, which trapped and also pissed it off. It started thrashing, the minivan started rocking, throwing out broken glass and metal all over the street.

I retreated under an awning, while Louis-Cesare grabbed two of the creatures, one under each arm. He broke their necks, only to have five more jump him in what looked like a feeding frenzy. He roared in outrage, but I knew him; he'd be all right.

Jason was another story.

I saw Ranbir grab Sarah and jerk her physically off the road, and into a shop. I saw Ev open up with a machine gun in each hand and rattle enough sheer brute force off of one creature's hide to send it screeching away. I saw Tomas get up from savaging his three, bloody and furious, and promptly get piled on by four more. Ranbir had been right: they were targeting the vamps, as they were the strongest magically among us.

And for that same reason, nobody was targeting me.

I ran through the hail of glass by the minibus and back into my arsenal, grabbing the only thing I could think of that might work. When I emerged, it was almost too late, as the now giant bird was taking off, headed this way and dragging Jason kicking and screaming into the air along with it. Ev caught hold of the boy, but all that resulted in was him getting dragged down the road, while Jason screamed at the added weight.

I put on a burst of speed, jumped out in front of them and lit a flare.

It wasn't magical and it wasn't a weapon. But it glowed a bright crimson in the murky air, shedding a red and orange banner of sparks behind me. And that was enough.

All along the street, the birds looked up, the light glinting redly in their eyes. And then they took off after me. Not one of them; *all* of them, because magic in Hong Kong was bright and colorful and moved a lot.

And I was suddenly the tastiest looking thing in sight.

"What the hell are you *doing*?" Louis-Cesare demanded, running up beside me.

"I saw this in *Jurassic Park*."

"Your strategy is based on a *movie*?"

"You have a better idea?"

He picked up a concrete shard left over from the battle and lobbed it at one of the birds— which caught it in a foot-long beak and bit it in two.

"No. But what happens now?"

"This," I said, and threw the flare down an alley. The flock, which had almost caught up with us, followed it, all except for the huge one. It tried, not seeming to realize that it was bigger now, and slammed into the bricks on both sides. Which was when the shit hit the fan.

Louis-Cesare and Tomas jumped it, ripping off the great wings in a sound like tearing metal. Ev opened up on the ones at the end of the alley, giving them both barrels past the thrashing body of the big bird, and then pulling out the rocket launcher. That didn't help much except to blow up the building at the end of the street, raining bricks and smoke everywhere and confusing the issue, but I didn't have time to complain.

Because they were on us.

There had to be ten or twelve of them left, maybe more. It was hard to tell as they were all about six feet tall and moving like lightning. All I saw was flapping, geometric shapes and stabbing, pointed beaks, and five-inch claws trying to shred.

They were doing a pretty good job of it.

They looked like paper, but felt more like steel, and when I reached for my purse and the lethal devices it contained, a long, savage beak plucked it away and flung it into the night, leaving me almost defenseless. So, the next bird head that slashed down at me got grabbed, twisted around, and its beak used like a dagger to stab at its fellows.

It didn't like that. *I* didn't like that I was already bleeding in half a dozen places and that my brand-new leather jacket was a couture rag. Louis-Cesare apparently felt the same way, judging by the amount of cursing and flailing and various bird parts that were flying from his direction.

In a minute or so, it was all over, leaving me panting and bleeding and plastered with fake feathers, but still on my feet. Louis-Cesare cracked the last long neck, then did one better and ripped the head clean off. At least they didn't bleed, I thought, as nothing spirted from the hole besides a little paper confetti.

Ranbir was back, along with Sarah, who ran past me to where her brother was lying on the sidewalk. He was bleeding profusely, but judging by the amount of swearing he was doing, he was going to be all right. Sarah seemed to realize this as well, and looked up at me, her face tear streaked and her hair everywhere, but her eyes shining.

"Whoever you are; whatever you're doing," she said shakily. "You've got yourself a team."

CHAPTER FORTY-ONE

Dorina, Faerie

*C*lump, drag, clump, drag, clump, drag.

    I awoke to the feeling of being pulled over wet stone, but I could not seem to gather the strength to open my eyes and see for myself. A cave, I thought, but it was a vague notion. I was aware of where I was only by the echoes that sounded back from far away, and the smells. The familiar scents of mineralized water, ammonia, and guano reached my nose, but the last two were distant, almost undetectable.

This cave was all about water.

Clump, drag, clump, drag, clump, drag.

We finally stopped, and I was left alone for a while. The strange sounds departed and faded away, and for a time there was only the faint drip, drip, drip of water over limestone. I drifted in and out of consciousness, but made no attempts to call anyone or anything to my aid. I did not have the strength, and, strangely, I did not feel the need.

This place was strangely peaceful.

Clump, drag, clump, drag, clump, drag.

Someone was coming back. I tried to raise my head, but did not succeed. I did manage to flutter my eyelashes, however, and found that there was not much difference to be had. The light was merely a few, watery reflections on cave walls, a dim, bluish gray against the darker eigengrau of the stone.

It almost felt like I hadn't opened my eyes at all.

Until I saw the creature that limped this way.

She was carrying a lantern, with a single candle dancing inside polished horn sides. But after the almost complete absence of other light, it was blinding. I didn't realize that I had raised a hand to shield my eyes, until I heard a cackle.

"Not dead, then. No, no. Not yet."

My eyes adjusted, and the creature became more visible. She was coming closer, and dragging something. I couldn't see what it was, but I started to be able to see her, little by little: a wild tangle of hair, half dark, half gray; a bent body, although that might have been from pulling a weight; a leg that dragged almost uselessly behind her, and was responsible for her shambling gait; a walking stick, which also supported the lantern in its wavy crook, and explained the clumping sound. She looked very old, and very witchy.

She also looked familiar.

I must have lost too much blood, I thought, as she bent over me.

And then I saw her blue-gray eyes, almost lost in folds of wrinkles. The eyes were the same, I thought, staring upwards. Nothing else was, but the eyes . . .

"Yes, it's me," Nimue said testily. "I know. I know. Not what you expected, hm?"

She dropped her burden, which turned out to be Ray. The many arrows were gone, but, alarmingly, the wounds were still open, splitting his flesh in terrible ways. He wasn't dead; he hadn't dusted away. But he was close.

"Removed the arrows," Nimue panted, squatting down beside him. "Didn't know what else to do. Don't have experience with these things."

She poked him.

"He needs blood," I croaked, wondering how much I had left.

Not enough.

But then a miracle happened, something that had me gasping in surprise and gratitude: she threw our three blood bags onto the stone. I managed to get a hand underneath me and reached for one. I tore it open with my teeth, and yes! It remained fresh.

"The waters still bring me things," she said, by way of explanation.

I did not know what she meant by that, nor did I question it. I focused on crawling over to Ray, before Nimue made a disgusted sound. "Some god-killer you are," she said nonsensically, and took the bag away.

She was no longer wearing seafoam, I noticed, but dirty, tattered robes of what might once have been silk. It was no longer possible to tell, as it looked like she had been wearing them for a while. But I doubted that Ray cared right now.

She dragged his head into her lap and looked at me expectantly.

"He needs—you just have to feed it to him," I panted.

She made a disgusted face, but did the job matter-of-factly enough, pulling his mouth open and drizzling a little of the blood inside.

"You must make him swallow it," I added, as most of it dribbled back out again.

"Oh, must I?" she replied testily.

"I'm sorry. I just . . . I meant—"

"Stop tearing up, girl. I'll make the creature drink. Here, take this."

She shoved a dirty vial into my hand, which I ignored. I needed to make sure that she did this properly. We had no blood to waste. She had to—

"Drink it, or he gets nothing," she told me flatly.

I drank.

It tasted vile, as most potions do, but I barely noticed. She made me upend the container to show that I'd finished it, then she started feeding Ray again, massaging his throat as I had once done to make sure that he ingested it all. Three bags later, his body had started to close some of the wounds, but he was still deathly pale and out cold, likely in a healing trance.

I relaxed back against the stone, feeling dizzy. I did not understand why, unless it was because of the potion Nimue had given me. I watched her through bleary eyes, as she less-than-gently pushed Ray back onto the floor.

Then, to my surprise, she lay back, too, obviously exhausted.

For a while, there was silence.

I was not sleepy, but I was so tired that the ceiling of the cave seemed to spin above me. I wondered if it would be the last thing I ever saw. Strangely, that thought did not fill me with the alarm I would have expected, but with a sense of wonder. I had seen so much, experienced so much, and in such a short time. I was greedy for more, and yet, it was enough. I was content.

Except for one thing.

"Please," I finally said. "If I die here, can you get my companion to a portal? He has family on Earth; they will find him—"

"You're not going to die," Nimue said, sounding annoyed. "Or else, what has this all been about? No, no. You don't get to die."

"I don't think . . . we have much choice there. I do not know what is wrong with me—"

She laughed, and it sounded genuine. It also went on for a very long time. It went on, in fact, until I began to worry for her. She had sat up slightly as we spoke, but now she lay back down and cackled at the ceiling.

"Do not know what is wrong," she finally gasped.

"I do not, unless the potion you gave me . . ."

"That was a healing potion, girl, and I went to a lot of trouble to get it. Hope it works, but with your strange composition, who knows? At the very least, it isn't hurting you."

"And yet, I feel like I might die," I said truthfully. "Hollowed out and . . . strange. Weak—"

"Of course, you're weak! You just summoned half the fauna in this part of Faerie to your aid! You're lucky it didn't kill you. But it didn't. You should be fine with some rest."

"Then . . .why did you bring me here?" I asked, but didn't get an answer to that.

Because someone else was coming, a lilting voice that echoed through the caves, as if singing. It was a woman's voice, and hauntingly beautiful, but Nimue did not seem to find it so. She jerked upright, into a full sitting position, then used her walking stick to help her back to her feet.

"What is it?" I asked, only to have her round on me.

"Be silent, girl!"

"Oh, let her speak," the lilting voice said. "It's not as if I don't know where you are. Nimue, daughter of the oceans, queen of the tides, leader of a people now scattered and broken . . . like herself."

The voice grew louder, which was a concern, as it was definitely getting closer. But Nimue's actions were more of one. She looked around frantically, stared at me for a moment, shook her head and raised her staff, lantern and all, sending flashes of light jumping about the cave.

I did not know what she was doing, but a moment later, a familiar sight came speeding this way—for an instant. Until it was stopped by a too-narrow gap in the walls, where it hung up. I stared at it, and at the little rocks tumbling around the edges of it, as it tried to push its way through. For a moment, I once again thought I was seeing things.

But no.

It was the little capsule.

I knew it was the same one, because I could see dark impact marks on it from the Svarestri weapons. The blue lights were also flooding the cave, spilling brilliant color onto the uneven floor and craggy walls. And onto Nimue's face as she uttered something that sounded like a curse.

"Should have left them outside, but you were afraid I'd find you, weren't you?" the lilting voice asked. It laughed. "How ironic."

Nimue cursed again, and the little capsule increased its efforts, judging by the amount of rocks suddenly hitting and then scattering over the floor. I couldn't hear anything that sounded like an engine, but if I could, it would have been racing. I could hear the walls begin to crack—

And then the capsule suddenly went dark.

"You forget, cousin," the woman's voice said. "I, too, can use our discarded toys. And, at present, I believe I am a little stronger than you."

I reached out, trying to add whatever strength I had to Nimue's, but she shot me a look over her shoulder and shook her head. "Save your strength, girl. You'll need it."

"Yes, do save it," the other voice said. "I don't want you any more beaten up than you already are."

"And whose fault was that?" Nimue demanded.

The voice laughed. "Yes, I admit it. Although, those were not my orders. The idiots were instructed merely to find her and alert me to her location. I was meant to do the retrieval."

"But you trusted them to do it, and now, what are you left with?"

"Enough."

There was an entrance at the opposite end of the cave that I hadn't seen, because it was hidden in shadow. But a pale, white light began to flicker against the walls of it as I watched. It was merely a dim haze at the moment, but getting brighter.

"Come, cousin," the woman's voice came again. "Let us not quarrel. I know what he did to you, how you've suffered. I will avenge you; this much I swear. After all, we both want the same thing."

The doorway suddenly flashed with silver fire, so brightly that I had to shield my eyes once more.

And when I looked again, a woman stood there.

A woman I knew.

She looked little different than the last time I had seen her. Long, golden blonde hair rippled almost down to her feet, unbound and beautiful. Her face was sweet, charming and as pale as the moon. Her dress was ludicrously fine for such a venue, with a pure white under gown in gossamer silk, and a silver overtunic of the same length, round necked and loose fitting, and made entirely of embroidery in a loose weave that showed the silk through the gaps.

Efridis. I felt my lips form the word, the name of Aeslinn's dead queen, but no sound came out. She was haloed by a wash of silvery light so bright that, for a moment, I thought that perhaps I was looking at a ghost. But then she stepped forward, dragging the trailing hem of her gown through a muddy puddle of water, and I frowned.

Ghosts did not get dirty. But if she was not a ghost, what was she? I had seen her die.

She came another few steps closer, but then stopped. "We both want Aeslinn dead," she said simply.

Nimue, who had been so agitated a moment ago, was suddenly calm. And more regal than I had seen her since that moment on the river. Filthy rags, lined face, frazzled hair and all, yet she was every inch a queen.

"Yes, we both want that," she said, her lips quirking slightly. "But tell me, *cousin*," and in her mouth, that simple word was obscene. "Will you give me back my ravaged soul, once you kill him? Will you return my power to me?"

Efridis laughed. "I am afraid it does not work that way."

"No, I don't suppose so. You'd put yourself in his place, wouldn't you? That's what you've always wanted—"

"What I deserve!" Efridis' eyes flashed silver fire. "My brother now rules two kingdoms; I have yet to hold one. Yet my abilities are as great as his."

"Not quite as great," Nimue said, "or you'd have defeated your husband ere this."

"You know why I did not—why I could not!"

"Yes, and now you would emulate him. Do you think it will not change you? Do you think you will not end up just like him?"

"I am *nothing* like him!"

"Not yet." And once again, Nimue changed. From imperious queen to something kinder, gentler, almost motherly. "You can still choose. He is too far gone in his delusion, but you . . . there is hope for you."

"What hope do you think there is?" Efridis strode back and forth, until the trailing hem of her lovely gown was almost black. "For me to slink home to my brother, beg his forgiveness, end my days in seclusion at court, shunned by all, paying for my sins? All hope of power—gone, glory—gone, renown—"

"Hope that you won't end up like me!" Nimue cut in, spreading her arms. "Look at me! See what I have become. You think it is because of what was stolen from me, what your husband did?" She shook her head. "No. I would like to think so, but years alone have forced me to face the truth, a truth I would not have you bear."

"And what truth is that?" Efridis asked, impatiently.

"That something ate my soul long before your husband came to take it. I was like you once; I wanted all the things you mention, not just for me, but for my people as well. I told myself that every compromise I made, every little cut I took to my honor, would all be worth it, someday . . .

"But instead, one compromise became a hundred, one cut a thousand. Until I knew nothing but compromise and my honor was in tatters. I hurt so many, telling myself that it was needful, asking myself what would happen otherwise to all those who depended on me, all those eyes constantly looking to me?"

"They would have died," Efridis said bluntly. "Some of them, possibly all of them—"

"And perhaps that would have been better. Look at them

now. Enslaving thousands, butchering millions—"

Efridis rolled her eyes. "Of dark fey. Those abominations —"

"And we're so much better? What Aeslinn did, in order to beat me; what you'll do, in order to beat him." Nimue suddenly looked at me, and her eyes were sorrowful. "What you'll do to her."

Efridis suddenly laughed, a startled, genuinely amused sound. "Look at this," she said, her voice marveling. "Look at this. I wish someone were here with me to see it, truly I do. The great Nimue, feared guardian of her people, the ruthless one, the vindictive one, the strong—"

"Those things didn't make me strong, any more than they will you," Nimue said, sitting on a rock.

"Oh, but you're wrong. There was a time I couldn't have touched you, a time when even Aeslinn feared you. And look at you now. Old, broken, weak, mewling over some abomination—"

"An abomination you would absorb into yourself." I made a small sound, and Nimue looked at me again. "Yes, child. That is what she plans for you."

"Enough of thissssssssssssss—" Efridis' voice began normally, then trailed off, yet it didn't stop. The last syllable was stretched into seeming infinity, something that . . . was a great deal more disturbing than I would have expected.

"I cannot hold her for long," Nimue said. "But you must know what she has planned for you—"

"I don't understand," I whispered, frightened and confused.

"I know that you don't! Something that will not change if you do not listen!"

I nodded, and bit my lip to stay silent.

"That device that broke you apart from your more human half?" Nimue said. "That is what she'll use to weld your soul to what remains of her own."

"What . . . remains?"

"She has already split her soul, with the same device that she used on you, shaving off a small piece of it to take solid form—"

"How?"

"Our souls are not like human's. They cannot exist separately from a body, to which they are fundamentally joined. Humans leave ghosts; we do not, as soul and body are one. Shaving off a piece of our soul, therefore, regenerates a body. Thus allowing Efridis to die ostentatiously on your world, yet still live here."

"But . . . why?"

"She wanted everyone to believe that she was dead, so that her brother, Caedmon, would not search for her. She had kidnapped and tried to kill him, hoping that her son could take his throne and that she could use her brother's armies against Aeslinn. She hates and fears her husband—she told you that true enough—and with Caedmon's forces at her back, she would have a chance to destroy him.

"But her attempt to take his throne failed, and she knew he would be hunting her. She therefore staged her death, gambling that, as distracted by the current war as he was, he might accept that story for the moment, leaving her time to do this."

"And what is this?" I asked, my head spinning. I did not know if Nimue was telling this badly, or if I was simply too tired to take it in. But I did not understand anything! Something she seemed to realize.

"Calm down, girl, and I'll explain. I forget: things that are common knowledge to us are unknown on your world. I—" She cut off abruptly, and her hand clutched her abdomen for a moment.

"Is something wrong?" I asked, putting a hand on her arm.

"Of course, something's wrong!" The blue-gray eyes glared up at me. "I'm dying."

CHAPTER FORTY-TWO

Dorina, Faerie

"Dying?" That did not make sense to me. How could such a being die? But then, how could such a being age, and in such ways?

I remembered the amazing creature I had seen on the river, and for some reason, I felt like weeping.

"Save your tears; you'll need them for yourself," Nimue said. "What Aeslinn did to me, his bitch of a wife wants to do to you."

"What did he do?"

She thought about it for a moment, as if trying to come up with words that I would understand. "The gods were energy beings," she finally said. "They battled other species and absorbed their energy into their own. What the old legends often forget to mention is that they didn't merely do it to outsiders, demon lords and such. But that they cannibalized each other, as well."

"They...cannibalized..."

"In war, when a god was overcome, he could expect to have his essence torn apart and absorbed by the victor. Energy was too precious to waste, it was thought, and they could often absorb another's abilities along with their essence, thereby making themselves stronger.

"But when they came here, to Faerie, and began to experiment with our people, they discovered that we did not work the same way. We were restricted by our bodies, whereas they could take any form they wished—"

"Zeus and the shower of gold," I said, remembering a strange story I had heard once.

"Yes. It didn't matter to them what form they took; it was all energy. But for us, it did matter. They could not bend us so easily into what they chose, and thus they came up with a device—"

"The one that was used on me."

She nodded. "It was employed in their experiments, to slice up souls and recombine them in new ways, and with new powers. For our people, a soul regenerates a body, so recombining souls changed the body that was produced as well. It allowed them to create amazing creatures, hybrids of many different species. As long as the root soul was fey, whatever they grafted onto it would manifest in the new body that the soul would form. You understand?"

I nodded; I thought so.

"Well, the god's device was left behind when they were banished by Artemis. It remained at Aeslinn's court, along with other godly instruments, until rediscovered by a human mage some years ago. He had been working to help bring back the gods, who Aeslinn assumed would fight on his side—their faithful worshipper—against all apostates, and hand him the whole of Faerie as a kingdom. The mage was in it more for power, but he found the godly instruments fascinating.

He began experimenting with them, grafting bits of soul onto himself, absorbing the new powers this gave him. And he began showing them off to his master, who started coveting the same for himself, but not for the same reason. Aeslinn went from worshipping the gods to wanting to be one, but the only godly energy left to absorb—"

"Was in you," I said, a hand to my mouth.

"And the other children they'd left behind," she agreed. "He began to follow their pattern of cannibalism, trying to drown out the fey in him with godly energy. Ten years ago, he took the device the gods once used in their experiments and turned it on me. And not just me. He has stripped any being he could find with godly blood of their power, ripping out the parts of us that we inherited from our divine parents and welding them onto his soul instead. He is a patchwork now, a corrupt, despicable creature who believes he is a god reborn.

"And while it has corrupted his own soul, and whatever goodness may once have lain within him, it has made him powerful. So much so that his own wife barely escaped with their child. He would have ripped the two of them apart, too, but she eluded him. I give her respect for that, but she was with him . . . too long . . ."

Nimue gasped, and her voice trailed off. She was fading. It did not take an expert on fey anatomy to see that. Her hands were shaking, her eyes were becoming dim, and her skin was sallow.

She would not last much longer.

But she was determined to have her say before she did, and I was grateful for it. I had so many questions, but chief among them was the obvious. "What does Efridis want with me?"

That won me what I was coming to know as her annoyed look. "What did I just say? She wants your power, girl, the same thing Aeslinn wanted from me."

"Yes, but why? And why did you call me god-killer? I have killed no gods."

She cackled at that, although it obviously hurt her. "Have killed . . . no gods . . . yet."

She slid down to the floor, where she could lean back against the rock instead of sitting on it. It seemed to buy her some respite, although for how long, I didn't know. She looked up at me and smiled slightly.

"Made a mistake with you, yes, I did. Should have taken

you on the river. Knew it then, but I've become cautious. Not so powerful anymore. Wanted to see . . ."

"See what?"

"What you could do. If it was really you." She shifted position slightly. "I received my answer, didn't I?"

Perhaps, but I was not receiving mine.

"Nimue—"

"Yes, yes, I know. Time is short. So many years, so many centuries, and it comes down to this." She looked about. "Fitting. I was born in a cave like this. And loved exploring them when I was a girl."

"You found the capsule in the cave," I said, leading her gently, because her mind had started to wander.

"Find it? I put it there. One of my old toys. Used it in my explorations. They call them *vimāna* where you come from. The gods made them for us, their children. We had bodies, you see, and could not travel as they did . . ."

"And you've been using this one again recently?"

She had been staring off into the distance, but the question focused her. "After Aeslinn's attack, I remembered it. It was made for me. Has my name on it, you know, in the old tongue. Aeslinn's people found and copied it, but it escaped them, returning to where I'd left it. I use it now to get around. What would your lot call it? My wheelchair." She laughed.

"Then the seahorse . . ."

"Was an illusion. My people are good with them. Especially in water."

So, what I had seen had been both an illusion and real. She had been there in her strange vehicle, but I had seen only what she wanted me to see. Finally, I understood something.

It made me bold.

"Why does it work for me?"

She arched an eyebrow, her expression droll. "Why do you think?"

"I do not know. It would not work for Ray—"

"You do know." She looked at me impatiently. "Come, come, girl. I'm not going to spoon feed it to you."

I thought this was exactly the time that she should be spoon feeding it to me, while she still could. But it would be impolite to say so. "I'm not a girl," I said instead. "I am more than five hundred years old—"

"And I am more than five thousand. And you do know."

I glanced at Efridis, who had yet to move. "You said something about godly experiments. I . . . am one of those?"

"No. You are an accident. Your mother was the experiment." She sighed and slumped a little more against the rock, to the point that she was almost lying down. "Quarrelsome, backbiting, thieving—we were not sired by the better sort of gods." Her lips curled. "No, not by half. They were constantly fighting each other, and doing experiments to make armies out of whatever they found, to give them an advantage."

"Whatever they found?"

"Whoever, would be more polite. But that's not how they thought, any more than it was how I did, once. People were commodities, tools, nothing more if they were not mine. Only my people were real; only my people mattered. Classic fallacy. We're all connected. But that isn't what you asked."

I shook my head.

"The armies didn't work out so well, and not merely due to flaws in the making. But also because they ended up fighting other armies, with nothing to show for it in the end but corpse-strewn battlefields. Eventually, someone asked the obvious question: why were they making armies when what they needed was an assassin? A single being with skills so great, and camouflage so perfect, that he or she could go after the real prey: their rival gods."

"God-killer," I whispered, and Nimue smiled.

"And so we come to it. It didn't work, not entirely. But they'd learned a great deal from their experiments, and they came close enough for Artemis to pull the trigger on her own plan—too early. But she had no choice. She had no doubt who they would have sent their assassins after, once they perfected them.

"Thus, she moved against her fellow gods, kicked them out, slammed a metaphysical door behind them. And, afterwards, destroyed their dangerous new prototypes—all but one."

"My mother." I repeated what Nimue had said, but it seemed unreal, a foreign word on my tongue. I had never had a mother.

"She hid out here for a time," Nimue said. "Blending in with the common sort of fey. Then escaped to Earth. No one knew what had happened to her, much less that she'd had a child. Not until—"

"I battled Efridis," I said, and suddenly understood.

Nimue nodded. "Efridis was always very good with things of the mind. I do not know what she saw in you that piqued her curiosity. But at some point, she realized that Earth had perfected what Faerie had begun, and given her the weapon she needed to move against her husband."

"She means to . . . join with me, as I was joined to Dory?" I asked, shivering a little, because the very idea was repellent.

"If that is what you call your other half, yes. But make no mistake, you will have no say in this union, any more than our stolen power gives us a say over what Aeslinn does with it. She would make herself into a god-killer, using your power, and destroy him. But once she has a taste . . ." Nimue shook her head. "It would truly be like the gods had returned. They couldn't handle that much power, and neither will she. It corrupted them, ah—"

For a second, I thought that she had broken off once more because she was tired. But then I saw Efridis beside her. I jumped slightly, because Efridis was still across the room— for an instant. Before the illusion that had allowed her to sneak up on us faded.

And only this one remained, holding a knife.

It was covered in blood—Nimue's. The gods bleed red, I thought blankly, staring at it. And then Nimue laughed, a retching sound, but strangely joyous, too.

"You don't swim, do you?" she asked her cousin.

"What?" Efridis looked confused.

I suppose that wasn't the reaction she'd expected.

"No, I don't suppose you do," Nimue chuckled. "Not ladylike, when you were growing up. And Aeslinn's lands are so cold. Pity."

"There's no water here for you to manipulate, old witch, even assuming you had the strength," Efridis snarled.

"No water," Nimue laughed again. "No water—did you hear what she said?"

I just stared at her. Efridis did, too, for a moment. And then she slammed the blade home again.

"So hard to hold form these days," Nimue whispered. "So very hard. So much easier to just . . . let go." She looked at me, and for a moment, her eyes were clear and brilliant once more, like a storm-tossed sea. "Remember what I told you."

And then, just that fast, she was gone. Only, no, that wasn't the right word. Because her body faded away but something remained. Something powerful.

So, this is what happens when a god dies, I thought, as the cave began to shake, as the rocks fell, and as the waters rushed in. Not some of them, all of them, what felt like all the water in the world. It came crashing through every doorway, spirting from every fissure, torrenting down from the ceiling—

Daughter of the oceans, and the oceans had come to mourn.

And more than that.

The ceiling abruptly fell in, causing waves to sweep up the walls, like the surf crashing onto a beach in a hurricane. It crushed Efridis under rocks and tides that went on and on, and certainly would have crushed me and Ray, too. But the little capsule suddenly appeared in my face; I supposed that it had had no more trouble getting through a door that had exploded around it.

I hauled Ray's body on board, how I didn't know. But the waves were rising all around us, and there was no more time. I threw myself in after him, grabbing one of the seats and pulling with everything I had. And as soon as I was onboard, I thought: Out!

We went out.

I did not know how the craft knew the way, as I could not help it. Perhaps it had some sort of memory, or perhaps some lingering piece of Nimue was guiding us. But we nonetheless went on the most frightening ride of my life, through a succession of interlocking caves, all of which were coming down on top of us.

Huge stalactites plummeted to the floor, which now looked more like an ocean. The waves they threw up crashed over top of our roof, threatening to swamp us. The little craft dodged this way and that, partly to avoid the rain of limestone, and partly from the battering it was taking. Ray and I were slung around the cabin, were almost tossed out of the missing shutter on the side of the little craft, and were sitting in at least a foot of water that sloshed around us.

But suddenly, we were out.

The tiny vessel burst out of the side of a hill, one of the mountains that bordered the river. We skimmed across the waves, which were almost as wild as the ones inside. It looked like the stream had been taken over by a flood. It washed across the banks, slammed against the trees, sprayed us in the face. And it was all done in dead silence, except for the rushing of the water.

The chittering things in the trees did not chitter; the birds did not call. It felt like the whole world was suddenly stunned and in mourning: the caves its eyes, the river its tears. Its creatures held their breath at the passing of a goddess and nothing seemed to be functioning right.

That included our little capsule.

It had been sagging lower and lower amidst the waves, until the cabin was flooded. I pulled Ray clear and swam to the shallows, not even realizing until I was halfway there that my legs were kicking. I could have cried at the realization, and then I did, because the whole world was weeping. Why shouldn't I?

I watched the last of her, the childhood toy she'd used to outwit them all for so long, slowly sink beneath the waves. It seemed fitting, that it go back to the waters. I watched until it was totally out of sight, bidding her farewell in the only way I knew how.

Then I turned my attention to the shore.

* * *

It was a long, hard swim against a raging current, as there were no areas of safe, dry land nearby. The tall trees hedged the river, and I would not go in there without a guide. Not even now.

It was fortunate that Ray did not need to breathe, or I would have drowned him a dozen times over. I barely managed to keep my own head above the choppy waves, and every time I looked back, it seemed that I found his face underwater yet again. But one of those times, his eyes were open.

I sucked in a breath, and a mouthful of river water along with it, then spat it out, coughing and hacking. He did not seem to notice or respond, but the eyes—that was a good sign, wasn't it? I decided to take it as such, and redoubled my efforts.

Finally, after what felt like an hour but was probably much less, a patch of sand appeared up ahead. I swam toward it as best as I could one handed, but didn't believe that it was real until my wobbly legs touched solid ground. I dragged Ray and I onto the little beach, and then just lay there, gasping and panting and laughing in uncontrollable spirts of giggles at the sky, I wasn't sure why.

The air was beautiful, the sun was beautiful, the world was beautiful, and we were alive! Somehow. I giggled again.

I should have been exhausted after our experience, and I was. But euphoria also buzzed in my veins, so much so that I could hardly lie still. I wiggled my toes against the sand, and felt the waves lap at them. I did not even try to process all that I had learned; it was too soon. And my mind was in no mood for it, no mood at all. Instead, I had a sense of expectancy running through me that I did not recognize. I finally realized that I was waiting for the next act of this strange play that I seemed to have stumbled into.

And judging by the spear that suddenly appeared in my face, it had arrived.

"*Gah!*" Ray yelled, suddenly coming alive and launching himself off of the sand. I managed to catch him by the hem of what remained of his tunic before he did anyone an injury, but it was a close thing.

"What are you doing? What's the matter with you?" he spluttered, turning to look at me, his face coated with sand.

I just nodded at the individual holding the spear. He had pale skin and gray eyes, and a shock of black hair that rather reminded me of Ray's. It was cut shorter, however, or was mostly bundled under the soft knitted cap he wore. His clothes marked him as a peasant: a tunic made from what looked like brown wool, tight, lightweight hose in scarlet, and a pair of old brown boots that sagged around his ankles.

They looked like he needed to grow into them, which was probably the case as he appeared to be about twelve years old. That explained why the spear was shaking so profoundly. And why an old man—or an old fey, I supposed—came running out of the woods a moment later.

He had a spear, too, and his did not shake, despite the age spots on his hands. There were also wrinkles on the weathered old face, and gray hair protruding like a scarecrow's from under a wide brimmed straw hat. He looked about eighty, although what that meant here, I had no idea.

There was a spluttering of words in a tongue that I didn't understand, and which, apparently, Ray didn't, either. The old man was gesturing at my tunic, or perhaps at the blood on it, I wasn't sure. It had been in water for much of the last day, but it still had a large stain on the side and several smaller ones that I had added to it.

The discolorations were brown now, the water having washed the red out, but I didn't think it fooled him. And I had no way to explain, or any clue as to whether I should. If they were vassals of the Svarestri, wearing a blood-stained, obviously stolen tunic might mark me as an enemy.

Perhaps I should have stayed naked, after all.

"Okay, so what?" Ray asked. "We just sit here like idiots?"

I glanced at him. "As opposed to?"

He waved a hand. "Take care of them."

I just looked at him.

"Not like that! I mean . . . we knock them out or something."

"And then what?"

"What?"

The old creature said something else. It did not sound friendly. "I don't think he likes us talking," I told Ray.

"And I give a shit because?"

"We are lost," I reminded him. "Perhaps they can help us find a portal."

"Yeah, or perhaps they can ransom us to the damned Svarestri and then we're really—"

But Ray never got a chance to finish his sentence. Because we had finally said a word that the old man knew. He scrunched up his face and spat on the sand, while thrusting the spear at us menacingly. "Svarestri!"

Ray and I looked at each other.

Then Ray did something that validated Dory's belief in him. He horked up a huge wad of spit, blood and phlegm, and spat it on the ground with enough force to make a divot in the sand. "Svarestri!"

The old man blinked, and regarded us narrowly for a moment. "Svarestri?"

Ray spat again. "Fuck the Svarestri!"

The old man thought some more, and eyed the large stain on my tunic again.

"Fuck the Svarestri," he finally agreed, pronouncing the words carefully, as if he liked the sound of them. "Fuck the Svarestri!"

He looked at me.

"Fuck the Svarestri," I agreed, and for the first time, he smiled.

He put his spear over his shoulder and clapped me on the shoulder. Then he decided it deserved more and grinned at me with a mouthful of gray and broken teeth. It appeared that we had made a friend.

"Fuck the Svarestri," he repeated, and led the way into the forest, beckoning us to follow.

Ray and I looked at each other again. "What the hell," Ray said.

I nodded.

We followed the old man and boy into the trees.

CHAPTER FORTY-THREE

Dory, Hong Kong

My new team raided my stash, and then took off through the streets, Ranbir in the lead with the activated charm in his hand. The hologram-type map glowed redly in the darkness, and it *was* dark. Magic and electricity don't play well together, so the street lights were out, and not a single lamp or lighted sign could be seen anywhere.

To make matters worse, there were plenty of reminders of the recent battle to get in our way and slow down progress. It had taken a week for anybody to notice that magic was going haywire in parts of the city, and not much clean-up had happened by then. And nothing had been done since.

That left piles of debris everywhere, high enough to fill whole alleyways in places and to spill out into the streets. There was also an ocean of shattered glass glinting in the occasional beam of moonlight, like new fallen snow. But that wasn't a frequent thing, as the cloud cover was thick overhead and completely opaque in the distance. Even up close, a thin mist hung in the air, silvering everything and reducing visibility to maybe a block.

The charmed map threw a red haze over Ranbir's face, which wasn't looking happy. He was trying to chart a path past the groups of moving dots, which none of us were enthusiastic about meeting. We couldn't use magical weapons against these things, but regular old bullets didn't do a lot, either.

What *did* work was vampire strength, but the vamps kept getting piled on, so evasion was definitely the way to go. Only with blocked off alleys, trash-filled streets, and destroyed buildings, that often wasn't so easy. It felt like an obstacle course where one wrong move could get us killed.

No wonder Ranbir was sweating.

And then an ominous rumble came from farther down our street, and suddenly everybody was.

"What was that?" Sarah asked shrilly. She'd followed her brother's example and loaded up on weapons, but it didn't look like they had made her feel any better. Her dark hair was up in a no-nonsense bun, to keep it out of her way in a fight, but her eyes were too-wide and her movements were jumpy.

Zheng had seemed to think that she and her team would be an asset, but he'd had false information. I honestly didn't know if it had been a good idea to sign these guys on or not, but what choice did we have? Nobody else was crazy enough to try this.

Of course, maybe that should have told me something.

"Fast moving bogeys, coming this way," Ranbir said, watching the map. And using the term we'd decided on for moving obstacles, because 'monster' made everybody nervous.

We dodged out of the street and into an alley—which turned out to be a dead end. It wasn't supposed to be, but it had been blocked by a mountain of bricks from a destroyed building. And the lane across from it was no better, leading to what the map showed as a massive battle going on between bogies on one of the main avenues. I could hear the screeching and caterwauling from here; I did not want to see it in person.

But the rumble was now loud enough to cause little avalanches on the garbage mountains and to vibrate under my feet. The streets were a warren, and the buildings made sound echo everywhere. It was impossible to tell where the noise was coming from.

"Where are they?" I asked, and Ranbir pointed at something I couldn't see, because we were running now and the map was jittering all over the place.

But a moment later, I didn't need an answer, because I saw them: vague figures appearing out of the mist behind us. But not vague enough. For a moment, I just stared at yet another example of how a lifetime of strange events had not prepared me for supernatural Hong Kong. Not even close.

Because we were being targeted by a group of motorcycle riding samurai.

They were 3-D, with bodies as solid as any of ours. But they were also black and white, as if the magic floating around the dead zones had activated a bunch of illustrations. The closer they got, the more likely that seemed, as they still had the sketch marks and the doesn't-change-with-the-lighting shading of a drawing.

It was like being charged by a bunch of cartoons.

Sword-wielding cartoons, I realized, as steel glinted in a stray beam of moonlight.

Okay. Running faster now, alongside Sarah, who had noticed our latest problem and was bitching about it in a high-pitched voice. And yeah. Totally not going to rag on her about that later. Assuming there *was* a later, because the messed-up street had hardly slowed our pursuers down at all, and in fact had helped them by providing a ramp in the form of a fallen wall—

And now they were arcing overhead.

"We can take them!" Tomas said, as the rest of us rolled into the shadow of a bunch of burnt-out cars.

Louis-Cesare reached out and grabbed him, jerking the idiot down as swords rattled against the rooftops overhead. Tomas threw off his hold and glared at us, and I made a be-my-guest gesture. He scowled.

"I thought dhampirs were supposed to be tough!"

"Tough, not stupid."

He frowned. "Are you calling me stupid?"

"No, just that the bonus stats all went to pretty."

Louis-Cesare laughed, and even Ranbir's lip twitched.

Tomas, luckily, took a moment to parse that, and as soon as the last rider arced overhead, we darted into a crumbling edifice.

We'd been trying to stay on the streets, because the structural soundness of a lot of the buildings was in question. Half of the obstructions were composed of the remains of fallen houses and shops, and even some of the ones still standing weren't looking like they'd be doing it much longer. Like this one, in fact.

But there wasn't a lot of choice, so we got busy wading through the almost knee-high soot in a lobby, then pelted down a smoke damaged corridor and through a door at the end that let out onto a narrow alley.

Only to find that our pursuers had flanked us.

Ev and Jason let off a barrage that would have discouraged a platoon, strafing them with suppressing fire, only it didn't suppress much. Bullets from my .44 Magnum likewise rattled off the samurai's armor, barely even leaving dents in the surface. And when I threw an incendiary, it had no effect at all.

Like the birds, they looked like paper but acted like high grade steel.

The kind that ricocheted weapons' fire.

"Don't shoot inside!" I yelled, as more bogies showed up behind us and we ducked into a building across the alley. But either nobody could hear me over the ringing in our ears, or the cluster of animated horrors had freaked them out. Because bullets were suddenly flying everywhere, with Ev and Jason letting loose with a weapon in each hand.

Sarah was yelling and crying and covering her ears, because it was loud enough to hurt. Louis-Cesare got in front of me and her, backing us toward the door to the next room, and taking a couple of bullets in the process. And then Sarah and I abruptly found ourselves standing in what looked like a nursery school.

I glanced back through the door to see that the two vamps had pulled swords, meaning that the sounds of steel on steel had probably just been added to the cacophony of engines revving, people yelling, and a sustained barrage, but I couldn't tell. My ears were temporarily out of commission, giving me back only ringing white noise.

Which was why I had nothing to distract me from our newest problem.

Sarah looked at me, her eyes huge, and yeah. Wasn't sure how bad this was gonna be, either. Because a bunch of faded, painted pandas on the walls had just brightened and turned their huge, fuzzy heads toward us.

They looked like a cutesy kid's mural, with a forest of bamboo trees in the background, some improbably large flowers, and some happy insect friends.

They weren't.

"No weapons," I mouthed, and I guessed she read lips, because she nodded slightly, and slipped her .357 back into its holster.

Bear #1 regarded me curiously, with a slightly tilted head. He was still chewing on some leaves, which I took to be a good sign. But the black eyes were shiny and suspicious as he checked me over.

"Get behind me," I told Sarah, because she was bristling with weapons and we were playing nice here. I had the arsenal with me, so I hadn't bothered with anything but the stuff concealed by my jacket and in the outer pockets of the bag. The jacket was pretty ripped up, thanks to the Stymphalian birds out there, but it covered the hardware.

Hers didn't.

She got behind me.

"Okay," I said, turning my face so that she could see my

lips move. "These things are popular protection wards. I saw some in a couple shops when I was here before. Play nice with them; they play nice with you."

"What happens if we don't play nice?" she screamed, because she couldn't hear shit right now.

It was right in my ear, and I guessed I'd had some hearing left, after all. But probably not now. I winced, and then immediately smiled again, because the bamboo chewing had just stopped.

"We get our asses kicked," I said. And since these things, like every-fucking-thing else in the dead zones, had been bathing in some high-quality magic for a while now, said ass kicking was likely to be epic.

"Okay," she yelled. "What's the plan?"

"We tell the guys. If they come in nice and easy, we can probably just walk on through. If not—"

And, of course, it was 'if not', because two first-level masters don't take long to deal with a room full of enemies. The next moment, our little group of Rambos came rushing in, guns and swords in hand. And immediately spotted the bright-eyed pandas on the wall.

"*No!*" Sarah and I yelled. "*Don't—*"

They did. Ev and Jason let loose and—yep. I hate being right, I thought as the walls went 3-D and in a hurry.

Black, fuzzy bodies suddenly jumped out everywhere, the size of grizzlies rather than pandas, and Sarah and I started backing up. But that was a nope as well, as the samurai weren't dead so much as in pieces, a scattering of lethal body parts across the outer room ready to slice and dice as soon as anything got close enough. Or to kick, I thought, as the bottom half of a rider nailed me in the shin.

"Other way!" I gasped at Sarah, who shook her head violently.

"No, no, this way!" And she stepped right in front of the top half of the samurai, who almost took her leg off with a sword swipe.

I pulled her back, just in time, leaving us stuck in the doorway between two kinds of hell.

Pick the way you want to die, I thought, as another panda leapt off of the wall, fluffed out from 2-D to 3-D, and immediately lunged at us. And reminded me that they are still bears when its paw tore a chunk out of Tomas, who'd dodged in between. And who was not nearly so pretty with half of his face missing.

Sarah screamed, loudly enough that I distantly heard it, a bright wave of blood spurted, and I threw a potion grenade into the middle of the room.

"What are you *doing*?" Louis-Cesare yelled, grabbing me. "No magic, remember?"

"I remember!" I yelled back, although I probably didn't need to, because vamp hearing—especially first-level master vamp hearing—heals itself almost before the gunfire stops. But it was a yelling kind of moment.

"Then what are you doing?"

"That," I said, as the potion's vapors boiled around the room.

It was a benign one, a smoke bomb meant for camouflage, but it was powerful, being designed to cover a whole block. Only it didn't cover this one. Billowing white clouds spread everywhere—and were immediately absorbed by the magic hungry bears.

And, oh, yeah, that made a difference.

That made a real difference, I thought, as they did the same thing that the bird had, only they had a lot more bulk to work with. The bird had mostly grown up, and they did that, too, their big, round heads suddenly hitting the ceiling and forcing them to bend over. But they also expanded the other way—big time.

I'd hoped for them to grow too big to maneuver in the small room, but this was ridiculous. Black, furry butts were suddenly everywhere, and getting larger. It was a sea of chubby cuteness that was already threatening to suffocate us. But at least they weren't swiping at us anymore, possibly because they appeared as confused as everybody else by what was happening.

And because there wasn't room.

The bears started fighting each other for space above our heads, but there were still spots of daylight around their chubby legs. Sarah saw her chance and took it. "The door!" she yelled, and lunged for it.

She was going for the one on the opposite side of the room, which looked like it let out into another alley. I dove after her, while I still could, and the guys finally seemed to get the idea, too. But had we left it too late?

Because the chub was taking over. I got halfway across the room, and found my way blocked by two giant, expanding asses. I tried going over, but they grew faster than I could leap, and I found myself bouncing back into Louis-Cesare.

"There!" I dimly heard him yell, and we dodged to the side, while gunfire broke out on the other side of the room.

But we couldn't help whoever it was. We were having enough trouble squeezing our way under some rapidly expanding stomachs, and even then, Louis-Cesare had to brute-force us a path to the door, shoving back what looked like a ton of blubber in the process. But through the enveloping love handles, I spotted a trash-strewn alley, littered with puddles from the last rain storm, and smelling like garbage.

Nothing had ever looked better in my life!

I started crawling for it, but before I could get there, here came Tomas.

I decided to start liking him again, because he had a gun-loving team member under each arm, and was fighting the chub for the door. He made it, and then so did I and Louis-Cesare. We hit the concrete outside, which I strongly considered kissing, and then had to immediately run again, because a truly massive rear end had just smashed through the windows and splintered the door.

It headed for a tattoo shop across the alley, and the next moment, a bunch of tiny tats came running out, fleeing the butt-pocalypse. I just stared at them for a moment, a bit overwhelmed in spite of myself. Until a tiny, adorable-looking bunny hopped over and nuzzled my leg.

And then bit the crap out of it.

Blood ran, the rabbit started growing, and Louis-Cesare smashed a foot down, grinding it into the pavement in a way that would normally have been gruesome, but all that came out from under his boot was squiggles.

We ran.

The team gathered at the end of the alley to catch our breaths, crowding under a dull green tarp stretched across some bamboo scaffolding because it had started raining. I was just able to hear the pitter patter of water on the green plastic overhead, which was a good sign. This was hard enough without being completely deaf.

But something was clearly wrong, because Sarah was looking frantic. "Wait. Where's Ranbir?"

We looked around, and damn it, the mage was missing!

"He was with us when we ran into the hotel," Tomas said. It was a bit hard to watch him talk, as his face hadn't healed yet, giving me an anatomy lesson every time he spoke. But he wasn't wrong.

"Was he with us in the last building, with the samurai?" Ev asked. "I don't remember."

"He didn't come into the nursery," I said.

Sarah nodded. "We assumed he was with you guys."

Louis-Cesare shook his head. "He may have been. It was difficult to keep track."

"And the weapon's fire burned my eyes," Jason added. "I couldn't see much of anything through the smoke."

"Yes, we know," Tomas said dourly. "That would explain why you kept shooting me in the ass."

"I did not!" It was indignant.

Tomas turned around, and sure enough, somebody had strafed him across the backside, leaving fluttering, bloody khakis and a bunch of healed skin.

Jason looked pointedly at Ev.

"I did not do that," Ev said placidly.

"How do you know?"

"I was using this," Ev produced my pride and joy: an AA-12 automated shotgun with its huge, round magazine. "It works better than the little bullets," he explained.

Tomas looked back at Jason.

"It must have been the ricochets," Jason insisted. "I'm an expert shot!"

"Yes," Tomas agreed. "I don't think you missed my ass once."

"Can we get back to the point?" Sarah said. "Ranbir is missing!"

"And?"

"And we have to go back for him!"

There was a sudden, uncomfortable silence.

"He'd do it for us!" she insisted.

"Would he?" Tomas asked. "He's a dark mage—"

"He isn't!"

"He sort of is, though," Ev pointed out. "He does blood magic—"

"Chickens! He kills chickens!"

"Have fun, then," Tomas said, leaning against the wall and crossing his arms.

Sarah glared at him. I had kind of gotten the impression that they were an item, since he moved to shelter her the way that Louis-Cesare did me. But it looked like there might be trouble in paradise.

Not that it mattered. "We have to go back," I pointed out.

Tomas cocked an eyebrow at me. "Oh, and why would that be?"

"Ranbir has the map."

CHAPTER FORTY-FOUR

Dory, Hong Kong

W e went back. It was useless, except that we discovered what happened to the samurai when they were carved into pieces. Best case scenario, they got confused and some parts ended up on the wrong bodies. In one case, that created an Indian-god-looking creature with a dozen arms, and in another, a monster where two non-matching halves had decided to come together. That left us being charged by something that walked on its hands like a circus performer, while its other pair tried to decapitate us with twin swords.

But you notice, I said "best case". Worst case scenario was all the other pieces, a couple hundred of them at a guess, which had decided not to bother looking for their missing bodies. They were just growing themselves new ones.

They weren't doing too well with that right now, but as soon as another magic cloud washed over them, we were going to have a *lot* more enemies. Only nobody intended to hang around for the show. Except possibly for Sarah, who was being stubborn.

"He ran off," Tomas said, when we stopped in a nearby side street to regroup, after the vamps hacked up the horrors. "He had the map; he lost his nerve; he ran. It's that simple."

"It's not that simple! He wouldn't just abandon us!" she

insisted.

Tomas spread his hands. "Did you see him?"

Sarah crossed her arms and frowned at him.

Tomas looked at Ev. "What about you?"

"I did not see him," Ev said.

Tomas looked at me. "How about you, Miss—"

"Basarab," Louis-Cesare said. "Lord Mircea's daughter."

"Bullshit." Tomas sneered. "Mircea doesn't have a daughter, much less a dirty—"

Louis-Cesare slammed him against the wall of a house, causing a bunch of ash to come raining down from the roof. "And my *wife*."

"Your what?" Tomas looked in shock at Louis-Cesare for a moment, looked back at me, and then at Louis-Cesare again—

And burst out laughing.

That had about the result you'd expect, but Sarah had clearly had enough. "Cut it out!" she yelled, getting in between them. And barely missing having Tomas put a fist through her face.

He pulled back with a curse, and starting yelling at her, but she wasn't having that, either. "I wouldn't have been in danger if you would control your temper! I know you don't like him, but insulting his wife is a low blow."

"That is *not* his—"

"How would you like it if someone insulted me? People don't exactly like jinxes, either—"

"That's completely diff—"

"It is not completely different. Jinxes are outlawed. I'm supposed to be locked up in some cell somewhere, living out my life staring at a wall like a good little freak of nature. And I probably will be if the Circle ever catches up with me. How would you like it if Louis-Cesare called me—"

"He calls you anything, and I cut his damned head off!" Tomas said fiercely.

Louis-Cesare started to comment, probably about how likely that was, but I beat him to it. "Louis-Cesare doesn't have to worry about that," I said. "He doesn't go around insulting women."

Tomas had the grace to blush, although it didn't last long.

"You're not a woman; you're a dhampir. And you aren't his wife—"

"What makes you so sure?"

"Because he's all but married to a bitch named Christine!"

Louis-Cesare started to say something, but I held up a hand and he backed off gracefully. He looked like he wanted to see this, too. I got in Tomas's space, not abruptly, but slowly, almost sinuously. I brushed my hand down the side of his pretty hair, to turn his face toward me. It had healed, and he was back to the show-stopper I'd first encountered.

I raised up on tiptoes so I could whisper directly into his ear. "I killed Christine. I blew her into a thousand pieces. From what I understand, they never even found them all."

Tomas stared at me, and for a moment, I thought I saw a flash of fear in his eyes. But then a wash of anger took its place. He abruptly stepped back. "You are insane!"

"Homicidal," I agreed. "Which is why you and my husband are going to stop antagonizing each other. It's bad enough that we're fighting a bunch of monsters; we don't have to fight each other, too."

"Or leave each other," Sarah said pointedly. "We have to find Ranbir."

We did not find Ranbir, although that was not our choice. We suddenly didn't have a choice. Because the whole damned street was coming alive.

The little road had a long brick wall on one side and a row of shuttered shops on the other. The one thing they had in common was graffiti: it covered the corrugated tin of the shutters, scrawled across the road, and had turned the long expanse of brick into an art gallery. One that was suddenly lighting up.

"What's . . . going on?" Jason asked.

"They usually do that before they attack," Ev said

helpfully.

"I know that!"

"Then why did you ask?"

"It was a rhetorical question!"

"Really?" Ev looked surprised. "This does not seem to be the time."

"Uh, retreat?" Sarah said.

"Retreat," I agreed, and turned around, only to find that there was nowhere to go. There was graffiti in the other direction, too, and on the street behind us—

"What the hell is this?" Sarah said, catching an eyeful of the mob headed our way.

I didn't answer, because I had no idea. For the last hour or so, we'd encountered problems, but we'd also avoided a lot of them. We'd opted for side streets and dodged anything we saw coming. I'd assumed that, once we found the mage, we'd reach our destination fairly quickly.

After all, we were learning how things worked around here.

Only apparently not. Because, suddenly, every creature in the place seemed to be focused on us. And if there were any benign ones in the crowd, I didn't see them.

"Incoming!" Ev yelled, and fired the rocket launcher at something screaming at us from overhead.

I didn't see what it was, but a second later, I was covered in blue goo, and so was everyone else. It wasn't sticky like the squid's had been, but it was gross. Not that I had time to worry about it.

A large, pink pig with anime character eyes jumped off of a wall and charged, its tusks threatening to gut us before Louis-Cesare grabbed them and launched it over a nearby building. A huge graffitied statue of David swept an arm out of a wall and sent a wave of garbage crashing into us, spilling us off our feet. And an equally giant fish came alive, its tail flicking acid instead of water and setting the trash alight.

But not for long. Because a great eye, big enough to have

belonged to Sauron himself, turned to look at us from the side of a nearby shop. Its pupil was as large as my whole face, and it had just pushed three-foot lashes out of the corrugated metal, which was strange enough. But then it began to cry, gushing with water like an open fire hydrant, and flooding the street a foot deep in seconds.

I stared at it, genuine panic rising in my throat. We'd stumbled into a supernatural obstacle course, filled with soldiers who couldn't die, and I didn't know how to fight this way! And neither did anybody else, the whole group stuck in indecision for a second, not knowing which way to turn.

Until Jason solved it for us.

"Pick a damned direction!" he screamed, and then let off a barrage at the crap headed our way down the alley, before running to the right.

"I guess we're going right," Louis-Cesare said dryly. But it wasn't any better or worse than the other options.

Of course, I could have been wrong about that, I thought, a moment later.

We had started pelting ahead with the two vamps on either side, to beat off attacks from the wall and shops; the two gunslingers in the back, to slow down the army; and me and Sarah in the middle, guns out, trying to pick off what we could of whatever was coming up in front. It was going pretty well until we approached a mural of a beautiful Chinese woman, who was reclining along the whole length of a building. She didn't bother to get up and chase us like half the city was doing, but then, she didn't need to. She had a child's bubble making toy, and was blowing iridescent spheres the size of beach balls that looked harmlessly ethereal until they floated into something solid.

And detonated like so many percussion grenades.

The street ahead was suddenly filled with explosions, which didn't rain shrapnel, but which did flash so brightly as to white out the landscape, and bang so loudly as to finish deafening us. They also played havoc with my sense of balance, sending me stumbling around like an old drunk, lurching from one explosion to the other. I ran into the side of the wall, almost broke my nose, staggered back and vaguely realized that . . .

It was coming with me.

I couldn't see shit, but I could feel, and that . . . wasn't brick. What felt like massive scales slid under my hands, thick and hard and smooth. A running river of them, but not snake-like. I'd felt something like them before, and the sensation was as visceral as it was memorable, chilling the blood in my veins and freezing my limbs, just when I needed them to move, damn it! Because that wasn't a snake, that was a—

"Dragon!" Tomas bellowed, right in my face, his vampire eyesight faring better than mine.

Along with his vampire reflexes. I was suddenly flying down the street, his arm around my waist and my feet barely touching the road. While, just behind us, something hit the ground, something like a giant foot followed by a colossal body, heavy enough to threaten to crack the road bed—

And, okay, I decided.

It was officially fuck it time.

"Get them to me," I told Tomas breathlessly. "Get the team!"

I couldn't even hear the words I was speaking, but he obviously could. Because a moment later, I felt bodies crowding me close, and while I couldn't see them or hear their breathing, the motion around me was indicative of panting or fear. Or, you know, both.

My hand found my bag, and the device holding pride of place in the biggest pocket of them all. I grabbed it, activating a personal shield worth the price of a house, and not a small one. I could never have afforded the Cadillac of shields, but then, I hadn't bought it.

I'd stolen it, from the consul's personal stash.

Here's hoping she spent more on herself than she did on

others, I thought, right before a burst of fire blasted us like we'd been caught in a volcanic eruption.

Or by an angry dragon.

"Auggghhhh!" Somebody screamed, as the transparent bubble of the shield showed a rain of flame that just kept coming and coming, even while the grenades' after effects jumped across my vision, leaving me half blind. But I had just enough eyesight left to read the shield's indicator bracelet wrapped around my wrist, and—

Shit.

"How much time do we have?" Louis-Cesare yelled.

"It was supposed to be half an hour," I babbled, thumping the thing because it had to be faulty. "But that was based on protecting twelve. With only six of us, it should last longer, although it depends on the level of power that it has to expend—"

"Damn it, how much?"

"Two minutes—"

"*Two minutes*? We have two minutes before we *die*?"

"One minute fifty seconds."

Louis-Cesare said a bad word in French, and looked at Tomas.

He didn't say anything out loud, but then, master vamps didn't have to. They were probably speaking mind to mind, and for once, they seemed to be in agreement. Because the next moment—

"I don't think it's supposed to be portable," I said breathlessly, as they *picked up the shield and started to take off with it.*

Only me, I thought, shell shocked. Only I could get stuck in a failing shield while being chased by a dragon. It . . . boggled the mind.

And it wasn't even a good chase, because the shield wasn't designed to be used while in motion. But when you pay the kind of money that the consul probably had, you get added features. Instead of staying put, and causing all of us to slam into it when we tried to run, it recalibrated as we moved, the way it had probably been designed to do in case somebody crashed into the thing and made it wobble.

But it didn't recalibrate fast. So, I had another odd experience to add to my collection: slowly shambling down a street from inside what felt like a giant balloon, while being whacked on by a pack of modern day Chinese soldiers, who might have looked real if they weren't twelve feet tall; by a group of abstract, Dali-esque monsters in neon colors; by a very un-pacifistic Buddha; by some video game characters I didn't recognize; by a couple of massive sumo wrestlers who kept trying to crush us with their huge bellies; and by a dragon. And a rainbow-colored rooster the size of a bus, who showed up out of nowhere and tried to peck our heads, only to have its beak slide off the shield and stab the dragon instead.

That did not please the dragon, who I could now tell was blue and snake-like, with a head that looked more like a lion than the typical western depiction. But the fire breathing attributes were right on point, and were abruptly turned on its attacker. Which took the heat off of us—literally—for a moment.

And that was enough.

Down a cross street just ahead, moving slowly to avoid the biggest trash heaps, rumbled an old, World War II era cargo truck with a cloth canopy and way more wheels than it needed. I had no idea who would be crazy enough to be driving around down here, and for a moment wondered if we were about to be targeted by the triad along with everything else. But then I saw what popped out of the cloth covered back.

"Bertha?"

I honestly wasn't sure if I was seeing things; it had been that kind of a day. But, yes, there they were, in all their glory, Bertha's massive assets, draped over with a couple dozen bandoliers of bullets. Somebody appeared to be using her as an ammunition mule, and I only knew one person alive who would think of something like that.

And then a head poked out of the passenger side window, and I was sure of it.

"Zheng!" I screamed, never so happy to see anyone in my life.

I saw his eyes widen and his mouth form a very bad word, and then I grabbed Louis-Cesare's arm and pointed. The truck didn't stop because it was already going fairly slow, and in fact, seemed to pick up speed as we tried to catch it, maybe because the driver had just spotted what was in the street behind us. But it didn't work. We shambled that way, but we shambled fast.

"Slow down, you bastards!" Tomas yelled, and half a dozen dark heads poked out of the cab to blink at us. Zheng's guys, I assumed. And then a dozen hands followed, trying to pull us on board.

And suddenly, we were having another reunion.

"Hello," Bahram said.

"You're not ditching us that easily," Rashid snarled.

"Oh, trust me," Louis-Cesare replied. "It hasn't been easy."

It looked like I'd been wrong, I thought, as the cloth side of the truck rolled up. There were a couple dozen of Zheng's guys in there, and they made my team look underdressed. Their hands slid off of our shield for a moment, but only for a moment. Then it gave up the ghost, and we were jerked into a truck already stuffed with heavily armed locals.

And a royally pissed-off master vamp who had the nerve to glare at me through the missing back window of the cab.

"*You're* the jinx!" he told me. "Every time I get involved with you—every time—"

"Then why are you here?" I asked breathlessly. I didn't know why I was gasping; I'd been moving—at best—at a brisk walking speed. But then, my usual workouts don't involve dragons.

"I didn't go to all the trouble to get a decent alliance to let it fall apart now! You do not get to die on me!"

"Okay," I said happily, as we rumbled off, while our pursuers devolved into a snarling, squealing, and roaring knot, too busy attacking each other to remember us. And blocking the road in the process, creating a natural barricade to anyone else joining in.

I felt my spine unclench.

"Where the hell's Ranbir?" Zheng demanded.

"We don't know," Sarah said. "We got separated—"

"He's dead," Tomas said flatly.

"You don't know that!" She turned on him.

"After what we just went through? Yes, I know that."

I was actually kind of with Tomas on this one, but didn't want to say so. Sarah looked like she might cry. I wondered if she'd ever lost a team member before.

It didn't look like it.

"Well, that's just great," Zheng said.

"It's worse than you think," Jason said. "He had the map. Without him—"

"What map?"

"The one they made from their past explorations," Louis-Cesare said smoothly, causing Tomas to do a double take. Probably because he wouldn't have been able to lie that quickly or that well. "The one to the approximate location of Eternity's base."

"But you know the general locale, right?" Zheng said. "I better not have come all this way for nothing!"

"I know it," Sarah said.

Everybody looked at her.

"He had it right out there in the open. We all saw it."

Yeah, but none of the rest of us had remembered.

I smiled at her. "Thanks."

She smiled back. "At least, I'm pretty sure—"

"Pretty sure?" Zheng said. "We can't roam around, looking for the damned thing! It's like the apocalypse out there! We get in, we get out, we get—"

He cut off abruptly, and one glance out of the open side of the truck told me why. Because in our relief at our getaway, we'd forgotten one, tiny thing. Dragons can fly.

CHAPTER FORTY-FIVE

Dory, Hong Kong

"**S**hit! Shit! Shit!" Zheng yelled, beating on his driver.
"Move! Move! Move!" I said, wishing I knew the
word in Cantonese.

I didn't need it. There are some reactions that
are universal, especially when a two-ton dragon comes
swooping after you. The men screamed, automatic weapons
fire tore through the night, and the big truck lurched ahead,
driving faster than I'd thought possible from its previous
performance. And then more than driving.

"Hold on," Zheng said.

I didn't have to ask why, because Bertha and the boys
were all cramming this way as a huge fan pushed up from the
back of the cargo area, and started blowing up a hurricane in
our wake. The device looked like the kind used on the local
rickshaws, only bigger, although it did not seem to faze our
pursuers. But then, that wasn't the point.

As demonstrated when the old truck, laden as it was,
slowly lifted off the roadbed and into the air.

I looked down to see the wheels turning flat and
retracting beneath the undercarriage, like landing gear on a
jet. Only this thing didn't seem to be nearly as well balanced,
because the movement sent us careening across the road. Or
maybe that was the driver, or should I say drivers, because

three different guys had their hands on the wheel.

"Zheng!" I yelled, because the dragon was matching our speed—and gaining.

But he was already on it.

"Get outta my way! You guys can't drive worth shit!"

Zheng took over, but it didn't seem to help much. The truck, while making considerably better time than it had while bouncing over piles of debris, was not getting away. Probably because the fan-driven contraptions they used around here were built on old rickshaw bodies for a reason: they were light and easily maneuverable. Neither was true for the truck.

It also seemed to have a steering issue. We ricocheted around the narrow street like a giant pinball, but couldn't seem to rise above it. Unlike our airborne pursuer.

A wash of fire rained down on us, hot as hell, for a split second. Then Zheng jerked the wheel, sending us scraping along a wall and plowing through a mountain of debris, throwing it up on all sides and discouraging our attacker. But not for long.

I saw it wheel away in an arc that clearly signified another attack incoming, one we couldn't survive considering that I was watching it through the burnt-edged holes that had been eaten through our roof by the last one.

"Dory!" Tomas grabbed my purse. "We can hide in here!"

"We can't!"

"It's the best chance we have. We can't fight that thing!"

"Listen to me. Fire will burn the purse to ashes—"

"But we won't be in the purse. It's just a gateway—"

"And what happens if a gateway is destroyed?" Louis-Cesare demanded. "It's what we tried to tell you before—"

Tomas scowled. "I don't need to be told anything by you!"

"Screw this," I said, and disappeared into my armory.

Tomas was right behind me as I threw open the door to my main stash of weapons. Something big, something big, something—okay, yeah. If those two didn't do it, nothing would.

"Why are you so resistant to this?" he demanded, catching my arm.

I would have had something to say—and possibly more than say—about that normally, but there wasn't time. "Because, if the doorway is destroyed, we are stuck in here, unable to get out. Me and Sarah and the other humans will asphyxiate quickly enough, when we run out of air. But you and the other vamps will be stuck *forever*. Do you get it now?"

I guess he got it, because he let go of my arm. Or maybe that was because Louis-Cesare had just shown up, and they wanted to try killing each other again. I left them to it, burst back outside, waded through the guys, and grabbed Ev.

"What are you doing?" he asked curiously.

"Can you launch this with one of your rockets?"

He looked at the small disk on my open palm. "Is it sticky? I could put it on the side of one of them—"

"Yes, yes, it's sticky!" I said, peeling off the little paper backing.

"I can try."

"What is it?" Louis-Cesare asked me. Because I guessed he'd decided that this was slightly more important than beating up Tomas.

"The biggest thing I've got."

If it didn't work . . .

I decided not to think about what would happen if it didn't work.

The dragon made its dive, Ev raised the launcher to his shoulder, being way too calm for any human blood to be flowing in those veins, and let loose. The recoil sent him stumbling back into us, putting all three of us on the floor. And giving me a perfect view of what happens when a two-ton paper dragon meets a device that magnifies an explosion by a hundred times.

"Yeah!" Zheng yelled, the guys whooped, and I continued to stare at the firework-sized confetti raining down everywhere, gobs and gobs of it, like we were flying through a ticker tape parade.

Only those usually follow a victory, don't they?

And ours wasn't won yet.

"Oh, come *on!*" Jason yelled. "This is *bullshit!*"

He had a point. Because the confetti was still blowing through the air when an army of motorcycle riding assholes pulled up alongside us. And in back. And for as far as I could see down the road, where they were running over our other pursuers, in some cases literally.

The samurai had returned for an encore, and this time, there had to be a couple hundred of them. I guessed they'd followed the dragon, who had thoughtfully led them right to us. And while this enemy couldn't fly, we weren't doing so hot at that right now, either.

The truck had levelled out at barely five feet off the ground, which didn't even clear some of the garbage piles. It definitely didn't put us out of the reach of our latest problem. Who were already climbing on board.

I grasped for my purse, had a boot stomp down on my hand, and grabbed an acid grenade off of Bertha instead. I shoved it in my attacker's unnaturally large mouth and as far down his throat as I could reach, then pulled the pin. And watched a miracle happen as Zheng's boys fought to wrestle him back off the truck.

Nothing had worked on these guys, absolutely nothing.

Until now.

The grenade went off and his "ink" started to smear, his eyes dripped down his face, and his features melted. The guys were forced to let him go after a moment, because there was literally nothing left to hold onto, just a black and white puddle of goo on the floor. They looked at me; I looked at them.

And then we were all throwing acid grenades.

The results, however, were mixed. The grenades flattened the samurai's tires, as their rides seemed to be made of the same stuff that they were, and turned them into monstrous versions of themselves, with greatly elongated noses, gaping maws for mouths, and earlobes that stretched halfway down their chests. But they didn't stop them. Maybe because the explosions were hitting the roadside or their armor, instead of discharging internally.

And then my hand reached for another grenade—and reached, and reached and reached, because we were out, damn it!

Even worse, we plowed into a garbage pile a second later that had completely blocked the street. The truck was tough; it made it through. But it caused an avalanche of soda cans, tumbled bricks, and charred roof tiles to hit the windshield, half of which lodged there, blocking Zheng's view ahead.

"Clear it off! Clear it off!" he yelled, but his guys were too busy unloading on the ever-growing field of monstrosities behind us.

And on both sides of us, I realized, as the road was just wide enough to allow them to pull alongside. They were threatening to swamp us, taking machine gun bursts directly to the face, which did little more than give them a bad case of acne. Yet their hands crumpled the guns they grabbed as if *they* were made out of paper.

The only reason we weren't already overrun were the two first-level masters, who were on opposite sides of the vehicle and raging like beasts. They were somehow keeping the sides clear all by themselves, allowing our firepower, for what it was worth, to be massed in back. Although how much longer that would last, I didn't know, as Bertha was quickly being denuded.

"Damn it, I can't see!" Zheng yelled, slinging us back and forth across the road, trying to dislodge the debris.

It didn't work.

So, I hopped up onto the roof to do it myself.

"Get back in here!" Zheng yelled, spotting me.

"In a sec."

I started throwing things off of the windshield, what I could reach, then slid down to the hood to get the rest. That would have been easier if a rider hadn't managed to find a way onto the top of the brick wall beside us, riding along the narrow edge to target Zheng. So, I sent a wrecked TV at his head.

It bounced off without unseating him, despite the fact that I had not lobbed it. I had sent it with the force of desperation, and at major league baseball speed. It would have killed a human; at the very least, the bogie should have been knocked off the wall.

Instead, he jumped his damned motorcycle *onto the hood*, and sent a sword slashing down at me, which I caught in a lead pipe and twisted away. Which would have been great, if he hadn't then used a gauntleted fist to punch a hole in the solid steel beside my head. And if he hadn't immediately grown another sword.

And that was what it looked like: as if the new sword had just sprouted straight out of his body. It reminded me of something, but I couldn't think what, as I was too busy getting my feet up and kicking the bastard off me. Dhampirs are strong, especially when we're about to get decapitated, so it actually worked.

He landed on his back against the windshield, but it sure didn't look like I'd damaged him. Luckily, Zheng took care of that, reaching out of the window and ripping the creature's damned head off. I fell back against the hood, feeling a surge of relief, until I noticed: the body didn't fall away. Instead, it lunged for me again, which was—

Really fucking creepy, I thought, getting arms up, but not because I was currently wrestling with a headless body. But because something was poking up out of the armor's neck hole. Something, I realized a moment later, that looked a lot like the top of one of their shiny helmets.

"Shit!" Zheng yelled, and yeah. That about summed it up. I kind of lost it at that point, something about seeing a creature regenerate a head doing bad things to my own. I started whaling on it, which unlike the bullets, did seem to have an effect.

But not enough of one.

A few seconds later, I was staring at a brand spanking new head, just like the sword, complete with an extra wide mouth full of teeth that started snapping at me like a dog.

I threw the creature back and screamed at it, in a cross between horror and disgust, and a sword came slashing through the air. But this time, it wasn't aimed at me. The bastard's second head went bouncing away into the night, and I looked up to see Louis-Cesare running along the top of the wall. He was hacking at the riders who were trying to flank us, and making it look like a ballet in the process.

"Show off," I heard Zheng mutter.

"What are you doing over there?" I yelled at my hubby.

"I might ask the same of you!" And then I had company, because he'd just run out of wall.

We screeched around a corner, onto another street, and Louis-Cesare leapt to the roof of the truck, pulling me up after him. He had one of the samurai's swords in his hand, which he sent flying at another rider. It skewered him, and the force behind it must have been pretty impressive. Because this time, the guy went swerving into a third, taking them both out.

But it didn't matter. There were so damned many. They must have been hit by a hell of a magic cloud to be able to regenerate like that. But if they could . . .

Then we didn't have an army of hundreds after us. We had an army of thousands. And we couldn't take them all.

That was evident by a single look at the back of the truck, which was getting boarded on all sides now. The new road was wider, allowing us to be flanked more easily, although Zheng's guys were doing amazingly well—he had obviously brought his A-Team. But the best they could manage was hold their own.

And they wouldn't be doing that for long, as we were almost out of ammo.

Bertha had a single necklace left, which somebody grabbed almost before I'd finished the thought. I should have been able to resupply everyone, having a damned arsenal with me, but most of my stash was magical and the rest had been taken by my team. I didn't know what we were supposed to do when we ran out.

But someone else did.

Jinxes are outlawed because they cause bad luck—really bad, in the case of talented ones. Which I assumed that Sarah was, or she wouldn't be able to target her gift. And she could absolutely target it, judging by the lightning that flashed overhead, and then speared down, straight at our enemies.

It burned through a couple dozen riders, turning them into blackened shells of themselves, which started to dust away even as they rode. But it wasn't done yet. It also leapt from them to those around them, hopping along rows until maybe thirty or forty had been sidelined. It gave us a short breather, mostly because the riders behind them had to navigate past the tumbled bikes and burnt bodies.

Which they did pretty damned fast.

It wasn't enough, but it gave me an idea.

I bent down and grabbed Zheng's shoulder through the window. "Floor it."

"It's already floored!"

"Through there!" I pointed ahead, to where a large building with double doors was looming at the far end of the street.

He stared back at me, his expression a cross between outrage and disbelief. "Have you seen this truck? It's not going to fit!"

"No, it isn't. That's the point."

"Have you lost it? 'Cause you need to tell me if—"

"Zheng! These things got distracted a minute ago and forgot about us—"

"So?"

I held up the second little disk I'd taken from my munition's stores. "So, we need them to forget again."

"Shit," he said. And then he was yelling a bunch of other stuff in Cantonese that I guessed was informing the guys or maybe cursing; it was hard to tell.

"Sarah!" I yelled.

She looked back.

"Can you do another lightning blast?"

"When?"

"Now!"

She nodded. "Thirty seconds!"

"Get ready," I told Zheng, and passed down my last two smoke bombs.

"What are you talking about?" Louis-Cesare asked. And then, when I pulled the bracelet for my one-person shield out of my purse, he grabbed it.

"What the—give it back!" I demanded.

"Not until you tell me what it's for."

I would have argued, but we didn't have time. "When the rooster attacked the dragon, it got the rest of the bogies off our back," I said quickly. "They got into a fight with each other and stopped pursuing us."

The blue eyes narrowed. "You want to start a fight?"

"No. I want them to believe that there's nothing left *to* fight." I grabbed for the cuff, but he was too fast. Damn it!

I glanced at the upcoming building, and there was no time to argue. It had to be now. And then lightning cleared a path around us, bright enough and powerful enough to cause all the hairs to stand up on my arms. I crawled into the cab and pushed at Zheng's huge shoulder. "Go!"

"They'll see us leave!"

"What the hell did I give you smoke bombs for?"

He cursed.

"Just make sure everyone gets clear!" I said, dropping into the driver's seat as he scooched over.

"They'll get clear." He grabbed my arm, his eyes serious. "Don't die."

"She won't." Someone said, as Zheng threw the bombs and bailed. Billowing white boiled up all around us, covering our team's flight. But, of course, one vamp hadn't bailed, and the damned building was coming up fast.

"Give me the cuff," I demanded.

"Give me the explosive." It was Louis-Cesare's implacable voice, and God, I was so sick of this shit! It felt like I had to fight him and our enemies, too!

"You can't do this!" I snapped. "You weigh ninety pounds more than me, and it was calibrated to my weight!"

"I will risk it."

"You'll be dead!"

"Better me than you." It was obdurate. And so stupid that it made me want to kiss him and kill him, at the same time.

So, I kissed him, tenderly, for a second, my hands sliding over his body, my tongue twining around his. Then I pulled back. "All right! But I need my bag! The charges are in there!"

I pointed to where it lay on the floor in back of the truck.

"I'll get it." He swung out of the cab, grabbed the bag and was back in a second, his body framed in the passenger side door.

"I love you," I said, and saw when his eyes caught the flash of white on my wrist—the bracelet I'd taken from his pocket when I kissed him.

But it was too late.

I lashed out with both feet and swerved at the same time, and he was gone, they were all gone. A moment later, I had my foot back on the gas with the second bomb like the one I'd used for the dragon pressed to the passenger side dash. It was just in time.

I sent thousands of pounds of solid steel crashing through the too small doors of the still-intact building. Or still-intact before I exploded the charge, because the only way to survive this was to make sure that our pursuers thought we hadn't. And then the world whited out.

CHAPTER FORTY-SIX

Dory, Hong Kong

Maybe I passed out, or maybe it was just the force of the blast making it feel that way. I didn't know. I just knew that I came back to myself inside a giant orange fireball, watching the seat flaring up around me, the rubber on the steering wheel melting onto my lap, and the now missing windshield showing nothing but a solid wall of flame.

It was mesmerizing. Until a huge piece of masonry caved in the passenger side roof, and I snapped out of it. I scrambled out of the now missing driver's side door, hit the floor and rolled through the fire.

I was all but blind from the smoke, but I was also almost out of time on the shield. So, I crawled, across a burning hellscape until I cleared the wreckage, although it was hard to tell exactly when that was. The whole world was on fire. But I kept on going, trying to get away from anything lethal.

I didn't make it.

When the smoke cleared enough to let me see anything, it wasn't another ruined lobby. It was an echoing space that looked more like a warehouse, with a high ceiling, red brick walls, and a concrete floor covered with burning debris and dead guys.

And fey.

A lot of fey.

They were not burning and they were not on the floor.

But I didn't immediately react because I was dizzy and my eyes kept wanting to cross. However, I'd have probably needed a moment, even on a good day.

It was a lot to take in: the human corpses on the floor, which I didn't think had gotten that way because of me, since I didn't recall shooting anybody full of arrows; the burnt concrete around the blast, radiating outward to burning detritus sticking out of the brick walls; the large group of Svarestri warriors, now headed this way.

I belatedly began to scramble for weapons, only to recall that I'd given most of them to Louis-Cesare. And it probably wouldn't have mattered in any case. There were twenty, maybe thirty fey here; I couldn't tell through all the drifting smoke.

Too many.

But I'd make them rue the day anyway.

I drew a gun and tried to remember how my feet worked, getting ready for the moment when my shield failed. I vaguely wondered why I hadn't been attacked already, while I was off-balance and vulnerable. But I hadn't, probably because they didn't view me as much of a threat.

Yeah, we'd see how much threat I was, I thought, surging to my feet.

And then abruptly plopping back down on my butt, when I almost blacked out.

I snarled at them like a wounded animal. Nobody snarled back. And they seemed to be taking an awfully long time to get to me, or was my brain playing tricks?

I blinked, trying to bring my fuzzy vision into better focus. And belatedly noticed something I'd missed. Because these . . . were not normal looking fey.

They kind of looked like they'd been hanging out in the dead zones a little too long. The bodies were mostly all right, except for one with a huge hunchback and what looked like some spines growing out of it. But everything else . . .

I scuttled out of the way of one with long, greasy white

locks that weren't the usual silver bright color I was used to, like moonlight distilled. Instead, these were flat and dead, like his face, which appeared to be sliding off the bones, with huge, red, gaping holes under the eyes. They weren't wounds, but rather the sockets, which had sagged an inch or more into his cheeks, leaving bloody half-moons under yellowed, bloodshot eyes. The irises were milky as if in death, but apparently still able to see. Because he followed me as I crab walked backwards, so freaked out that I couldn't get back to my feet.

He bent down, that horrible, dead face in mine. And, of course, just about that time, my shield gave out. I felt like screaming, but I didn't have the breath. And before I could get it, he spoke, in a horrible, dry rattle, completely unlike any voice I'd ever heard, human or fey.

Although it didn't matter, as I couldn't focus on the words anyway, since the stench of his breath almost had me passing out again.

It smelled like death. It smelled like *old* death, weeks past its prime, full of rot and decay. It smelled—

I couldn't describe how it smelled.

I rolled away, desperate to get out of range of that stench, but now they were all coming at me. Not quickly, not with weapons, and not in any other way threatening. Just coming.

And it was worse than any attack I'd ever suffered.

"What the *fuck*?" That was Tomas's voice, and then Louis-Cesare's arms were around me, pulling me up.

I knew him instinctively, and assumed that the rest of the team was here, too, but I didn't turn to see. I couldn't seem to move. Because the fey were still coming, only not with the springy grace they usually had, but with a shuffling, halting sort of walk. Even worse, they were speaking.

I didn't know the language; didn't know what they said.

But Tomas seemed to.

"What do they want?" Louis-Cesare rasped. And, for once, the two weren't arguing. Petty, or even not so petty, emotions just didn't hold up in here.

"They want us to kill them," Tomas said blankly, as if he couldn't believe what he was seeing, either.

"Not a problem," Jason said harshly, and raised his gun.

Tomas shoved it down. "They want to die in Faerie! That's the only way their souls can be reborn. It's their religion."

"*Fuck* their religion."

But Sarah was a little more generous of heart. She didn't say anything, but she came forward and put a hand on her brother's shoulder. And, without a word being spoken, Jason holstered the gun.

"You're the expert," he said to Tomas. But he was still fingering his weapon, as if he'd enjoy granting their request.

Only, it looked to me like somebody already had.

"Jonathan," Louis-Cesare said.

And, yeah, obviously.

But Tomas didn't seem to agree. "No," he said, because of course, he'd know the story. They had been master and servant for something like a century, whether Tomas had liked it or not. And he seemed generous enough not to make fun of that, at least. "He isn't behind this."

"He is. He's here."

And something about the way Louis-Cesare said it, made shivers go down my spine.

"You can't make zombies out of fey," Tomas insisted. "They're not like us. Their bodies and souls . . . they are linked in a way that ours just aren't. Necromancers don't want a soul in house. They want to put a bit of their soul into an empty vessel, to control the creature they've created."

"And . . . what would happen . . . if there was already a soul in place?" Sarah asked.

We looked at the horrible creatures in front of us.

I thought we had our answer.

Someone suddenly screamed. It was a high-pitched sound that could have come from either a man or a woman, and it was loud enough that everybody jumped. Even the vamps.

"Shit!" Sarah said. "Shit, shit, shit!"

I'd never agreed with anything more.

We moved back to the area around the burning truck and mostly destroyed entryway of the warehouse. There were a lot more bodies there, but they weren't fey and they weren't moving. Zheng turned one over. A little gold charm was on the ground under the corpse. I guessed it was one of the kinds that came off after death.

He picked it up.

"Eternity," he said, turning it over in his fingers.

"So . . . the fey killed the triad?" Jason asked, sounding dubious. Maybe because those fey didn't look capable of killing anyone.

"They're supposed to be working together," Louis-Cesare said. "They hit Hassani's court together."

"Seems like they've had a bit of a falling out," Zheng said dryly.

And then the scream came again, and this time, it was possible to tell the direction. We looked at each other, but we'd come this far. We cautiously followed some stairs down to a basement.

It seemed intact, if dank, with water spots on the walls and suspicious scurrying in the corners. It would have been perfect as an old, horror movie set. All it needed was a monster.

Only, it had one of those, too.

"See? *See?*" There was a creature on the floor, at the far end of the large space, but the acoustics were good enough for the voice to carry. "There they are! Just as I promised. My creatures didn't manage to find it at Hassani's court, but they have it. *They have it!* They think the girl is here, so they must have brought—"

"I don't care about the device!" a woman hissed.

"But—but you must. Isn't that what all this has been about?" The voice turned angry. "You've been beating me up for half an hour because I lost the damned thing and now you tell me—"

A large fey stepped forward, and the creature put its hands over its head, cowering.

The woman who had been standing over it turned, and I froze. Long, floor-length blonde hair, beautiful, sweet face, faint silver light spilling everywhere. I knew her.

But . . . that was impossible.

"Efridis," I whispered, and felt Louis-Cesare stiffen beside me.

She looked at me blankly for a moment, then turned back to what she was doing. Which appeared to be torturing who or whatever was on the floor. There were some fey around her, healthy, normal looking ones, maybe a dozen.

They didn't react to our presence, either.

I looked at Louis-Cesare; he looked at me. "Stay here," he told the others.

"Gladly," Zheng said.

We walked forward.

Efridis was looking a little worse for the wear herself. Her usually perfect hair was tangled and wild, and her normally silk clad body was dressed in a woolen tunic and leggings, much like those that the male fey wore. But there was something else, something . . . almost raw on her face. I couldn't describe it; didn't understand it.

But it was not the look of a well woman.

Which was fair, as she was supposed to be dead.

"Please," the creature on the floor said plaintively. "Please, I don't understand. I did all that you asked—"

"And more." Her voice, too, was a rasp, so different from her usual, melodic tones. She knelt down, and turned his face up to the light. "I saw your creatures," she whispered.

I gasped; I admit it. Because that was also someone I knew. And someone else who was supposed to be dead.

Jonathan.

I glanced at Louis-Cesare. I didn't know what expression

I'd expected, when he came face to face with his old nemesis again, but it wasn't that one. He'd looked blank for a moment, and then a succession of emotions had flashed across his face, too fast to read. But in the end, he settled on . . . puzzled.

Okay, I guessed that . . . was an emotion. It wasn't the one that I was experiencing, though. Not even close.

My hand went to my knife, because I wanted to feel this kill. No easy gunshot, simple and bloodless, at least if you managed to stay out of the splatter zone. No, I wanted—

And then I stopped, my hand still on the hilt of my weapon, because I'd begun to understand my husband's expression. This wasn't the man I remembered. That man had been frighteningly talented, brash, more than a little crazy, and above all, scary. This . . .

What the hell was this?

He looked more like the shambling, possible-zombies outside than anything I remembered. His face was sallow and heavily creased; his eyes sunken and dull; his hair thin and gray, as if he'd aged decades since we saw his body in the Circle's dank holding cell. That had been the man I remembered; this—

"No," I said, the word bursting out of me on a puff of air, a single, visceral reaction.

Efridis glanced at me. "Yes, he hurt you, too, did he not? You may have him when I am done, if there is anything left."

I looked at Louis-Cesare. I understood exactly nothing, but I knew he would have at least one answer for me. "Is it . . .?"

He didn't immediately reply. He knelt down, putting him and maybe-Jonathan's head on a level, and searched those too-dull eyes. Then he did what I couldn't have, and leaned in. And sniffed him.

I doubted that it was a pleasant experience, although the man appeared relatively clean, except for spots where it looked like the fey had been throwing him around the basement floor. But there was something unsavory about him. The stench of dark magic, Louis-Cesare had always said, but Ranbir was supposedly a dark mage, and he'd smelled like sweat and fried chicken. Not like . . .

"He's dead," I said, finally placing that smell. It was the same one that the fey had been giving off upstairs, only fainter. And underneath a boatload of cologne that only made it worse by contrast.

"Yes, I'm dead!" Jonathan snarled, some of the old fire coming back into his eyes. "That damned Pythia—she killed me! She killed me *twice*!"

"Apparently she needed to do it a third time," I said, feeling dizzy. I looked at Louis-Cesare. "Is it him?"

He nodded.

"Tell them," Efridis said, looking at Jonathan. "Tell them what you have done."

And, immediately, there was a change of demeanor. From outraged pride to groveling pathos. "Please, Lady, we can make some kind of accommodation between us. I can help you—"

"You've 'helped me' enough. Tell them!"

It was not a request.

But Jonathan seemed confused and vaguely petulant. "I can't confess if I don't know what I did!"

"Don't *know*?" It was almost a yell. And it was accompanied by a lovely, manicured hand reaching down, grabbing the huddled figure by the hair, and jerking him upward. "What you did, was to butcher our people. What you did, was to make monsters out of our dead! Desecrating their bodies and endangering their very souls!"

"Oh." Jonathan swallowed. "I'm . . . sorry?"

She just stared at him, her face a mix of shock, disbelief and revulsion. I took my chance. "How are you still walking around?"

He scowled at me. "I could ask you the same thing. Louis-Cesare should have been able to battle his way through that, but not you. I sent repeated bursts of magic at you; those things should have eaten you alive."

So that was why we'd suddenly been so popular, I thought, and barely refrained from kicking him.

But he noticed, and his expression sharpened. "I bet your bitch sister is having fun in Faerie, if she's still alive. I bet—"

He broke off with a scream, probably because Efridis had just torn out a handful of his hair. She did not seem to be in a good mood. And Jonathan, however much pain he was in, knew it.

"Tell us what you did!"

"All right, all right!" he glared up at her. "I was doing an experiment—with permission, of course. King Aeslinn lost a lot of fey at the recent battle over his capitol. I asked if I could have some, for an experiment I wanted to run—"

"Some . . . what?" I asked.

Those creepy, colorless eyes turned to me. "Bodies. What else? He said yes."

There was a change in the air of the room suddenly. I couldn't have said exactly what it was, as no sounds were uttered that were audible to me, and nobody appeared to have moved. But there was an element of menace that hadn't been there before.

Jonathan felt it, too.

"I'm not lying!" he said, sending his eyes around. "He said it. He said he didn't care. And how was I supposed to know about your religion?"

"You've lived in Faerie long enough," Efridis hissed.

"But I don't pay attention to those sorts of things! I was there to get godly tech, to help with my experiments. As far as I knew, they were just dead bodies. Stronger, more resilient, but dead, all right? I wasn't—I didn't mean—"

"What in the hell were you doing with them?" I asked.

Jonathan looked annoyed. "The obvious, I should think. I am, as you can see, very dead. That puts me in a bit of a bind. Luckily, I had already started the aforementioned experiments, to see whether fey could make decent zombies.

The answer is no, by the way—"

"That isn't all you were doing," Efridis said. "You *changed* them."

"Yes, well, that's what experimentation *is*. I was trying out different possibilities. Fortunately, I had put a bit of my soul into several, to see if I could control them. It didn't work very well, but it meant that, once I died, there was a tiny bit of me still around. But it's very little. I basically had to make a zombie out of myself in order to—"

"Wait," I said. "Wait."

Jonathan waited.

"You put the bits of your soul . . . from the fey experiments . . . into your dead body and . . . reanimated it?"

Jonathan blinked at me. "Isn't that what I just said?"

"I think I need to sit down."

To my surprise, one of the fey brought me over a chair.

I took it, because this was so surreal, nothing surprised me anymore.

"So, I'm dead," Jonathan continued, like this was a perfectly normal conversation to be having. "But I'm still useful. I did a great deal for the Svarestri royal house, and I can do much more. These idiots have the device, so I can do the operation as soon as you find the girl. Plus, you know what I've made here." And no, we didn't, but then, he wasn't talking to us anymore. His eyes had slid over to Efridis, who was standing there, as still as a statue. "I can give it to you instead of him. I can hand you your husband's throne; the thrones of all the great houses of Faerie. I can give you honor, fame, renown for the ages—anything you want.

"And all I want in return," he said, looking at Louis-Cesare. "Is him."

CHAPTER FORTY-SEVEN

Dory, Hong Kong

"Why?" I said, getting in Jonathan's face. "What do you need with him? You have all the magic that anyone could possibly want—"

"Caveat: it's not life magic," he said pedantically. "It runs things, not people, but I see your point. I could buy all the life magic I want with what I've collected here."

"Then why do you want him?"

He looked at me like I was crazy. "Why do you think? I want his body."

Louis-Cesare shifted slightly, but he made no other sign that he'd heard. I, on the other hand, had had enough. I slugged Jonathan, as hard as I could, right across the face. It was fortunate for Efridis that she was no longer holding his head, or the force might have broken her wrist. It was fortunate for him that he was already dead, or he likely would have been.

"You stupid bitch!" He spit out three teeth, but there was no other sign that anything had happened. No blood, no discoloration, no swelling. It was eerily similar to hitting a side of meat. "I think you broke my jaw!"

"I'm going to break a lot more than that!"

"Why?" He looked genuinely confused. "You asked a question; I answered it. It's not like I don't need one. Look at me! And his will never age."

"What?" I said, confused myself now.

Jonathan looked at me. "Are you slow?"

"What?"

"Yes, I can see that you are. Okay, let's see what I can do here." He pointed at himself. "Me dead. Body fall apart. Need new one. He," a finger pointed at Louis-Cesare, "has immortal body. Me take, live forever. Do you get it now? Or do I need to draw you a picture?"

I just stared at him for a moment. And then I started to hit him again, but Louis-Cesare pulled me back. I made him work for it, because I really, *really*—

"That's why you were doing your experiments on the fey," Louis-Cesare said. "They are body and soul combined, like vampires. You thought, if you could control one of them, you could control me."

Jonathan nodded. He didn't smile; he probably couldn't right now. But he seemed vaguely pleased that someone was following his logic.

"Yes, exactly. I am—or was, before my recent, unfortunate demise—over nine hundred years old. Do you have any idea how much magic it requires to stay alive at that age? Let me clue you in—it's a lot. It makes you have to do all kinds of things you don't want to do, because if you don't, you just stop living. You can't spend your time on your experiments, like you'd prefer, because you're constantly scrounging around for new sources of magic. And making deals with people to get it that you can't get out of afterwards. It's a lot like being in jail—"

"Or in a loveless marriage to a monster."

He glanced at Efridis. She looked back, expressionless. He frowned.

"Anyway, I thought, wouldn't it be nice if I could have a body that just keeps going? Drink a little blood now and again, and its all good. I became fascinated with your body when I held you captive briefly," he told Louis-Cesare. "So handsome, so strong, so sturdy. I told you I'd have you one day, and now I know how. I can't control the fey; they're not human enough. But you—I think I've finally figured out how to take you.

"And in return, I'm willing to be extremely generous," he said, his eyes going to Efridis. "I'm very sorry about the bodies. I truly meant no disrespect. I will return them, for the proper burial or funeral rites or whatever you do. I just need —"

He broke off as two large fey came forward, and snatched him up by the arms. Efridis had given no sign discernable to me, but I didn't think they were acting on their own. There was no surprise on her face, and she made no attempt to stop them.

"Wait! Wait!" Jonathan said.

They did not wait.

"What is this? I can make you rich," he yelled, as they dragged him off. "I can give you whatever you want! All you have to do—"

"Is make a compromise," Efridis said softly. "A little cut to my honor. Just a small one . . ."

Jonathan looked relieved. "Yes, if you want to put it that way. I can—"

They jerked him out the door.

For a long moment, nobody spoke.

Finally, Efridis looked at me, and sighed. "Jonathan lied. As far as I know, your sister lives. She is lost in Faerie, however; I do not know where. And I doubt that I, of all people, will be able to find her, as she has every reason to hate and fear me. I can, however, give you the location where I saw her last, and anything else that you require to help you find her."

I blinked a couple of times. "What?"

She smiled slightly. "You may also take whatever you find here. Jonathan included. He has been helping my husband to create . . . things . . . to use against you in the war. But he would not say where they are. I believe he wishes to use them to bargain for his life.

"Or what is left of it."

She was handed a piece of paper and a quill by one of her fey, and she scribbled on it. She handed it to me, and it appeared to be a map. "I would give you safe passage," she added, "but coming from me, it would likely do you more harm than good."

I stared at the paper blankly, and then back up at her. "Why are you doing this? You fought against us. You tried to kill us—"

"I did a great many things," she agreed. "Thinking it would all be shown to have been right in the end. I was wrong. And now a great jewel of Faerie is dead at my hand, while I consorted with a monster. I cannot bring her back—"

She cut off, and for a moment, the beautiful, serene mask fell, and I saw another face beneath it. One that looked more like a little girl's: confused, sorrowful, in agony. And then determined, too, as she regained control.

"I cannot bring her back," she repeated. "I would give my life to do it, if it would suffice, but it will not. She is gone, and I . . . have to find a way to atone for that." She had been staring at the floor, but now she looked at me suddenly. "Do you think there is such a thing? A way back?"

"I . . . don't know."

"No more do I. But I will find out."

And then she was gone.

* * *

Efridis didn't disappear, but she may as well have done. She and her fey could move like lightning when they chose, scooping up their misbegotten brothers and disappearing through a portal. Their speed said that they'd about had enough of Hong Kong. Frankly, so had I, but I had a mess to clean up.

And what a mess it was.

"So Aeslinn was behind the new triad that was leeching all the magic," I said to Zheng, who had only understood about half of what we'd been told.

"Yeah," he paused to kick one of the dead bodies. "Only that Efridis bitch butchered the lot of them before we could ask any questions, so how are we supposed to find the army? We don't even know what the hell it looks like!"

"They're still sort of warm," one of his vamps said, kneeling by one of the corpses. "If we had a *bokor*—"

"Do you see any *bokors* around here?" Zheng snapped. He was in a temper, and I didn't blame him. The consul was going to thank him very prettily for finding out all about Eternity—which I assumed was Jonathan's idea of a joke, since that was what he had been after—but in her very next breath, she was going to inquire about this magical army. And when he couldn't tell her . . .

Yeah.

"Maybe it's all the crazy shit we've been fighting," Jason said. "That stuff looked like an army to me."

"Too random," Tomas said. "The fey like organized, disciplined troops. The stuff we've been seeing . . ." he shook his head. "Some of that might have been discards, things Jonathan couldn't use and released to keep people scared and away from here. But it's not an army."

"How do you know so much about Faerie?" I asked.

He shrugged. "That's where I went, to escape your husband." He hesitated, and then blurted out. "Are you really married?"

"Yes, why?"

"You don't bear his mark."

I looked at him levelly. "I bit him."

Tomas just stared at me for a moment, and then he laughed. "Okay, don't tell me. Who knew a dhampir would have a sense of humor?"

"Yeah, who knew." I handed him my card.

"What's this?"

"I might have a job for you, and your team, if you want it."

He tilted his head. "What kind of a job?"

"The kind that pays a lot of money and might get you killed."

He grinned. "Right up our alley, then."

He walked off.

"What was that all about?" Louis-Cesare asked, coming up behind me.

"Thinking about hiring the team to help me go get Dorina."

"And you trust them with that?"

I shrugged. "You know how it goes. Where else am I going to get a bunch crazy enough to go in there?"

He smiled slightly. "I suppose so."

I looked back at him, but didn't turn around, because he'd started to give me a shoulder massage and it felt good. "You don't mind?"

"Why would I mind?"

"It's just that, you and Tomas—"

"That was over as soon as Christine died. I need to explain that to him, but talking to the man for more than a minute without wanting to belt him—"

"He does have a certain charm." I paused. I didn't want to ask if we were all right, but I needed to. "Like me?"

He kissed the top of my head. "Later."

Now what did that mean?

Not that I could blame him for not wanting to get into personal matters right now. Zheng was on a tear, which in his case, meant dragging the freshest of the bodies around and yelling. "Damn it, find me a *bokor*!"

"I thought you didn't want one?" Sarah said.

Zheng snarled at her, and she put up her hands. "Okay, okay. We're going. We'll be by to pick up that reward tomorrow."

"What reward?"

"The one you're going to pay us to keep our mouths shut."
They left.

One of Zheng's braver boys edged up. "Sir, by the time a *bokor* could get here, the mind will have decomposed to the point—"

"Do it anyway!" he growled. "Not that we should have to. If that bitch Ranbir isn't dead, I swear—"

"Did I hear someone take my name in vain?"

I looked up, and so did everyone else, to see Ranbir himself coming down a set of metal stairs from what looked like an office. Only, if I'd been him, I'd have been headed back up, instead, because Zheng was Not Feeling It. But Ranbir tripped happily downward anyway, a small leather pouch in his hand.

"Nice of you to join us," I said. "Your team just left."

"Yes, I know. I was waiting for that."

"Too ashamed to face them?" Zheng demanded, with a sneer.

"No, I thought you might want to decide this without an audience." He held up the bag.

* * *

Zheng still had an audience, but only of three. His boys were downstairs with strict orders that we not be disturbed. Louis-Cesare, Zheng, Ranbir and I were up in the office, making decisions that all of us were far too tired for.

"This is above my paygrade," Zheng said, striding back and forth. That was a good trick, as the office was small, and Zheng took up the space of two. The bag was there as well, sitting in the middle of the desk. It was nothing special, just the type that medieval people kept money in, and that somebody like Jonathan kept an army in.

It was, of course, fey tech, the same kind that my arsenal was composed of. Only this one was much, much bigger. I opened it up again, even though it was a little dizzying to look down into a space that your brain expected to be small, and see a vast hangar, of the type that they keep jumbo jets in, teeming with Jonathan's handiwork.

It was even stranger to think that all of this—the original attack on Hong Kong, the study and exploitation of its magical system, and the design of the super soldiers down there—all of it, had just been the day job to Jonathan. He was a necromancer; he specialized in studying the dead. He could give a damn about any of this, but as he'd admitted to us, he'd needed life magic, a huge amount of it, to sustain him, and so he'd been chained.

It didn't make me feel sorry for him; I didn't think there was anything that could do that. But I did understand him a little better now. I just didn't know what to do about any of this.

"It's above all our paygrades," I said, dropping the army back onto the desk. "But it fell in our lap. We have to decide this."

"Easy for you to say," Zheng snarled. He'd been doing that a lot. "I'm the one who'll take the heat for this!"

"Is there another option?" I asked.

"Hell, yes, there's another option! I turn it over to the consul and reap massive rewards. She could end the war with this. She could rule the world with this!"

"Exactly," Louis-Cesare said, and said no more.

Zheng threw himself into a pathetically inadequate desk chair and glowered at us. "I hate you both."

"We're not trying to tell you what to do," I began.

Zheng said a bad word.

"Okay, we are. But . . . you do realize that no good will come of this, right? Give the consul that much power—hell, give any vamp that much—"

"I have that much, right now, and yet I'm sitting here, listening to you."

"But you can't use it."

"Like hell I couldn't. I could . . . I could take over the world myself. I could run this shit!"

I looked at him. "Do you want to run this shit?"

"Hell, no. I have enough trouble running Lily's, and she does most of it." A huge hand pushed up the hair over his forehead. "I just wanted some respect. That's how I got into this mess. I'm an ex-pirate and a gangster. I am not supposed to have to make these kinds of decisions!"

"You're also a senator," Louis-Cesare commented.

"Yeah, for a hot minute." He picked up the bag and tossed it to him. "You deal with it!"

"We could destroy it," I said. "Just burn the bag and destroy the gateway—"

Zheng grabbed it back. "Talk sense. We're in the middle of a war. We need this."

"Nobody needs this," Louis-Cesare said, sitting forward. "You know that. This kind of power could unbalance everything."

"And not having it could end up costing us the war. Not to mention the fact that I know it's here, okay? I can't unknow that. The first time someone like Ming-de scans me—or your father, or anybody else with mental abilities—you think it's not going to get out? It's getting out."

"He has a point," I told Louis-Cesare.

My husband frowned. "If your father were here, or Dorina—"

"But they're not. And I wouldn't trust Mircea with this, any farther than I could throw him. He's the general for this war. You think he's going to throw away an advantage like that?"

Louis-Cesare frowned some more.

"Okay, so we turn it over," Zheng said. "At least we know Aeslinn goes night-night—"

"And how many of his people?" I demanded. "How many of the fey in general? You've seen those things! We can't turn them loose on anyone, not to mention that the only person who can control them is their maker—"

"We don't know that!"

"—who is a dangerous dark mage!"

"*He's* a dark mage." Zheng hiked a thumb at Ranbir, who'd been sitting quietly all this time. "But he turned this over to us."

"I'm more of a medium gray," Ranbir said modestly.

"Why did you turn it over?" I asked. "And why did you leave us, anyway?"

"I had the map. It also serves as a communication device, and Jonathan texted me. He offered me a fortune to betray you—"

"But you betrayed him instead."

He shrugged. "I know the type. This much power in his hands?" He shook his head. "I like money, but it doesn't do you much good if there's no world left to spend it in."

Zheng scowled. "Tree hugger."

"Pragmatist."

"Whatever. Point is, I am not going to burn for this, okay?" Zheng looked at Louis-Cesare and I. "You want it your way, fine, then pull my nuts out of the fire. And you might want to think about your own while you're at it. The consul isn't going to be any happier with either of you."

He glanced at Ranbir. "And she'll outright kill you."

"That would be . . . distressing."

"So, what do you want?" I asked. "A next level mentalist who can erase this from all our memories, someone we trust enough to do it, and somebody who isn't gonna do it, and then abscond with an army and take over the world. Is *that* what you're asking for?"

Zheng crossed his arms and gave me his best glare. "I will not burn. Find a—"

There was a knock on the door.

"What the hell?" Zheng was on his feet in an instant, furious. "When I say we're not to be disturbed, I mean it, damn it!"

"Please do not blame your men," came a familiar,

soothing voice through the flimsy wood. "They simply . . . forgot."

The door opened and I turned around to see Hassani standing there, looking like an angel in brilliantly white robes.

"How did you get here?" I asked.

"Bahram and Rashid are good boys. A bit rambunctious at times, it is true, but they have a useful talent. Together, they can summon a portal from anywhere they have been to anywhere they are. They cannot hold it for long and it takes two of them to channel enough power, so it is not a very useful master's gift for them. But I have made use of it, many times."

"You said to call you—"

"And I am sure you would have, eventually. But it seems that you need my help now."

"Your help?"

I suddenly remembered what he'd said when he came in. And then I remembered something else: all that he'd suffered, and that his people had suffered, at the hand of a so-called god. There was nobody in the world I trusted more to know the dangers of absolute power, and to avoid them like the fucking plague.

"Tell me you're a mentalist," I said, fervently.

"I am not, as it happens. I do know one, however." He stepped aside, and—

"Maha?"

"I always was good with the mind," she said, apologetically.

"How good?" Zheng said.

EPILOGUE

Dory, Cairo

"Our host is very strange," Louis-Cesare said, sliding into the bath alongside me.

"Tell me about it."

We were back at "work" in Egypt, finishing out our time here while our team geared up for the next adventure. I was glad for the brief break, which both of us needed. And also glad to be with vamps who didn't scowl when they saw me.

I could get used to that.

But there were still . . . let's call them peculiarities . . . about this place. I guessed every court had its quirks, and all things considered, this one was way less weird than our own. But it was still weird.

Take tonight, for instance.

Hassani had invited us to his study after dinner, to watch him burn some old bag. He'd been cackling the whole time, like a mad thing, like he had the day he'd burned the great snakeskin. Hassani, I was starting to think, maybe needed a vacation, too.

Maha had been there, as well, I had no idea why. But after all the leather pieces were curled up and black, and half of the bag was simply powder on the desk, Hassani had looked at her. "Are they?"

She'd nodded. "Still there, all of them. The man, the creatures, and . . . him. They will always be there."

"Eternity," Hassani had said obliquely. "But perhaps not

the way he'd envisioned it."

She had stepped closer to him. "Do you want me to—"

"Not now. Take it from me tomorrow, as we discussed. For tonight . . . I wish to remember."

She had bowed silently and left.

I'd noticed a small pot on the floor, the one I'd seen glowing with blue light the last time I was in these rooms. Its cover was off now, and it was empty. Hassani saw me looking and smiled.

"Another problem solved. Amazing how things dovetail, isn't it?"

"A problem?"

"The *col de mort*, as you call it, did not work on our friend Sokkwi. It killed him, but he has died many times. The wood, I am afraid, was no different to him than any other stab wound."

"You mean, he could come back?" I said, already halfway out of my chair.

Hassani made a calming motion. "He could have. Not now." He chuckled again and swept the ashes of the little bag into a garbage can by his desk.

"Why not now?"

"Oh, let's just say, I sent him off to enjoy his endless rebirths with someone who could appreciate his unusual talent."

And then he'd cackled again.

Louis-Cesare and I had gotten out of there as soon as possible, because seriously? Diplomacy has limits. Although, I thought now, relaxing back into my husband's arms, it had its perks, too.

"I'm getting one of these pool tubs when we get back," I told him.

"And put it where?" he murmured, against my hair. "It would be more than half as large as your room at Claire's."

I sighed. I didn't want to do this now. I didn't want to do anything now, except appropriate honeymoon activities.

But I guessed we had to.

"We don't have to do this," he told me.

I turned around. "Did you just read my mind?"

"No. I just think I have harangued you enough."

I lifted an eyebrow, dislodging some water that trickled down my face. He moved closer, to kiss it off, but I stopped him with a hand on his chest. "Wait. Does this mean no more freak outs? No more knight in shining armor bullshit? No more talk of locking me up to keep me safe?"

He winced slightly at that, which he damned well should have.

I pressed my advantage, and pressed myself against him at the same time, because it felt good.

"No more 'oh, no, my weak little wife is in danger'? No more, 'I married a dhampir, but I wanted a Christine'?"

"That's unfair. I *never* wanted Christine."

"And me?"

"I wanted you from the first moment I set eyes on you, however I may have acted at the time. This wasn't about you."

"Then what was it about? And why the change?"

He looked like he was struggling, so I pushed him around to soap up his back. And to give him some time. He took it; that was the cleanest back ever by the time he finally spoke.

"I'll start with when it changed."

"Which was?"

"When I saw him with Efridis. When I saw the man who had captured me, had humiliated me, had hurt my family and had threatened . . . who I thought had threatened . . ." he trailed off, but I didn't need the help.

"To rape you." I finally said the words that we'd been dancing around for a while now.

Louis-Cesare didn't say them himself, but his head nodded. "It happened before, not with him, but when I was a boy . . ."

"You don't have to tell me about that." I already knew the

story. Not in detail, but enough. He'd been a captive; his jailer had done what jailers sometimes do, him and some friends. It had left deep scars that still surfaced occasionally.

Like with Jonathan, I assumed.

"You thought it was going to happen again."

He nodded. "He had me utterly in his power. I could not have resisted him. And he kept touching me, talking about wanting my body . . . what else was I to think?"

"Not that he meant it literally," I said. "The man was insane."

"But brilliant, and intelligent, and strong . . . or so I thought."

"Until you saw him groveling at Efridis' feet."

"Yes. It changed everything. I had been so afraid of him, for so long, and so ashamed of myself for it. Everyone always talked about how strong I was, but if they could have seen me with him . . . they would not have thought so."

"Then they're fools," I said, brushing damp hair off his forehead. "You went to him the first time to save Christine; you were going back this time for me. How is that not strong?"

He looked surprised at that, which pissed me off, although not at him. Jonathan was dead, killed by the fey before we could get to him, and so yet again, Louis-Cesare had been denied his revenge. He deserved it, like he deserved to not have to feel like this.

"You knew he might capture you again. You knew, if he did capture you, what might happen. But you went back anyway, because he had Dorina's location and you needed that information. Not for you, but for me. You were willing to risk so much, for me . . ."

"You are a part of me," he said hoarsely, his Adam's apple working. "So, it was for me as well."

I kissed him then, because a girl can only take so much.

But then I drew back, because I still didn't get one thing. "Why the overprotective father bit? Was it just about the leg?

Or were you afraid that Jonathan would get his claws in me, too? Or does battling would-be gods give you as much of a headache as it does me?"

He sighed, and sagged back against the tub. "All of the above. And . . . more. So much more."

I stopped and I waited, because getting him to talk was rare, while I talked all the time. The least I could do was to be silent for once, while he had his chance. So I was, and it worked.

After a moment, he sighed and then spoke again. "So much has happened recently. So much change. Some of it bad, with the war and the constant fighting. But much of it, for me personally, has been good. And some of that has been beyond good. I was afraid, no, I was sure, that the other shoe was soon to drop.

"My life has always been a rollercoaster, one with far more lows than highs. I suppose I have gotten into the habit of assuming that it will always be so, and that any high is begging for a correction. And meeting you, all that we are together, all that we could become—"

"Is a hell of a high." I felt a little dizzy with it myself, half of the time.

He nodded. "I don't doubt your abilities—yours, apart from Dorina. I was simply afraid, and I did not know what to do about it. I wanted to protect the most important person in my life, but . . . I acted badly."

"I forgive you."

He quirked a brow. "That was fast. You should make me work for it a little more. I am, after all, rarely wrong."

I managed not to roll my eyes—just. "I intend to," I said. "We're going to get Dorina back so you can bite me and I can stop having idiots like Tomas ask if we're 'really married'."

He smiled.

"But, since that may be a while, I think you owe me a little down payment."

He looked slightly wary. "In the form of?"

I smiled and put my arms around his neck. "We can start with what you heard in that room at Lily's."

Dorina, Faerie

The crab was as large as a car, but mottled green and brown, which was why it could not easily be seen among the treetops. It had been fitted with two seats in front and a long, bench type one in back. Ray and I were on the back one, with ropes across our laps to help us keep our seats. Our guide, who occupied one of the front seats, had informed us that these creatures could climb up completely perpendicular trunks as easily as they could skitter through the forest canopy above, so we would have to hold on.

The camp was a flurry of activity, as everyone packed up their substitute for horses. The group of fey we had met with were hunters, on a food-finding trip for a larger gathering —much larger, from what I understood. And now we were going back.

"How are the legs?" Ray asked, looking at the bright green leggings I had acquired.

"They are well."

"Are you sure? I mean, I know you've been walking around and all, but can you run? Fight?"

I looked at him curiously. "I have been quite active all week. Why do you ask?"

"It's just . . . we don't know what we'll find at this new camp, okay? We need to be ready for anything."

"Did the fey say something to upset you?" I could not talk to them as yet, but Ray had been working hard to learn the local language. It had some things in common with a widespread trade dialect that he had used before, although not as much as he would have liked.

"I can't be sure, since I get all of one word in ten," he said fretfully.

"But?"

"But it sounded like . . ." He repeated a word in their tongue that I didn't know. "It means 'similar', or 'like you'," he explained. "They said we were going to meet someone like us."

Now I was the one frowning. "That could be either good or bad."

"Yes! Yes, it could. So be ready."

I nodded, and then said no more, as our unusual ride suddenly rose from a crouch to its full height. And immediately took off for the trunk of a very large tree. Our guide said something in their language, and Ray gripped the side of the seat.

"What did he say?" I asked, as the pincers grasped the wood.

"He said hold on!"

And then we were climbing. It was so fast that I barely realized what was happening before we were bursting out above the tree line. It was a beautiful view, with vividly colored trees—green and yellow and orange and deep purple —spreading out all around us and thick with leaves, like the most luxurious of carpets. Some startled birds—vividly blue with a yellow chest and long, trailing tails—added to the scene, flying up and then off at our appearance, into the perfect cerulean of the sky.

The voyage took the better part of a day, despite the fact that the crabs were extremely fast. They explained the strange rustlings I'd seen in the treetops, shortly after we'd arrived. The common folk seemed to use them in these parts like horses, and the trees like highways, allowing them to swiftly travel across long distances.

I found the trip quite pleasant, and quite easy. There

was nothing to impede us here, no mountains to climb or enemies to avoid. I saw a dragon in the distance once, fiery red and easily visible against the pale blue of the sky. But our ride dipped below the leafy canopy for a little while, and when we emerged again, it was gone.

We finally reached our destination in early afternoon, with the climb backwards down another great trunk a new pleasure. In no time, we were on the ground, amid a huge forest of a different kind. Silver gray bark, blue skies and bright yellow leaves, many of the latter swirling down around us as we gazed about in wonder.

"Have you ever seen the like?" I asked Ray.

He just shook his head.

Our guide took us forward. He was the same old man we'd met on the riverbank, and he seemed to have developed a fondness for us. He beckoned us along, while the rest of the party hugged family and friends, and chatted—about the hunt, I presumed—while unloading their beasts.

The forest was a wonder, but I did not have long to marvel at the height of the trees, or the thickness of their trunks, or at the size of their leaves, which were feet across in some cases. Or at the many tents that had been set up beneath them, some on the forest floor and some farther up, on branches so broad that they could be used as additional "stories." Some of the tents were hide, but many more were in colorful fabrics that added to the festive nature of things.

Ray did not seem so impressed, looking around suspiciously as we moved ahead, watching the people so closely that he did not even bother to swear at the size of the roots we often had to clamber over or pass under, or the floor covering of massive, decomposing leaves that we waded through in places, up to our thighs.

Everything was so beautiful, but so alien . . .

Almost.

I paused at the edge of a small clearing. There were no tents here. Instead, a small group of thatched huts clustered closely together, around a central fire. A handful of women, one of them gray haired, were bustling about, fixing a meal. The smell of roasting meat hit my nose, as well as that of some strange vegetables bubbling away in a pot of soup and an open container of hoppy beer.

The beer was more or less familiar, although it wasn't what had me pausing again, half way to the fire, to sniff the air.

Ray noticed the same time I did, and his face flushed. "No. No, no, no, no, no!"

"Ray—"

"I won't have it, do you understand?" he yelled, causing the people to pause and look at him oddly. But I didn't think he was talking to them. "I've been ripped to pieces," he raged. "I've been kidnapped, thrown all over a ley line, and almost stomped to death by a dragon! And that was before being shot full of arrows and practically drowned—"

"You can't drown," I said, but he wasn't listening.

"I have put up with it all, but this—I will not do this. Fuck it, I'm done."

And I supposed he meant it, because he sat right down in the dirt, arms crossed, face mulish, and refused to go another step.

"Raymond?" A familiar male voice carried from somewhere inside one of the huts. "Raymond Lu? Is that you?"

"Not doing it," Ray muttered, hands going over his ears. "La la la, can't hear you."

The old man was looking from me to Ray and back again, as if he was starting to regret bringing us here. I couldn't really blame him. And then the voice came again. It was slightly muffled, but was nonetheless perfectly understandable.

"Damn it! Stop horsing around and get over here!"

I went over there. The voice was emanating from the third hut I peered into, which should have been the first since it was the only one with guards outside the door. They crossed spears when I approached, and I did not attempt to remove them.

We were guests.

It would have been rude.

It was gloomy in the hut, especially when standing outside, but my eyes adjusted after a moment. This allowed me to see the figure of a man, lashed against the central pole of the structure. I assumed there must also be some magic involved, because otherwise, the flimsy ropes would not have held him for an instant. Because he wasn't just a man, he was a vampire, one with curly hair and a familiar scent in my nose.

"Oh, god damn it!" he said, catching sight of me. "What the devil are you doing here?"

It was Kit Marlowe, the consul's chief spy. It did not appear that his spying was going very well, if that was indeed, why he was here. "I could ask the same of you," I pointed out, only to have the usually brown eyes flash fire.

"I'm looking for your damned father! He ran off without a word and we're running out of ways to cover for him. Now get me out!"

I did not point out the obvious fact that I had no way to do that. Instead, I focused on the main issue. "Father is here?"

"Yes, father is here," Marlowe said sarcastically.

"Why?" Unless . . . could he possibly be here for me? The thought flashed across my mind—foolishly, because I knew better. But then Marlowe said something even more amazing.

"Why? He's looking for your mother, that's why! And he's likely to start another war in the process, if we don't stop him!"

"My mother?"

"Damn it, Dory! We can talk about this later. Now, are you going to help me or not?"

I stared at him for a long moment, until he began to look

slightly nervous. But I could not seem to help it. In the space of a few days, my life had gone from almost completely shut down to dizzyingly, wondrously open, and now I learned . . .

I could not take it in.

Marlowe swallowed, loudly enough that I could hear it. "You're . . . not Dory. Are you?"

"No. I am Dorina." I smiled at him, and he reared back slightly for some reason. "And I will help you."

Dorina Basarab Series

Midnight's Daughter
Death's Mistress
Fury's Kiss
Shadow's Bane
Queen's Gambit

Cassandra Palmer Series
(same universe)

Touch the Dark
Claimed by Shadow
Embrace the Night
Curse the Dawn
Hunt the Moon
Tempt the Stars
Reap the Wind
Ride the Storm
Brave the Tempest
Shatter the Earth

Author's Website

KarenChance.com/Books

Printed in Great Britain
by Amazon

32568581R00300